# She was not for him.

He knew that, and not just because of the voices, but getting his body to agree was a different matter. Her scent numbed him like good whiskey. Made him feel needy. Reckless. Finding some shred of control, he shadowed her out of the club, away from the mob awaiting entrance, and herded her deep into the alley. He scanned in both directions. Nothing. They hadn't been followed. He could get her somewhere safe. Not that he knew where that might be.

"No one saw us leave."

She backed away, hugging herself beneath her coat. Her chest rose and fell as though she'd run a marathon. Fear soured her sweet perfume. She had to be in some kind of trouble. Why else would she be here without an escort? Without her patron?

"Trust me, we're completely alone." He reached awkwardly to put his arm around her, the first attempt at comfort he'd made in years.

Quicker than a human eye could track, her arm snapped from under the coat, something dark clutched in her hand. The side of her fist slammed into his chest. Whatever she held pierced him, missing his heart by inches. The voices shrieked, deafening him. Corrosive pain erupted where she made contact.

He froze, immobilized by hellfire scorching his insides. He fell to his knees and collapsed against the damp pavement. Foul water soaked his clothing as he lay there, her fading footfalls drowned out by the howling in his head.

# BLOOD RIGHTS

House of Comarré: Book 1

## KRISTEN PAINTER

orbit

www.orbitbooks.net

This book is a work of fiction. Names, characters, places, and incidents are the product of the author's imagination or are used fictitiously. Any resemblance to actual events, locales, or persons, living or dead, is coincidental.

Copyright © 2011 by Kristen Painter
Excerpt from *Flesh and Blood* copyright © 2011 by Kristen Painter
All rights reserved. Except as permitted under the U.S. Copyright Act of 1976, no part of this publication may be reproduced, distributed, or transmitted in any form or by any means, or stored in a database or retrieval system, without the prior written permission of the publisher.

*Book design by Giorgetta Bell McRee*

Orbit
Hachette Book Group
237 Park Avenue
New York, NY 10017
Visit our website at www.orbitbooks.net.

Orbit is an imprint of Hachette Book Group. The Orbit name and logo are trademarks of Little, Brown Book Group Limited.

The publisher is not responsible for websites (or their content) that are not owned by the publisher.

Printed in the United States of America

First edition: October 2011

10 9 8 7 6 5 4 3 2 1

*For Grandma B,*
*who instilled in me in my early years*
*the power of a good story well told.*
*I wish you were here to see this.*

# BLOOD RIGHTS

In this shall the coming of the end of days be revealed: the light and the dark shall collide, and the covenant shall be broken. Sorrow shall bind the darkness, and he shall devour the light and arise reborn. Then blood and sorrow will be his mistress.

—SCROLL OF THANICUS (13, 175–176)

# Prologue

*Corvinestri, Romania, 2067*

The servant trembled in front of the grand fireplace that had never been lit and never would be. "The girl...the girl is, well, it seems...that is, we cannot..." He bit at his lip.

The gilded mantel clock ticked toward sunrise. Tatiana yawned and rolled her hand through the air. "Go on."

His hands twisted, fingers knotting. "We cannot find the comarré, my lady."

Tatiana's veins iced and she stilled at the mention of the female blood whore. "What do you mean, you cannot find her?"

"We've searched Lord Algernon's manor, and she isn't there."

Tatiana and Lord Ivan had discovered Algernon's body just that evening, a rather unusual occurrence in a vampire death. Ashes yes, bodies no. "How long do you suppose he's been dead? Not more than a few hours, surely."

His hands fisted at his sides. "We believe two days, perhaps three. We think it happened just after the Century Ball, my lady. Perhaps that night or the next morning. We have no way of knowing exactly."

A spark of pain lit her palms. She glanced down at the tiny crescents of blood left by her nails, watched them vanish as she forced herself to relax against the velvet upholstered chair. Algernon's death meant the Elder position could be hers, but proving herself worthy of that title would require this chit to be brought to justice. The girl *would* be found. Even with a three-day lead, how far could she travel alone and unprotected? She was a simple comarré, bred for her blood and her social skills, little more than the vampire's equivalent of a geisha. The girl knew nothing of the kine world, just as humans knew nothing of this one. The girl would be simple to find among the kine. Like a sparkling gem in a mud puddle.

"Search again. Search the grounds as well."

"Yes, my lady."

"Now. Begone." Tatiana leaned her head into her hand. With Algernon's death, the council would have little choice but to appoint her Elder. Her reign would be a very different one from that old fool's. She would start with bringing that thin-witted girl before the council. By making an example of her to the other comarré. A dark joy lifted Tatiana's thoughts. When she was appointed Elder, Algernon's manor would be hers. Along with all his property in it. Not that she cared for any of his baubles and treasures but one, the one she and Lord Ivan had come to fetch when they'd found Algernon's body.

At last, the pieces were knitting together. All her work, her meticulous attention to detail, her endless studying of the prophecies, her personal sacrifices... finally, she would wear the mantle of power she'd been stitching these many years.

The taint of her past, the human years spent in poverty and squalor, those wounds could only be salved by the protection of great power. The ghosts of those who had used her, treated her like rubbish, those ghosts still haunted her, as spectral as the lost loves of her human life. Power could exorcise them, once and for all. She had to believe that. Or go madder still. Her fingers drifted to the locket around her neck.

The scent of kine had not dissipated. She looked up at the servant, dropping her hand from the locket. "Why are you still here?"

He shifted from one foot to the other. His head stayed bowed. "There is one other thing, my lady."

Tatiana sighed out the end of her patience. "What?"

"She appears to have taken a few of Lord Algernon's possessions."

Her nails drummed the chair's carved arm, wounding the old wood. "Such as?"

"As best we can tell, some jewels, gold coins—"

"Insignificant. Now go, search again." Finally, she could join Mikkel in bed, where he undoubtedly already chilled the sheets for her. Of all the paramours she'd had since her turning, he'd lasted the longest. Perhaps it was his youthful exuberance.

The minion stayed put. Fear wafted off him in delicious waves. Her stomach growled, causing him to jump.

"What else?" Bothersome mortal. Kine really were good for one thing and one thing only.

The servant shivered. "The ring you asked me to look

for? It was not on Algernon's person or anywhere else in the house. I believe that the girl has taken it."

Bloody hell. The ring of sorrows, gone. Wood splintered beneath Tatiana's grip. That old dolt must have shown the girl the ring. Probably bragged about it. Algernon deserved to have his head removed from his neck. Unfortunately, the girl had beaten Tatiana to it. She forced the tip of her tongue against the razor point of one fang until blood coated her mouth. With pain came clarity. "How many searched with you?"

"Twelve."

She tested him. "And they also know the ring is missing?"

"No, my lady." Concern lined his forehead. "I told no one else, just as you instructed me."

She smiled. "You did well."

He relaxed and tentatively returned her smile. "Thank you, my lady."

In one lightning-quick move, she was beside him, her fingers threaded through his black curls. She snapped his head back, exposing his throat. His pulse fluttered like a wounded sparrow, his heart pounded wildly. Deliciously.

"My lady?" He paled beneath skin that showed an arrogant hint of tan. Did he think his ability to face daylight something to flaunt before her?

The tremor in his voice stroked pleasure over her skin. The clock chimed 6 a.m. Nearly sunrise, but she had work to do. Loose ends to tie up. A lifetime of planning to protect. The Nothos must be sent after the girl immediately. The unnatural creatures enjoyed a good hunt now and then, especially when put to the task by their vampire half-brethren. "You're positive no one else knows the ring is missing?"

"Yes, my lady, I swear it on my life." Indeed, he reeked of truth.

"You would mention that." She trailed a finger down the minion's neck. "Seeing as it's about to be required of you."

With a rabid growl, her human features disappeared as her facial bones shifted and her fangs descended fully. She sank them into her servant's throat, his cries filling her ears like chamber music, his blood disappearing down her gullet along with the secret of the missing ring.

She dropped his limp body to the hand-knotted Turkish carpet, licked a bead of blood from the corner of her mouth, and headed to her office. She'd make a note for Octavian, the head of her household staff, to remunerate the dead kine's family, but the cost was worth it. Killing soothed the painful memories of her past and what had been taken from her. It gave her the strength to face the enormous amount of work ahead.

She stopped at the door and glanced at the lifeless form fouling the perfection of her sitting room. She'd worked so hard to get where she was and sacrificed so much, she hated to see anything mar her home. She shook her head at the dead kine. Had she been that vulnerable as a human? No. The streets had beaten the soft edges and innocence out of her before she'd lost her baby teeth. Humans were like that, turning on each other, picking the weakest among them apart, using one another for their own means. They deserved what they got at vampire hands.

Would the comarré be that vulnerable? Probably. The pampered creature had little chance of realizing what she possessed in that ring. Not even Algernon had fully understood it until Lord Ivan's explanation. How would a comarré know she held the key to a prophecy that might change the world? She was nothing but a blood whore. A piece of property, no different from the ring she'd stolen.

Tatiana smiled grimly. Well now, that wasn't true at all.

The ring had a future.

# Chapter One

*Paradise City, New Florida, 2067*

The cheap lace and single-sewn seams pressed into Chrysabelle's flesh, weighed down by the uncomfortable tapestry jacket that finished her disguise. Her training kept her from fidgeting with the shirt's tag even as it bit into her skin. She studied those around her. How curious that the kine perceived her world this way. No, *this* was her world, not the one she'd left behind. And she had to stop thinking of humans as kine. She was one of them now. Free. Independent. Owned by no one.

She forced a weak smile as the club's heavy electronic beat ricocheted through her bones. Lights flickered and strobed, casting shadows and angles that paid no compliments to the faces around her. She cringed as a few bodies collided with her in the surrounding crush. Nothing in her years of training had prepared her for immersion in a crowd of mortals. She recognized the warm, earthy smell of them from the human servants her patron and the other nobles had kept, but acclimating to their noise and their

boisterous behavior was going to take time. Perhaps
humans lived so hard because they had so little of that
very thing.

Something she was coming to understand.

The names on the slip of paper in her pocket were
memorized, but she pulled it out and read them again.
*Jonas Sweets,* and beneath it, *Nyssa,* both written in her
aunt's flowery script. Just the sight of the handwriting
calmed her a little. She folded the note and tucked it
away. If Aunt Maris said Jonas could connect her with
help, Chrysabelle would trust that he could, even though
the idea of trusting a kine—no, a human—seemed
untenable.

She pushed through to the bar, failing in her attempt to
avoid more contact but happy at how little attention she
attracted. The foundation Maris had applied to her hands,
face and neck, the only skin left visible by her clothing,
covered her signum perfectly. No longer did the multitude
of gold markings she bore identify her as an object to be
possessed. She was her own person now, passing easily as
human.

The feat split her in two. While part of her thrilled to
be free of the stifling propriety that governed her every
move and rejoiced that she was no longer property,
another part of her felt wholly unprepared for this existence. There was no denying life in Algernon's manor had
been one of shelter and privilege.

Enough wallowing. She hadn't the time and there was
no going back, even if she could. Which she wouldn't.
And it wasn't as if Aunt Maris hadn't provided for her and
wouldn't continue to do so, if Chrysabelle could just take
care of this one small problem. Finding a space between

two bodies, she squeezed in and waited for the bartender's attention.

He nodded at her. "What can I get you?"

She slid the first plastic fifty across the bar as Maris had instructed. "I need to find Jonas Sweets."

He took the bill, smiling enough to display canines capped into points. Ridiculous. "Haven't seen him in a few days, but he'll show up eventually."

Eventually was too late. She added a second bill. "What time does he usually come in?"

The bartender removed the empty glasses in front of her, snatched up the money, and leaned in. "Midnight. Sometimes sooner. Sometimes later."

It was nearly 1 a.m. now. "How about his assistant, Nyssa? The mute girl?"

"She won't show without him." He tapped the bar with damp fingers. "I can give Jonas a message for you, if he turns up. What's your name?"

She shook her head. No names. No clues. No trail. The bartender shrugged and hustled away. She slumped against the bar and rested her hand over her eyes. At least she could get out of here now. Or maybe she should stay. The Nothos wouldn't attempt anything in so public a place, would they?

A bitter laugh stalled in her throat. She knew better. The hellhounds could kill her in a single pass, without a noise or a struggle or her even knowing what had happened until the pain lit every nerve in her body or her heart shuddered to a stop. She'd never seen one of the horrible creatures, but she didn't need to in order to understand what one was capable of.

They could walk among this crowd without detection, hidden by the covenant that protected humans from the othernaturals, the vampires, varcolai, fae, and such that coexisted with them. She would be the only one to see them coming.

The certainty of her death echoed in her marrow. She shoved the thought away and lifted her head, scanning the crowd, inhaling the earthy human aroma in search of the signature reek of brimstone. Were they already here? Had they tracked her this far, this fast? She wouldn't go back to her aunt's if they had. Couldn't risk bringing that danger to her only family. Maris was not the strong young woman she'd once been.

Her gaze skipped from face to face. So many powdered cheeks and blood red lips. Mouths full of false fangs. Cultivated widow's peaks. All in an attempt to what? Replicate the very beings who would drain the lifeblood from their mortal bodies before they could utter a single word of sycophantic praise? Poor, misguided fools. She felt sorry for them, really. They worshipped their own deaths, lulled into thinking beauty and perfection were just a bite away. She would never think that. Never fall under the spell of those manufactured lies. No matter how long or how short her new life was.

She knew too much.


Malkolm hated Puncture with every undead fiber of his being. If it weren't for the bloodlust crazing his brain—which kicked the ever-present voices into a frenzy—he'd be home, sipping the single malt he could no longer afford, maybe listening to Fauré or Tchaikovsky while searching his books for a way to empty his head of all thoughts but his own.

Damn Jonas for disappearing without setting up another reliable source. Mal cracked his knuckles, thinking about the beating that idiot was in for when he showed up again. It wasn't like the local Quik-E-Mart carried pints of fresh, clean, human blood. Unfortunately.

The warm, delicious scent of the very thing he craved hit full force as he pushed through the heavy velvet drapes curtaining the VIP section. In here, his real face, the face of the monster he'd been turned into, made him the very best of their pretenders and got him access to any area of the nightclub he wanted. Ironic, considering how showing his real face anywhere else would probably get him locked up as a mental patient. He shuddered and inhaled without thinking. His body tensed with the seductive aroma of thriving, vibrating life. The voices went mad, pounding against his skull. A multitude of heartbeats filled his ears, pulses around him calling out like siren songs. *Bite me, drink me, swallow me whole.*

Damn Sweets.

A petite redhead with a jeweled cross dangling between her breasts stopped dead in front of him. Like an actual vampire could ever tolerate the touch of that sacred symbol. Dumb git. But then how was she to know the origins of creatures she only hoped were real? She appraised him from head to toe, running her tongue over a set of resin fangs. "You're new here, huh? I love your look. Are those contacts? I haven't seen any metallic ones like that. Kinda different, but totally hot."

She reached out to touch the hard ridge of his cheekbone and he snapped back, baring his teeth and growling softly. *Eat her.* She scowled. "Chill, dude." Pouting, she skulked away, muttering "freak" under her breath.

Fine. Let her think what she wanted. A human's touch might push him over the edge. No, he reassured himself, it wouldn't. *Yes.* He wouldn't let it. *Do.* He wouldn't get that far gone. *Go.* But in truth, he balanced on the edge. *Fall.* He needed to feed. *To kill.* To shut the voices up.

With that thought he shoved his way to the bar, disgusted things had gotten this dire. He got the bartender's attention, then pushed some persuasion into his voice. "Hey." It was one of the few powers that hadn't blinked out on him yet. Good old family genes.

His head turned in Mal's direction, eyes slightly glazed. Mal eased off. Humans were so suggestible. "What'll it be?"

"Give me a Vlad." Inwardly, he died a little. Metaphorically speaking. The whole idea of doing this here, in full view of a human audience, made him sick. But not as sick as going without. How fortunate that humans wanted to mimic his kind to the full extent.

"A shot?"

"A pint."

The bartender's brows lifted. "Looking to get laid, huh? A pint should keep you busy all night. These chicks get seriously damp over that action. Not that anyone's managed to drink the pint and keep it down." He hesitated. "You gotta puke, you head for the john, you got me?"

"Not going to happen."

"Yeah, right." The bartender opened a small black fridge and took out a plastic bag fat with red liquid.

Mal swallowed the saliva coating his tongue, unable to focus his gaze elsewhere, despite the fact he preferred his sustenance body temperature and not chilled. A few of the voices wept softly. "That's human, right? And fresh?"

The bartender laughed. "Chickening out?"

"No. Just making sure."

"Yeah, it's fresh and it's human. That's why it's $250 a pop." He squirted the liquid into a pilsner. It oozed down the glass thick and viscous, sending a bittersweet aroma into the air. Even here in the VIP lounge, heads turned. Several women and at least one man radiated hard lust in his direction. The scent of human desire was like dying roses, and right now, Puncture's VIP lounge smelled like a funeral parlor. He hadn't anticipated such a rapt audience, but the ache in his gut stuck up a big middle finger to caring what the humans around him thought. At least there weren't any fringe vamps here tonight. Despite his status as an outcast anathema, the lesser-class vampires only saw him as nobility. He wasn't in the mood to be sucked up to. Ever.

The bartender slid the glass his way. "There you go. Will that be cash?"

"Start a tab."

"I don't think so, buddy."

Mal refocused his power. "I've already paid you."

The man's jaw loosened and the tension lines in his forehead disappeared. "You've already paid."

"That's a good little human," Mal muttered. He grabbed the pilsner and walked toward an empty stretch of railing for a little privacy. The air behind him heated up. He glanced over his shoulder. A set of twins with blue-black hair, jet lips, and matching leather corsets stood waiting.

"Hi," they said in unison.

*Eat them. Drain them.*

"No." He filled his voice with power, hoping that would be enough.

They stepped forward. Behind them, the bartender watched with obvious interest.

Damn Sweets.

The blood warmed in his grasp, its tang filling his nose, but feeding would have to wait a moment longer. Using charm this time, he spoke. "I am not the one you seek. Pleasure awaits you elsewhere. Leave me now."

They nodded sleepily and moved away.

The effort exhausted him. He was too weak to use so much power in such a short span of time. He gripped the railing, waiting for the dizziness in his head to abate. He stared into the crowd below. Scanned for Nyssa, but he knew better. She only left Sweets' side when she had a delivery. The moving bodies blurred until they were an undulating mass, each one undistinguishable from the next until a muted flash of gold stopped his gaze. His entire being froze. Not here. Couldn't be.

He blinked, then stared harder. The flickering glow remained. It reminded him of a dying firefly. Instinct kicked in. Sparks of need exploded in his gut. His gums ached, causing him to pop his jaw. The small hairs on the back of his neck lifted and the voices went oddly quiet, save an occasional whimper. His world converged down to the soft light emanating from the crowd near the downstairs bar.

He had to find the source, see if it really was what he thought. If it was, he had to get to it before anyone else did. The urge drove him inexplicably forward.

All traces of exhaustion disappeared. The glass in his hand fell to the floor, splattering blood that no longer called to him. He vaulted over the railing and dropped effortlessly to the dance floor below. The crush parted to let him through as he strode toward the gentle beacon.

She stood at the bar, her back to him. The generous fall of sunlight-blonde hair stopped him, but the fabled luminescence brought him back to reality. So beautiful this close. He rubbed at his aching jaw. *You'll scare her like this, you fool. You're all fang and hunger. Show some respect.*

He assumed his human face, then approached. "Looking for someone?"

She tensed, going statue still. Even with the heavy bass, he felt her heartbeat shoot up a notch. He moved closer and leaned forward to speak without human ears hearing. Bad move. Her scent plunged into him dagger sharp, its honeyed perfume nearly doubling him with hunger pains. The whimpering in his head increased. Catching himself, he staggered for the bar behind her and reached out for support.

His hand closed over her wrist. Her pulse thrummed beneath his fingertips. Welcoming heat blazed up his arm. A chorus of fearful voices sang out in his head. *Get away, get away, get away…*

She spun, eyes fear-wide, heart thudding. "You're…" She hesitated then mouthed the words "not human."

Beneath his grip, she trembled. He pulled his hand away and stared. Had he been wrong? No marks adorned her face or hands. Maybe…but no. She had the blonde hair, the glow, the carmine lips. She hid the marks somehow. He wasn't wrong. He knew enough of the history, the lore, the traditions. Besides, he'd seen her kind before. Just the once, but it wasn't something you ever forgot no matter how long you lived. Only one thing caused that glow.

She bent her head. "Master," she whispered.

"Don't. Don't call me that. It's not necessary." She thought him nobility? Why not assume he was fringe? Or worse, anathema? But she'd addressed him with the respect due her better. A noble with all rights and privileges. Which he wasn't. And she'd surely guessed he was here to feed. Which he was.

She nodded. "As you wish, mast—" Visibly flustered, she cut herself off. "As you wish."

He gestured toward the exit. "Outside. You don't belong here." Anyone could get to her here. Like Preacher. It wasn't safe. How she'd ended up here, he couldn't fathom. Finding a live rabbit in a den of lions would have been less surprising.

"I'm sure my patron will be back in just a—"

"We both know I'm the only real vampire here." For now. "Let's go."

Her gaze wandered to the surrounding crowd, then past him. She sucked her lower lip between her teeth and twisted her hands together. Hesitantly, she brushed past, painting a line of hunger across his chest with the curve of her shoulder. *Get away, get away, get away…*

She was not for him. He knew that, and not just because of the voices, but getting his body to agree was a different matter. Her scent numbed him like good whiskey. Made him feel needy. Reckless. Finding some shred of control, he shadowed her out of the club, away from the mob awaiting entrance, and herded her deep into the alley. He scanned in both directions. Nothing. They hadn't been followed. He could get her somewhere safe. Not that he knew where that might be.

"No one saw us leave."

She backed away, hugging herself beneath her coat.

Her chest rose and fell as though she'd run a marathon. Fear soured her sweet perfume. She had to be in some kind of trouble. Why else would she be here without an escort? Without her patron?

"Trust me, we're completely alone." He reached awkwardly to put his arm around her, the first attempt at comfort he'd made in years.

Quicker than a human eye could track, her arm snapped from under the coat, something dark and slim clutched in her hand. The side of her fist slammed into his chest. Whatever she held pierced him, missing his heart by inches. The voices shrieked, deafening him. Corrosive pain erupted where she made contact.

He froze, immobilized by hellfire scorching his insides. He fell to his knees and collapsed against the damp pavement. Foul water soaked his clothing as he lay there, her fading footfalls drowned out by the howling in his head.

# Chapter Two

A few hours until sunset and Tatiana had yet to succumb to daysleep, but she would give in to its siren call upon completion of this last chore. Through the smoked, helioglazed glass of her Bentley, she watched her driver speak to the headmistress of the Primoris Domus, the house of the renegade comarré. Madame Rennata looked past the driver at the car, then nodded.

With gloved hands, Tatiana pulled the deep hood of her floor-length cape over her head and adjusted her dark sunglasses. Her driver extended a wide black umbrella before opening her door and escorting her to the portico. The strip of shade it offered was far too narrow for her comfort.

"That will be all," Tatiana dismissed him.

She extended one hand and spoke in the most pleasant tone she could manage when dealing with lesser beings. "Madame Rennata, so good of you to take my call."

Rennata eyed her warily and kept her own lace-gloved fingers wrapped securely around the crook of her ivory cane. "Rather an unusual visit, Mistress Tatiana. I do hope all is well with Damien."

Tatiana dropped her hand to her side. "With whom?"

Rennata tilted her face to one side, causing the delicate gold signum curling across her brow and cheekbones to glint. "Damien? Your comar?"

"Ah, yes. He's fine. I'm not good with names." Not when it came to servants anyway.

"What can I do for you, then?"

Tatiana glanced at the line of approaching sunlight. "Perhaps we could go inside?"

Rennata's spine stiffened as rigidly as the elaborate coif confining her pale blonde hair. "You know our rules don't allow for random visits. As you've already purchased your comar, you've no need to be here."

Tatiana suppressed the desire to tear the woman's throat from her neck. How dare this glorified whore tell a noble what she could and could not do? Tatiana chose her words carefully, steadying her voice to hide the distaste on her tongue. "This is an unusual situation."

"Indeed, it must be to bring you here."

"Please." Was there a more bitter word? How she longed for a draught of blood to rinse it from her mouth.

Rennata unpursed her lips. "You may enter the foyer and great hall, as those are common areas. You will not be invited farther."

"Of course." She followed the woman over the threshold, pulling off her shades and pushing back her hood. She'd not been here in many years, not since coming to purchase her own comar with Lord Ivan, but the aroma was the same. Dark, seductive, sweet...it sank into the vein like a velvet needle. Her mouth watered, and her head spun. She swallowed, blinked hard.

"Does the light bother your eyes, mistress?"

"No, I . . . yes, it *is* a little too bright."

Rennata gestured and white-robed comarré dimmed the lamps in the great hall, then vanished. She moved toward a pair of tapestry chairs near a crackling fire. "Sit, won't you?"

Tatiana took the chair farthest from the flames. Fire was not a vampire's friend.

"Now then. What brings you here?"

Right to it. Good enough. Tatiana had no desire for small talk either. "I'm looking for Algernon's comarré."

"She's not here. I imagine she's with her patron."

"Ah, then you haven't heard. Algernon's dead and the girl is gone."

To Rennata's credit, her face showed no reaction, good or bad. "That is unfortunate, but technically she would be considered released."

"Technically, yes. But at the moment she's considered the prime suspect in his murder."

"You think a comarré capable of such an act? We are hardly our patrons' equals, mistress."

"Comarré are trained in swords, are they not?"

Rennata shrugged and a wisp of a smile played on her lips. "All for ceremony and show. Our skills lie in other, more delicate areas." She turned her face toward the hearth and the firelight brought her signum to life like bright, golden vines unfurling across her skin. "Was there blood on her sword?"

"I don't know." Damnation. She hadn't asked the servants to check that. Tatiana leaned back and sighed. "I would like to see her room."

"That access is not mine to grant."

"I merely wish to see if I can cross the threshold. If so,

I will not disturb anything within." This charade of polite-
ness wearied her. For all her power, she was bound by an
age-old pact with these creatures. Had the comarré forgotten they were, at heart, still kine? If not for the vampires, they would be ordinary mortals. Ripe for plucking,
like the rest of the kine. If not for that ridiculous covenant.

"You want to know if the girl lives."

"Yes."

"Let me confer with the others and I shall return with
an answer." Rennata pushed to her feet, leaning heavily
on her cane.

As soon as she left the room, Tatiana closed her eyes
and concentrated, listening, sensing, trying to eavesdrop
as best her abilities would allow. The house was strangely
quiet. At any given time there might be several hundred
comarré here, and yet she heard nothing. No voices, no
movement, no breathing. Not even a heartbeat. Still, she
could sense she was not alone. She opened her eyes and
studied the room's opulent appointments. Crystal and
silk, gilding and exotic woods, rare paintings and priceless sculptures. Comarré were well compensated for their
services, that much was plain. Granted, blood from this
house had been proven to be the best of the best and so
these comarré demanded the highest price of all, but still
the grandness of it gnawed at her cold heart.

For the donation of blood, they lived like nobility. Was
what beat in their veins that special? Unfortunately, it
was. The purity was unmatched. The power it gave was
remarkable. The taste—her cheeks ached—was richer
than the finest wine, more succulent than any ordinary
mortal could ever be. And merely owning a comarré indicated a vampire's wealth and status. She eased her grip on

the chair and tried to remain calm. She was almost done here. Then she could return home. To her own comar. What had Rennata called him? David? Daniel?

"Mistress Tatiana, we will grant you access this once."

She stood and nodded. "Very kind of you."

Rennata's eyes flashed. "If you would follow me."

The halls they traveled were dim, the adjoining doors closed. Occasionally, Tatiana picked up what might have been a heartbeat or distant pulse, but for the most part silence shrouded the house.

At last, they stopped before a simply carved door, no different from the multitude of others they'd passed.

Rennata unlocked it with a long, ornate key, then stepped out of the way. Tatiana twisted the knob and pushed the door open. It swung slowly, revealing a narrow cell, austerely furnished. The crest of Algernon's house hung over the bed and a pair of diamond-crusted slippers sat beneath it, the only two indicators that the occupant had some means. She looked at Rennata. "This is typical?"

"Yes. While a comarré's true home remains in their house of origin, most of their possessions are kept in the quarters provided by their patrons. Where they spend the most time."

Tatiana turned back to the room. Only if the girl were dead would no invitation be necessary to enter her room. If the girl was alive, Tatiana would be knocked back. Entering would not be impossible, but the consequences would be horrific. Fatal, if endured long enough. She straightened, stepped forward, and crossed the threshold with ease.

Rennata swallowed and exhaled a shuddering breath.

An angry mix of satisfaction and disappointment

welled inside Tatiana as she twisted to face the madam. "The girl is dead then."

"So it appears." Rennata rubbed a knuckle against the corner of her eye.

The need for sleep pulled at the edges of Tatiana's consciousness. Time to wrap this up before she went comatose where she stood. "Does the girl have any living family?"

"We are all her family. No comarré knows her birth parents."

Tatiana's brow wrinkled as she fought the creeping fog of daysleep. "I am certain there was someone. A sister... or an aunt, perhaps..."

"Every comar and comarré of her age is a sibling. Every older comarré her aunt, every older comar her uncle."

Tatiana's frustration grew. "There was one. No longer with you."

"Not that we remember."

"Ah, yes, I forgot you have your own sort of anathema. Those who leave are never spoken of again, isn't that right?" She waved her hand through the air. "Stricken from all records, that sort of thing? While I completely understand the need to remove the weaker members of your family, this is vital information. I'm sure the council will find a way to get it out of you."

Rennata's jaw tightened for a split second. "There was an aunt. All record of her has been destroyed."

Tatiana couldn't help but smile at how easy that had been. "Very well. Lead me out. I'm ready to go." She'd have to send word to the Nothos, redirect them to search for the ring. They might balk at being used as a lost-and-found service, but not for long if they valued their undead lives.

When they reached the great hall, Tatiana strode past Rennata, stopping only at the front door. She stabbed a warning finger toward the woman. "Don't touch that room. The council will undoubtedly wish to inspect it as well. Her death doesn't make her innocent, only dead."

Rennata bowed her head. "Yes, mistress."

Tatiana pulled up her hood and slid her sunglasses into place before charging out and slamming the door. She skidded to a halt on the shaded side of the portico. Her driver was already out and rushing toward her, umbrella at the ready to shield her from the sun's killing rays.

"Home, mistress?" He lifted the broad stretch of silk above her as she stepped off the portico toward the car.

Secure in a wide circle of shadow, she nodded, too exhausted to say anything. Staying awake this long had been draining but very worthwhile. Her hand found the locket around her neck, her fingers smoothing across the single ruby on the locket's front. The original was gone, this one the closest replica she'd been able to find.

Painful memories kept her focused. She kissed the locket and tucked it away. Things were going to be much easier once the ring was hers.


*That fool girl.* Rennata slumped onto one of the window-front settees, peering through the sheers until Tatiana's car wheeled away from the house and down the tree-lined drive. Finally. She stood, shoved her cane into the umbrella stand, and strode back to the great room. She clapped her hands. A trio of comarré came forth out of the shadows.

"Put a few of Chrysabelle's oldest robes in the closet of

that spare room, perhaps add a few insignificant personal items to the dresser drawers, a book, a drawing, that sort of thing. If the council comes, they will inspect more thoroughly. The crest and slippers alone will not convince them."

Saraphina nodded. "What of her suite?"

"Leave it be. No one but us can touch it anyway."

"Yes, Madame." Saraphina and the other two bowed and headed off to the work at hand.

"Jessika."

The girl stopped. "Yes, Madame?"

"Fetch me paper and pen and find me a messenger going to the Americas." Times like this she wished the comarré ignored the nobility's edict that banned modern technology. She had to get word to Maris immediately. Tatiana's history in dealing with those who crossed her was dark and bloody. Maris would understand. Chrysabelle could not be allowed to damage everything they'd worked so hard to establish. Maris had done the right thing once. Certainly she could be counted on to do it again.

# Chapter Three

Hesitating at the door to her aunt's house, Chrysabelle checked over her shoulder. Nothing moved but the water bubbling from the three-tiered fountain at the center of the circular drive. Satisfied she hadn't been followed, she punched in the alarm code to unlock the entry.

The cab had dropped her off two blocks from the bridge into the private gated community of Mephisto Island, then she'd run the rest of the way, swimming the canal beneath the guardhouse and scaling the perimeter wall surrounding her aunt's estate without incident. Ever since the occurrence at the hellhole otherwise known as Puncture, it couldn't hurt to be too careful.

If she never set foot in Paradise City again, that was fine with her. For a town with such a lovely name, that place was remarkably deficient in anything close to perfect bliss.

The door slid open. She zipped in and punched the button to lock it again. Must be after 2 a.m. Hopefully, she wouldn't wake her aunt—

"You're all wet!" Maris's iBot wheelchair was in balance mode, putting her at eye level.

Chrysabelle jumped, her heart thudding. "I swam the canal."

Maris's brows rose.

"Don't look at me that way. I'll do what I see fit to keep you safe. Anyway, I was trying to be quiet."

"You were, love. Sorry to startle you." Maris grinned. Velimai, her aunt's assistant, wavered behind her. Velimai was a wysper fae. Wavering was the closest she came to standing still unless she was in solid form.

Chrysabelle sighed. "But I still woke you and Velimai."

Velimai signed *yes*.

Maris patted her side. "No, it's this damn hip. Velimai, go on back to bed."

Velimai signed *good night* and vanished into mist. Chrysabelle restrained a shudder. Wyspers were unstable creatures at best. The fae breed was small and wiry when not ethereal, light as a breeze and destructive as a hurricane. They could vocalize sounds but had no speech. Their screams were fatal to vampires, and clearly the reason her aunt employed one.

With the slightest twist of her upper body, Maris turned her iBot toward the kitchen. "Come on, you can tell me what happened over a cup of tea."

"Tea would be good." Chrysabelle kicked off her wet shoes and hung up her damp brocade jacket, then followed, her bare feet padding softly on the wood floors.

Maris flipped on the light. "I'll put some whiskey in it."

"Maris, you know I can't partake."

"You're not bound by those rules anymore, my darling."

"Yes, I know, but adjusting to that will take some time." Just like not calling every vampire she ran into mistress or master. Not that she hoped to be running into any more. Chrysabelle went to sit, then thought better of it. "I'll get the kettle."

Maris waved her off. "Have a seat. This kitchen is set up for me, you'd just get in my way." She winked, then looked at her niece a little harder. "Didn't go that well, I take it?"

Chrysabelle sank into a chair and leaned her arms on the table. "The man you sent me to talk to wasn't there."

Maris sighed as she took out two cups. "Jonas always has been a tricky one. You'll have to go back tomorrow."

"No. I mean, I can't. They ... might have found me. I need to gather my things and go somewhere else."

"Already?" Fear flickered over her aunt's face for a brief moment, then vanished, hidden by a mask of determination just as her signum were hidden under a layer of foundation. "Don't go yet. I'll call Jonas. Make one more attempt. I didn't want to do this over the phone, but I can't see another way."

"He's kine—I mean, human. I don't know how you think he can help." Human *and* he employed a remnant, Nyssa. Her hybrid of wysper and shadeux fae had apparently rendered her mute. In the world of vampire nobility, remnants didn't even register.

Maris tsked. "Jonas is a tremendous resource. You'll see."

Chrysabelle sighed. "I don't want to put you in any more danger than I already have."

"My darling girl, you worry for nothing. I can take care of myself and you." Maris added a scoop of loose tea to the teapot, put the pot and a sterling silver flask of single malt on a tray with the cups, and wheeled it to the table. "You should know that this house is as secure as money can buy, and thanks to my time at Primoris Domus and my talent for turning some of those comarré secrets into Lapointe Cosmetics, that's an ungodly sum of money."

Chrysabelle stretched out her hands, studying the backs of them—or rather the Lapointe foundation that still covered them. "That makeup certainly did the trick."

Maris headed back for the whistling kettle. "Sometimes there are things about a woman best kept secret."

"Do you ever not cover yours?"

"No. Never. I've put that life behind me. I don't need to be reminded of it every time I look in the mirror."

"Sorry, I—"

Maris laughed softly. "My apologies. I didn't mean to sound sharp. I just . . . I just don't care to see them is all."

Chrysabelle understood, a little. She knew Maris's exit from comarré life had not been an easy one, knew that she'd chosen libertas, the comarré ritual of fighting for one's freedom, but not the reason why Maris had nearly sacrificed her life to leave behind everything she'd ever known. Perhaps, like Chrysabelle, Maris had simply wanted more than a life of servitude. That was enough, wasn't it?

They had their tea and chatted about the night's events. Mostly about the human world and the club patrons' desire to mimic vampires. Chrysabelle glossed over the vampire she'd stabbed, saying instead that she'd ducked out unnoticed when she'd seen him. She claimed he'd been fringe too, not the possible Nothos she'd encountered masquerading as nobility. Her aunt's claims of security aside, Chrysabelle saw no reason to put Maris at unnecessary risk, especially if the hellhounds were already on Chrysabelle's trail.

When they turned in, she resolved to give her aunt's connection one more try, but after that she would move on, go underground if she could, and truly disappear until it was safe to return. Maris had been through enough in her life. She shouldn't have to suffer through her niece's troubles as well.

The next two nights, Chrysabelle barely slept. Every tick of the house, every breeze that sighed over the roof, every imagined footstep woke her. And every time she woke, she saw the face of the vampire she'd stabbed. The surprise in his dark, silvered eyes when her blade connected. The haunting look of disbelief. The pain—more than she'd expected, as if he carried it constantly within him. But worst of all, the hunger. That she'd not only seen, but felt the moment he'd laid his cold hand over her wrist.

He'd been five, maybe six nights without feeding. She hadn't been comarré this long without learning to read temperatures. He'd probably planned to drink her dry, then take her body back to the council as proof. She should have killed him, but another death attributed to her would not help her cause.

And there was something about him that seemed broken. Not the way she'd imagined a Nothos at all. Nor had she ever imagined one of the Nothos to be so…so… magnetic. In the tales she'd heard, they were savage mutants, not the creature she'd met. She squeezed her eyes shut. Had she really just felt a minute hint of attraction to the monster that would have killed her? Maybe it was one of his powers. Just like the way he had changed his scent to portray himself as nobility. She breathed out. Yes, that was much easier to believe. Pretend he was Nothos. Lay the blame with him, not her fragile mind.

Light filtered in beneath the heavy drapes. Enough feigning sleep. She rose, donned her white cotton gi, and padded out to the balcony to begin her morning exercises. The sun glinted off the blue-green water of the bay. So peaceful, so beautiful. She pushed through each form, holding, tensing, feeling the strength in her muscles and taking comfort in her years of training. Slow and easy, but strong and exact. Now more than ever she needed the calm and center the movement brought to shut out the reality slicing toward her like an executioner's blade.

Energized and sweaty, she showered, dressed in her usual white tunic and pants, and went out to start some coffee.

The rich aroma greeted her as she walked into the kitchen. Her aunt had beaten her to it for the first time in three days.

Velimai's diminutive form flitted about the kitchen preparing breakfast. Maris set her e-reader down. "You're up early. I figured you were still programmed to nights."

"I am. Mostly. I didn't sleep well. Again. Finally decided to stop fighting it and get up. How about you? I haven't seen you up this early either."

"A late night turned to an early morning. I haven't been to bed yet, but I was able to finally contact Jonas. He knows of someone who can help you." Maris pushed a piece of paper across the table. On it were an address and a few instructions. "Go to this location at any time during daylight, but not within an hour of sunset. Tell him Jonas sent you."

"Any time during daylight sounds good to me. I'll go this afternoon." She took the slip. If this didn't work, she wouldn't be coming back here. "Maybe we could have lunch together first?"

Maris narrowed her gaze and smiled gently. "You're making plans."

Chrysabelle turned away to get coffee and hide her face. Maris was too perceptive. Farther down the counter, Velimai sliced cantaloupe as rapidly as a machine. "I shouldn't have stayed here as long as I have. It's a wonder there hasn't been some sort of movement already. How do you know your source won't give me up?"

"For one thing, he doesn't know any details, just that you need help. And for another, he's left the city. I don't know where he's gone, but I wired him enough money to ensure it was far away. You're safe, my darling, I swear it. And I insist you stay here with me." Her aunt sniffed.

A twirl of a spoon and Chrysabelle returned to the table. Her aunt's eyes glistened with moisture.

"I need you, Chrysabelle. I'm an old woman. I'm tired of being alone."

Chrysabelle nodded toward Velimai. "You're not alone. And you're not that old."

"You're my family. Please, as long as there is no immediate danger, stay." She reached across the table and clasped her hand over Chrysabelle's. The pulse that beat beneath the hidden signum was strong, the skin firm, the joints smooth. Maris might consider herself an old woman, but by human standards she looked barely middle-aged. Granted, she was paralyzed from the waist down, but she'd been willing to pay that price for her freedom. Velimai set a crystal bowl of fruit salad on the table, along with smaller dishes of organic yogurt. Life here was good, luxurious to a fault, thanks to her aunt's impressive cosmetics fortune.

"I'll stay. But if anything happens, anything that

makes me think I've brought danger to your doorstep, I'm gone."

Maris patted her hand. "Nothing will happen. You'll see."

"I'm sure you're right." Although she wasn't. Not at all. Nothing had seemed safe since that night.

Velimai signed something Chrysabelle didn't quite catch. Maris nodded and the wysper left.

Maris turned back and stroked her thumb over Chrysabelle's wrist. "Are you... taking care of yourself? Without a patron, the buildup can make you sick."

Chrysabelle nodded, her thumb worrying the band on her right middle finger. A twist to the side and a flip of the tiny mechanism released a hidden blade sharp enough to open a vein. "I drained once in Paris. I feel fine, but I'll probably do it again tonight when I get back." Or wherever she ended up.

Maris patted her hand again. "Forgive me for mothering you, I can't help myself."

"It's okay. It's kind of nice, actually."

After a long breakfast, she packed a few things and dropped the bag out the window. Later, she'd skirt around and pick it up. Having a backup plan was never a bad idea.

She tried to read for a while but concentration eluded her. Finally, she excused herself to get ready. Back in her room, she strapped on her carved bone wrist daggers, then tucked a different blade into the sheath on her waistband. If only she had her sacre, but hiding a sword was a little trickier.

Saying good-bye to Maris without tearing up was difficult. Hopefully, the person Chrysabelle was going to meet would help her prove her innocence. Then her new life could truly begin and she could keep the only family she had.

She took a cab into the city, then walked a block over and up to a new street. There she hailed another cab to her final destination, satisfied she'd left no easy trail.

The cab wound through the marine district, past the small portion of the port still in use and into the depths of the shipyard where weeds sprang from the sunbaked concrete and warehouse doors hung off hinges. Finally, the driver stopped in front of a docked freighter that looked as though it hadn't been to sea since the End War. Rust spotted the sides like a rash. Debris-free solar tiles sparkled on the main deck, the only indication the ship was in use. She checked the slip of paper.

"Are you sure this is the place?"

"That's the address you gave me, sweetheart. You change your mind? Couldn't say I blame you, the docks are no place for a woman like you. Nothing but skeletons and bad news down here."

"No, I haven't changed my mind." Although she'd begun to have questions. "I will pay you to stay here and wait for me though."

"I hope you got deep pockets, 'cause I charge extra for ghost towns like this. Plus, I only got about three hours of running time after the solar juice disappears. You ain't back before then, I'm gone." He buzzed the window down, turned the vehicle off, and fished a cigar nub out of his pocket.

"Understood." Not really, but this was no time for a lesson in alternate fuels.

"Then we got a deal." He tapped the com cell behind his left ear and checked in with someone named Dispatch.

Nobility didn't allow those in their employ to have the com chips embedded, nor did they use them themselves. Supposedly the chips could be used to gather a multitude of information from the user. Maybe she would get one when this was all over. When her life was her own again.

She shouldered her bag and got out. The stench of decay and rancid crude wrinkled her nose before a shift in the breeze replaced it with salt and sea. A seabird circled, then dove and came up with a wriggling silver fish. She headed for the gangplank, squinting against the sun and, despite the haze of smog, a brilliant blue sky.

No wonder the vampire from the club hadn't come after her again. With this much sun, he'd probably been unable to find a safe place to recover from the wound she'd given him and turned to ash with the sunrise. Comarré one, Nothos zero.

She smiled. Maybe Paradise City wasn't such a bad place after all.

# Chapter Four

Three days. Three long, pain-filled days since the mystery woman had tried to stake him, and the wound below Mal's heart still throbbed. It should be long healed. At least the screaming in his head was back to its usual almost tolerable level. If Doc hadn't known he'd gone to Puncture that night, hadn't found him in that alley, Mal would have been toast come sunrise. Literally. He'd shake his head if not for the chance it might wake the voices.

Damn that Sweets. Mal had had enough pig's blood in the last week to fill a swimming pool, but it was like Chinese food. An hour later and you were hungry again. Now, if he'd eaten the cook instead...

That jack-off had better show up with a serious amount of fresh, human red. The thought eased the ache in Mal's chest. He'd heal up fine after that. Not to mention being able to go out without wanting to drain every human who crossed his path.

Then he'd deal with his female problem. His beautiful, deadly, sweet-scented female problem. He tapped his fingers on the book he should have been reading and reminded himself she'd nearly turned him to dust.

"Hey." Doc stuck his shaved head through the door. In the ship's dim interior, his almost blue-black skin rendered him nearly invisible. Only his green-gold eyes gave him away with their hint at his varcolai heritage. At the moment, they held a suggestion of worry. "You don't look so hot. Want me roll to the butcher's again?"

"Not unless you're bringing back the butcher."

Doc furrowed his brow, his dark skin reflecting the room's soft light. "I thought you weren't drinking straight from the tap."

"I'm not." *You should.*

"Oh. That was a joke, right?" He leaned against the door frame, nearly filling it. "Kinda sorry, you ask me."

"I didn't." Mal spun his chair toward the porthole that overlooked the distant ocean. Those waters would be a brilliant blue-green on a day like today, if he remembered correctly. Even through the nailed-up boards, the sun made him itch. He should be deep in daysleep, recovering, but the bloodlust made it impossible. Might as well get lost in the next ancient, answerless book. "We're even now. You don't need to be here anymore."

"What are you talking about, bro?"

"You saved my skin. That makes us even. Your debt is paid. You can get back to your own life." Not that Mal really wanted to lose Doc. Having someone around who was daylight capable made life a little easier. And Fi would kill him if Doc left, but fair was fair.

"Like hell. You met me? I'm a little handicapped at the moment. I'd rather hang here." He paused for a moment. "Unless you're saying you don't have my back anymore."

"I'm not saying that. And you're not handicapped." Mal scrubbed a hand over his chin. The growth had moved past stubble and was approaching beard. If he cared, it would have been time to shave.

"Really? What else would you call a were-leopard who can't shift into anything more than a house cat? If it's all the same to you, I'll hang 'til my curse is lifted." He paused. "Or yours. So long as that's cool with you." He shrugged. "Actually, it don't matter. I'm here 'til Fi tells me otherwise."

Mal eased the chair around halfway. "Take money out of the safe and buy the heaviest chains and padlocks you can find. I need you to restrain me before the sun goes down."

"I'll assume that's a yes on having my back." Doc crossed his arms. "Based on the S&M request, I'll also assume you don't think you can hang much longer without something a little more human in your system. I wasn't going to say anything until I had some proof, but word on the street says Nyssa's been spotted running deliveries."

"She better run one here." Mal turned to face Doc. "Find Jonas. Now." He growled softly in his throat. "No, wait. You better chain me up first, in case you can't track him down." *No!* "There's got to be a reason he hasn't contacted me yet."

"Yeah, my gut tells me he's laying low. Not sure why, other than the fact that you're ready to eat his liver." He smoothed the sides of his goatee and grinned. "I'll hit the hardware store and be back in a few."

Doc returned around noon. "I've got good news and bad news."

"And..." Mal gestured for him to go on.

"Shackles are ready to go in the hold. But there's no

four one one on Sweets, sorry. Nobody's talking. He's definitely keeping things on the DL." He planted one large hand on the desk. "You sure you don't want to hit the streets yourself tonight?"

"Not until I find a new blood source."

"There's always Puncture. I could go with you this time. Keep a look out."

*Yes. Go.* "Not again." He twirled a pen through his fingers. The chrome tip glinted dully in the solars.

Doc slouched into the chair across from Mal's desk. "I could jack that blood bank on Nineteenth."

*Do it.* "If anyone's going to do that, it should be me. And trust me, I've thought about it. But that might arouse civilian suspicion."

Doc sat forward. "Maybe I could find a willing subject. This city is lousy with people down on their luck. Offer them some coin. It's not much different than letting the Red Cross have a pint."

Mal glared at him. "You want to add to the voices in my head?" *Yes.* "The names on my body?" *Yes.* "Give Fi a playmate?" *Sure.* "What's one more soul to bear, is that it? No. Never. Don't ever suggest it again. I haven't drunk from the vein in almost fifty years, I'm not about to start now."

"I never said drain them dry. Just take a little."

"I don't have it in me to just take a little. You know that." *Take it all. That's all you've ever done. All you know how to do.* He slammed his head down onto his fists, trying to shut the voices up.

"You shouldn't have let it go this long."

"Thanks for pointing out the obvious."

They stared at each other for a moment, the other

option hanging in the air between them unspoken. Mal knew Doc wouldn't suggest Seven, and Doc undoubtedly knew Mal wouldn't go there, even if he did. That club was out of the question for a multitude of reasons.

Doc cleared his throat. "Speaking of souls, where's Fi? I haven't seen my girl in a few hours."

"She can't be far." Fiona was the first human Mal had drunk to death after being cursed and imprisoned some fifty years ago. She was also the last, since Mal had discovered every life he took after her would manifest in spirit form just as she had. Being haunted by one ghost was one too many. Fortunately, the rest of the lives he'd taken stayed in his head, their voices a constant torment, their names inked across his body. He wore Fi's name across his left forearm, a few inches above his wrist. "I'm not her keeper."

"Well, you kind of are, aren't you? Otherwise, she would have bugged out of here a long time ago."

"Just because she can't leave me doesn't make me her keeper."

"Did I hear you talking about me?" Fi floated in wearing her spirit form. "Miss me, huh?" She propped herself against a wall of conveniently located daggers, swords both long and short, crossbows and throwing stars, and gave Doc a wink. "Hiya."

Mal eyed his ghostly companion, wishing for the millionth time he hadn't sucked the life out of her. "Just wondered where you were is all."

"You get cranky when you haven't fed. I was looking at the fall fashion mags Doc brought me." She spun to show off the clingy dress and high boots she wore.

"This is New Florida." Doc laughed. "We don't have fall."

She frowned at him. "In case you've forgotten, I'm a ghost, pussycat. I don't feel temperature. If I want to pretend to wear wool, I will. You should at least tell me I look pretty." She planted her hands on her hips. "Don't you have mice to catch?"

Doc's pupils narrowed into slits. "You're the only mouse I want to eat."

Fi giggled.

Mal groaned. "Get a room."

Fi opened her mouth to retaliate when the door on the deck below them creaked open.

Mal shot Doc a look. "Forget to lock up again?"

"Hey, I had my hands full." He jumped out of his chair. "Welcome wagon on the way."

A minute later, he bounded back up the stairs. "There's a fine female downstairs. Says Jonas sent her, but she's definitely not Nyssa. Nothing remnant about this chick. She's carrying a bag too. I think your *vino de vena* has finally arrived."

"Tip her, get the goods, and bring them up here, now." His stomach knotted with hunger, and his fangs dropped. A split second later his facial bones shifted. Just as well. Maintaining his human face was wearing him out. He needed that blood. Desperately.

Doc reappeared empty-handed. "I tried. Says she'll only talk to you."

"Son of a priest. Jonas must want a report on how I can't do without him."

"Probably going to jack up his price." Doc tipped his head toward the door. "You want me to bring her up?"

Mal spun toward the overflowing bookcase behind his desk, using the tall back of his leather chair to screen himself from the door. The voices clamored for blood. "Bring her up, but you two get lost. I don't need an audience for this."

"Sure thing, boss." Doc curled his finger at Fi. "C'mon, baby."

The door clicked shut. Several long minutes later, it opened again.

"Hello?"

The dark, taunting perfume of blood and honey choked Mal like a silk noose. His hands dug into the leather. His wound throbbed anew. *Get away, get away, get away…*

He twisted his chair around, already knowing who stood at his door.

"You," he snarled, reaching under the desk for his hidden blade. "Come back to finish what you started?"

# Chapter Five

Mikkel squeezed Tatiana's hand. She responded to the gesture with a stifling glance. Didn't he understand this was neither the time nor the place to display such affections? Perhaps she shouldn't have brought him at all. He'd been turned barely seventy-five years now. Hardly more than a vampling, he still acted like the traveling magician he'd once been. She bit back a smile, remembering the nights they'd spent in Rome. Of course, those youthful appetites were exactly what had drawn her to him in the first place. Now his lineage kept her interest. Mikkel was from the House of Bathory, known for its powerful skills in the black arts. Besides being a strong family, they were the only one that rivaled the bloodthirstiness of her own family, Tepes.

Tepes, as in directly descended from Lord Vlad Tepes. The very count made world-renowned by the kine Bram Stoker and his infamous novel. A purer bloodline one would be hard-pressed to find.

Lord Timotheius, Dominus of the House of Paole, rapped his signet ring on the burled wood table, shivering the flames on the center candelabra. "I hereby call to order this meeting of the Families. May it be noted each house is in attendance."

Tatiana closed her eyes for a brief moment. No matter how hard she tried, she couldn't sense Timotheius the way she could the others. How the House of Paole had managed to cultivate their certain type of invisibility confounded her.

One by one, Timotheius nodded to the Dominus of each family. If the Elder could be equated with the prince of a Family, the Dominus was the king. The always *male* king. "Lord Ivan, Dominus of the House of Tepes, your graciousness in hosting this meeting is much appreciated."

Ivan nodded and motioned for Timotheius to continue as though the five Families met in his mansion every day. Tatiana tried to catch his eye, but his gaze didn't go beyond those gathered at the table. Still, she knew she had his support. After all, Ivan had been with her from the start. He was the one who had tipped her off about Algernon having the ring and advised her about the covenant. How long had he been planning this? Since he first offered her navitas in secret? The resiring had been a difficult, painful process—dying often was—but at least she had come through the ritual with none of the madness often touted as a side effect.

"Lord Syler, Dominus of the House of Bathory."

"Lord Timotheius." Syler waved a hand in response. Curls of dark energy spun off his fingers. Such a deliberate display of power was obviously meant to remind the others of who he was and what he wielded, but to her it recalled a fat old peacock spreading his vulgar feathers. No one needed reminding. Bathory's dark arts shielded the home city of each Family from kine senses, save those mortals who lived within the walls and worked as staff for the nobility.

"Lord Grigor, Dominus of the House of Rasputin."

His face propped against his ring-encrusted hand, Grigor said nothing, just stared with his intense, probing eyes. His house was the youngest, and perhaps the most despised. Of all the gifts of all the houses, those of the Rasputin family made the others most uneasy. No one cared to have their mind read. Tatiana tightened her mental defenses, as invariably all the others in the room did as well.

"And Lord Zephrim, Dominus of the House of St. Germain."

Zephrim bowed slightly, smoothing his robes. In her opinion, St. Germain held the least effectual power of all the houses. Alchemy was as useful as wings on a frog. She much preferred the Tepes gift of persuasion. How could she not? Bending others to her will filled her with a deliciously wicked warmth.

Each Family leader occupied his space like a king, face stoic and full of self-importance. Blighty old ratbags, the whole lot of them. Whether they were dancing with their paramours at a ball, chastising a servant or deciding policy, they were no better than she.

"Tatiana of the House of Tepes, you may bring your petition before the council."

She rose and bowed slightly. "Thank you, Lord Timotheius, esteemed members of the council." Besides the Dominus of her own house, she hoped she had the support of Bathory as well. "I come before you due to the most unfortunate circumstances, the death of my house's Elder, Lord Algernon. It is with great sadness but a sense of duty that I petition the council to appoint me Elder in his stead. In doing so, it is my deepest desire that I may prevent any chaos that might erupt from these circumstances and destroy the great name of the House of Tepes."

Timotheius spoke first. "You are the eldest female, but there is an elder male, Crotius, is there not?"

Zephrim laughed. "Crotius is a babbling idiot who never should have been turned. Still, he is the eldest—"

"Tatiana is a wise choice," Ivan said.

"Of course you would side with her," Timotheius argued. "You are her sire."

Ivan turned, face indignant. "I have sired many of the House of Tepes. I am not recommending any of *them*."

How many had he resired? Was that why Crotius was insane?

"Sire or not, Lord Ivan has a right to his opinion," Syler added. There, that was a modicum of support. Not as much as she'd hoped, but something.

Zephrim pounded his fist on the table. "I call for Lord Ivan to recuse himself."

"And I you," Ivan shot back.

"On what grounds?"

"On the grounds that your precious potions and chemicals have turned you into an addle-brained idiot."

Tatiana quelled the urge to nod.

Zephrim jumped up, drawing an amulet from his belt and shaking it at Ivan. "Someday, you will bow at the feet of my achievements. Alchemy is our only salvation."

"My lords, if I may." Tatiana lifted her palms up, a traditional sign of submission. It pained her deeply to posture this way in front of such ancient fools. "It is not my wish to create such discord."

"Or perhaps it is exactly your wish." Grigor eyed her warily from his seat. He hadn't moved once, just stared at her. Damn his preternatural gift of sight. Had he looked into her? Seen her true purpose? She'd done her best to bury that information. The other lords sat and collected themselves.

Grigor's gaze continued to bore into her. "I suggest we make no decision until Lord Algernon's murderer is brought to justice."

Tatiana drew her spine straighter and faced Grigor directly. "I believe justice, in its own way, has already been served." She turned slowly, making eye contact with each of the Dominus. "I visited the comarré's quarters personally. Stepped over the threshold without need of invitation." She finished her sweep by returning to Grigor and opening herself up so that he might see her memories for himself. "The comarré is dead."

"Death is not an indicator of guilt." Grigor's eyes went down to thin slits.

"Are you accusing me of something?" Rage bubbled up in Tatiana's gut.

Ivan shoved back his chair. "That is uncalled for, Lord Grigor."

Grigor raised his shoulders, then let them fall. "There is but one fatal sin among our kind."

Syler scrolled his finger through the air and words appeared behind it, drawn out by his powerful black magic. *Thou shalt not kill thy brethren.* One by one, the words dripped away until the air cleared.

She trembled at what was being suggested. "I had nothing to do with Lord Algernon's death. Nothing. He was...a friend."

Zephrim snorted. "You have no friends, Tatiana. You have acquaintances, those who tolerate you, those who fear you." He looked behind her at Mikkel. "Those who enjoy your good favor and pray it lasts." He shook his head. "You are exactly what you've striven to become. The best of the worst. The cruelest of the noble. You've not only lived up to your house's reputation, you've surpassed it." His fingers tapped the tabletop. "I believe you recently killed one of your servants, did you not?"

"Remuneration has already been sent to the family," she said. Those who came to work for the Families knew what they were getting into. Most hoped to earn the bite that would forever change their future.

He stood. "As to Grigor's suggestion that no decision be made until Lord Algernon's murderer is found...I second it."

"Motion passed." Timotheius rapped his ring on the table again. "The council is adjourned."


"Nothos," Chrysabelle spat out the word. "I thought you were dead."

The assassin rose from his chair without the grace most vampires usually possessed. A blade flashed in one hand. By the looks of him, he still hadn't fed. And by the smell of him, her dagger had left a lasting impression in that alley. He was weak. Easy to take down.

"Nothos? Not hardly. And as blood delivery girls go, you fail. Unless Jonas meant *you* were the delivery." He made an attempt to retract his fangs, got them halfway gone, and failed. Could Nothos do that? She didn't think so. "Not going to happen."

"You've got that right." She straightened her arms, unsnapping the locking mechanism on her wrist blades. They shot forward and she snagged them in her fists. "Guess I will finish what I started after all."

She threw the first blade, but he ducked, letting it thwack into a copy of *Schender's Compendium of Pandimensional Beings*. No loss. *Schender's Compendium* was first-year stuff at best. The second dagger found its mark in the vampire's shoulder. A thin wisp of smoke curled off the new wound. Varcolai bone blades had that effect. She snatched a third from her ankle holster.

He leaped over the desk, arms out to grab her, but the wince when he landed gave him away. He was more than hurt. He was about to collapse. His eyes rolled back in his head.

Check that.

He *was* collapsing. Definitely not Nothos then.

A half second after he thudded to the floor, his face went from human to full on noble vampire, proving her right about him not being Nothos. The big man who'd let her in came charging through the door. He was varcolai— or shifter in human terms, and of the feline variety by the scent of him. Another being followed him in. Chrysabelle blinked as the temperature dropped a few degrees—a ghost? What kind of vampire kept this sort of company?

"What did you do to him?" The man ripped the dagger out of her hand.

"Hey!" She grabbed for the blade, but he was quicker than she anticipated.

"Sorry, princess. Can't have you perforating the boss." He threw it out the door and, by the clattering, down the steps. "Fi, get corporeal and give me a hand."

"On it."

With a quick shimmer like rising heat, the ghost was suddenly earthbound. She grabbed Chrysabelle and held her arms tight to her sides. The ghost's cold touch reminded her of Lord Algernon. Fi leaned in, eyes flinty with anger. "You stake him dead, and I disappear. I'm not cool with that, you comprehend?"

Chrysabelle head butted Fi and knocked her backward.

"Ow." Fi tumbled into a bookcase. She shook herself and felt her forehead. "I'm bleeding! I'm not supposed to bleed."

"We better get a look at that wound." The varcolai knelt beside the vampire.

"I'm right here, kitty cat," Fi said.

"Not you, babe. Him. And I told you about calling me that when we're not alone." He turned his attention back to the vampire. "Hang on, boss, this is gonna sting." He pulled the pale dagger out of the vampire's shoulder and turned it over in his hands. "What kind of bone is this?"

Chrysabelle reached for it, but he tossed it over his shoulder before she could grab it. He growled and his eyes glimmered gold.

"Move and I'll tear your throat out, got it?"

She nodded, pretending to be scared as she slowly reached for the blade in her back waistband.

He went back to work on the vampire, ripping his T-shirt down the front.

Chrysabelle froze, blade forgotten, and stared at the vampire's bare chest. Except it wasn't bare. A lacework of script decorated his flesh. Names, in a multitude of languages, covered almost every inch of skin and muscle. Her mouth opened, and for a moment, no sound came out.

She pointed. "Vampires can't be tattooed. The skin heals them away."

"They're not exactly your typical ink." The varcolai glanced toward Fi. "We've got to try to clean this or something. It's not getting any better."

Chrysabelle backed up. The weapon-laden walls started to close in. "It won't."

The man and woman simultaneously turned to look at her. The vampire groaned and struggled to sit. The varcolai helped him to a chair, but Fi kept glaring.

"What do you mean, it won't? How do you know?"

Chrysabelle backed up a little farther and hit the desk. She had to get out of here. "It won't heal, unless he feeds. Or—"

"Or what?" The vampire stood, one hand on the varcolai's shoulder. This close, he seemed taller. And bigger. And not nearly as weak.

This wasn't going to be well received. Call it a hunch. "Or you wash it out with holy water."

The vampire snarled. "What the—"

"And us, fresh out." The varcolai reached for her, but she bobbed to the side and spun past him.

"He's a vampire. Why do you care what happens to him?" They must be his minions, enthralled by his power.

"Because he's straight up." Anger flashed in the varcolai's eyes.

"He's straight up what?"

The varcolai rolled his eyes. "One of the good guys."

One of the good guys? Since when did that apply to vampires trying to kill her?

The vampire, face back to human, grabbed a short sword off the wall and positioned the point at the hollow of her throat. His hand trembled slightly, clearly weaker than he let on. "You're not exactly supposed to be trying to kill me either. Comarré."

He spoke the word like an accusation. Had he read her mind? Maybe he was from the Rasputin bloodline. Must be careful. Relax. So he knew what she was. What vampire didn't? "I came here for help, not to find the monster who tried to kill me in that alley. You can tell your friend Jonas he did a great job of setting me up. Twice."

"Jonas isn't his friend—" The varcolai's brows rose. "Wait, this the chick who stabbed you?" He whistled out a breath. "You really do need to feed."

Fatigue bracketed the vampire's mouth. "Me try to kill you? Other way around. I was trying to protect you. An unescorted comarré has the same chance for survival in this city as a duckling in a snake pit." The sword glimmered in the overheads. "Swear you'll behave and I'll put this down. I really don't want to have to kill you."

She grabbed the wrist holding the sword and did a fast calculation. No wonder he was on the verge of shutting down. "Big words from someone who hasn't fed in eight or nine days."

"How do you know that?" His voice held a small tremor. Not just weakness. By now, bloodlust would be crazing him. She knew what her scent did to his kind. Her touch could multiply that. He fought it well for one so hungry.

She released him. "Comarré know a lot of things." Shouldn't he know that too? Most nobles did.

He kept the sword raised, the tendons in his wrist cording with the effort, but put a little distance between them as he went to sit behind the desk. He tipped his chin at the chair across from him. "Sit."

She did, reluctantly.

"What's all this comarré business?" the varcolai asked. "And what exactly did you stab him with?"

She reached into the back waistband of her trousers. The varcolai grabbed her elbow. "Easy now."

"I was only going to show you the weapon."

He released her. "Fine, but nice and slow."

Carefully, she pulled out the dagger she'd used in the alley and held it flat on her palm. "Golgotha steel."

Fi, now hovering near the ceiling again, shook her head. "Looks like wood to me."

"Golgotha steel is wood." The varcolai's eyes rounded as he took the blade and tossed it onto the desk. "Carved from the True Cross or the Tree of Life. I thought those blades were just stories." His gaze went back to Chrysabelle. "Someone's well connected."

The vampire swiped his free hand across his stubbled chin. His eyes fixed on the weapon. No doubt at close range he could sense its power. "And has deep pockets. A weapon like that could buy some serious muscle." He stood and leaned forward, keeping a firm grip on the sword and a reasonable distance from the Golgotha blade.

"It's time we started from the beginning. And by we"—he narrowed his eyes on Chrysabelle and raised the sword to throat level again—"I mean you."

# Chapter Six

I'm not telling you anything," the comarré said.

"Fine." Mal nodded to Doc seated in the chair next to her. "Lock her in one of the storage containers until she decides to get chatty." Then he could stop imagining his teeth sinking into her pretty neck and drinking until his brain floated. *Drain her.* He could give up the pretense of being fine too and go collapse somewhere. Golgotha steel. *Bad, bad, bad...* It was a wonder he'd lasted this long. Not that he hadn't survived worse. He dropped back into his desk chair.

"You got it, bro." Doc rubbed his hands together in overacted glee.

The comarré didn't budge. "If you're trying to scare me, it won't work. I don't frighten easily."

The tough act was hot, he'd give her that. "What's your name?"

"A-Anna."

*She lies.* He closed his eyes for a moment. He didn't need the voices telling him what he already knew. "You scared pretty easily in that alley, Anna. I could taste the fear coming off you." *Should've tasted more.*

She crossed her arms. "I thought you were trying to kill me."

He gestured with the sword. "And you don't feel that way now because . . . ?"

She smirked. "How's your shoulder?"

Doc failed to stop a laugh. It came out a snort. Fi elbowed him in the ribs, but since she'd returned to ghost form, her arm went right through him. Unfortunately.

"Did Jonas really send you?"

"Yes."

Damn Sweets. What was he thinking? "What for? And how did you come by that blade? Just knowing what you are raises a multitude of questions."

Doc raised his hand. "We back to that comarré thing again?"

Anna, or whatever her real name was, ignored Doc.

"Jonas said you could help. And I could say the same thing for you, vampire. Besides those impossible markings you wear, your being here"—she glanced around, clearly unimpressed—"raises a few questions as well. Where's your luxury? Your display of wealth? Your servants? If this ghost and this varcolai are the best you could do, then I pity you."

"I could be fringe," Mal said. If only his life were that simple.

Anna didn't look convinced. "Fringe can't shift their faces."

Fi shot forward. "I'm no one's servant." She jerked a thumb at Mal. "Especially not his."

"Don't get too close," Doc mumbled, waving the ghost back and staring hard at Anna. "How'd you know I'm varcolai?"

Anna slanted her eyes at him. "You smell like a shifter."

Doc growled softly.

"Enough." Mal shot him a visual dagger before looking at Anna again. Her glow was impossible to ignore. Worse still, the pulse at her neck beckoned. *Drain her. Quiet her.* He shifted his gaze. "I have my reasons for being here. What are yours?"

She kept her bloodred lips firmly shut.

"Storage container." He kicked his feet up onto the desk, leaned back, and picked up the book he'd been about to read earlier. The movement sent fireworks through his field of vision.

Doc jumped to his feet. "Let's bounce, princess." He grabbed Anna's arm and yanked her up.

"I knew Jonas was no good. *Mortal.*" She filled the word with the same disgust Mal felt toward the being responsible for his curse.

"But you are one." Couldn't hurt to remind her. *Couldn't hurt to drain her.*

"What?" Doc looked at Anna a little harder. "Princess is mortal?"

"Sure," she said, staring Mal down. "As much as the vampire used to be."

Doc jerked her once. "Chill with 'the vampire.' He has a name—"

"Doc, storage container, now." The last thing she needed to know was who he was. Comarré knew their history, or were supposed to. He wasn't sure of anything about them based on this one. Unless she was some sort of renegade.

"Wait." His feet went back to the floor. If she was renegade, there might be someone after her. He stood, digging the point of the sword into the desk for support.

"Tie her to the chair. If she fights, knock her out. Then run the perimeter. Make sure Anna came alone."

"Shouldn't one of us check her for weapons?" Fi asked. "She seems to have a serious stash of them."

"I'll take care of that when I get back, just get her tied up." He made it to the downstairs fridge without passing out. Seemed like a good sign. He drained the last quart of pig's blood, hating every drop and wishing with each swallow it was the blood of the woman upstairs. *Take her. Drain her.* He'd never tasted comarré blood, but he'd heard stories. It wasn't just nourishment; it was power, prestige, protection. If you could afford it.

He headed back up feeling marginally better. Doc and Fi waited at the door.

"She's trussed like a Sunday goose," Fi said.

*Perfect for the eating.*

Doc winked at Fi. "Yeah, Fi's pretty good with the knots."

"Doc, you sweep the ship. Fi, haunt the incoming streets. Look for any strange vehicles, scents, beings—anything out of the ordinary. Report only if you find something. Otherwise, I'll let you know when I'm done with her."

They nodded and took off. He gave up on hiding his true face—after all, she'd seen it already. Not masking it would help him conserve some energy. With that, he pushed through the door and locked it behind him. Anna's arms and legs were tied to those of the chair.

She sneered at him, all blonde rage, pale anger, and shimmering glow. Her pulse boiled through him. "Does this make you feel strong and powerful, vampire? Binding a gentle comarré like some great enemy?"

"Considering you've sunk two blades into me, gentle left the picture a long time ago." He kneeled in front of her, putting them at eye level. Time to see what else she might be hiding, starting from the ankles.

She sniffed at him. "You just fed and yet you still smell hungry. Animal blood will not sustain you. Why don't you take what you really need?" The question brought his head up. Her eyes were the pale blue of the last dawn he remembered.

"Is that an invitation?" *Take it.* He eased his hands over her right ankle, then worked up her calf over her trousers. So warm. *So ripe.*

She stiffened at his touch. "I meant why have you not fed properly for so long?"

"I don't drink from the vein, and my source hasn't come through." A little honesty given might a little honesty get. He stopped midthigh and switched to her left ankle.

"You'd be much stronger if you took from the vein. You're barely surviving."

"I've survived just fine for the past fifty years or so, thanks." He glanced up. She was staring. Hard.

She leaned in, studying his contorted facial bones. "When the bloodlust is this strong, it keeps you from hiding your true face."

With great effort, he shifted to his human face, then let it go, just to prove he could. "I can hide it if I need to." The exertion cost him a chunk of his control, just what he hadn't wanted to do. His hands stopped above her right knee. *So full of blood.* Her body heat sank into his skin through her thin silk trousers like tiny, licking flames. Her heart's rhythm pulsed into his gut, tightening it, making him want. This close, she seemed bathed in sunlight. He suffocated a groan. *Drain her. Drink her. Hot, sweet, yours.*

Her mouth moved, but the voices in his head drowned out the words.

"What?" Concentrate.

"I said why do you wear those marks?" Her eyes studied the strip of skin visible where his ripped shirt hung open. He should have changed.

He skimmed one finger down the back of her naked hand. "Why do you hide yours?"

She dropped her chin, breaking eye contact. "I do what I must to pass."

At last, a little piece of her puzzle revealed. "Why do you need to pass as human?"

For the span of three breaths, she stayed silent. "How do I know I can trust you?" Her voice was softer. Almost touching. If this was a ruse, it was a very artful one. Practiced. But of course it would be. She was comarré.

His hands slid up her arms, gently squeezing, feeling the mechanisms that had held the hidden wrist blades, then going higher. "You can't. Just like I don't know if I can trust you. You can take the chance though. See if it pays off."

"And if it doesn't, I end up dead."

"Who would want to kill you, Anna? You're comarré, not exactly the scourge of the vampire world." That was his job.

She tipped her head back, exposing the length of her pale, beckoning neck. If he'd had breath, it would have caught in his throat. Most likely the exact response she'd been going for. The voices begged.

"My patron is dead."

Blood coursed beneath her delicate skin. Think. *Drink.* Respond. *With fangs.* Find words. He stared at the ceiling along with her. "So...dead. Then...you're free, right? Isn't that how it works?"

"He was murdered."

Mal took his hands off her and rocked back on his heels. Another piece of her puzzle clicked into place. "And they think you did it."

# Chapter Seven

The cobra nudged Tatiana's fingers, traveling over her palm to rest his heavy mother-of-pearl head against her wrist and forearm. She learned long ago her pet's affection came easier if she fed before visiting him. Nehebkau preferred her warm.

His tongue flicked her skin, and she smiled. "My darling," she whispered. "Can you tell I've missed you?"

She stroked his smooth back as he slithered his meter-long body around her arm. In the two years since his hatching, the albino serpent had become her favorite companion, and the room she'd turned into his home, her sanctuary. The space had been transformed into the perfect habitat with all the appropriate jungle flora and fauna and elaborate systems designed to re-create the proper humidity and ultraviolet light. When Tatiana came to visit, the replicator automatically shifted to night. Overhead, a false sky twinkled with fiber-optic stars.

"Those suckwits think I killed him. Can you imagine? I am nothing if not patient. The ruins prove that, don't they?" She shook her head. "Makes me want to drain the life out of something."

Bloodred eyes met hers expectantly as he raised his head. She smiled. Her anger cooled.

"My sweet boy. At least you listen." Not that he had a choice. "We cold-blooded creatures have to stick together, don't we?" He hadn't struck her since the first few months of his life, and those times were inconsequential. The venom had no effect on the already dead.

"Come, let's sit and you can tell me all about your day." She patted a lump in his midsection. "I see you got the rat I sent you." She'd begun feeding him rats injected with her own blood in an effort to make her pet as immortal as she was. Nehebkau was her fourth cobra and she hoped her last. Losing the first three had hurt, not as bad as losing a child, but close. As mementos, she'd had a belt and slippers made from the skins. A little macabre, perhaps, but such things did wonders for one's intimidation factor. Everything for a purpose.

She carried her precious boy to the teak chaise and lay down beneath the special circulating heat lamps. Nehebkau stretched, uncoiling from her arm to wind across her belly and chest until his head nestled at the hollow of her throat.

She pulled her locket out from under him and unsnapped it, studying the painted portrait inside. A wistful smile crossed her mouth as a twist of pain knotted her belly. She snapped the locket shut and tucked it into her blouse.

Closing her eyes, she slid into her favorite fantasy, imagining herself as some great Egyptian pharaoh-queen. Not Hatshepsut or Nefertiti or even Cleopatra, but one greater still. A true goddess come to rule on earth. She caressed Nehebkau's drowsy form. In her mind, sparkling jewels and beads of gold adorned her, showering her in reflected sunlight.

Her lids lifted. That was always where her fantasy ran aground. Those wretched Egyptians and their stupid sun god. For all their dreams of immortality, they'd been headed in the wrong direction. She twirled the end of Nehebkau's tail through her fingers.

Perhaps she should be Eve instead. An immortal Eve, unafraid of the apple, unashamed of her nakedness, and all too willing to corrupt man. She laughed. Nehebkau shifted.

Footsteps approached, followed a moment later by a knock on the door. It had best be a dire emergency. She was not to be disturbed when she was in her sanctuary.

"What is it?"

"Mistress, there is news."

"Of what?"

"The girl."

The girl? The girl was dead. Wasn't she? Tatiana bolted upright, tumbling Nehebkau to her lap. He hissed like a distant tornado, raising his head and flaring his hood. "Now, now, Nehebie, this is very important. I won't be a minute."

She scooped him to the side, where he wound around himself to bask in the heat, then she went to the door.

"Well, what news?"

The minion handed her a sealed note. "This just came from the Nothos dispatched to the IRF."

She snatched the paper. "I don't care if it is the Islamic Republic of France, just call it bloody France, you prat." If the kine grew a backbone, they might stop being overthrown by whichever one of them had the bigger gun or the more frightening god.

"Yes, mistress. France it is from now—"

She shut the door and strolled back to the chaise. Nehebkau hadn't moved. She sat next to him and tore open the note.

*Found traces of comarré blood in the Paris sewers. Believe the girl alive and fled overseas. No sign of ring. Proceeding as discussed.*

Bollocks. What proof did the Nothos have that the girl was alive? Or were they just assuming? Not that she trusted Madame Rennata either. If the blood whore was alive, that would change everything. Because thanks to the council's insistence on justice, she was now going to have to bring the girl in, still alive, to be tried. And to prove her own innocence so she could be made Elder.

So much for proceeding as discussed.

"Why do you automatically assume they've decided I'm the murderer?" If they hadn't been tied to the arms of the chair, Chrysabelle would have put her hands on her hips.

"You've attacked me twice. Seems a natural conclusion to me." The vampire had been struggling to keep his hungry, silvery eyes off her throat ever since she'd tipped her head back. The distraction had worked beautifully. She almost had the knot around her right wrist undone.

"I was only defending myself."

"Really? Is that what they teach in those comarré houses?"

She froze. Did he know? She exhaled. Of course not, he was just talking. She laughed. "Yes, that's right. We're lethal killers, trained from birth in the dark art of assassination. Because we have so much free time between etiquette, history studies, and music lessons."

He half-smiled at that. Good. "Where did you get the hidden blades then? And the Golgotha steel?"

"The wrist daggers were…a gift. The Golgotha is standard comarré issue." The knot loosened beneath her stealthy fingers. "It's our cyanide pill."

His brow furrowed. "Is there a big call for ritual suicide among the comarré?"

"It isn't unknown." She shrugged, the perfect opportunity to work her hand a little farther out.

"So you carry a blade known to be not only exceptionally rare and expensive, but extraordinarily dangerous to vampires, just in case you might need to die an honorable death?" In one quick move, he was inches from her face, those eerie silver eyes shining on her. "Not bloody likely."

Someone knocked on the door. She inhaled. The varcolai. The vampire unbent himself slowly until he towered over her.

"Come in, Doc."

Doc? The varcolai was a physician, but he couldn't supply the vampire with human blood?

The varcolai opened the door. "Bad time?"

"No. What is it?"

"Can we convo?" He nodded behind him.

"Sure." The vampire left, closing the door.

She shut her eyes and listened. They stayed just outside the door but kept their voices down. They might know what she was, but they obviously underestimated her capabilities. A smile curved her mouth. Eavesdropping at this distance wasn't even a challenge.

"We didn't find squat, 'cept for a cab hanging at the end of the pier. I sent him away."

The smile vanished. No cab meant a long walk back to

somewhere safe. She could do it, but it would be dark soon. Not exactly the time she wanted to be alone and on foot in this wretched place. Her fingers worked harder on the knot.

"Where's Fi?"

"Patrolling the top deck. Did you get any more weapons off her?"

"No. I'm going to move her to one of the crew rooms, get her settled in for the night. Tell Fi I want her to research everything she can find on the comarré. This girl is one lie after another."

Chrysabelle bristled at his accusation, even if it was accurate. She worked her wrist back and forth until the rope grazed her knuckles.

"Once I get her down there, I'll probably talk to her a little more, but then I'm definitely going to need you to lock me up. Opposite end of the ship, secure as you can. Having her on board right now is like storing lighter fluid next to open flame, but I can't see sending her back out there."

A change of scenery meant a good chance to escape. She tugged her hand free, chafing the skin but thankfully not breaking it. The scent of her spilled blood might push him over the edge. Her fingers flew to the second knot.

"You got it."

"She'll need food too." The doorknob clicked a half turn. Forget the food, she needed more time.

"Don't worry, Fi and I will hook her up."

The second knot came easier. She bent to use her teeth. The rope tasted of salt and something oily. Her head snapped back as the knot came loose.

"I'm serious about securing me. It has to hold. I don't

need another name on me or another ghost haunting me. Especially not a comarré."

Frantically, she went to work with both hands on the rope around her ankles.

"We won't let you. I swear it."

One of her fingernails broke with the effort to get the first knot undone. Faster, faster... The door opened. The vampire filled the passage, outlined by the light from the hallway. He shut the door and leaned against it. "Your heart rate sped up the minute I stepped outside. I figured you'd have all four of those knots untied by now."

Ankles still tied, she lunged toward the desk and the Golgotha dagger. He reached it first, snatching it up. The sizzling started as soon as it made contact with his skin. Snarling, he pitched it away. A long red weal marred the length of his palm. He turned to face her.

She sank back into the chair, the first real trickle of fear running down her spine.

"I'm done playing games with you, comarré."

He gathered both her wrists into his injured hand, reaching down with his other to tear the rope from her ankles in one clean swipe. He yanked her to her feet, opened the door, and shoved her out ahead of him. "Run and I will hunt you down and eat you for dinner."

She didn't know him well enough to know if he was lying or not, so she went with not. Just in case.

Together, they marched down two flights of stairs and through numerous hallways and turns. She tried to memorize the labyrinth, but the ship was massive and completely unfamiliar territory.

He stopped her in front of a small door that locked from the outside. "In."

She fumbled with the dead bolts, hating that her nerves were showing. He reached past her and popped the door open, brushing his cold arm against her shoulder. She stepped through, glad to put some distance between them.

He followed, ducking to fit, and flipped on the light.

She clutched her chest in mock surprise. "All this? For me? You shouldn't have." The room held nothing but a narrow fold-down bunk and a wooden chair. The built-in bookcases were empty save for a yellowed Russian newspaper.

He grabbed the chair and tossed it out the door, which bore an equal number of locks on the inside.

"You're right, that's a huge improvement." She crossed her arms and did her best to look like she didn't care. It was better than crying. Not that she would. Not in front of him. Comarré were built of stronger stuff.

He faced her, the mask of anger still firmly in place, those silver eyes bright and piercing. "Sun goes down in less than an hour, so you're here for the night."

"People will be looking for me if I don't return."

"I'll put an end to the looking if they get this far." He moved to the door.

She took a step forward. "I thought you wanted to talk to me some more." Some perverse part of her wasn't ready for him to leave.

"I've had enough lies for one day. Maybe you'll feel more truthful tomorrow." He ducked out. "Lock this behind me. Don't unlock it for anyone but Doc or Fi. Doc will bring you food later."

"Lock myself in?" For some reason, maybe the line of dead bolts on the outside of the door, she hadn't expected that. She took another step forward. "In case you break out of your shackles and come after me?" Adrenaline pumped through her, making her reckless. Pushing her to dare him. She no longer cared if he knew what she'd over-heard or what power she possessed. "Afraid I might end up another name on your skin?"

He was suddenly in front of her, eyes platinum bright and feral with hunger. He inhaled, opening his mouth as if to taste her scent on his tongue. His lids half-shut, his fangs gleamed white as bone. Then he was out the door again, jaw tightening as he swallowed.

"Yes. That. Exactly."

# Chapter Eight

Mal made the trek to the far hold on autopilot. The way there disappeared in a mind-numbing, head-spinning golden haze of summer sky eyes, sun-blonde hair, and honey-fragranced blood. Fortunately, she was now three decks above and at the other end of the ship. Far enough so he could pretend her perfume no longer curled around him like warm smoke. Far enough for the voices to stop chattering about her. Around the comarré they alternated between frenzied need and cowering panic.

Doc was in one of the empty boxcars that filled hold number five, threading the wrist-thick chains through some tie-downs in the interior of the container. "You get anything else out of her?"

"No." He shoved a hand through his hair. It was as overgrown as his beard. "Hurry up."

"Sun's not down for another thirty." Doc adjusted something for a second time. "You sure you're cool with this? I mean, considering your history and all—"

"Now." The idea of voluntarily putting himself in shackles seemed like madness until he considered the alternative. He would not have her death on his hands.

"Cripes, she's made a mess of you." Doc looked up. "Well, a bigger mess." Chains rattled and clanked with what sounded like safety. "All right, let's go."

Mal walked to the center of the hardware and lay down while Doc secured his ankles. The floor of the storage container reeked of chemicals and rust. Good. Maybe that would block out the perfume he was desperate to ignore.

"You gave Fi my instructions?" he asked.

The first shackle clunked into place. Darkness swirled through his brain, snapping at his sanity like a pack of wild dogs. He stared into the light beyond the container's open door. Doc added the chain and padlock before answering.

"Yeah, about that…"

"What?" The air-temperature metal cooled against his skin. *Always cold.*

"She said she'd get to it at her earliest convenience." Doc fastened the other shackle into place quicker than the first.

"In English."

"She said she had something to do and I should leave her alone." He shrugged. "Not like I can keep up with her when she's slipping through walls anyway."

Mal placed his wrist onto the next steel band. "Why couldn't the soul destined to plague me for the rest of eternity have belonged to a little old man who just wanted to sit in an easy chair and nap?"

Doc shook his head as he clicked the padlock shut. "Women. They're man's downfall, that's for sure. All those curves and attitude. No good can come of that."

Images of Anna filled Mal's head. Her scent swirled around him anew. A low growl vibrated out of his throat.

*Always hungry.* He jerked against the shackles. Doc jumped away.

"Seriously, bro, you give me the freakin' creeps when you're like this."

"Finish." A feral edge serrated the voice rumbling out of him. "Now."

Doc closed the last shackle around Mal's wrist and locked it. "I'm outa here. See you in the a.m." He backed out of the storage container and slammed the door. *Always dark.*

Mal listened as Doc ran a length of chain through the handle and secured it. His footsteps faded. He would lock the hold doors as well. Possibly sit guard outside.

Darkness cocooned him in isolation. He lay there trying to imagine a sky of stars above, trying to hold on to his sanity, but his mind's eye twisted the blackness into difficult memories. As the beast inside roared with hunger, the walls around him became a stone pit slick with scum. The shackles bit into his skin, echoing the pain he'd endured all those years in that ruined dungeon. The boxcar disappeared, transformed into the place he'd been cursed. The hellhole that still tormented him in nightmares.

Foul air filled his mouth, coating his tongue like spoiled milk. Rats scuttled along the walls. *Stay still. Let them come to you.* Their bones crunched beneath his teeth, their gamey blood spilling down his throat, keeping him on the razor's edge of existence.

He pulled against the shackles until they bit through flesh. Until they scraped bone. Until the bone cracked.

His bed of straw deteriorated into dust. His clothes to rags, then threads, then nothing. Day or night, May or December, one year or five, five years or fifteen, he couldn't tell. Always hungry. Always cold. Always dark.

At first, he refused to call out for help. Then he tested the walls with a bellow that had the power to shatter glass. No one came. In the end, his voice left him, his tongue little more than leather, his throat a useless passage. The rats were gone, long consumed. His muscle thinned to strips of sinew barely holding his brittle bones together under withered skin.

Hallucinations plagued his atrophied brain. Memories of his human life flitted in and out like tortured butterflies. The moan of pleasure from his wife's lips. His daughter's laugh. The wildflower scent of their chestnut curls. Their dying pleas. Their torn throats. Their blood. His past became a torturous mix of dreams and delusions. Had he done those things? He couldn't remember. Couldn't tell truth from lie. He wept dry tears over the chaos in his head.

It wasn't until he heard her voice that he realized his sight was gone. So sweet, that voice. Sweeter still, the siren call of her beating heart. *Blood.* Hope stirred inside. He'd learned his lesson with the rats. Didn't move until she was upon him, nudging his remains with her foot, no doubt thinking him the dungeon's last victim.

How wrong she was.

He lunged with power borrowed against the promise of blood. She beat her small fists against him, breaking bones, tearing skin, shrieking, crying. He held fast. Sank his gumless fangs into her soft, pliant neck. Her backpack slipped from her shoulders. He drank deep her throbbing, pulsing life. Drank until he almost swallowed her death.

Her dead body fell limp and warm across his rejuvenating form. Pain flashed over his body but he ignored it. After so much hurt, what was a little more? He shoved her aside and pulled his scrawny wrists through the shackles before the flesh filled out. A pool of light spilled from somewhere, hurting his eyes. He felt for it. No fire greeted him. Not sun. A flashlight. Hers.

With new strength, he smashed the shackles at his ankles with the steel torch.

It wasn't until he heard her voice the second time that he realized the extent of the curse.

"Vampire," she screamed at him.

He nearly toppled over he twisted so fast. Was there life in her still? That meant more blood.

A transparent, female image hovered over the girl's lifeless form, pointing a finger at him. Accusing. "You killed me. All I wanted was to find a shard of pottery or a coin and now I'm dead." She flew at him, cutting through him like a gust of winter wind. A ghost.

He stumbled to his knees, gutted by the burst of cold after her blood had begun to warm him. The flashlight fell, its light directed at him. He stared at his shriveled forearms. Had his skin decayed that much? He stared harder and the bruises separated into names. Up his arms. Across his belly. Covering his chest.

The mother of three he'd taken in 1811. Her three he'd taken right after. The miller in 1860. The miller's plump wife. The shipbuilder. The passel of street urchins. The farmer's son in 1920. The whore in New Orleans not long after that. The midnight raid through a boarding school dorm. The policeman who'd tracked him...

The ghost girl hovered before him. "Killing me has activated a curse placed upon you. Blood magic. Black magic." She shook her head. "Monster," she screamed. "And now you're going to pay. For every life you've already taken you'll hear their voices in your head. For every new life you take, you'll be haunted by their spirit. I am the first of those."

She pointed at him. "I'm going to make your life a living hell. All of us are." She howled in rage as she hung over him, her ruined throat weeping bloody tears. "Can't you hear them? The voices of everyone you've murdered. So many..." She clutched at her head.

Whispers echoed through his brain. *The voices of his kills*. The souls waking. Crying for vengeance. Screaming for blood. Berating him. Lashing him. A multitude of voices. A multitude of languages. Nagging, punishing, cursing. A fissure of pain threatened to split his head open.

"Mal."

That voice. Her voice.

"Mal, you awake?"

He lunged upward. The shackles wrenched him back. Sweat soaked his clothing. His chest ached. He would kill her again if that would shut her up.

"Mal, it's Fi. Snap out of it."

Light shattered his vision. He blinked and struggled to sit. "Where..." The voices laughed at him. His body shuddered with exertion. He was in the storage container, not the pit. Fi stood in the open door. Light filtered through her diaphanous form.

"Go away," he snarled. As if she could. The curse had trapped her. Bound her to him. He turned away as much as the chains would allow. *Go away*, the voices mocked. *Weak. Broken. Pitiful—*

"Trust me, I would if I could." She drifted closer. "Snap out of it. I have blood." She stopped and peered at him. "You look like hell and your nightmares are wrecking my head. We share that crap, remember?"

He nodded, not trusting his voice.

"Hurry up," she called over her shoulder. Her image wavered.

"I'm here." Doc came in carrying a clear plastic pitcher stained with crimson.

"Take care of him. I need to go lie down..." Her voice trailed off.

"Will do," he answered, but she'd vanished. He kneeled at Mal's side. "Here, drink up." He lifted the pitcher to Mal's lips.

He drank without tasting, gulping it down until there was no more. Familiar warmth flooded his body. He lay back, sated for the first time in many days. Warmth and relief. And worry. That blood had tasted—"Where did Fi get human blood?"

Doc set the pitcher aside and went to work unlocking the shackles. "You know Fi, she's sly like that."

"Where did she get it?"

"You know where she got it."

The leg bands came off first. "She can't do that. I told her after the last time—"

"You don't know by now she doesn't listen to you? Or anyone for that matter."

Fi had done this two years ago. Slit her wrist and drained blood for him. Problem was her solid form took forever to replenish the fluid. No wonder she'd disappeared so quickly to rest. They'd all be better off if she couldn't become corporeal. Could real ghosts do that? Fi was the first he'd come across of any variety. He rotated his unlocked arm while Doc undid the other. Felt good to be whole again. But not at Fi's expense. Their relationship was tenuous enough already. Not that he blamed her. Living with your murderer had to wear on you.

He watched Doc work. "You knew she was going to do that."

"Don't lay that on me. You think I wanted her to hurt herself for you? I'm not the one who needed the juice." Doc tossed the key at him and hopped to his feet. "Unlock yourself."

Mal grabbed the key. "I didn't mean—"

"Yeah, you did." He prowled toward the door. "Thanks for reminding me what a jerk you can be."

"Unlike Fi, you stay here of your own choice."

Doc didn't look back. "I stay here for *her*."

Mal unlocked the last shackle and pocketed the key. Doc would cool off, no matter how much Fi's actions had upset him.

Mal stretched, feeling better than he had in a long while. Human blood did an undead body good. He hiked up his shirt. The wound was gone. Only a fading bruise marked where the comarré's blade had pierced his skin. The blood would quiet the voices for at least a day, maybe two, and with the hunger under control, she could no longer tempt him. Perfect time for a visit.

Why put off until tomorrow what could be interrogated today?


From the outside, Hôtel de la Belle Etoile had changed very little since the last time Tatiana visited Paris several decades ago. She left Mikkel to direct the unloading of the car and went inside, pulling off the mandatory burqa once she entered the lobby. Some of the staff were different.

And now the windows sported the latest in helioglazing, as did all the hotels run by and reserved for vampire nobility. Gone were the days of suffocating velvet drapes and interior rooms.

Other than those changes, it was still the same beautifully maintained interior, decorated in unrelenting Charles X style. The lush drapery, expanses of marble, gilt chandeliers, and yards of carved paneling suited her perfectly. This was the level of style a woman of her rank should enjoy when traveling. Still, being here meant the blood whore might yet breathe.

That was enough to ruin her trip.

Maybe she'd recover the ring. A potential bright spot. She relaxed as Mikkel joined her and the fringe concierge bowed his greeting. "Mistress Tatiana, how lovely to see you and your guest."

"I'm tired. Where's my room?" Fawning bored her, unless she was in the mood for it. Which she wasn't, strangely enough. Must be stress.

"Of course. We have the Empress Suite prepared for you." He smiled like a dog waiting for a biscuit. "I see the bellman is taking your things up. Is there anything we can do or provide to help you settle in? Anything at all?"

Sycophant. She smiled back, perfectly willing to test his mettle. "Female twins. No blondes. Not older than twenty-five, and still virgins." She glanced at her diamond and platinum Cartier. "Say...half an hour? I'd hate to spend my first night in Paris without a proper French meal."

"Good choice, darling," Mikkel said, giving her a wink. She returned his gaze and rested her hand on his forearm, imagining how delicious that blood would taste and how earth-shattering the sex would be afterward. There was nothing like a good scrog with virgin blood in your veins.

The concierge's head bobbed in agreement. "Children then, my lady?"

A harsh memory flipped her smile to a frown. "Never children. Ever. Do you understand me?"

The concierge's beatific glow faltered for a moment, then he recovered. "Of course, my lady, never. I shall make your request my number one priority."

Muscle quivered beneath her hand. She relaxed her grip on Mikkel's arm. "You do that."

# Chapter Nine

Eight feet by ten feet.

Chrysabelle counted off the room in steps. Slightly smaller than the guest cells at the Primoris Domus.

Not a useful tool anywhere. Not since Doc had taken the dinner fork back. Black paint obscured the single porthole. She used her nail to scratch near the edge. A thin line of paint came away. Well, that had potential.

Dismantling the fold-down bed was another option, but it seemed pretty sturdy. Her one attempt to rip the metal structure free had ended with her losing her grip and smacking her head on the opposite wall. The effort had also scraped the foundation off the backs of her hands. Hopefully, her face was still covered. Hard to tell without a mirror, but the chances this vampire would have one of those lying around was slim. Traditional silver-backed mirrors reflected a vampire's true visage—the demon side of them. Not pretty. Not the way most nobles wanted to think of themselves, which is why they favored the pricey gold-backed mirrors. But this vampire wouldn't have the money for a luxury like that.

She paced, getting angrier with each step. What had

made her test him like that? With that much bloodlust in him, he could have killed her.

Maybe she didn't care if he drained the life out of her.

Maybe he still would.

She stopped pacing. Her hand strayed to her throat. She rubbed at the curve of flesh between ear and shoulder. He would come to her angry. Punishing. He'd strike fast, his fangs sliding in with that white-hot spark of pleasure, breaking her open, sucking her in. Yes...

*No.*

She shuddered, instantly repulsed and compelled by the thought. How could she entertain such a fantasy? She was free. The days of servitude ended. Her blood rights were finally hers again. So why the drift into the ways of the past?

She knew why. Rushing to the single wall sconce, she thrust her wrist toward it. *Holy mother, get me through this.* Her veins pulsed fat and blue. Hypervolemia was setting in. Without a patron, without some way to rid her system of the extra blood, the buildup would continue to muddle her brain. Make her crave the delicate pain of fangs piercing her skin.

His fangs.

Her release.

Shame crept over her tightening body, even though she knew she couldn't help herself. For the hundredth time, she scanned the room. No place to dispose of the excess. Not to mention that opening a vein in scent range of her vampire warden had "disastrous idea" stamped all over it. She had to escape before she did something she might not live to regret. One by one, she unbolted the locks and eased the door open.

Doc leaned against the wall across from her cell. He gave her a little wave. "Going somewhere?"

She slammed the door shut. The varcolai couldn't be out there all night. Could he? She took her frustration out on the porthole.

Finally, she turned off the light and lay down. The cot's thin, itchy blanket stank of unwashed wool. Doing her best to ignore it, she closed her eyes and listened as hard as she could for any sign her guard might leave.

Nothing.

Then nothing turned into sleep.


At this late hour, the nearly depleted solar meant only the faint running lights along the corridor floor remained, and they weakened even as Mal passed. Not that he needed the light. These passageways were imprinted into his memory, and with the fresh blood in his system his eyesight was crystalline, lights or no.

Before he made the turn into the hall where Anna was being kept, he registered Doc's slowed heartbeat and relaxed breathing. Mal padded around the bend and stopped. Despite snoozing, Doc's feline balance kept him upright. A deep, throaty rumble purred out of him. Maintaining human form took the same effort in varcolai as it did vampires. Asleep, Doc had shifted to an in-between state, the closest he could get to his true form under the witch's curse he lived with.

His flattened nose and split lip disappeared as he shook himself awake, apparently sensing Mal's presence. With a few blinks, his pupils rounded and his fangs receded. "S'up?"

Mal nodded.

Doc yawned and arched his back with remarkable flexibility, then rubbed the back of his neck. He stared at the floor. "About earlier—"

"Forgotten." Mal tipped his head toward the locked door. "Anything?"

"Stuck her head out once. But she's been in sand land now for"—Doc checked his watch—"almost three hours."

"I'll take over."

"I'm cool." Doc eyed Mal as though his beast was about to rip through his skin and devour the city.

"I'm fine." He forced his human face into place. "Go check on Fi."

Doc ran his tongue over his teeth and, after another hard look at Mal, shrugged. "Later." With a quick wave over his shoulder, he jogged down the corridor, his stride long and quiet.

As Doc disappeared, Mal opened himself to the woman on the other side of the steel door. The blood made everything easier. His senses slid over her like a wisp of satin. Her breathing and heart rate mimicked what Doc's had just been. She slept.

He splayed his hands on the door and inhaled, testing himself. Her perfume sang through his veins, and suddenly the blood he'd consumed seemed inadequate. *Need.* The golden haze was back, hugging his bones, making him ache for her. *More.*

How could her scent affect him this much after he'd just fed? The realization that he still wanted her chilled him, then he relaxed and accepted it. She was comarré. No vampire could be near her and not hunger. Not want to claim her.

Her patron was dead. Her blood rights were her own. Unless she chose to sell them again. Or give them away. *Take them. Drain her.*

A needy flame ignited in his belly. He doused it in reality. *Imbecile.* For once, he agreed with the voices. He was anathema. She was as close to vampire nobility as a human could get. The chance she'd share her blood with him was...nonexistent.

He inhaled again, drugging himself with her scent, pressing his cheek to the door. If anything, her scent seemed stronger, sweeter, more forceful. He tipped his head back and opened his mouth. She tasted of power and promise and blood as hot and sugary as a summer plum. The voices went dead silent.

He shook himself. Took his hands off the door and backed away. Where was this coming from? He wasn't hungry. He was sated. Complete. He needed to snap out of it. *Get away, get away, get away...*

Maybe he should. Talking to her when he felt like this was a very bad idea. She was sleeping anyway. He should skip the talking. His hand strayed to the handle, surprised when it turned. She'd left the door unlocked even after he'd warned her. If she wasn't afraid of him, she was a fool.

A little push and the door swung open. The paint had been scraped off the porthole in thin lines. Moonlight sifted through the scratches, suffusing the room with an underwater glow. She sprawled on the bunk, gleaming softly, her face toward the far wall, one arm in his direction, palm up, her fingers half-curled. Like she was beckoning him.

He stepped through. There would be plenty of time for talking in the morning.

He stood beside the cot and watched her sleep. Had her patron ever stood at her bed like this? Some old fanged creature with Lucifer's bank account and a false idea of his importance. Had he been kind to her? Or treated her like one more possession? Used her? Mal hoped to hell not.

"She's not yours anymore," he whispered, hating the image in his head of some noble prat floundering on top of her. Rough when he should be gentle because he owned her and it was his due. Mal's fists tightened with the need to shatter something. That was what he did best anyway. Not protecting. Not comforting. Destroying. Killing. That's what he knew. What he'd always known. Mortal or immortal, death was his legacy.

She'd leave when she found out. He couldn't blame her.

He needed to go. He shouldn't be this close to her. Couldn't be trusted. He'd told her that and yet she'd left the door unlocked. Pretty little fool.

Something glistened on her cheek. He leaned in and brushed her hair out of the way, the strands like cool water. The makeup covering her marks had worn off. The moonlight caught her signum and brought them to life in a subtle dance of gold across her cheekbone that turned into vines and flowers scrolling up her temple and arching over her brow.

Beautiful. Wrenching. Like he'd been privileged to see something both intimate and sacred. He should go.

He couldn't.

Not until he saw the others. From what he knew about the comarré there should be more signum on her hands and feet. He desperately wanted to see them. Needed to. He kneeled beside the bed and slid his hand beneath her upturned palm. The veins at her wrist throbbed. Not delicate like he'd expected, but thick. Lush with blood. He should go.

He lifted her hand to his face, closed his eyes, and took her scent into his body. It plunged into his gut. His fangs dropped as his face revealed his true nature. He rested her smooth palm against the hard plane of his cheek and pressed his closed mouth to the soft, warm flesh of her wrist. His gums ached. His body throbbed. His brain found a hundred reasons to sink his teeth into her.

A moment longer and he would go.

A whispery moan opened his eyes. She shifted half an inch, then lay still. He froze. Her palm flexed against his cheek, molding to the ridges of his face. Her fingers twined in his hair. He leaned into her caress, not caring what dream made her touch him like this. Pretending not to care she might be dreaming of her lost patron.

It didn't matter. Not at this moment. Not when she was touching him in a way no one had since his turning. The contact made his eyes sting and his muscles taut. It felt so good and hurt so bad. The kind of hurt that razored away all pretense and left him bare and unworthy. The kind of pleasure that weighed him and found him wanting. The names burned like brands on his body, reminding him.

He was the desiccated creature in the pit again. Stripped back to base urges and animal instincts. Humiliated. Wounded. Broken. *Worthless.*

He should drain her. *Do it.* Take away the possibility that she could make him feel like this again. *Yes.* He was anathema.

Death was his legacy.

No one would expect different.

# Chapter Ten

The second time Doc knocked and got no answer, he stopped waiting for an invitation and just opened the door to Fi's room. She was there, as he'd known she would be.

His heart dropped. She wore the jeans and sweatshirt her body had been found in.

"Fi?" His breath spun out in curls of vapor. The room had to be ten degrees below freezing.

Still no answer. She hovered, back to him, near a portion of the wall she'd covered with newspaper clippings. Her body was flimsy enough that he could read the yellowing scraps through her. Not that he needed to read them again. He knew the headlines by heart. Knew the dreams that her death had put an end to.

*Graduate Student Missing After Research Trip. Search Covers Northern England. Body Recovered in Ruins. Parents Mourn Student's Death.*

"He killed me," she whispered.

"I know he did." He ached seeing her like this. Not just faint and wispy, but lost in the past. She sounded far away. Like she was ... down in a hole.

"It hurt." Her voice wavered. Like it might disappear altogether.

"I know, baby." He reached a hand out to her. "C'mon, now. You should rest."

She didn't move. "Maddoc?"

"Right here, Fiona."

"It still hurts." She turned toward him, eyes blank and staring. A gash opened her throat from ear to collarbone. Blood stained the right side of her university sweatshirt.

He did his best not to wince. It was a manifestation of her pain. He'd seen it once before when he'd happened upon her topside studying herself in the water's reflection. She'd flashed it away instantly, but he knew. This was what she'd looked like when the search party had found her in the pit. How that bloodsucking monster had left her.

Doc forced the anger out of his voice. Fi didn't need that right now. Times like this, the witch's curse he was under served as a mixed blessing. If he were able to shift into his true form, he might go leopard and tear Mal to shreds. Or die trying.

"You should rest. That will make the hurt go away." He hoped. He went to her bed and pulled her covers back. Not that she could get under them. Maybe he should try to get her into the room they usually shared and away from all these memories.

"I can't find my backpack." Her bottom lip wavered. "My parents gave it to me for the trip."

"I'll find it while you snooze, I promise. You want to go into our room? Hang in there?"

"No." She whirled, her face distorted with anger.

"You're right, bad idea. Let's stay here." He patted the mattress and tried to ignore that maybe Mal was right.

Fi's current condition was Doc's fault. He'd known that she'd intended to drain blood for Mal and he'd let her do it anyway. Now she was so weak from the blood loss, she couldn't escape her own nightmare.

"I need my passport." She floated toward him. "I have to have it to get home."

He nodded, swallowing. "I'll make sure you have it."

"Promise?"

"Cross my heart." He patted the bed again. "Just a little nap."

She glided to the bed and lay down as best as a spirit could.

"That's my girl." He backed toward the door. "I'll turn the light off for you."

"No." She started to weep softly. "No more dark."

"Okay, lights on. No worries." Except when the solar ran out in the next half an hour or so. Screw it. He'd get candles.

A tear rolled off her cheek and hit the pillow, leaving a wet spot. He looked at her more closely. She was flickering between her spirit and corporeal forms. If he could keep her whole, she could rest. Forget the torment of her spirit form.

"Fi? You cool?"

"No." She shook her head. "I'm scared."

"I'm right here. I won't let anything happen to you. I got you." Whatever that meant. What could he really do? He hated that she'd helped Mal, but he also understood it. Without Mal, Fi would cease to exist, but when his voices got wound up, she had to hear them too. No wonder she wanted to shut them down as much as Mal did.

"Stay with me."

"I ain't never gonna leave you." He folded his six-foot five-inch frame cross-legged on the floor. She'd saved his life in a way. If Mal hadn't brought the torn-up alley cat he'd found back to Fi, thinking a pet would mellow her out, Doc would've been kibble by now.

"Here," she said, longing in her liquid eyes. "With me." She rested her hand on the curve of space near her stomach. "Please."

He knew what she wanted. Inwardly, he clenched his teeth and buried his pride. The things a man did for a woman. But only this woman.

With the power of a thought, he shifted into the only feline form he could. A tiny smile lit her face, erasing a small part of his humiliation. He jumped onto the bed beside her and curled into a ball, his spine to her stomach, his tail hooked over his paws. She was soft and warm and smelled of fading roses.

She wrapped her arm around him, kissed the top of his head and scratched behind his ear. "Pretty boy," she whispered, sniffling. "My pretty, pretty boy."

Unable to help himself, he started to purr.

Tatiana stood calf-deep in French sewage. She'd insisted on seeing the evidence site and the Nothos had dutifully escorted her into the belly of the Parisian waste system. Mikkel was probably trolling the nearest nightclub for his breakfast. Bloodthirsty devil. How she adored him.

The decaying carcass of something floated by. She rolled her eyes. This was not where she wanted to be. Her expensive coat would have to be thrown out. There was no way this smell could be removed from the unborn varcolai hides. Unless Mikkel had some black magic that might do the trick. She should have worn that stupid burqa.

"There, my lady." The Nothos pointed a claw at an incoming pipe. Sweat dripped off its massive forearm.

She inhaled. Over the foul stench of the sewer and the heavy brimstone of the Nothos, she smelled the faintest hint of rich, sweet comarré blood. The trail grew warm. She smiled and nodded. "Well done."

"Thank you, my lady." It bowed with the litheness born of an excess of bones and double-hinged joints.

She scowled at the Nothos. "I was talking to myself. If I hadn't sent you out, you wouldn't have found this, would you?"

"No, my lady." A growl rumbled out of it. The creature clenched and unclenched massive clawed hands. Steam snorted from its nostrils.

Filthy beast. They were almost as horrible as the Castus that had spawned them, but far less intelligent.

"Where does this pipe lead?"

"A hotel."

She turned to stare up at the abomination she'd hired. "What hotel? Did you find out if she stayed there?"

It blinked yellow eyes at her. "Not yet."

Anger drove her body forward. She slammed her fist into its face, knocking it into the muddy sludge. Some of it splashed onto the hem of her coat, marring the skins. "You stupid ogre. What am I paying you for? So I can do the work myself?"

Its eyes glittered beneath a layer of muck. "No, my lady."

"Get it done. Now." She flexed the hand she'd punched with, then spread her fingers and checked herself for damage. Hitting a Nothos was like ramming your fist into a block of granite. She frowned at her fingers. "Bloody hell. You made me break a nail. Do you see this?" She waved her hand in front of its face. It grunted. Not the response she'd hoped for. Disappointed, she kicked it in the groin. Something popped, and it howled.

"On second thought, you're fired. Unless you bring me the ring." She stood over the Nothos, shaking her head and muttering under her breath. She should have brought Octavian with her. He was always willing to do the dirtiest of deeds for her. "If you want something done right, you have to do it yourself."

With that, she scattered into a cloud of black wasps and flew back to the hotel.

Heat stroked the soles of Chrysabelle's feet. Swirled around her ankles and up her calves, kissed the smooth hollows at the backs of her knees. Delicious and taunting. Wrapping her in pleasure.

"Mmmm." She shifted under his hands. The heat moved to her thighs. Touch as soft as a whispered promise.

"More," she told him. He was a shadow of silver. A fevered caress. A flicker of sensation. The breath tumbled ragged from her throat.

She tucked her hand beneath her cheek. His raw, dark scent coiled around her, turning her body liquid with craving. Her wrist throbbed, steeped in the smell of him. His mouth had been there, soft lips barely masking the hard fangs she desperately needed.

"Pierce me," she whispered, drawing the words out like a prayer.

He didn't answer.

Her skin erupted in flames.

She opened her eyes and squinted at the pink-tinged sun streaming through the porthole where the paint had been scratched away. The light abraded her legs, even through the long trousers she wore. So hot. She bent her knees, pulling her legs toward her. Better out of the sun. She breathed openmouthed as she pushed up and swung her feet over the side of the bunk. Still hard to think. Where was she?

She blinked a few times and stared at the small, sparse room. A trail of dead bolts decorated one side of the door.

She nodded, remembering pieces. The room spun. She tried a deep breath in and out. The air carried a sweet, dark spice. Him. Her belly tightened. That's what she needed. Him. His mouth. His hunger.

Getting off the bed made her dizzy. She held on to the empty shelves until her body balanced itself. So hot.

Her long-sleeved tunic was damp with sweat. She grabbed it at the neck, tore it down the front, and shimmied out of it. Good. Her trousers went next. Better. She grabbed up the tunic and ripped a strip of silk from it, then used it to tie up her hair on top of her head. Much cooler. Much better.

Now in her white cami bra and bikini underwear, she approached the door. Careful steps so she didn't fall. Everything needed extra concentration in this much heat.

The dead bolts weren't locked. She tried to open the door, but it wouldn't budge. Think. Locks on the other side? That seemed right. Her head felt thick and flighty, full of moths and molasses.

Locks were no problem. Needed shoes first. She circled slowly, eyes on the floor. There. Her kidskin slippers sat under the bunk. She fished them out and tugged them on. Hot hot hot. She paused to fan her neck. That felt good. Back to the door. She positioned herself in front of it, lined up just right, and channeled her years of training. Deep breath. Centered and calm.

She side-kicked, shifting her weight into the movement, and connected with the door just below the handle. With a metallic gasp, it buckled outward. A second kick and the bent metal collapsed into the hallway.

She smiled, despite the sharp ache across the arch of her foot. Maybe it was the slippers. She stepped out of them, hopped over the broken door, and went in search of the vampire who'd left his scent all over her.

He could fix what was wrong with her. She felt it in her blood.

# Chapter Eleven

Mal had run through the streets of Paradise City until the first line of pink fired the horizon. Not jogging like the white-collar office jockeys he passed in the early hours before dawn, but real running. Flat-out. As fast as he could. As far as he could. He'd outsweated a racehorse. Definitely outpaced one. He'd come back, showered, scrubbed his fevered body, and still her scent leeched onto him, sucking away the will to keep his fangs out of her pale skin. How many times during that run had he imagined her beneath him, pliant and willing? Begging for his mouth. How many times had he imagined the taste of her, as sweet and rich as her scent?

Now in the hold-turned-gymnasium, his bare fists pounded the heavy bag. Thinking about the taste of her during the run was why he was here. And thinking about it now wasn't making things better.

The seams of the bag strained. Jab, hook, cross. The force she'd exerted over him last night had scared him. And nothing scared him. Sweat rolled down his temple. He ignored it. The way she'd been, the way she'd affected him... he'd felt possessed.

The thoughts he'd had. Jab. The urges. Hook. That's what scared him. Cross. Not the taking of blood, but the completion of the taking. She'd almost compelled him to…Enough. Maybe he should spend the day in a bottle of whiskey and just forget. Maybe he should get Doc to take her into the city and turn her loose. He had enough problems of his own without protecting some runaway comarré who didn't seem to want the protection anyway. Jab, hook, cro—

"Vampire." The word wafted past him like a plea.

His fist hung in midair. For the first time, that name didn't drip with disgust. On the contrary, it drifted round and ripe through the shadowy space. Spoken with a smile. Full of the kind of promise his body didn't need to hear. Especially not now.

He turned.

Holy Hades.

The comarré strolled toward him in nothing but two slips of white silk and a spacey smile. More white bundled her blonde hair in a messy knot. Somewhere inside him, buried under his black heart, the miniscule piece of him that remembered being a man woke up.

"I've been looking for you," she said.

"I…" Forget it. He had nothing.

She passed through one of the circles of light cast by the large overheads. Sparks shot off her. He scrubbed a hand over his face, not believing what he was seeing. She had more signum than just what was on her hands, feet, and face. The lacy gold mapped her entire body. A finely wrought filigree of stars, vines, flowers, butterflies, ancient symbols, and words ran from her feet, up her legs, over her narrow waist, spanned her chest, and finished down her arms to the tips of her fingers. Gilded, head to toe. No wonder she glittered like lost treasure.

He moved backward as she came nearer, bringing that narcotic scent with her. "Where are your clothes?"

"I'm hot." She laughed. Her eyes were pale, glassy lavender. Lavender?

"Doc," he called. This might require backup.

"Do you need a doctor, vampire? Are you sick?" She sauntered closer. "I know how to heal you."

He put power into his voice. "Stay where you are."

She giggled. "You think you can use your persuasion on me, silly devil?" She shook her head, blonde tendrils quivering around her face. "My patron had those gifts too. That means I'm immune."

"Anna, stay." His fangs punched through his gums.

Her eyes fixed on him, barely blinking. "My name's not Anna. It's Chrysabelle."

"Okay."

"Say it." The tone of her voice shifted in an instant from satin smooth to steel hard. "Say it."

Alarms went off in his brain as his body went up in flames. His human face disappeared into ridged bone and sharp fangs. "Chrysabelle."

"Even better with that face." She purred a low, throaty hum of approval. The sound sent a chill skittering down his spine. No way was this typical comarré behavior. Something was very wrong.

He looked past her. Still no sign of him. "Doc, where the hell are you?"

Raising her right wrist to her face, she closed her eyes briefly and inhaled. "I smell you on me." She clucked her tongue. "Come for a visit last night? Maybe next time you'll wake me up so we can both enjoy it, hmm?"

Even as he tried to shut his imagination down, the images of what might have happened if she'd been awake played out. They burned phosphorescent in the blackness of his tortured mind. Hot skin against cold. Blood. Sweat.

He exhaled long and hard. The voices clawed at his skull. *Get away, get away, get away…*

They skirted each other in a slow, predatory dance. Except Mal had become the prey. Something told him this version of Chrysabelle wouldn't have any qualms about eating him either. The hell of it was he might let her. There were worse ways to die. He knew. He'd tried most of them.

"Who let you out of your room?"

"Afraid you forgot to lock the door after you left?" She licked her lips while one hand massaged the slope of her neck. Keeping his eyes off her throat became increasingly difficult. "Don't worry. You didn't forget. I let myself out."

Doc barreled through the makeshift gym's door. "What's the nine one one—holy mother Bast." He skidded to a stop.

Chrysabelle turned around. The signum covered her back as heavily as her front. Runes Mal didn't recognize decorated the sides of her spine from the base of her skull to the small of her back. "Hello, kitty cat."

Figuring this might be his one shot, Mal leaped forward and grabbed her. "Doc, get something to tie her up—"

She bent forward and tossed him to the ground like he was a plaything. Okay, he hadn't seen that coming. She planted her hands on her hips, still smiling. "Naughty vampire. That's no way to treat a guest."

Doc's mouth had yet to close.

Mal flipped to his feet and twisted to face her. His ears rang with the thump of her heart. Maybe he should bite her. Drain enough to knock her out. *Drain her enough to kill her.* Because that's all he could do, kill her. "Doc, get her clothes out of her room."

"Um. Yeah. Okay." He shuffled backward out the door.

Chrysabelle's eyes were preternaturally bright. "You want to play?" She loosened her stance as though preparing for battle. Except she staggered slightly. "Or would you rather fight?"

"I don't want to fight you."

"Fight me or bite me." She laughed. Were those tiny points tipping her canines? "I think you want to do both." She waggled her finger as if he was a disobedient child. "You should just bite me. Why deny your instinct?" She tipped her head to one side, exposing her throat. "You can hear the blood in my veins, can't you? Smell the scent surrounding me. You've imagined it. I know you have. I see it in your eyes when you look at me. That first moment when your fangs sink into my skin." Her fingers stroked the pale arc of her neck. "The hot, sweet spill of blood." She moaned softly. Or maybe he did. "The heat pouring through you. The way I taste. Better than anything you've ever had before. The way your name sighs off my lips—"

"Enough," he snarled. "I will not drink from you."

She stiffened like she'd been slapped. "You don't want me? Are you a fool? Do you know who I am? I am not just any comarré, I am the purest there has ever been. From the Primoris Domus." Indignation twisted her pretty mouth. "Do you know what my blood rights went for? Twenty-two million. *Euros.* The highest price any comarré has ever fetched."

Wobbling to the side, she stabbed a finger at his chest. He backed up to keep her from touching him. "I can give you power beyond your—"

Doc ran back in, her clothes in his hands. "Her door was pretty jacked up. Kicked down from the inside by the looks of it."

She nodded, looking pleased. "It was."

Mal moved so he could see Doc and Chrysabelle at the same time. "If I didn't know better, I'd think she was drunk."

Doc held her clothes out like an offering and came toward her while talking to Mal. "I did some reading this morning. Think she might have blood poisoning."

"Who would have poisoned her?" Mal asked.

"Her own body. Too much blood." Doc tried to give her the clothes, but she wouldn't take them.

"So hot," she whispered. Her scent shifted. The sweetness went sour.

Mal realized the shine on her was more than just gold. A thin layer of sweat covered her skin. Her eyes rolled back and she crumpled forward. Mal caught her before she hit the floor. He turned her hand over. Fat, blue veins corded tight beneath the skin of her wrist like they might pop at any moment. "Get Preacher."

"You get him. I'll hang with her."

"I can't." He ground the words out. "It's daylight and he lives on hallowed ground." Chrysabelle's skin felt like the surface of the sun. She moaned in his arms.

Doc shook his head. "You should have thought of that before—"

"Before what? I didn't do this to her." Anger tinted his vision. "Send Fi if you're too yellow."

"Screw you." A vein in Doc's forehead twitched. His

pupils narrowed to vertical slits. "She's too sick." The *because of you* hung in the air between them.

"Then we need him more than ever, don't we?"

Doc stared daggers at him, shook his head in obvious disgust, and stormed out.

"Make sure he brings his bag," Mal called after him.

So what if Doc was pissed. Let him be. Anger got things accomplished. If Doc failed—he couldn't—but if he did...Mal looked down at the unconscious woman on his lap. He wasn't going to bear this death alone.

One useless Nothos. One lying comarré madam. One list of hotel guests that Mikkel was checking through, but no real leads in the whole lot. Tatiana considered confronting Madame Rennata, but knew that would only get her more lies and misdirection. Not to mention the woman might warn the missing girl, if she was still alive. The other two Nothos awaited orders.

Once again, the real work was left to her.

The lights outside Algernon's manor remained lit, despite Algernon's demise. They cast half-moons over the mammoth stone house, illuminating the late hour. She'd had Octavian drive her, and right now he unlocked the manor's massive front doors and held them open. She lifted her palm in his direction. He dropped the key into it. Good help was not impossible to find, just hard.

"Wait in the car."

"Yes, my lady." He bowed deeply and returned to the Bentley parked in the center of the circular drive. Probably to dream of the day she'd turn him. As if that would ever happen.

She walked in and shut the door. How many times had she been here? How many balls had she attended? Too many. She stood for a moment in the foyer. It was twice as big as hers. This manor would go to the next Elder elected.

Unfortunately, correcting the horrible taste with which it had been decorated was going to take a considerable sum of money. Algernon's legacy was his excess. If one crystal chandelier was good, ten must be excellent. If owning a comarré spoke of your wealth, a Primoris Domus comarré screamed the depth of your pockets to the world. Especially when the bidding price exceeded that of any other comarré in history. The fool. She hadn't paid half as much for her comar, but then the males weren't in such high demand.

She walked slowly, taking in the surroundings with new eyes. Things crammed every inch of the property. Granted, possessions were all well and good, but moderation was key. She'd have to study the floor plan. Find a suitable room for Nehebkau's new enclosure. She wouldn't move until he could move with her.

As she strolled through the great hall, she ran her finger over a tabletop. Dust. Had the house sat that long? Or perhaps Algernon's staff lacked the necessary skills to keep a manor this size. They'd have to be fired.

The house needed a good airing as well. Death lingered in the air.

She continued to the comarré's rooms. They sat in the wing opposite Algernon's living quarters. The door was ajar. She went in. The familiar blood scent was fading, but still there. Without having personally drunk the comarré's blood, she couldn't distinguish the particulars of her scent over another's. The only one that smelled different to her was her own.

The search her servants had performed had left the place a mess. Clothing and books strewn everywhere. She sifted through a few pieces. The comarré's clothes were easy to spot. Silk, linen, wool, suede. All white. All meant to cover every bit of skin except for the hands, face, and feet. The more intimate signum were kept for the patron's eyes only. Not that she'd ever cared to see her comar's.

The books she flipped through held nothing but pages. No cutaway compartments or damning slips of paper.

The comarré's sacre hung on the wall displayed by a thick red satin cord that matched the red leather-wrapped hilt. The gold-etched length mocked her with its bright shine. She leaned in toward the ceremonial sword, careful not to touch any part of it, and inhaled. The holy water used to quench the steel stung her nostrils, but there was no blood scent.

Nothing. Not a single tiny clue. Frustrated, she sat on the bed.

"If I were a comarré, where would I hide my most personal things?" Her eyes skimmed the room. The shelves were bare now that the books had been tossed to the floor. The drawers all dumped out. Where, where, where? How, in this mess, could she be expected to find anything?

She got up and walked through the dressing area to the bathroom. Another mess. Towels, toiletries, and brushes lay scattered about. Shampoo oozed from toppled containers. A cracked bottle of perfume leaked its contents onto the floor. She caught a whiff and sneezed. The whole apartment should be shoveled out. She grabbed a tissue to hold over her nose as she investigated, but nothing seemed pertinent here either. She wadded up the tissue and tossed it in the trash on her way out.

A metallic glimmer among the refuse caught her eye.

She backtracked, grabbed the wastebasket, and dumped it on the counter. She picked up the glossy white box that had stopped her. The gold-foil design on the front looked very much like the swirling sun signum every comarré received as the first marking. Beneath the sun were the words Lapointe Cosmetics Complete Coverage Foundation.

When was lazy staff not a bad thing? When their failure to do their job left evidence behind. Foundation. How very out of place. No self-respecting comarré would hide the markings they took such pride in. Unless they intended to disappear into the kine world.

And imagine, a cosmetic company using a design so close to comarré signum.

She laughed. "Stupid, stupid blood whore. I'm going to find you. And as soon as I claim what's mine, I'm going to drink every last drop of you."

# Chapter Twelve

Same military buzz cut. Same holier than thou attitude.
Preacher hadn't changed since the last time Mal had
seen him, which was once, right after he'd moved into the
old freighter. Preacher had tried to cleanse him. With a stake.

Not exactly the kind of behavior he'd expected from
another vampire. But Preacher wasn't exactly just another
vampire.

As far as Mal knew, Preacher was the only vampire
turned without ingesting the blood of his sire. For that
matter, he was the only vampire who had technically
turned himself. Either way, he was fringe—a lesser class
of vampire descended from the betrayer Judas Iscariot.
Noble vampires came from a much darker source, the Castus Sanguis. The ancient ones who'd fallen from heaven.
They'd raped and warred and used Earth as their play-
ground, begetting the nobility, the varcolai, and the fae.

But the End War was what brought about the rise of
the fringe. They took advantage of the chaos, turning or
trying to turn any human they could. Those who didn't
survive the turning, and there were many, blended into
the casualties of war. Before that, fringe numbers had

been a fraction of the nobility's. Preacher was one of those turned during that great upheaval.

That's where things went left of center. Story went that during a skirmish, Preacher's World Corps unit took a direct hit under enemy fire, leaving Preacher and a few other survivors wounded but alive. When a pack of fringe vamps dressed as insurgents converged, looking for human spoils, Preacher was bitten, but emptied enough rounds into his attacker to incapacitate the creature. Being both a chaplain and a medic due to the need for double-duty troops, he knew his blood loss would kill him before help arrived. Instead of administering his own last rites, he helped himself to a field transfusion from his subdued attacker, not realizing what the result would be.

Of all the tales surrounding him, one truth was that Preacher lacked a few of the regular vampire characteristics. Like the one concerning sacred symbols. Which explained how he made his home in an abandoned Catholic church in the ruins of Little Havana.

Most bizarre was his ability to daywalk, something no other vampire could manage without some serious protection and abundant shade. So even though he could have come immediately to help Fi and Chrysabelle, he'd made them wait until after sundown. On purpose.

Mal hated waiting. "What's taking so long?"

Preacher unhooked the stethoscope from his ears and rested Chrysabelle's hand back on top of the sheet Mal had covered her with. He met Mal's eyes with suspicion. "Beside the hypervolemia, she's got a broken foot. Been playing with your food, Malkolm?"

"She's not my—screw you." Mal glared right back. "She kicked a door down."

"Trying to get away?"

"Shouldn't you be saving her life?"

"I'm pretty sure I can save the comarré, but…" Preacher nodded to Fiona's comatose form resting on the second cot parallel to Chrysabelle's. "Can't say for sure about the spirit. The only undead I know about are the fanged kind."

Doc snarled. He was as close to shifting as he could be without going house pet. Eyes like slits, the bridge of his nose flattened, teeth needle-sharp with fangs like a tiger. "You find a way to help her or—"

Preacher snorted. "Or what, varcolai? You'll use my couch as a scratching post?"

Mal stepped between them. "You'd better help both of them."

Preacher's nostrils flared. "I should have cleansed you when I had the chance."

"You had the chance. You failed. Fix them and I'll give you another shot." Mal crossed his arms to keep from throttling Preacher until he begged for a stake.

"Well then." Preacher rolled up his sleeves and went back to his work. "That's a paycheck I look forward to cashing." He unpacked the rest of his bag, laying out tubing, needles, and a blood bag on a clean towel. "I'll wrap her foot first. She should keep it elevated for a few days." Preacher went to work.

"What's your beef with him?" Doc asked Preacher, tilting his head at Mal. "What's he ever done to you?"

Preacher answered without turning and secured the bandages in place. "He's a vampire."

"So are you, foolio," Doc said.

"He's unclean. And unrepentant." Preacher went back

to his bag and added more tubing and alcohol swabs to the towel.

Doc raised his brows. "You better check yourself."

He snapped the bag shut. "Unlike Malkolm, I dedicated my life to a higher purpose. I have not faltered from that mission."

Doc scoffed. "You're crazy as a crack whore."

"And you're a house cat. We all have our crosses to bear." Preacher shot a look at Mal. "Metaphorically speaking."

Mal narrowed his eyes at the crucifix that swung with the dog tags around Preacher's neck. "Or not."

"You have any more lights you could turn on?"

Mal shook his head. "You could have had all the light you wanted a few hours ago. You chose to show up this late."

"You're lucky I showed up at all. I owe you nothing." Preacher scowled, reached into his bag, and pulled out a headlamp. He adjusted it over his buzz cut and flipped on the LED.

Mal uncrossed his arms, blinking in the sudden brightness. "Do it already. Before there's no reason to. Because then I'll be forced to *cleanse* you."

"Patience." Preacher sprayed his hands and forearms with latex then bowed his head in prayer.

"Freak," Doc muttered from his spot at Fi's shoulders. His thumbs stroked her skin.

How Doc kept Fi corporeal, Mal had no idea. Just like he didn't understand how the ex-Marine could pray without his tongue bursting into flames. Mal walked past Doc and placed his hands on Chrysabelle's burning skin. Her lips parted, but no sound came out. Light from Preacher's headlamp sparkled off her signum as the man bent over Fiona's arm and studied her veins. Something between Chrysabelle's parted lips caught Mal's eye. Tiny. Pointed. White.

He grabbed Doc's arm and motioned with his head at her mouth. Doc followed Mal's gesture. He stared, then looked back at Mal and mouthed the word "fangs" like a question.

Mal shrugged and shut Chrysabelle's jaw before Preacher noticed. Preacher thought he was helping a human. If he thought she was a vampire, he might not. Mal wasn't taking the chance. Why would the comarré have fangs? Granted, they looked more like the baby teeth version, but still. Was she human or not?

Preacher lifted his head and twisted his headlamp to focus the beam. He moved to Chrysabelle first, securing a tourniquet of rubber tubing around her arm. Her vein popped up instantly. He repeated the process on Fi, slapping her arm to bring the vein up. Nothing. He shifted her arm to hang off the cot.

"I may not get a vein on her. Leave her arm like that and I'll try again when I'm ready."

Moving back to Chrysabelle, he grabbed another length of tubing, attached the collection bag at one end and a needle at the other. He caught Mal's eyes. "I don't know how she'll react, so be ready for anything."

No kidding. Mal nodded. "I've been ready. Waiting on you."

"Beginning." Preacher swabbed the inside of her elbow with alcohol. He slid the needle into Chrysabelle's protruding vein and let the bag rest on the floor. Blood spurted through the tubing and started filling the bag, thick and violet red. "The blood's not getting oxygenated fast enough.

Too much volume. Her body can't keep up." He shook his head. "I'm not sure putting this blood into the other one is going to help."

Doc's head snapped up. "Quit jawing and hurry up. It's the best chance Fi has."

"Your loss." Preacher shrugged.

The bag continued to fill. Despite the off-color, Mal's fangs ached. So much blood. Right in front of him. The angry buzz in his head said the voices were aware of it too. He shifted his gaze to her signum until the gold marks blurred into a shimmery glaze.

"Done." Preacher taped a cotton ball over the puncture site then slid the needle out, carefully holding it higher than the bag, and returned to Fi. He handed the needle and bag to Doc. "Keep the needle high."

He lifted Fi's arm and slapped it a few more times. "All right, drop the bag to the floor and give me the needle."

Doc handed over the needle and moved to the head of Fi's cot. His hands went back to her shoulders. Preacher slid the needle into Fi's vein and lifted the bag to shoulder height. Blood flowed through the tube and vanished into her. For a long minute, nothing happened. Blood fluxed from the bag to Fi. Both girls lay still. Mal watched. Listened. No change. Then another minute went by.

And another.

"It's not working." Doc's head dropped to his chest. Anger radiated off him hot and sharp. "You son of a—"

"Oh." Fiona's eyes fluttered open with a gasp. "Wow," she whispered. "I feel...alive."

Doc let go of her shoulders and grabbed her hand. "You are. Sort of." He looked at Preacher. "Get that thing out of her arm."

"Not yet, I need to—"

"No, now. You don't know what too much of that blood could do to her." Doc yanked the line out and pressed his fingers to the spot on Fi's arm.

Everything decelerated into frame-by-frame slow motion. A crimson thread of liquid jetted through the needle. The scent of Chrysabelle's blood replaced the air in the room. Mal's head came up at the same time as Preacher's. Fangs pierced the gaping maw of his mouth. Mal knew his face had gone feral and his eyes silver, a sure reminder to Preacher of the difference between them.

Mal snarled a warning. Her scent alone was enough to intoxicate him, but the smell of her uncontained blood infected him like a virus. Her scent *became* his blood, his reason, his brain. Every inch of his flesh hummed with the drive to protect. Possess. The voices crammed his cerebrum with a frantic, high-pitched, jet engine whine. Blackness edged his vision, but this was no time to lose control. He shoved his demons back into his brain.

"Mine," Preacher snarled back. "I need her."

"You need to be put down." Strength born of the moment surged through Mal. He landed a fist across Preacher's jaw, throwing him into the wall. "Stay away from her."

The needle lay on the floor leaking an ever-widening pool across the linoleum. Preacher jumped to his feet, eyes flicking from Mal to Chrysabelle to the blood and back again. Mal vaulted over Chrysabelle and landed squarely between her and Preacher.

Mal clenched his fists and roared, baring his fangs. "Back. Off."

Preacher threw a punch. Mal blocked with his left forearm and rammed his right fist into Preacher's gut. He retched and went to his knees, bile dripping from his mouth.

"Praying's not going to help you now," Mal growled. In his peripheral vision, Doc helped Fi off the cot.

"Preacher's here?" Fi asked, narrowing her eyes at the other vampire.

"Yeah." Doc pushed her behind him. "I'll explain later."

"Doc," Mal called over his shoulder. "Take both girls below."

Doc nodded as Preacher lunged to his feet and sprang forward. "She's mine."

Mal snagged him around the neck and hurled him to the floor. Preacher hung on and they rolled together. Fi shrieked. Doc scooped a limp Chrysabelle into his arms and hustled her and Fi out the door as Mal came to his knees.

"Hell spawn." Preacher's fist pounded Mal's cheek.

Mal shook off the pain. "That the best you can do, jarhead?" Amateur. What he wouldn't give for a weapon. Or a quart of blood. His muscles were starting to tremble from exhaustion.

"Get staked, anathema," Preacher growled.

"You fringe don't know when to quit." Mal clipped Preacher in the temple, opening a cut and snapping his head back until the floor stopped it. Hitting something beside the heavy bag, something that bled, felt good. With Chrysabelle out of the room, and the added bitterness of Preacher's blood, his brain was starting to clear.

"Her blood is pure. She should belong to someone worthy." Preacher shoved his combat boots into Mal's chest, thrusting him back and cracking a few ribs. The pain barely registered.

"You've outstayed your welcome, altar boy." Mal rolled to his feet. Preacher was a second behind him. They faced off, circling.

"Give her to me and I'll leave."

Mal realized he had no idea if the transfusion had helped Chrysabelle or not. Time to bring this to a close. "You go home alone."

Mimicking the combo he'd used on the bag earlier, he hit Preacher again and again until blood covered his fists. His or Preacher's, he wasn't sure. Preacher staggered back against the wall. His head wobbled on his neck like a doll's, then he slumped to the floor.

"Age plus nobility always equals a win. I tried to tell you that last time." Mal grabbed Preacher by the belt, his doctor bag by the handles, and dragged them both out of the room. He kept going until he hit the end of the pier, then he dumped Preacher and threw his bag to the ground beside him. "Consider that your last chance to cleanse me."

He slogged back to the ship to check on Chrysabelle. Fatigue overtook him as the exhilaration from the fight disappeared. Pain started to register. His right eye was swelling. He probed his ribs through his shirt. Two broken. Good thing he didn't have to breathe. That was going to hurt in the morning. Or whenever he woke up after he collapsed into bed.

Back on board, he winced as he wiped his bloody hands on his pants. He followed Chrysabelle's scent toward the room Doc had taken her to. A few doors away, and he knew Doc wasn't done punishing him for what happened to Fi.

Sleeping in his own bed was no longer an option.

Chrysabelle was already in it.

*  *  *

Tatiana couldn't take her eyes off the mansion even as she slipped through the car door Octavian held open. Hers. Very soon. Especially now that she had a possible clue as to where the comarré might—

"Hello, child."

If she'd been less focused on the future and more on the present, she would have recognized his scent before she'd heard his voice. If the sound of words being dragged over gravel and broken glass could be called a voice.

Not now. She didn't have time for this now. Not when she was so close to finding the comarré. She could scatter, but they'd find her. They always did. There was no running from the Castus Sanguis. She bowed her head in obeisance and shifted on the leather seat to face him.

"My lord."

He offered his hand. Dutifully, she kissed his ring, careful to touch as little of his skin as possible.

"You seem troubled." The voice came from deep within the hooded black cape. No visible face, which suited her fine. She'd seen his face. Once was enough.

"No, my lord, just…I have a lot on my mind." She concentrated on not gagging from the stench of sulfur and gangrenous flesh.

"Ah. Then you may not be able to focus as much as I'd like on this plane."

After her first trip to his dimension, she'd vowed never to return if she could help it. "My lord, please, I'm fine." She reached behind her neck, found the clasp of her locket, and released it, letting it fall from beneath her blouse to the car's seat. She would not lose that memory again.

He twisted the amber gem in his ring and the world around her swirled away. She fought to maintain consciousness but when the blackness lightened to charcoal, she knew she hadn't. The glassy black walls and disappearing corners were not her dimension. She was in theirs. And at their will.

She tested her surroundings. Not bound. That was something. Not that she could run. Where would she go? She was a rat, confined by an inescapable maze. She stretched her arms out, feeling for what was beneath her.

A bed. Her stomach churned. Not again. Please, not again. The last time it had taken her nearly a month to recover.

He approached, robe gone. Her memories of him had not been exaggerated. Veins throbbed with blood so powerful and ancient it had given birth to three races. A skirt of shadows covered him from the waist down, hiding his hooved feet. Behind him, knots of darkness hovered. His brethren. He circled the bed, giving her a glimpse of his back where the blackened stumps from his torn-away wings still thrust from his shoulders.

"We sense that the ring has not come into your possession as promised."

"It will, master. I will have it very soon."

He spun, jaws extended, rows of fangs jutting forward. "You should have it already." Spittle stung her face.

"It was…" No, no, that was not the right answer. If the Castus Sanguis found out about the girl, they would be furious. If they got to her first… "Yes, master, I should. I failed you, but I will redeem myself."

He relaxed. "Yes, we have faith you will. Or we will

find another." He continued circling. The scrape of his hooves abraded her nerves.

"We don't want to find another, child. You understand that. But we want the covenant abolished as soon as possible."

"As do I, my liege." Neither did she want to give up the power that would be hers. She'd been through too much already. She braced herself for whatever he might deal her. For such power, she could withstand anything. She repeated the word like a mantra. Anything, anything...

"Good. Do you have a sacrifice in place? You know what we require—"

*"The light and the dark shall collide, and the covenant shall be broken."* She quoted the old text, knowing it would please him and hoping it would hide the fact that she had no sacrifice and no idea where to get it.

"Yes, that is the way of it. You are the darkest of all our children, the one in whom we are most pleased." The shadows disappeared from his lower half. An unstoppable shudder ran through her at the sight of him. Her words had pleased him more than she'd expected. She swallowed a mouthful of bile. He kneeled on the bed and ran a claw up her thigh. She shivered and his mouth pulled back in a frightening smile.

"Your pound of flesh is due."

# Chapter Thirteen

Mal's scent tugged Chrysabelle from her dreams, waking her with the cool promise of more. She opened her eyes to slits. Definitely not the cot she'd slept in the other night. Too comfortable. She was on her side in this strange bed, staring at a wall of old books. A soft circle of light washed over her from a squat candle under a hurricane lantern on the night table.

And everything—the bed linens, the air, her skin—smelled like the vampire's dark, spicy scent. Wait. That must mean this was his bed. Oh no. No, no, no. She held her breath for a moment as the possibilities made her blush with horror. The blood sickness. Sweet holy mother, what had she done?

She forced that horrible prospect out of her head and took stock of herself. Her head was clear. The fever gone. Her body held no unfamiliar soreness, except…a faint pang in her arm and a dull throb in her foot.

Using her elbows, she pushed to a sitting position and extended her bare arm. The covers fell down around her waist. Air cooled her skin and her signum winked back in the candlelight. Why was she only in her bra and—she lifted the sheet—underwear? First things first. On her arm, medical tape held a puff of cotton to the inside of her elbow. She hooked her nail underneath and peeled it off. A tiny pinpoint of red marked her skin.

Not only had someone stripped her down to her underwear, they'd drained her. At once she felt relieved and violated and scared. Who had undressed her? How had they . . . disposed of the excess blood? That blood was hers to give or not. Those rights reverted back to her with Algernon's death. Had the vampire . . . she closed her eyes against the thought and inhaled in hopes of finding some calm before investigating her foot. The thickness of his scent spoiled the air for a proper breath. *Please, don't let my freedom be so short-lived.*

The tiniest sound, like skin brushing leather, brought her head up. Beyond the circle of light, all was black, but in the far corner, the shadows were darker than the rest.

No wonder his scent choked her. He was in the room, watching.

She tugged the sheet to her throat, covering all but the signum on her hands. She glared in his direction. "Show yourself."

Light flared as he struck a match and lit a squat candle on the small table beside him. "Didn't want to disturb your sleep." He shook the match out. The extra glow illuminated more of the room. Additional shelves, all packed with books. Any bare space on the walls held a collection of long swords. Other than that, there was nothing personal, nothing to indicate the room's occupant held anything or anyone dear.

"So you left a candle burning on the table next to me?" She tucked her knees to her chest. "Your concern is touching." And his need to watch her unnerving. He'd left that candle lit to see her better. And her signum too, no doubt.

Silver shifted through his eyes. "You're feeling better." He stood, and without invitation moved his leather chair next to the bed. A bruise grayed his left cheek and surrounded his eye. And he'd shaved, revealing a hard jaw.

"Who undressed me?"

"You did."

She didn't remember doing that, but better than at someone else's hands. She peered over the edge of the bed. Nothing. "Where are my clothes? I'd like to put them back on."

"They're in the gym." Mal's eyes stayed on her face, but he'd probably seen his fill of the rest of her last night.

"Why are they—"

"You didn't want them, and when you passed out, it became a nonissue."

"I took my clothes off in the gym." And he'd obviously been there to witness it, which meant he'd seen her signum. All of them. Mortification heated her cheeks.

"No, you took your clothes off in the holding cell. Not sure if that happened before or after you kicked the door down."

She pressed her forehead to her knees and fought the shame burning her eyes. "Leave me alone."

"No."

"Get out." She yelled the words into the sheet.

"Not until we talk."

"I'm done talking." She sniffed, hating her own weakness.

"You haven't begun to talk, Chrysabelle."

She looked up. "How do you know that name?"

"You corrected me when I called you Anna yesterday."

Self-pity turned to anger. "Did everyone get a good look at my signum yesterday too? I'm sure that gave you a nice thrill, hmm? Watching the blood-drunk comarré stumble around half-naked?" She clenched her jaw against the rage. She wanted to hit something. Anything. Him. "You're a monster."

"Yes, I am." He leaned back. "And yet you're in my bed, broken foot tended, fever free, and clearheaded enough to vent all over me." He kicked his feet up on the edge of the mattress. "Go ahead, I think I can manage not to walk into the sun from the guilt."

"You think this is funny?" She tugged the sheet free, knocking his legs off the bed, and wrapped it around herself. "I'm leaving."

"Suit yourself." He grabbed the corner of the sheet and yanked it off her, spinning her on her good foot. "But the sheet is mine. It stays."

His eyes didn't keep to her face this time. "Not sure which one of us has more marks. I like yours a hell of a lot more than mine." Tossing the sheet to the foot of the bed, he got up, walked back to the small table, and picked up a book. He kept his back to her while he paged through it. "You can get back in bed and rest, or I'll carry you to another room and you can rest there, but you're not leaving and we both know it."

Carry her? "I am leaving." Although her foot had begun to throb harder.

"To go where?"

"Back to my au—my friend's house."

"If someone's after you, would you take that danger

back to your friend?" He waited and when she didn't answer, continued. "You obviously came here for a reason. What is it?"

She tried to see into his thick head. "Why do you want to help me all of a sudden?"

He flipped a page. "Didn't say I would help. But I will listen. After what you did for Fi, I'll do that much."

"I want my clothes." She paused. "After I did what for Fi?"

"You tore your shirt down the middle, but your pants are still—"

"After I did *what* for Fi?"

"Your blood. She's been solid ever since. Without working at it either."

"You...you put my blood into her?" She collapsed onto the bed, no longer caring if she was half-naked. He'd taken her blood, then given it away like it was his to give. That was not supposed to happen. Did that even count? "My blood. You put my blood into a ghost?"

"She was corporeal at the time." He turned around. "It seemed like the best solution for both of you." He scowled. "Plus I owed Fi."

She shook her head, disbelief clogging her throat. "That was my blood. Mine to give or not. You had no right to do what you did."

He took a step toward her. "So we should have let you die? Because that's the direction you were headed in." Then another step. "Or are you just disappointed because I didn't personally suck it out of you? Maybe I should have given in to you in the gym and done what you were begging me to do."

"Stop." She bent her head and wished she could hide.

Wished she'd never come to this horrid city. Wished Algernon was still alive. "No."

"We did what we thought best. None of us are comarré experts, and you haven't exactly given us much to go on."

She studied the leafy tendrils of signum curling up her thighs. Loathing the way they tied her to so much power and responsibility. She didn't want it. Not anymore. Not ever again. "I want my clothes."

"Here." A flutter of movement, and a black T-shirt landed in her lap. It was oddly cool and redolent with his scent. She glanced up. He was bare-chested. The names written on him seemed as much a part of the shadows as he was, moving and flickering with the candlelight. Pulling her gaze from him was difficult, but she knew what it meant to be stared at. Neither did she want to give him the satisfaction of thinking she found anything about him interesting. Because she didn't, despite the fact that she'd never seen a naked male torso before his.

"I don't wear black." She bent down to hide herself and pulled the shirt on anyway.

"Some of us have no choice." Book under his arm, he returned to the chair and settled in. He put the book on his lap and held out his hand. "Give me one of those pillows."

She tossed one to him, then pointed at the bruise on his cheek. "Did I do that?"

"No, but it amuses me that you think you could have. You have a rather lofty opinion of yourself, don't you, comarré?" He arranged the pillow at the bottom of the bed, then patted it. "Foot."

She kept her mouth shut and frowned. He read her curious look correctly. "It's supposed to be elevated."

Reluctantly, she stretched her leg across the sateen sheets. Not silk, but not a bad substitute. At least he found money for the important things. He caught her ankle and held it in his hand as he stuffed the pillow beneath. The touch was less unpleasant than she'd hoped it would be. "There. Now, who's after you?"

Her fingers worried the shirt's hem. "I don't even know your name."

He sat still, staring at her like he was thinking. Too long, she thought. "Why don't you want me to know your name?"

"I'm…anathema."

*"Quelle surprise."* She stared back, incredulous. "You think I haven't figured that out?"

"I could be fringe."

"Nice try, but your eyes go silver and you can shift your face."

"Then how do you know I'm not nobility?"

"Living here?" She laughed at the absurdity of him thinking she might mistake him for anything else but anathema. At this point, finding anything funny was a gift. "Look around you. This isn't the Grand Palace. You have no staff—"

"I have Doc and Fi."

"Like I said, no staff. No blood source. You're about as anathema as a vampire can get, I imagine."

He shrugged. "So the freighter's a tip-off. Big deal."

"Please. I've basically known since that night at the club."

"How?"

She lifted one shoulder. "A vamp who drinks animal blood smells different. Nobility never drink animal blood.

Plus, you were very hungry that night, and nobility never get to that point. Also, you were alone. I figured you were either Nothos or anathema."

"How could you think I was Nothos?"

"I've never seen one. Of course, when I dropped you in that alley like a used tissue—"

"Lucky shot." A vein popped out on his forehead. "Plus I was weak."

"You still are."

He growled softly. She put her hands up. "I just mean you don't drink enough human blood and you don't drink it from the vein. You're not half the strength you could be."

"I do what I have to."

"Why?" What was he hiding? No vampire abjured human blood without an exceptionally good reason. And there really were no good reasons when it came to vampires.

"Don't worry about it."

She wouldn't. Not really. It was his business. She understood the need to keep secrets. Besides, she'd know his soon enough. "Ready to tell me your name yet? I'm very willing to call you Fluffy if I have to. Maybe Rufus. Or how about Bunny?" She tapped her chin. "Captain Bunny of the Ship of Fools. That has a nice ring to—"

"Mal."

She raised her brows. Mal could be short for only a few names she could think of.

"—achi. Malachi."

Her brain searched every bit of vampire history she knew. The only Malachis she could come up with were nobility. If he really was such a low-level, unregistered anathema, what harm could he be? Maybe she should take a chance and trust him. Maybe she should tell him everything. He had taken care of her so far, in his own way. That was worth something, wasn't it?

What did she have to lose, really? She picked at a loose thread on the T-shirt's hem.

Besides her life.

No, she refused to think that way. She would play his game until it no longer suited her. And if she had to, she'd end it her way. With a blade to his neck or a stake through his heart.

*Liar, liar, liar.* Better a small lie than a truth that might send her running again. Getting her to talk was the most important thing. That was why he wanted to keep her here. Not because being near her brought him a foreign sense of serenity or because the voices didn't like her or because she made him strive to be more than he was. No. She needed help.

And help was his middle name. Right after loner and miscreant. *And killer. So kill her.*

She tugged the T-shirt down again, but it refused to cover any farther than the tops of her thighs. Fine with him. He could look at her all day and not get tired. There was something mesmerizing about those bright metallic marks. *Drinkable.* Something that made her seem both fragile and indestructible. *Drainable.* An angel spun from gold.

Hades on a cracker, she made his brain mush. If it wasn't her scent, it was something else. Her mouth was moving again. If he didn't pay attention, she was going to think she was affecting him. Which she wasn't. "What?"

"I said I don't know where to start."

"Oh." He forced himself to look into her eyes. "Start from the beginning."

"I found him the morning after the Century Ball." She paused. "You know the significance of that event?"

"No."

"After comarré have been with their patrons for a hundred years, a chance comes for the patron to offer freedom to his comarré. The comarré almost always declines and stays with the patron, so much so that it's become something of a foregone conclusion."

She glanced away as if remembering. "I had planned to accept. It was going to be my way out." She caught his gaze again. "Instead, Algernon made a long, flowery speech about how he knew where I was happiest and therefore saw no reason to extend something that would insult my good graces." Her lip curled. "He presented me with this enormous, gaudy gold heart on a chain. Just what I needed. More gold on my body."

Mal bit back a snicker. She had a point.

"Anyway, that's what goes on at the Century Ball." Her jaw tightened a fraction. "After we returned to Algernon's estate, I immediately went to my suite. I had already packed a few things in anticipation and seeing those bags made me realize what I was giving up if I stayed. I decided to run. I waited until I was sure daysleep had him, then I headed out. I planned to tell the servants I was headed to Primoris Domus. There would be nothing unusual about that. And that's when I found him in the great hall." She shifted uncomfortably. "He'd been murdered. Beheaded."

"The body was still tangible?" The older a vampire was, the faster they went to ash. *Fast, fast, fast for you.* "How young was your patron?"

"He wasn't young." She shook her head. "He was—"

"There's only one way—"

"—killed with a hot blade."

Mal studied her face. Dread etched the corners of her mouth. That revelation had cost her something. Good. About time she started telling a few truths. "Vampires can't use hot blades."

"No." She didn't meet his eyes.

"You think a mortal killed him? A slayer?" There hadn't been a successful human slayer since...ever, really. The covenant prevented it.

"No." Still no visual contact. So much for truth.

He leaned forward, forcing himself not to inhale. "Then what *do* you think?"

"That it looks like it was meant to put the blame on a comarré."

"Then they did a poor job. That Golgotha dagger is too small for a beheading."

One quick glance up, then her gaze went right back to her fingers. "That's not the only hot weapon we have. The sacre, our ceremonial sword, is quenched in holy water."

What other fun toys did she have up her sleeve? "Where's your sword?"

"Unless someone moved it, it still hangs in my patron's house on the wall of my apartment."

"Was it used?" A blade made hot with magic or something sacred left a wound that would fester unhealed for a very long time. In a clean cut, it seared the flesh as it passed through. If the flesh belonged to a vampire, that meant leaving a corpse or a stump behind. A great way to send a message, or set someone up.

"I don't know. I didn't think to go back and see if there

was blood scent on it and there was no way to take it with me, so I just ran. I swear I'm innocent. I had no reason to do this."

"You had reason. He didn't offer you freedom."

"I planned to leave anyway. Why would I kill him and complicate things?" She glanced up. "And just because I own such a sword doesn't mean—"

"What happened after you saw the body?"

"I was scared, but I went to the Primoris Domus as planned, grabbed a few more things, then went to the airport." She brushed the ends of her hair back and forth over her fingers.

Scared, but not so scared she couldn't formulate a plan. "Why go to your house at all?"

She stared at the backs of her hands, but her eyes had a very faraway look. "To get cash for the ticket and to cover my signum with the foundation my friend had sent me. And to buy myself some time. It's not unusual for one of us to spend several days at our house."

"Why would your friend send you makeup to cover your marks? How would she know you'd need to cover them?"

That made her look up. "How do you know my friend is a she?"

"Who else would send you makeup?" He shifted, crossed his legs. "Now answer the question. How did this friend know you'd need to cover them?"

"She didn't know. She works at a big cosmetics company, and every once in a while she'd send me samples like that."

He watched her for a moment. She kept eye contact with him. Maybe she was telling the truth about the foundation. Still, it was a pretty interesting coincidence. "What did you use for ID at the airport?"

More fidgeting with the hair.

"Whether or not I help you depends a lot on how much truth you give me."

She worried her bottom lip between her teeth. "All comarré have false papers."

More fun toys. He leaned back. "In case you behead someone and need to flee the country?"

"In case our patrons need us to travel," she snapped back. "I am *not* guilty."

"You realize trying to kill me in that alley doesn't help your case." He could still see her in that dim light, the speed at which she'd come at him, the sleekness of her movements. That was no lucky shot. That was practice. Most likely years of it.

Fire lit her eyes. She bowed toward him, fists planted on the mattress. "I didn't intend to kill you. If I had, I would've moved the blade up two inches. I know more ways to kill a vampire than you'll ever…" Her jaw went slack, her eyes unblinking. Closing her mouth, she sat back.

And there was the proof. Nodding slowly, he watched the anger fade into the sinking realization of what she'd just said. He lifted his palms nonchalantly. "But you're innocent."

"Yes," she whispered, slumping against the headboard. She covered her face with her hands.

Time to change the subject before she shut down. "A hundred years with your patron. That's a long time to be with one person."

"I'm not sure what you're implying." She uncovered her face to look at him.

Mal shrugged. "Just saying you look good for an old broad."

Steel glinted in her eyes. "Comarré age very slowly."

Hmm. Anger brought the truth out of her. Might be worth another shot. "How old were you when he first sucked your brains out?"

A spark of that rage returned. Her chin lifted. "You needn't be vulgar. He purchased my blood rights when I was fifteen."

Ouch. "So...was he your first?" He hated the images those words brought, but took pleasure that her patron's head was no longer intimate with his spine.

"And my last."

Only one. That was something then. Easier to take. Not that it mattered if she'd serviced the whole bloody council. Because it didn't. He decided to test her, to see how much truth she was telling. "What Family was he?"

She pursed her mouth. Like she was about to be kissed. Or stalling.

Mal put his hands on the chair's arms and pushed up. "If you're done, I'm leav—"

A sigh ended the silence. "Tepes."

Great, she hadn't been lying in the gym when she'd said his power wouldn't work on her. Why, of the five Families, did it have to be that one? "And his name?"

More sighing. "Algernon."

"As in the Elder of the Tepes Family?" Hell and damnation. This couldn't get worse.

She shrugged. "Yes, but, well, not anymore. Obviously."

He stood and paced to the far end of the room, then back again. How convenient that the prize comarré of the Elder of the Tepes Family should somehow end up in New

Florida. On his doorstep. She probably didn't even know she was being played for a pawn. How bloody perfect. It stank like a setup, because it probably was. Somehow, despite everything he'd done to stay off the radar, someone had found out he'd escaped the imprisonment. Someone who still wanted him dead. Someone who obviously thought he was stupid enough to fall for a game like this. Damsel in distress worked better if the damsel wasn't trying to kill you.

"No." He waved his hand at her. "I've made my decision. I'm not getting involved in this. Nice try, though."

Her mouth opened, most likely to protest, then she crossed her arms. The movement inched the T-shirt higher. "Would you say that Fi belongs to you?"

"No. Of course not."

"Then she's free to leave whenever she wants?"

"No." He scowled. "She's bound to me."

Chrysabelle rolled her eyes. "So she belongs to you. Have you noticed that the urges you feel around me, the way the scent of my blood affects you, those things, have you noticed they're a little less aggressive today?"

Actually, they were. "Yeah, so?"

"Then you have no choice but to help me." She couldn't have looked more smug if she'd tried.

"How the hell do you figure that?"

"The first to blood a free comarré takes that comarré's blood rights. Technically, that would be you, via Fi. Even though, technically, you stole them." She scowled and started muttering to herself. "A ghost. How does that even happen? I hate this city."

"You mean I'm your new patron because of Fi getting your blood?"

Chrysabelle glared daggers at him. "Great. Anathema and slow. This just gets better and better."

"No, this isn't happening. There's got to be a way around this. I'll give them back. Go. You're free. I release you." He waved his hands at her like shooing a fly.

"I'm not a sparrow. You can't just release me into the wild and hope for the best." She shook her head, looking at him like he was a world-class idiot. "There are two ways to give me my rights back."

He waited. "And those would be?"

"You can die on your own. Or I can kill you."

# Chapter Fourteen

The red-black haze numbed Tatiana like a paralyzing poison. She welcomed the respite from the pain and the punishing use of her body and allowed herself to float. As long as she fought her way back to consciousness when the time came to drink in the power she'd earned. The kind of power only the blood of the Castus Sanguis could supply. Such power was priceless. Painless.

A hand slapped her face, tugging her back to reality. *No*, she whispered to the fading numbness, but already it dissolved around the edges. She reached for the remains of her self-imposed oblivion, but it was too late. The pain sifted the haze out of reach. Blood trickled from the corner of her mouth. Hungry tongues lapped it up. She gasped, desperate for the darkness. Clawed fingers dug into her flesh. Every slice registered with unnatural clarity. *Must . . . return . . . to the nothing.*

Greedy mouths worked the cuts for more blood. A whimper built in her throat, but she refused to give it voice. They might bend her, but they would not break her. She would prove herself worthy of the power they had to bestow.

A body leaned into her, heavy, unrelenting, weighing on every sore spot. She pushed the pain away, sought the haze, opened herself up to it, and forced her way into the fog's sweet relief.

The reward was all that mattered.

The door chimes sang out at dusk. Maris wheeled to the door ahead of Velimai and opened it, hoping for Chrysabelle, but knowing it wouldn't be.

It wasn't. She fought to keep her face steady.

"Hello, Dominic. Punctual, as always."

"*Ciao,* Marissa. For you, would I be anything less?" He stood outlined by the darkening sky and the landscape lighting, his hair just as black, his eyes just as mossy green. Her gut clenched from the scent of him. She fought against the tide of past memories sucking at her emotions, just as she did every time he came to visit. She would not give in, even if he was as beautiful as she'd remembered. Maybe more. And hopefully as willing to help her.

"It's Maris now, you know that." How many times must she correct him?

"You will always be Marissa to me." His slight smile opened another chink in her armor. She missed him and hated herself for it. "May I come in?"

She leaned back and the iBot retreated a few paces accordingly. He knew better. But that didn't stop him from asking. "You know the rules haven't changed. Meet me on the patio."

He clutched his dead heart, always the dramatic. "*Tesora,* you wound me."

"You'll live." She shut the door and spun toward the

rear of the house. The distance allowed her to breathe again. Velimai hung near the patio sliders, a disapproving look on her face.

Maris nodded. "I know how you feel. So noted." Dominic would never harm her. Not any more than he already had.

Velimai's storm-colored eyes narrowed, and she signed that Maris wasn't the only one living in the house.

"He's never so much as raised a finger in your direction. Now shoo."

When Maris opened the sliders and rolled through, he was there, stretched out on one of the chaises and looking like a Roman god. She angled her iBot toward him.

He tucked his arms behind his head, careless with the suit that must have cost a mortal's fortune. "You've cut your hair." He shrugged. "Still *bella*. Like the day you broke my heart."

"Your heart was broken long before me." She smiled indulgently, as she might with a child. "Dominic, I haven't called you here for the usual reason." Although undoubtedly, it would lead to that. "I need a favor, and I know you owe me nothing, so..." This was far more difficult than she'd thought it would be, especially with him so close and so unchanged.

"Well, that explains why you called me so soon after our last visit." One black, winged brow lifted. "Although I didn't think your pretty mouth could form the words for help."

"I'm serious." What had she thought? That he'd age in the short time since she'd last seen him? That time would temper his addictive beauty into something easier to deny? That her body would forget everything that had happened between them?

"So am I." He sat up. "You must need the help desperately."

She powered the iBot down to a seated position, folded her hands in her lap and took a deep breath. Her lungs filled with his seductive aroma. She exhaled. "It's not for me, it's for my niece. Who is also ... who is still comarré. And, I fear, in terrible danger." She shook her head, thinking of the note of warning she'd received from Rennata. *Trouble comes your way.* This was not what she'd wanted for Chrysabelle. Not at all.

"What do you need from me?" He leaned forward. "Protection?"

"No." She rested her hand on his, knowing how persuasive her touch could be to a vampire. Especially this one. "I have to find her."

"Do you think I need to be reminded of your allure?" He pulled his hand away. "Why not send your wysper?"

"And leave myself defenseless?"

Dominic laughed. "We both know you're not defenseless. Does your sacre still hang above your bed?"

"Yes." His remembering where she kept her weapon should not be reason enough for her cheeks to heat, but it was. The memory of when they'd shared a home nearly broke her. She bent her head to remove an imaginary piece of lint from her linen pants.

"Please, Dominic," she whispered, bracing herself for the lie she hoped would sway him. "She is like a daughter to me. The child we ... could never have."

He went rigid at those words, then stood and strode to the edge of the pavers. A shard of light from the young moon filtered through the palms, tipping his hair silver. Beyond him, the patio curved around the infinity edge pool and down to the deep water slip holding her favorite way to escape, the *Heliotrope*. He stared at the yacht. Was he remembering the last time they'd been aboard her? The last time they'd made love? "Twenty years since you walked away from me, but I remember as though it were yesterday." When he turned, his eyes matched the moon glow. "Come back to me, *cara mia*. Not the way things are now, but the way they were."

Of course he remembered. She focused on his tie. Looking there was easier than looking into his handsome face. Did she look older to him? She must. "Dominic, please. We've been down that road. I can't. That life," she sighed, "it holds too many bad memories for me."

He came and kneeled at her feet. "I can erase those memories, Marissa. Give you new ones. What we had—"

"What we had was wonderful, but brought too much pain. Dominic, I've changed. You've changed." Although not physically. She cupped his cheek as the old feelings swirled through her. For her, he had willingly become anathema, accepting the banishment the nobility inflicted on those who fell out of favor for one reason or another. For Maris, Dominic had made it so much easier to walk away from everything she'd ever known all those years ago. He'd been her safety net. She had loved Dominic, once.

Now, the older she got, the further away she wanted to be from the past and the pain it held. And unfortunately, that included Dominic. They'd both gone too far in opposite directions to meet at any kind of middle now.

"I had to change in order to survive. To take care of us." He pressed his cheek into her hand, then turned his face and kissed her palm before rising to his feet again. He smoothed his suit. The lines of sentimentality disappeared from his face as well. This was not a new conversation for them, but they'd not repeated it in several years. "Of course, we have moved beyond the past, you and me. What falls between us now is business. Duty. Nothing more."

Cursing the bitterness of her own heart while praising the coldness of his, she nodded. "Yes, Dominic. That is the way of it."

He put distance between them again and stared out to sea. "What is it you wish me to do?"

She held out a copy of the address Jonas had given her. "She went there, two days ago, and has not returned. Jonas is not returning my calls and I am tired of imagining what has happened. I want to know if…things have not gone well."

He walked over, took the paper without looking at it, and tucked it into the inside pocket of his jacket. "I will find out tonight."

"*Grazie,* Dominic."

"And in return for this information?"

She'd known he'd expect payment. Prepared herself for it. After all, this was business now. She unbuttoned a few buttons, spread her shirt collar, and tilted her head back. At the edge of her vision, she spotted Velimai whirling like a hurricane behind the sheers. "I trust you will be gentle."

His fangs gleamed. Her weak body betrayed her with its eager response, tightening in anticipation. He leaned in. "Ah, *bella mia,* as always."

"I own you?" Fi almost bounced on her toes.

"You don't own *me,* only my blood rights," Chrysabelle explained for the third time. Why the ghost took such happiness in this, Chrysabelle didn't understand. "And actually Mal owns them. Stole them, really."

"Enough with the stealing. We didn't know." Mal ground his teeth and glared heavenward. "I need sleep." He shoved a hand through his black hair. "I should be getting up at sundown, not going to bed." His gaze shifted from Fi to Chrysabelle. "Try not to kill each other for the next four or five hours. Or do, I don't care. Doc, you're in charge." Shaking his head, he left.

"Whatever that's worth," Doc called after him from the kitchen, where he was fixing plates of something he optimistically termed dinner.

Chrysabelle sank into one of the chairs surrounding the worn table. She rested her head on her hands and stared at the scarred surface. This really wasn't the new life she'd envisioned for herself. In that life, she wasn't wearing a black T-shirt and baggy pajama pants that reeked of male vampire. A male who had not only stolen her blood rights, but didn't seem to care one way or the other what that meant. She glanced at Fi. "Why are you so excited about this anyway?"

Fi cocked an eyebrow. "You don't get it, do you?" She leaned in. "Those voices in Mal's head? I'm one of them, or at least I was until I got your blood in me. Since he killed me, I've had to listen to that chaos just like him."

"Why do you stay?"

"Like I have a choice?" Fi's gaze strayed to Doc. "Mal's not so bad. Not since he stopped killing. And look, being a ghost is better than being dead altogether." She glanced at Doc again, a slight smile on her face. What a strange pairing, the varcolai and the ghost. "Things aren't so awful here."

Chrysabelle kept her voice low. "You love him?"

"Yes, she does, and I can hear you, you know," Doc called out from the kitchen.

Fi laughed as she turned back. "I can't leave anyway, so might as well make the best of it. I tried once. Went corporeal and started walking. Six blocks and I got snapped back, like some big metaphysical rubber band attached us." She sat back. "So now, with your blood in me, I can't hear the chaos anymore." She grinned. "Thanks."

"You're welcome. I guess." Chrysabelle studied the girl, feeling a sense of sympathy she hadn't before. What a strange existence.

Doc put plates of pasta in front of her and Fi. "Eat up. You must be jonesin' for food big-time."

"I am, but"—Chrysabelle poked at it with a fork—"where's the meat?"

"Beggars can't be choosers," Fi said.

"I am not a beggar." She wanted to add *you little thief,* but it was Mal's fault, not Fi's, that this had happened. "I need protein. It's kind of important for someone like me."

He squeezed Fi's shoulder but spoke to Chrysabelle. "Meat's spendy, especially when there are three of us now."

"Varcolai need meat, too."

He shrugged and took the chair beside Fi. "I eat it every few days."

Chrysabelle raised her brows. "Please tell me this ship is just naturally rat-free."

"I *buy* the meat," Doc said, stabbing his pasta. Clearly, she'd hit a nerve.

"Every few days isn't really enough, is it? Just because Malachi chooses to starve himself doesn't mean you have to."

Fi's expression wrinkled. "Malachi?"

Doc shot the ghost a look. "We call him Mal. That's what he likes."

Fi shot the look back but stayed silent. Something wasn't right.

"Regardless," Chrysabelle continued. "I...we don't need to suffer too. If money is a concern, I'm willing to help out."

Fi laughed. "With what?"

"Where's the bag I brought with me?" Chrysabelle asked Doc.

"Should still be in Mal's office," Doc answered.

"All right, I'll just be a moment." She pushed her chair back.

"Where do you think you're going? We're supposed to watch you." Fi's indignant look made Chrysabelle stifle a laugh. She had to give Fi points for trying.

"What are you? Twenty-three? Twenty-four?" She slanted her eyes at Doc. "You're not much older, are you? I don't need children minding me." She strolled toward the door, hiding her slight limp as much as possible. Her broken foot already felt better than it had when she'd woken up.

"Children?" Fi scoffed. "Pot meet kettle."

Chrysabelle paused. "I am one hundred fifteen years old." She flicked a glanced at Doc and tried not to smile. "That's in human years."

Doc jumped up and grabbed her arm. "I'll get your bag. Wouldn't want you wearing out those old bones."

She tugged her arm out of his grasp and forced down the surge of fighting instinct that had arisen at his touch. She had to stop reacting like that. Humans touched each other. She had to get used to it. "That would be nice of you."

Thankfully, Fi kept quiet. Maybe she sensed Chrysabelle's struggle.

Chrysabelle went back to her place and sat down. The food barely registered on the scale of what she was used to. Comarré ate well. The best foods made for the best-tasting blood. But that was her old life, this was her new.

She spun the noodles around her fork and took a bite. Jarred sauce. No meat except what had been used to flavor it. Fi wolfed hers down like it was foie gras. "You really like spaghetti, huh?"

Fi swallowed her current mouthful. "I like everything. Ghosts don't really get to eat, you know? Since I became alive again, I just want to eat everything. We had the best tuna melts yesterday. Doc loves tuna. Guess it's a cat thing." She stuffed another forkful in.

"What do you mean, alive again?"

"Since I got your blood. I don't even have to think about staying corporeal, I just am. Used to be I had to work at it, think about it, you know?" She shrugged. "I haven't been in my spirit form since."

Warning bells clanged in Chrysabelle's brain. "Have you tried?"

Fi didn't bother swallowing this time. "Nope."

"Could you try now?"

"You're a fat pain in the ectoplasm, you know that?" Fi smirked, took a long drink of water, then closed her eyes. A moment later, she opened them. "Did I go fuzzy?"

"No."

"Are you sure?" Fi's eyes sparkled. "Wait, let me try

again." Another interlude of eyes opening and closing. "Well?"

"Not even a flicker."

"Wow! This is awesome. I really am alive again. I can't wait to tell my parents!" Her fingers strayed to the back of her right ear. "I wonder if my com cell still works."

Chrysabelle leaned back slightly. "I don't think telling your parents is such a hot idea and I wouldn't let Mal know if your com cell does work. He might make you take it out."

"Why shouldn't I tell them?" Fi's nose wrinkled. "And why would Mal make me—"

"Tell who what? What about Mal?" Doc walked in carrying Chrysabelle's bag. He set it beside her chair, then retook his. "What did I miss?"

Chrysabelle pulled her bag onto her lap. "I was saying Fi shouldn't tell her parents she's alive again because it might not be permanent, and if her com cell works, she probably shouldn't mention it. You know how othernaturals are about that stuff." None of them, vampire, fae, or varcolai, used the devices. The tracking potential was too great.

Fi's hand came away from her ear. "Doesn't work anyway." She turned to Doc. "I'm not a ghost anymore."

"I know. I hung with your unghosty self all day yesterday." He gave her a wink and picked up his fork.

Chrysabelle pressed her thumb to the bag's scanlock. It recognized her and clicked open. She checked through it. Everything was there.

Fi kept talking. "No, I mean like not at all. I'm completely alive again. I can't become a ghost even if I try. Which I just did. Twice."

Chrysabelle pulled out a fat velvet pouch and removed one of the jewels.

Doc put his fork down. "How? You sure?"

"Totally sure." Fi tipped her head at Chrysabelle. "Her blood."

His brows rose. "Wow. Cool."

"That's what I said."

"Here you are." Chrysabelle slid the gem across the table to Doc. "Sell that for whatever you can get and then fill the larders. I'd love steak for dinner tomorrow. Get everything you like. Lots of produce, fresh vegetables, and meat. Lots of meat. Organic when you can. Game hens, steaks, lots of steaks—Kobe if you can get it, wild salmon—none of that cloned stuff either."

Doc grimaced. "I agree, I hate that crap." He picked up the stone. "This what I think it is?"

Chrysabelle tied the pouch and tucked it away in her bag. "What do you think it is?"

"Some fat pink ice." He turned the gem in his fingers, holding it up to the light. Fi was blissfully silent, mesmerized by the sparkle.

"You're right. Fancy Intense Pink. Not quite two and a half carats. It was a gift from my patron. Cost him nearly two million almost seventy years ago. Get as much as you can."

Fi's mouth dropped open. "Two mil? He must have been filthy rich."

Chrysabelle laughed joylessly. "That's nothing compared to what he paid for my blood rights."

Both Fi and Doc looked at her expectantly. She shook her head. "Please, I don't wish to discuss him anymore."

Doc rolled the diamond around on his palm. It glittered against his dark skin. "Why you trust me with this?"

"Trust is earned, right? We have to start somewhere." She lifted her hands in a gesture of surrender. "I'm not used to this life enough yet, I know that. I like to live well, but I guess that makes me soft. I just need time to adjust." She half-smiled and lifted a shoulder. "Buy whatever else you need with what's left over, all right?" She plucked at her borrowed T-shirt. "Although I could use some new clothes too."

Fi stuck her hand up like schoolgirl. "I can buy those. I'm good at clothes."

"I thought you couldn't get more than six blocks away from Mal?"

"I have a feeling this permanent corporeal state will change that. If not, I'll send Doc."

Chrysabelle nodded. "Okay, that would be wonderful. I'll have to measure myself, all I know are comarré sizes. I'll make a list for you." White clothing shouldn't be too hard to come by in this warm locale. "I think I'll go for a walk around the deck, if that's okay with both of you."

"No can do." Doc shook his head as he pocketed the gem. "Sorry, but you outside is a bad idea. Especially with Mal counting sheep."

She sighed. "I really can take care of myself."

"Really?" Doc raised a brow. "Then why'd you come to him in the first place?"

"I meant physically." Chrysabelle pushed her plate away. "I'm done, thank you." She stood, testing her weight on her broken foot. Barely a twinge. She bent and picked up her bag. And realized she had nowhere to go. "It's occurred to me I don't actually have a room on the *Titanic*."

Doc tried not to smile. "Shouldn't have kicked that door down, GI Jane."

"Thanks for the reminder. I need to add shoes to the list. Something sturdy." She slung the bag over her shoulder and stared at him expectantly.

"What?" Doc asked.

"Is there a room I can use or should I just pick one out? I'd like one without all the locks. On the outside. Inside locks I'm okay with."

Doc dipped his napkin in his water and wiped his mouth with it, then stood. Chrysabelle chalked up the extra cleanliness to his feline bloodlines. "Follow me. There's a bunch of empty cabins you can pick from."

Fi jumped up. "I'm coming too. I don't want her too close to ours in case she snores."

"I don't snore but I'm happy to have a little space." Except maybe from Mal. Despite his contribution to her losing her blood rights, she couldn't help but feel some comfort in the fact that he'd done what he thought best and taken care of her afterward.

The three of them walked down the hall, Doc in front, Fi behind. Chrysabelle decided to subtly test the waters.

"So... what's Mal's story?"

"What do you mean?" Doc asked.

"Where's he from, what Family is he, that sort of thing."

Fi snorted. "You mean how'd he get those names all over him?"

So much for subtle. "Yes, that too."

Doc shook his head. "He'll spill his info when he wants, if he wants."

Which is exactly what Chrysabelle had assumed.

"He's anathema, you know," Fi added, like that was news.

Chrysabelle looked over her shoulder and laughed.

"You don't say? Living here with you two? I thought perhaps he was preparing to ascend to Dominus any day now."

Fi's brow wrinkled. "Dominus?"

"Big-time head vampire," Doc explained. Chrysabelle let it go. She was in no mood to give a primer in vampire politics. Instead, she changed the subject.

"Why do you stay, shifter? Did your pride kick you out?"

"As a matter of fact, they did. Plus Mal and Fi saved my life. You got a problem with varcolai?"

Obviously, he knew what nobles thought of his kind and must think she felt that way too. Which she didn't. "Not at all, I was just wonder—"

Mal burst through a door ahead of them. One hand held a crossbow, the other a pair of mismatched swords. A leather strap of throwing stars crossed his chest. He tossed the crossbow to Doc. "We've got company."

Doc tipped his head and listened for a second, then nodded. "Not sure how I missed that."

Chrysabelle inhaled. The new vampire's scent was faint but present. And somehow familiar. Nothos maybe, if it was covering its scent with something else. "We missed it by talking."

Mal jerked his thumb down the hall behind him. "Fi, get to your room and lock the door. Stay there until Doc or I come for you."

"But I—"

"But nothing. You're mortal." Mal's gaze went to Doc next. "Kill the lights, then come around the other way. Chrysabelle's with me."

"Will do." He grabbed Fi's arm and pulled her down the hall with him.

"Good luck." Fi pouted on her way out.

Mal turned back to Chrysabelle. "You can handle a sword, I take it?"

She nodded. If this new vampire was here for her, this was no time to hide her abilities. Mal handed her a rusty dagger. Instead of taking it, she pointed to the long, curved sword in his hand. "You're kidding, right? Give me the katana."

"You sure you—fine, here." In a flash, he turned the slender blade over to her. "I attack first. You stay back, understood?"

"I want my dagger." She tossed her bag into his room for safekeeping.

"No time. Follow me."

A second later the lights went out. "Can you see?" he whispered, creeping forward.

She followed close behind. "Perfectly." In truth, her night vision was starting to dim. Nearly a week without a true patron and without the bite—that life-prolonging, sense-enhancing input of vampire saliva into her system— her exceptional senses would diminish until she was as human as Fi. When would she begin to age again? Maris looked remarkable for someone who'd been without a patron for nearly fifty years.

She ran into Mal's outstretched arm. He put a finger to his lips, then gestured for her to stay while he went ahead. She nodded. He slipped around the bend. Fresh air filled the passage. They must be close to an outside door. She flattened against the wall, sword at the ready, wishing she was fully armed. Not having a backup weapon meant no second chances. Hand-to-hand with a Nothos wasn't going to be fun.

A singing hiss broke the silence, followed by the clang of two swords biting into each other. She took a deep breath and eased forward as a blade sliced toward Mal's neck. Suddenly, the new vampire's familiar scent registered.

Not brimstone. Comarré blood.

# Chapter Fifteen

Mal ducked and the intruder's sword whistled by Mal's ear. Chrysabelle shoved past, slicing her blade between them and pinning the other vampire to the door he'd just come through. His blade clattered to the ground while hers gleamed against his throat, just above the collar of a very expensive suit.

Mal lifted a brow. The comarré was fast, he'd give her that. Then his focus shifted to the vampire she'd pinned, and he scowled. Some vampires never changed. Dominic was one of those.

The other anathema held his hands up. "Watch the threads, *cara mia*. This just arrived from my tailor in Bangkok."

Chrysabelle pressed the blade into his skin. "Like I care."

The lights flickered on. To Chrysabelle's credit, she didn't falter when Doc strolled out from the opposite hall and cast a shadow on her and Dominic. Doc shouldered the crossbow and stared hard at the creature under Chrysabelle's sword. The rancor in his eyes was unmistakable, but then Dominic was the reason Doc had been cursed.

Bad drugs had a way of making people angry. And vengeful. Doc had just been the unfortunate delivery boy.

Doc's finger caressed the crossbow's trigger. "Looks like you got this under control. I'll check the perimeter. Unless you need something staked. Then gimme a yell."

Dominic wisely kept his mouth shut while he watched Doc disappear down the passage.

Mal kept his sword up. "What are you doing here, Dominic?" As though he didn't know what had brought the biggest crime boss in Paradise City sniffing around. Mal's freighter stank of comarré. Speaking of which—

"Dominic Falconetti?" Chrysabelle glanced over her shoulder, then back at the vampire under her blade.

"You know him?" Mal asked. Comarré knowledge was scary. Another reason for her not to know his real name.

"Scarnato, now," Dominic answered. He smiled at Chrysabelle like an indulgent parent.

She eased her sword back. "You're supposed to be dead."

"I am." His smile widened. "And have been for nearly two hundred years now." His gaze slid to Mal, but he spoke to her. "Drop the blade, *bella*. I've come to help you."

"Keep the blade where it is," Mal said. "He's no help to anyone." Dominic Scarnato was the largest black market alchemist in New Florida. Probably in the whole Southern Union. His drugs altered the minds of humans and othernaturals alike. As far as Mal had uncovered, he'd come out of nowhere but made a real name for himself in a short period of time. In fact, Dominic's presence was one reason Mal had moved to Paradise City, figuring the man's black cloud would offer some cover.

Dominic shrugged. The subtle movement against the weapon's edge opened a thin slice in his throat. Blood pearled on the blade, its aroma filling the air.

Chrysabelle reeled backward, gagging and taking her weapon with her. The cut vanished a second after her sword pulled away. "You've had—"

"Comarré blood," Mal finished. Son of a priest. He lunged, sword in hand, and grabbed Dominic by the collar with both hands. The move notched Mal's blade against Dominic's face, opening a fresh cut on his cheek. Another wave of scent rolled over them, a heady mix of comarré-sweet, vampire-spicy. "Explain. Now."

Dominic's eyes shifted to Chrysabelle. "You have somewhere we could talk?"

Mal jerked Dominic against the metal door, cutting a new line into the man's face. "Here works for me."

"Then stop wrinkling my suit. The fabric alone cost more than this dinghy." He grimaced at the dim passageway. "How you can live like this...*pazzo*." He rolled his eyes.

Being called crazy had little effect when that was a known quantity. Mal stepped back but aimed the sword at Dominic's throat. "Talk."

The cut on Dominic's cheek zipped closed. "I'm here on behalf of Chrysabelle's aunt. She got worried. Hasn't heard from her niece. She needs some reassurance the girl is in good hands." He laughed humorlessly. "She'll be so disappointed."

Chrysabelle inched forward. "How did you get her blood?" Her voice trembled with what sounded like fear and anger. Mal understood both.

Dominic smoothed an eyebrow with his ring finger. "You think I work for free?"

With a noise that was part sob, part gasp, Chrysabelle charged. Mal caught her around the waist with his free arm. She vibrated with anger.

How long had he lived in the same city with another comarré and not known? "Your aunt is comarré? And she lives here?" He really needed to get out more.

"Yes," she hissed, nearly breaking his hold. So, fast *and* strong. Noted.

"Enough," he whispered in her ear. "This is not the time."

She glared at him, but he released her anyway. "You can flay him when I'm done."

Her glare shifted to Dominic. "I will, too."

Dominic had the stones to laugh. "Yes, I'm sure you will, *cara mia.*"

Pointing with her blade, she narrowed her eyes. "Don't patronize me, leech." Her signum glinted dangerous sparks.

Mal forced himself not to laugh. Angry Chrysabelle was something to behold—especially when it wasn't directed at him. "You can tell her aunt everything is fine."

Dominic's brows lifted. "Is that so, Chrysabelle? I am perfectly capable of freeing you from this black-hearted beast." He leaned past Mal's sword as though about to impart some great, secret wisdom. "You do realize Malkolm will kill you sooner or later, don't you? Comarré or not, it won't stop him. Death and madness, those are Mr. Bourreau's only mistresses." Dominic grinned at Mal. "Or don't you know the anathema you're keeping company with?"

Over the screeching voices in his head, Mal could hear Chrysabelle thinking, checking every jot of information stored in her head for an anathema named Malkolm Bourreau. It shouldn't take long to determine who he was, although certainly most nobility assumed him dead or, at the least, permanently indisposed. Would she raise her sword against him? His fingers loosened on his own weapon. There was no desire in him to fight her or be responsible for her death. He prepared for the killing blow, sure she would slice his head from his neck as she probably had her patron's.

Then the strangest sound reached his ears.

Her laughter.

"Of course, I know who he is. Why do you think I hired him to protect me? I'm not stupid, Dominic." She dropped her sword to her side. "Neither is he foolish enough to accept something so fleeting as blood in payment."

Dominic couldn't hide his amazement. "Have you given him the ring?"

Chrysabelle's eyes widened a fraction. "How do you know about that?"

A ring? Mal would get that information out of her later, when he'd recovered from the fact that he had somehow become the lesser of two evils.

"A very disgruntled Nothos came to me a few days ago looking for something to enhance its tracking abilities. I gave it what it wanted. With a little truth amplifier mixed in. Then I asked some questions. Seems it'd failed to bring back a missing comarré who'd not only killed her patron but stolen a very valuable ring."

"Where is this Nothos?" Panic sheared Chrysabelle's voice.

"By now, I'd guess in the belly of a gator. I don't need Nothos in this city any more than you do. I dumped it unconscious in the glades." Dominic checked his watch. "Well, it's been a distinct lack of pleasure talking to the two of you, but I have other business to attend to." He nodded to Chrysabelle. "I'll give your best to your aunt."

Her sword came up again. "Keep your filthy hands off her."

Gripping the door handle, he smirked. "I don't use my hands. Unless she asks."

Chrysabelle threw her sword like a javelin, but Dominic was already gone. The blade screeched halfway through the closed metal door before it stopped.

Mal yanked it out, then faced her. "You and I need to talk."

She grabbed the scarred blade from his hand and angled the point at his heart. "You first, *Malkolm*."

Pain filled Tatiana like mortal breath once had. No longer could she reach the safe haven of the distant haze. Agony owned her. Each stabbing thrust branded her skin. Clawed hands opened new wounds and freshened old bruises. The screaming left her throat raw until she ceased any effort for sound. By now her body was little more than a purpling rag, torn and wasted. Still, the Castus Sanguis persisted. With each movement, the bed seeped dampness onto her skin. Blood, tears, or worse, she didn't know. Didn't care.

The reward would be hers. She clung to that certainty, let it blunt the jagged edge of her reality. She would survive, stronger than before. She would break those who opposed her. Destroy them. Suck the marrow from their bones and grind them into dust.

*Dominus dominus dominus.* Over and over like a prayer, she chanted the title that would someday be hers. When this hell was extinguished and she'd received her reward.

The Castus bit into her shoulder and drank, his large body heavy on hers. His forked tongue flicked against her skin. She laughed hoarsely, openmouthed and drunk with the promise of power.

*Dominus dominus dominus.*


Malkolm tried to insist they talk in his room. Chrysabelle refused. No way was she following the most notorious fallen vampire into a place he considered safe ever again. Malkolm Bourreau, vampire killer. The name Bourreau meant executioner in French. He'd been named for his human profession. Ironic how well it suited him now. Even so, her knowledge of him was a mere fragment of his shadowed story.

They'd ended up in one of the ship's holds that had been converted into a mammoth gym. It suited her. Being able to put space between them was a very good thing. The massive overheads shed half their normal light and flickered as they dwindled further. This dependence on solar made her miss the wealth of the world she'd left behind. Adjustment took time, she reminded herself.

"Talk," she said, not caring that her feet stayed planted in a fighting stance or the sword remained lifted, ready to strike. Whether it was the adrenaline or her body's vampire-given ability to heal itself, her broken foot felt whole. Not that pain would stop her from fighting. She was tougher than that. And if he hadn't learned by now that she could defend herself, it was time he figured it out.

"You think I care what you know about me? I don't." He prowled back and forth like a caged beast.

"Then tell me."

He snarled. "I'm cursed."

"So I've heard." She shifted slightly, keeping her body aligned with his movements.

He tore his shirt off as he turned, giving her another glimpse of the black scrawling that covered him. "Every life I've taken I wear on my skin. Every one. Every father, every mother, every child." He dropped the shirt and slapped his open palm against his chest. "Every name haunts me. The voices..." His hands tightened on his skull as he circled back. "They never shut up. Taunting me. Pushing me."

She stared at his black-inked skin. How many lives did he bear? Thousands? Tens of thousands? "That must be difficult beyond words." She couldn't fathom how he hadn't gone insane.

"It is." He spun on his heels to face her. "Especially around you." He came as close as her blade would let him. "Do you know what they tell me to do with you? Do you?"

She shook her head, unwilling to say anything that might stop him. There was power in knowing an opponent's secrets.

"Kill her, drain her, get away." Silver eyes drilled into her. "That's what they scream into my ears when you're around."

She tried to steady her breathing and failed. Her pulse must be slamming into his head like a jackhammer. He stalked closer. The sword point scratched a bloody line into his skin, but she refused to back up even though the smell of him—bitter, spicy, and yet deficient—shredded her nerves. The desire to feed him, to give of herself, made her want to weep with disgust.

He stabbed his fingers at his temples. "That's what they hiss into my ears around you. Over and over until I want to do it just to shut them up."

His face contorted and he retreated a single step, pointing a finger at her. "You're trouble and they know it."

"Me? Trouble?" She forced a laugh, but it sounded feeble even to her ears. "I'm not trouble, I'm *in* trouble." Seriously in trouble if she didn't get some distance, but backing up would make her look weak.

"I should," he muttered like he was talking to himself. Or maybe the voices. "I should drink you dry and be done with you." He paced the floor, thankfully away from her.

She waved the sword after him. "Try it and I'll be forced to defend myself." Of course, if what she knew about him was true, try might be all she did.

"Don't you mean behead me? Like you did your patron?" He turned, hands clenched. His body tensed, cording the muscles in his chest. The names danced with the movement.

"You're the expert on beheading. You really think I'm capable of that?"

The silver in his eyes darkened for a second then flared back to life. "Yes." He shrugged while he walked. "No. I don't know. Don't care. Go back to your aunt." He crisscrossed his hands over each other. "I'm done with this. With you."

She lowered the sword. "It's not that easy. I need help, and you own my blood rights. That makes you responsible for me."

"I don't want you or your blood rights. I just want to be left alone."

Despite the situation, the rejection still stung. No lucid vampire turned down a comarré's blood rights. Especially a Primoris Domus comarré. She almost laughed at herself. Yes, being a Primoris Domus comarré had really paid off, hadn't it? How pathetic. "I told you it doesn't work that way."

"Then find a way to make it work." He halted, his back to her, and stayed that way while he spoke. "How did your aunt get out of it?"

Chrysabelle hesitated. There was no reason not to tell him. He wouldn't suggest it. "Libertas."

"What's that?" He rotated and shoved a hand through his hair, pushing the long black strands out of his eyes.

"She asked for her freedom." So she could leave her patron and be with the man she loved. That much Chrysabelle knew from the letters she'd received.

"So ask." Frustration bracketed his mouth as his steps brought him closer. "Why haven't you done that alread—"

"It means one of us dies. Remember how I said you could die or I could kill you? This is the I could kill you part." She waited, but he kept silent as he turned to pace the other way. "Libertas is a battle to the death. If the comarré survives, she goes free. If the patron survives, he gets his choice of a new comarré."

He reached the far wall, planted his hands on it and leaned in. "That seems fair."

She agreed with his sarcasm. "I wasn't suggesting it."

For a moment, he didn't say a word, his head bowed. Then he lifted it and spun to rest his back against the wall. Promise glittered in his eyes. "You would lose."

She took a breath. Then another. "You don't know that."

"Yes, I do. I'm vampire. Anathema, but noble nonetheless. You're human. Basically. I'm stronger, faster, older—"

"I know what you are, and what you were." Death dealer. Headsman. Executioner. "But now, you're not half the strength you could be. Can you use your inherent Family gifts? Can you scatter?"

"Not all vampires can scatter. You should know that."

That wasn't an answer. "What about healing then? You saw how quickly Dominic healed. How long does it take you?" The scratch on his chest from the sword was already gone, but that had just been a scratch.

"That has nothing to do with my fighting ability."

She snorted a soft breath. "You're easy to weaken."

The glitter darkened. "You're easy to kill."

Truth rose in her throat like bile. She lifted her chin and began to chip away at the solid gold fortress she'd been raised in. "Comarré train all their lives. Swords, crossbow, close range weapons. Hand-to-hand. Linear, circular, hard, soft, internal, external." She shook her head. "There's not a martial art or fighting style I haven't studied. A block or thrust I don't know."

He laughed, a thin, cagey sound. "You weren't kidding, were you?"

"About what?"

"You said comarré were lethal killers trained from birth in the dark art of assassination. That wasn't a lie, was it?"

A chill racked her body. These were sacred truths she'd sworn to take to her grave. Speaking them aloud violated every tenet she'd had thrummed into her these last one hundred fifteen years. What did it matter? That life was her past. And without him helping her, she'd have no future. No matter what he was, anathema, killer, head case, she couldn't do this alone. Not for long anyway. And her inborn will to survive overrode all other options.

"No," she whispered. Any hope of returning to the life she'd left, however infinitesimal, vanished with that word. Her safety net had been cut away. "It wasn't a lie. But it is the most closely guarded secret of the comarré."

He beckoned her closer. "Then show me."

"What?" He couldn't mean what she thought he—

"Drop the katana and show me," he urged. The names on his body seemed to swim before her eyes. "I won't hurt you, I promise."

"Why?"

"Because I can't take another voice in my head."

"No." She frowned, taking comfort from his confession nonetheless. "Why do you want me to show you these skills?"

His mouth twisted cruelly. "Because everything out of your mouth has been a lie."

"Not everything. Not this." Withholding full truths wasn't the same as lying. Not when you were protecting yourself.

"Then prove it. Prove it and I'll help you. You have my word."

His word. As though the vow of an anathema meant anything. She relaxed her grip on the curved blade anyway and let it fall. It thunked against the padded floor, throwing sparks of light as it settled. She closed her eyes and took a deep breath. This was insane. And dangerous. For both of them.

As her eyes opened, she shifted to fighting stance, her dominant side toward him.

He mimicked her, standing loose and ready, feet planted, fingers curled in easy fists. A dubious half smile, half smirk curved his mouth.

Fine. She'd remove that first.

He motioned her forward with an open hand. "I'm not going to make the first move, so it's up to you—"

She lunged forward, popping her right fist into his jaw. His head snapped back. She followed with a hard left to his solar plexus. He stumbled, hit the floor hard. If he'd been mortal, the move would have emptied his lungs. She stood over him, ready for more.

"Get up, vampire." Easy to kill. Ha!

He did, almost quicker than her eye could follow. The smirk was gone. She shot a rapid combination of punches toward him, but he blocked them. Was he taking her seriously yet? She couldn't tell, so she backflipped to gain some space, then leaned into her rear leg and nailed a side kick to his ribs. The crunch of bone and his wince rewarded her. Adrenaline flooded her system. She smiled.

"Twice in two days." He shook his head, muttering curses under his breath. "Fine, I get it. You can fight. But your fancy moves aren't going to kill a vampire."

"If I had my blades, I would have staked you already. I did it once, remember?" She crouched and swept her leg out, knocking him off his feet a second time. He rolled to his side and back to his feet faster than she'd toppled him. Okay, he still had a vampire's speed, she'd give him that.

"Enough," he growled. "I'm not going to fight you."

"I can see that. Too scared?"

He snorted. "I don't want to hurt you."

"You'd have to catch me first." Speed wasn't exclusive to vampires.

He reached out to grab her, and she darted away, laughing. Sweat tickled her neck. Sparring this way exhilarated her after such a long period of inactivity. If you didn't count the night she'd stabbed him in the alley.

With a lightning-quick move, he latched on to her, clipping her arms to her sides. She was completely enveloped. Breath caught in her throat as her lungs struggled to expand. Nothing but his borrowed T-shirt between her skin and his cold, bare chest. She swore she could feel the names writhe against her, wriggling like maggots seeking carrion.

"Enough, comarré. Be still."

She lifted onto her tiptoes, arched back and rammed the crown of her head into his nose.

He grunted but held on. A thin line of blood trickled from one nostril. "You're a freaking pain, you know that?" His arms tightened, decreasing her air further. "In a real fight, you'd never get close enough to do that." His jaw cocked to one side. "You've never fought a real vampire, have you?"

"Yes, I have." Not technically a lie if you considered the fringe that the comarré trained with as real vampires. She inhaled as deeply as she could.

"Besides me."

"Let go of me." Small spots danced at the corners of her vision as it became harder to breathe. She dropped her chin and slanted her eyes, trying to find the sword she'd tossed. It was about a foot behind her. Her fingers reflexively went for her missing wrist blades. If he'd been anyone else, he would be ash right now.

"I thought not." A soft growl lifted her head. His face was inches from hers. "You think asking to be let go works with most vampires?" He shifted, giving her a little more breathing room while moving impossibly closer. His legs straddled hers. As though he owned her. "You think it's going to work with me?"

"Yes," she whispered, magnetized by his gleaming metal gaze. For all his protests, he certainly took to the role of patron with ease. She forced her eyes down. Fangs jutted behind his top lip. His tongue flicked over them. Would he bite her? Kiss her? Did he even know how a patron should behave? Not that proper behavior or protocol mattered to one like him. He was more beast than brains.

His head moved back and forth a millimeter in each direction. "This means you lose."

"No." If she could distract him, she could get free, and if she could get free, she could grab the sword and turn things to her advantage. "The fight's not over yet."

"I think it is." Mouth open, his head bent toward her in that way of his, like he was trying to inhale her and taste her at the same time. The hunger must be growing in him. He'd need to feed again soon, and she was the most accessible source of blood.

Of course. Why hadn't she thought of it sooner? She'd told him that owning her blood rights diminished the power of her scent over him. He was right about her lying in that instance. If a patron didn't drink from his comarré soon after taking blood rights, the urge to consume only increased. By now, Mal's head must be swimming.

She needed him to drown.

With her thumb, she released the tiny blade hidden in

her ring, flattened her palm, and shoved the pin dagger through the thin pajama pants and into her thigh. A brief flash of pain. Then she yanked it out.

Wet heat trickled down her leg. Blood scent blossomed around them like hothouse gardenias, sweet and rich and unexpected.

"What did you—" Mal's body went taut. The muscles in his neck tensed into bands. He shook his head. Whispered, "No."

He released her and backed away. The silver in his gaze tarnished to black as his eyes threatened to roll into his head. This was not quite the effect she'd imagined, but she'd gotten free, so that was—

He crouched onto all fours. "Get out." The words sounded like they'd been spoken by several voices in unison.

"Why? What's wrong?"

"Go!" The names that covered him began to shift and grow. The swirling letters expanded into inky puddles, spilling over his skin and turning every visible inch black as night. His back arched, his muscles flexing and contracting like someone else controlled them. He lifted his head. Not a glint of white remained in his eyes. His face had shifted beyond the hard ridges and predatory angles of a vampire in full regalia to something far more frightening. Something born of the devil's nightmares.

His fangs were longer than any she'd ever seen, his body somehow larger, more muscled. A wall-shaking roar bellowed out of him. The freighter rocked like a cradle. He pushed to his feet, as dark and fearsome as a sudden storm.

She backed up. Nothing in her training had prepared her for this. "You know, maybe I will go—"

"Too late." His voice was a chorus of thousands. He strode forward. "We've had enough of you, comarré whore. The vampire is ours, do you understand?"

"Yes, of course. All yours." The sword twisted under her slippers, tripping her retreating feet. She went down.

He grinned and stalked closer.

Her breath caught in her throat, her pulse racing. If she could just reach the katana...

"Too late for you," the voices singsonged.

Her fingers curved around the hilt as a thundercloud of fangs and muscle lunged.

# Chapter Sixteen

Tatiana blinked hard against the artificial light. It stung her eyes, so she closed them again and reached out to test her surroundings.

The sheets beneath her were soft and dry, the bed empty save her. She inhaled a familiar fragrance. Mikkel. She was home.

"Are you awake, darling?" Mikkel's voice played over her like a lullaby.

She opened her eyes to thin slits, and his handsome face came into view. The tension that had tightened her body like a bowstring since the Castus had taken her finally dissipated. "I'm home."

"Yes." The bed dipped as he sat. He curled his fingers under her hand, lifted it to his mouth, and kissed her knuckles.

Contact was the last thing she wanted, but she stopped herself from pulling away when she saw the look of concern on his face. She needed Mikkel. "How long?"

"You've only been gone two days."

Two days in real time, but with the Castus it was hard to tell. Time meant nothing to them. A day, a year, a century…one was just the same as another. "When did I return?"

"Midnight last."

Three days she'd been kept from the hunt. She sighed in frustration.

"Darling?" His eyes filled with concern.

Her lids closed. She didn't want to see the horrors of her body reflected in his pitying gaze or to be reminded of how they'd used her. Let what had passed stay that way. "How long before I'm healed?"

"Don't you feel healed?" He stroked her arm. "Do you still hurt?"

The touch made her want to retch. She rolled to her side, using the movement to turn out of his grasp. "I don't know…"

Taking stock of herself, she found only the softest echoes of discomfort. Her fingers crested the hills and valleys of her body. Her eyes and mouth opened on a gasp. No welts, no crusted cuts, no tender spots. It was one thing to heal quickly from an ordinary wound, but a mark made by the Castus took time. And blood.

Which meant they'd fed her. She'd gotten her reward. She didn't remember it or much of her last hours with them, but no other explanation could justify her current health. In fact, she felt good. Strong. Full of power. The kind of power only original blood could bring. She still didn't know what she was supposed to sacrifice to engage the ring, but perhaps this new power would bring the answer with it.

She bolted upright, the sheets falling away from her naked body. She glanced down. Flawless, as always. She grabbed Mikkel, kissed him hard, then shoved him out of the way and leaped from the bed.

He laughed, his eyes hungry on her body. "I take it you feel well, then?"

"I feel better than well. I feel as though I could devour nations." She turned before her gold-foiled mirror, checking herself. "Not a mark." She turned to look at her back. "Not a scratch." She faced forward again. Her hands smoothed the taut skin of her belly. She almost missed the stretch marks from her human pregnancy. She pushed that memory away and compelled herself to smile. "You are a lucky sod, aren't you, darling?"

Mikkel shook his head and grinned. "I am indeed. I take it your time with the Castus wasn't so bad, then?"

With a snarl, she spun to face him. "Hell would have been more enjoyable. Speak of it again and I will rip your throat out." She might do it anyway, just to watch him suffer while he healed. See how he liked it.

"Of course, not again." His smile vanished as he straightened. He cleared his throat. "When you disappeared from your car, you left behind your locket and a cosmetics box. Octavian brought them to me."

"Give me my locket."

"It's in your jewelry drawer."

She hurried to her dresser and retrieved the locket, fixing the long chain around her neck with a sense of relief. She rubbed the gold oval between her fingers. "What of the box?"

"I took the liberty of doing some research on the cosmetics company since I assumed you'd found it at Algernon's. Headquarters for the company are in Paradise City, New Florida. The company's female CEO lives there as well. Does that mean anything to you?"

That got her attention. "Oh yes. It means a great deal.

It means we're going to the Southern Union." It also meant she hadn't lost as much time in the hunt as she'd imagined. She smiled. "What a good boy you are." Mikkel was worth his weight in blood. Speaking of which...

"Get my comar. I'm hungry. Then send word to ready my jet. I want to depart as soon as possible." After she fed, she would visit Nehebkau. She couldn't leave for the Americas without seeing her precious pet.

"Yes, my love." Nodding, he hurried from the room.

Her gaze returned to the mirror. "Let's see what this new power can do, shall we?"

Tipping her head back, she opened herself to the delicious darkness that owned her undead soul and waited for the surge of something unfamiliar, a thread of fresh ability, that welcome burst of new power.

Her face shifted, her fangs dropped, and hunger wound through her belly like Nehebkau's twin. She looked into the mirror. Nothing else had changed that she could see. Maybe the power wouldn't manifest physically.

She stretched her hand toward the Fabergé egg on her nightstand and willed it to come to her. It didn't move. She tried to transform it into a dagger. It stayed an egg. She attempted to make it vanish. It remained.

Bloody hell. What good was having a new power and not knowing what it was? She needed every edge to help her track down the ring. Anger coursed in her veins, filling her with a potent urge to destroy. She scowled at her reflection in the mirror. If she'd gone through all of that suffering for nothing... Her fist shot out and shattered the glass, leaving a spiderweb of cuts on her hand.

A door opened behind her. She scented Mikkel. He'd returned with her comar.

"Leave the boy in the other room and come here." The gashes on her skin knit closed, leaving traces of blood behind.

"Yes?" Mikkel was at her side instantly. He took her hand and licked the blood away.

"Don't." She shivered in revulsion and yanked her hand back. Clutching it to her chest, she peered at him. Tried to read his thoughts. To get him to react in some way. Even setting him on fire would be a start.

Nothing. She cupped his face between her hands and stared into his gray eyes.

He smiled and reached for her hips. "That's my girl—"

"Quiet." She slapped his hands away, then replaced hers. She needed to think, to figure out what this new gift was. It would come to her. She just had to try harder. Maybe she could get into his head, see through his eyes. Become him.

Her spine tingled with energy. He jerked out of her grasp, his eyes wide. "How...what...you're me."

"What?" Her eyes refocused on her hands. Dark hair sprinkled wide knuckles and thick fingers. These were not her hands.

"You're me. Look." He pointed into the cracked mirror.

She turned. In a thousand different shards, two Mikkels stared back at her, one clothed, one not. She stared down at her transformed body. Mikkel's body. Immediately, she imagined herself back in her own skin and just like that, she was. Without touching Mikkel, she tried to become him again. And did. She shifted back and forth a few times, then tried a few of the Dominus. Timotheius, Grigor, Syler...none were beyond her power. Her head spun and she tilted, catching hold of Mikkel as the dizziness took her. No power came without price.

"Amazing," she whispered. "My new gift is mimicry."

Laughter bubbled out of her throat as she changed back to her own form with a small amount of effort. "Get my robe. After I feed, we leave for the Americas."

Mikkel nodded and held out the heavy crimson satin for her, helping her into it. She tied the robe's sash and glanced once more into the shattered glass.

"You will be unstoppable," he said.

"Unstoppable? I will be the greatest ruler the vampire nation has ever seen." She smoothed her hair. "Lucky sod, indeed."

"Get off her," Fi yelled as she and Doc ran into the gym. She skidded to a stop at the scene before her.

"Don't think he's listening." Doc pointed with the crossbow he still carried from patrolling.

Mal's beast, as they'd named this curse-born rage state, crouched overtop Chrysabelle, looking at her like she was an all-you-can-eat buffet. He must have scratched her, because blood stained the fabric of her pajama pants. Not a good sign. Neither was the way Chrysabelle's fingers were tightening around the handle of a nearby sword.

"Doc, get the weapon."

"I think it's fine where it is."

"You're such a help." Fi realized Doc had probably never seen this side of Mal. She turned her attention to the beast. "I said, get off. Now." Mal had enough voices in his warped brain without adding another one. Plus there was the whole question of what might happen to her corporeal status if Chrysabelle lost hers. Or if Chrysabelle put that sword through his neck. As much as Fi hated being dead, being *really* dead would be worse.

Mal's beast growled, his jaws inches from Chrysabelle's face, but his words were aimed at Fi. "You're not one of us anymore, mortal."

"Crap." That was exactly what Fi had been afraid of. In the past, she'd been able to talk to him from the inside, calm him down before the rage engulfed him and the beast took over. Being corporeal via Chrysabelle's blood seemed to have rectified that. At least Fi didn't have to hear those other voices anymore. They were enough to drive a person crazy. Obviously.

"Everything's fine," Chrysabelle whispered as she worked her fingers around the sword's hilt.

"Girl, you do *not* want to do that," Doc whispered back.

The beast dragged a clawed finger down her cheek and bared his fangs in a wicked snarl. "Everything *is* fine, isn't it? You won't like our version of fine, though."

Fi edged closer. "Mal, I know you're in there. Fight the voices. You can do it, you've done it before."

His head whipped toward her. An eerie grin spread across his mutated face. "Malkolm is dead."

"No kidding, he's a vampire. It's a big part of the job description." Fi motioned behind her back for Doc to move in. She had to distract Mal enough to get him away from Chrysabelle before she took a swipe at him with that sword. "What are you after? Blood? I've got tons of that now."

Mal shook his head. "This one needs to die."

Fi caught Chrysabelle's gaze, held up three fingers, and

hoped to high heaven the comarré could take a hint. "What makes you so afraid of her, huh? She's just a measly mortal, like me. Do you really want her in your head too?"

Doc was at her side now. She pressed against him and reached for the switchblade he kept hooked on his belt. She tapped his back three times. He nodded slightly as she took the blade, then moved away.

She flicked it open and streaked the edge across her palm. Pain and a line of red welled up. Mal's black gaze narrowed on the new blood.

Memories painted a haze around Fi's vision. Memories of when Mal had attacked her. The way his fangs had torn through her skin. She swallowed and, for a moment, thought she saw a flicker of silver in those eyes. "C'mon, Mal. You know you want it. You can smell it, can't you? Pure mortal blood, untainted by all that gold. You know what it tastes like, don't you? This blood saved your life *one* time before. It can do it again."

Fear rounded Doc's eyes, probably because he knew as well as she did that if Mal reached her in his current state, he'd tear her arm from her body to get what he wanted. Or worse. If everything went according to the quickly sketched plan in her head, that wouldn't happen. Probably.

Her heart thudded hard in her chest. The room seemed darker. More like the ruins.

Mal swallowed and flicked his tongue over his lips. With a shuddering breath, Fi squeezed her hand into a fist and let the blood drip onto the mats. The shroud of names on his skin began to waver and separate. Doc slowly shifted around behind Mal, hefting the crossbow into position. "That's it," she cajoled, sending the next signal. "The *two* of us can do this together."

Mal inched forward and Fi yelled, "Three!"

Chrysabelle bucked Mal into the air. Doc squeezed the trigger. The bolt caught Mal in the shoulder and thrust him away. A multitude of voices cried out in rage as he fell to the ground at Fi's feet. She got out of the way as Chrysabelle flipped to a crouched position, her chest heaving, sword in hand and pointed at Mal. Frozen with tenuous relief, the three stared at him, waiting to see what would happen next.

Thankfully, the blackness bled away into the familiar pattern of names. Mal lay prone for a moment, then reached back and yanked out the bolt with a grunt. He tossed it without lifting his face off the mat. Blood oozed from the wound. "Leave me. Now."

Doc looked at Fi, then Mal. He shifted to his other foot. "Sorry, bro, I didn't know what else—"

"Get out." Shame made Mal's words quiet and still. Fi understood, and new emotion filled her. Elation that she'd survived. Sorrow that she hadn't been as successful the first time. But not the hatred that usually welled up. Pity had taken its place. Pity that Mal would never want to know about. The curse was a mammoth burden to bear. She knew what a horror show went on in that head of his. A lesser creature would have killed himself long before now. Not just thought about it or tried it but done it.

Doc thrust his lower jaw forward. "You would have torn Fi's arm off."

"Get. Out."

"Doc..." Fi tried to catch Doc's eyes but he was intently staring daggers at Mal's prostrate form. Doc might be cursed too, but his was nothing like Mal's. Chrysabelle quietly set the sword down and pushed to her feet.

"Not you, comarré." Mal eased to his knees. The oozing blood turned into a thin trickle as he stood. His fists clenched tight to his sides. The voices must be tearing his head to pieces. Chrysabelle glanced at Fi.

Fi shuddered, then caught Doc's gaze. His pupils were down to slits. He'd been ready to attack on her behalf. "C'mon, let's get out of here." If Mal wanted to talk to Chrysabelle, Fi wasn't about to stand in his way. Whatever he needed to discuss with the comarré, he was in decent shape to do it now. And hopefully, a more sane frame of mind. Fi knew that her survival depended on his. No matter how much strange blood ran through her system, how long could she last without Mal?

Doc walked out with her, his hand comfortably on the small of her back. Ever since she'd gotten fully corporeal, the varcolai's attitude toward her had changed a little. He'd gotten sweeter, more demonstrative, and not just when they were alone either. She tucked his switchblade back into his belt and, giving his side a little pinch, whispered, "Thanks."

They went single file up the narrow stairs to the next deck, coming side by side again when the passage widened. Doc's hand returned to rest on the waistband of her jeans. "We need to bandage that hand of yours, but leaving them alone is a bad idea."

"They'll be fine. My hand too." She was sure about her hand, not so much about Mal and Chrysabelle, but this was Mal's problem and he had to deal with it or it was likely to happen again. Her uninjured hand slid up Doc's back to rest at the nape of his neck, about as far as she could reach without going onto her toes. The man was sleek, hard muscle from stem to stern. Too bad about his curse. Just once she'd like to see him in his true form. She'd love to snuggle up next to a big black leopard. Not that she'd ever admit that to him while his curse prevented it. Curse or not, she was never leaving him.

Doc opened his mouth, most likely to talk her into going back to check on them, but her fingers drifted over his back, her nails scratching lazily at his skin. His lids drooped, drugged by her caresses. "That's cheating," he mumbled.

Sometimes a girl had to do what a girl had to do. Especially when the joy in her life centered on the subject at hand. How lucky was she that Mal had decided she needed a cat? How lucky was Doc that Mal had decided to save him from those mangy street mutts? Everything happened for a reason, even if those reasons didn't always make sense at the time. "I just thought my kitty cat needed a little reward for his help."

Doc's eyes flicked open, warm green-gold in the dim lighting. "I told you about calling me—"

"Hush now. Unless you'd rather sleep alone?" Fi dug her nails in a little more, dragging them over his body with purpose. His mouth stayed open, but the words stopped, replaced by the low undercurrent of a motor running. He shook his head like a drunken man. Drunk on pleasure.

"I thought so." She laughed softly. Dead or alive, she'd never felt this way about a man before. Made her want to hold on to life more than ever.

# Chapter Seventeen

Mal waited to speak until Doc and Fi had left and shut the door behind them. His eyes stung with the need for sleep, his shoulder burned from the puncture wound, and humiliation shredded his gut. He'd lost control. *Weakling.* Let the voices best him. *Obey us.* For a creature who'd once been so feared, he was now as helpless as a child. *Impotent.* Doc had done what was necessary. Too bad that bolt hadn't found his heart. Things would be so much easier that way. "You see now why I can't help you."

"No." Thinly veiled anger lowered Chrysabelle's voice. "I almost killed you."

"And I you. But neither of us did." She sighed. "Besides, that wasn't really you."

"It *was* me." He turned, tired of her eyes watching the wound on his back not heal. "I can't control the curse when it takes over."

"You could stop it from taking over."

"No, I can't." *Powerless, powerless, powerless.* He wanted to be alone, not to stand here and explain himself to a woman-child who knew nothing but privilege and pampering. Unless that was a disguise to mask who she really was. She *had* fought well. Surprised him. But there was time for figuring that out tomorrow. "I'm going to bed."

"If you fed properly—"

"Enough." The word came out in an angry rumble, and she had the good sense to flinch. Then her good sense disappeared.

She walked toward him, her face a mask of determination. Foolish woman. She opened her mouth, but he held his palms up, forcing her to stop. "Go home. To your aunt's. Wherever. Just leave."

"You own my—"

"I don't give a damn about your blood rights. I don't want them. Or you." He spun and walked toward the door and away from the lie he'd just told. He could be in bed in minutes, asleep seconds after that. *To sleep, perchance to nightmare...*

Again, she started after him. Desperation and self-loathing wafted off her, souring her alluring scent. Of course. When had a comarré ever chased an anathema? It must be torture for her to need the help of someone so far beneath her. "They'll kill us both, my aunt and me. Do you want that on your head?"

"As long as you don't come back to haunt me, I'm okay with it." She'd definitely end up dead if she stayed here. *Yes, yes, yes.*

"You don't mean that."

He kept walking.

"You said you'd help me if I proved my fight training to you."

"I lied. You should understand that."

Anger must have cleared her mind of all reasonable thought, because she charged after him, tackling him and taking them both to the ground. "You need me, you stupid man. Don't you see that?"

He pushed her off and rolled on top of her, pinning her to the floor. *Kill her, drain her.* "I don't need anyone." Except maybe Doc. And occasionally Fi. Not that Mal would admit that on point of death.

"Help me, and I'll give you blood."

"By blood rights, it's mine anyway, isn't it?" *Take, take it all.*

Her mouth bent into a frown, her hair splayed out around her head like rays of light. "I don't want to be around you any more than you want to be around me, but as much as I'd like to get on with my vampire-free life, I can't until I'm cleared of this murder. And you, unfortunately, are my best chance of that. My means to an end." She turned her face away, exposing her neck. "Take the blood in payment if it makes you feel better."

"It wouldn't." He leaned down, erasing the space between them. The voices thrashed at the sweetness of her perfume. "I don't want your blood. Not ever. Understand? The only thing I need is to get these voices out of my head." He jumped up, earning himself a stab of pain from his wounded shoulder, and stalked off.

Of course, she followed.

He needed air. And space. Anything to separate himself from the blood scent filling the gym. With a speed she couldn't duplicate, he raced to the nearest deck that overlooked the sea. Right after making this ship his home, he'd discovered that even the somewhat polluted mix of night air and salt tang helped subdue the voices.

"You can't lose me that easily." Her chest rose and fell with the effort of chasing him. Good. She needed to know she was not his equal. He stared out at the black water. If she expected him to hold up his end of the conversation, she was going to be heartily disappointed.

She wasn't quiet long. "What if I said I might know a way to break your curse? You know, it's kind of pretty out here."

He whipped around. "How? Break it how?"

She gazed toward the sea. Past the wharf and the now-dark tenements beyond it, expensive lights pocked the curve of shoreline where the homes of wealthy mortals sat like temples of excess. The crescent moon's reflection shattered on the dark, rippling water, and its weak light outlined the corpses of the other abandoned ships. Pretty was not a word he'd use to describe this landscape.

She wrested a piece of hair from the night breeze and tucked it behind her ear as she faced him. Even in the thin light, her signum glittered and her skin glowed. Hell. There was no denying she affected him. Who wouldn't be affected by a beautiful woman who effervesced light and life? Except she couldn't give him either of those things. No one could. And all he could offer her was darkness and death. Not that he was offering her anything. Or even thinking about it.

"I *might* know a way to break your curse. Or at least, know someone who might know."

"Who?"

She crossed her arms and leaned against the rail. "The comarré have a kind of historian who keeps our records. The Aurelian."

"I don't need a librarian." Books he could go through

on his own. Just as he had been since he'd gotten free of the ruins and found a thread of sanity.

Chrysabelle uncrossed her arms and inched closer, one hand wrapping the railing. "She's more than that. She's an annalist, a keeper of spells, an ancient mind, a source of knowledge that goes beyond the books she keeps."

"A witch."

Her face remained impassive. "She's been called that."

"What makes you think she'd know something about what was done to me?"

"Your legend says your second curse was placed upon you by nobility."

"I wasn't aware anyone knew that." Maybe the source of that information was the source of his curse. Who else would know but someone connected?

She shrugged. "Comarré know a lot of things that aren't common knowledge. Our scribes document anything that involves the vampire nation. And the Aurelian knows all of it."

He snorted air through his nose. "Basic vampire history isn't hard to find if you know where to look." And he did. Because he had.

She shook her head. "It's so much more than basic vampire history. It's legends, ancient texts, prophecies—"

"I get it." He held up his palm. "I've been through all those books."

"No, you haven't." Her hand slid toward his on the railing. "And those books in your room and your office are worthless."

He scowled, then wondered if she could see his expression in the dim light.

"Don't look at me that way."

Question answered. "What makes you think those books are worthless?"

Her eyes widened in mock disbelief as she shook her head and sighed. "You're still cursed, Einstein."

Maybe he'd just kill her a little. "There are some I haven't read yet."

"Don't bother. Unless you like wasting your time." She stepped onto the lowest rung of the railing, leaned her torso over, and inhaled with her eyes closed, as though the smell of the sea was something special. Maybe it was, but not here where the rainbow sheen of leaking oil clogged most life into a decaying mess.

"Why would your Aurelian have anything different?"

She hopped back onto the deck. "There are books, scrolls really, long lost to the vampire histories."

"I doubt that. Vampire history goes back to the beginning of time. To the Castus Sang—"

"Quiet. Never say that name out loud." Fear flared in her eyes. She glanced from side to side, as if expecting the ancient creatures to come rushing in and swoop her up.

"I don't think they're much concerned with anathema these days."

She glared at him. "Really? Are you willing to test that theory?"

In truth, no. "What about these long-lost scrolls? How does the vampire nation not have them?"

The shift in subject seemed to calm her down. She exhaled and twisted the hem of her T-shirt around her fingers. *His* T-shirt. The black fabric swallowed her. *Like you should.* "The vampire nation doesn't have them, because the comarré have kept them hidden. Over the years, we've plucked every existing copy we could find from the libraries of our patrons." The hem tore in her fingers. "These are secrets even some lesser comarré don't know. I shouldn't be telling you, of all people."

"But you are."

She shook her head, tucking her chin against her chest, and went quiet for a long minute. "Things will never be okay again, will they?"

The question threw him. He didn't know what to say, how to answer. "Things change." Yeah, that was brilliant. A real epiphany for the ages.

"I just wanted to be free. Now that may never happen." She lifted the hem to her face and wiped her eyes.

The smooth gold-inscribed expanse of her stomach distracted him, and too late he realized she was trying to hide tears. Son of a priest. "Look, don't do that. Everything will be . . . fine."

She tilted her head to look at him. Her eyes were round and liquid. And angry. "Everything will be *fine*?" She stood straighter, tears forgotten. "I've been accused of murdering a high-ranking vampire and stealing a very valuable ring, neither of which I did. I'm being hunted by Nothos that will assuredly kill me when they catch me. If they don't, then the power-hungry vampire they work for will. And my best chance of survival is a half-starved, fully-mental outcast with a head full of voices who refuses to help me and, oh, might *also* kill me. Everything is *not* going to be fine."

He stared at her for a moment, trying to deny how accurate her assessment was. "It's not that—"

"Stop, please. You're not going to help me. I get it." She leaned her elbows on the railing and cupped her head in her hands. The breeze shifted and wrapped him in her scent.

He swallowed down the saliva pooling in his mouth. He wanted her, and the admission filled him with bitterness. She wasn't for him. He knew that.

He asked anyway. "You really think the Aurelian could help?"

"Yes." She went still. "Are you saying what I think you are?"

Lifting his chin slightly, he peered into the night. "Helping you would take funds I don't have."

She straightened but didn't look at him. "I can fund whatever we need. I've already given Doc some assets to cash in to help out. Plus I'll pay you whatever you think your time is worth." She turned, eyes regrettably hopeful. "And I'll give you blood. You're going to need the strength. I have to drain it anyway, so why not take it?"

The part of him that had begun to warm went cold again at her offer. "Since you know so much about me, you must know why I'm anathema." And what he'd been in his human past. Not that he'd been so different.

"I know in order to become anathema, you killed another vampire, but not the details. I'm sure they're in your file. I just don't recall." Snowy teeth worried her bottom lip.

"Let me help then." He crossed his arms. Memories of that night burned the backs of his eyes. "The vampire I killed was my sire. Would you like to know how I killed him?"

Her breathing increased. "I'm sure you had your reasons—"

"Reason had nothing to do with it." He leaned in and

lowered his voice, purposefully trying to shock her. "He turned me, and I drank him to death."

The lip dropped away from her teeth, and she stepped back with a little gasp.

He watched her expression as the full meaning of his confession registered.

"Oh," she whispered again, and wrapped her arms around herself. Her eyes searched the air around her, for what he didn't know. She swallowed. "Oh."

Mal had not just killed some random vampire, but his sire, and not just killed him, but drank him to death. She shuddered and looked anywhere but at him. If that was true, and she had no reason to doubt him, he was doubly cursed. First because any vampire who committed parricide was cursed to kill every being he sank his fangs into. That part seemed to hold true, but the other belief, that a vampire who drank his sire also gained that sire's power, didn't seem evidenced in him. Perhaps because of his perpetually weak state. Or maybe he *had* been that powerful before he'd been cursed the second time. No wonder the nobility had tried to put a stop to him. A vampire that destructive would be bad for all of them, but like typical nobility, they'd held fast to the law that no vampire should ever kill another and so they'd just cursed Mal and let him live.

But the nobility's curse, the second one that had brought about the names on his skin and the voices in his head, would be almost powerless if not for the first. Whoever had placed that curse had known him well enough to know how effective it would be.

"You still want my help?" He watched her. She could

feel it. Maybe he thought she might bolt. But running was pointless and not what she'd been trained for. This was one of those times in a person's life when the hard choice was the only choice.

She stared at the ring on her finger that hid the tiny blade. "I don't think I can clear my name on my own. If I could stay alive long enough, maybe, but having a vampire on my side would be a big help. So, if you'll help me, I'll take it." Chances were good she'd die one way or the other. If Mal killed her, maybe she'd get to come back as a ghost like Fi.

It took him a moment to respond, like he hadn't expected to still be having this conversation. "Tell me about this ring you've been accused of taking."

Exhaling softly, she pressed her hip to the rail and ran her fingers over the peeling paint. Rust had turned it into snakeskin. She was glad for something else to focus on. "I don't know much about it, except that two very ambitious vampires, Lord Ivan, whom I'm sure you know, and Lady Tatiana, believe it to be extremely powerful."

His face darkened. "I know who Ivan is."

"Well, I overhead them speaking about it. The female tried to persuade Algernon to give it to them for research." A partial smile lifted her mouth. "She's one of those vampires who thinks all other creatures are beneath her. She barely notices comarré, forget acknowledging that our senses are nearly as good as our patrons'."

"Typical nobility." He spoke the words with such rancor, she wondered if his agreeing to help wasn't partially motivated by his own hatred of the noble Families. Did he hope to somehow extract his revenge while helping her? If that's what it took to get his help, so be it.

"She claimed the ring was very old and very important and told Algernon he shouldn't show it to anyone else or even speak of it. Lord Ivan told Algernon he was never to put the ring on. Tatiana told him doing so would mean death. I don't know if she meant because of the ring's power or because she'd kill him for doing it."

Chrysabelle flicked a curl of paint into the sea. It fluttered down to float on the black water. "Algernon laughed them off, but I don't doubt he knew they were serious. Lord Ivan might be Dominus of the House of Tepes, but Tatiana isn't someone you want to cross either."

"And yet you have the ring."

"Not because I wanted it, believe me." Her fingers worried the railing, nails digging into the rusty metal. "Remember how I told you Algernon put that horrible necklace on me at the Century Ball? Well, after I found him dead and went to gather the rest of my things from the Primoris Domus, I ripped the hideous thing off my neck and threw it against the wall in anger. It cracked open." A shower of chips drifted from her fingernails. "The ring was inside."

She laughed bitterly. "Just one possession guarding another."

He shifted uncomfortably. Did her past bother him? A moment of silence passed before he spoke again. "What power does this ring have?"

"No idea. I started researching it after I overheard the conversation, but I didn't get far before Algernon was murdered, and I ran. Now that I've had it in my hands, I can tell you it's pure gold, sacred gold like what's used for comarré signum, with script on the outside in a language I don't recognize. Inside, it looks like . . . fish scales, sort of.

Like interwoven pieces of gold. But it's completely smooth on the outside, except for the writing." Brushing her hands off, she shrugged. "Whatever power it has, it's got to be strong. Tatiana wouldn't waste her time on it otherwise."

"How do you know it's Tatiana and not Lord Ivan? He's a vicious bastard, he could be the one hunting you."

"Because Lord Ivan hasn't done so much as raise his voice since Tatiana came into the picture. He leaves all his dirty work to his pet."

"Which is why you think this Tatiana will do anything to get the ring back."

"Yes. I'm sure the Nothos Dominic killed was one of hers. And with Algernon dead, her next step will be forcing herself into Algernon's position of Elder. It's no secret she wants to rule."

"A female Elder? That's a stretch."

Chrysabelle flicked the switch on her ring back and forth, clicking the tiny blade in and out. "Puts her in place to become Dominus."

He raised his brows. "Dominus? She is ambitious."

"More than ambitious. She wants to break the covenant." The covenant protected humans, kept them from seeing the truth of the world around them. If humans knew their nightmares were based in reality, the fear alone could destroy them. Or, as in the days of old, rouse them to gather their torches and pitchforks. It protected both sides, really.

His brows lifted another millimeter. "So she's *also* insane."

"Quite literally if the rumors of her undergoing navitas are true."

"She voluntarily got resired?"

"Or Lord Ivan forced her to. We can't find the truth of the incident. But Tatiana definitely thinks the time is ripe for vampires to stop living in secret and start ruling the mortal world. She's thought that since the days of the End War. Perhaps even before."

"The fae will think otherwise." He paused for a moment. "She'll start a war."

"Which is why she wants to reenslave the varcolai. They'll be her army." Chrysabelle had overheard that part of the conversation too.

Mal scratched his jaw. "She sounds bloodthirsty enough to have killed Algernon."

"With a hot blade? She couldn't hold it long enough."

"Does she have a comar?"

"Yes." That made Chrysabelle think. "He's from the same house as I am, Primoris Domus, but a few years older." She shook her head. "I don't know him well, but Damien doesn't seem the type to even hurt a fly."

"If he's had the same training as you, he'd not only hurt the fly, but fillet it like a side of beef while kicking it repeatedly."

She covered her half smile with her hand. His acknowledgment of her skills was a welcome thing. "You have a point."

"Would giving the ring back be enough for Tatiana?"

"Hard to say with her. She's not really the type to just let something go, and I'm sure she wouldn't want anyone else to know about the ring." She sighed. "Plus, I don't exactly have the ring with me."

"Where is it?"

"Hidden." Why not tell him? Wasn't like he could get to it anyway. "In my suite. At the Primoris Domus."

"You left it there?"

"You think bringing it with me would have been a better idea? We'll have to go there anyway to contact the Aurelian." She sneaked a look and caught him staring back. She shifted her gaze to the deck.

"Am I that hard to look at?"

"No, I...it's just..."

A low, gravelly noise rumbled out of him. "You judge me while you have no idea what it's like. My head is never quiet. Never. You try spending just twenty-four hours without a moment's privacy and see if it doesn't make you a little crazy. I live that every day and night." His hands, the only part of him she dared look at, squeezed the railing until the metal groaned.

"How long have you carried these voices?"

"Since I killed Fi. The second curse kicked in with her death."

She nodded. "In my own way, I do understand."

"How could you? How could your pampered, privileged life even begin to compare?"

She lifted her head, forcing herself to look into the murderous black depths of his eyes. "In my *pampered, privileged* life, comarré are never alone. Other comarré act as our handlers from the moment we're born until we receive patronage. We live, study, and train in groups of fifty or more. When we're in our patron's home, we're on constant guard that every emotion and feeling we give off is proper and respectful. Our lives are lived not for ourselves, but for the good of our house and to serve your kind."

His eyes held a little more starlight and a little less anger. "They're not my kind."

"Shades of gray." She rubbed at her shoulder. The muscles were balled into knots and had been for days.

"Tell me about those." He nodded in her direction and she knew exactly what he referred to.

Lifting her hair and turning slightly, she patted the sun gilded onto the nape of her neck. "There is only one signum required to be comarré, the phoebus."

He notched his head with what seemed like genuine interest. She took it as an indicator to go on.

"Signum are extraordinarily painful. We are taught to meditate into a trancelike state, but nothing keeps the bite of the signumist's needle from getting through. The sacred gold is heated to a threadlike consistency so it can be stitched into the skin."

A grimace twisted his mouth. "Why not just numb yourself with drugs or booze?"

She slanted her eyes at him. "Because we must keep our blood pure for your kin—for the nobility."

If her slip upset him, he didn't show it. "Do any comarré get just one? You're covered with them."

This time he looked away, but not before silver sparked in his eyes. Was he remembering her blood-drunk nakedness when he'd seen exactly how many signum she had? Her nails stung her palms. She relaxed the fists she'd made. "There are seven sets, but they're not all required. Most comarré get as many as they can handle."

"Because they make your blood more desirable."

"In part, yes. The more signum, the purer our blood, the higher our blood price. But we continue to get them after we receive patronage."

"Why?"

The water lapped gently at the ship's hull, soothing her

memories. "Because for the time it takes to recover, we are left alone. For those few days, we meditate and heal. Only a skeleton staff attend us and then only when we require it. In pain, we find a fleeting peace." Confessing such things was wrong but powerful. The comarré did not even speak this way among themselves. If Mal ever revealed what he knew, she would be ostracized for sure, but sharing made the burden—and her mood—lighter.

She laughed softly. "I am the worst comarré to ever draw breath."

"Why do you say that?" His expression held genuine disbelief.

"I reveal too much. They say the comarré's mystery is a great part of our beauty. I must seem rather ordinary to you right now, hmm, vampire?"

Before she drew a second breath, he was in front of her, so close only moonlight separated them. "There is nothing ordinary about you. Knowing the pain you've endured for those marks only makes them that much more impressive, because pain is one thing I most definitely understand."

When he was this close, it was nearly impossible to deny her training. Her instinct took over, bowing her head, dropping her gaze. She fought to keep from calling him master, finally raising her face to his again after she squelched her inbred impulses.

He lifted a strand of her hair and held it to his nose, closing his eyes on the inhale. His lips parted enough to give her a glimpse of fangs. "Everything about you reminds me of the sun. The way you smell, the color of your hair, the glow that surrounds you, the warmth of your skin..."

*It's the gold,* she wanted to say, *and that is our purpose,* but his nearness muted her tongue. Her heart was as restless in her chest as a feral cat. Her body's want and her mind's fear made her tremble. Such a reaction was weakness and she willed it from her body.

"It's no wonder I want to devour you," he growled softly. He twisted the hair around his finger. "Aren't you afraid of me?"

"Yes," she whispered. Afraid she might have to kill him. Afraid she might not be able to.

"Wise," he whispered back, dropping the strand to coast his cool fingers down the curve of her neck. "I'm not a champion. I don't know any other way to be but this thing I've become." His hand stopped, his thumb pressing lightly over her jugular, perhaps to absorb her quivering pulse. "And yet, you scare me too."

His admission calmed her. "I scare you?"

He nodded, barely moving his head. "I don't want to hurt you, but I'm afraid I will." The words seemed spoken to himself more than to her.

"You won't." But no faith backed the words she desperately wanted to believe.

A breeze blew the loose strand across her face. His hand moved from her throat to tuck it behind her ear, then he stroked his palm down the length of her hair to her hip. His hand stayed there, fingers firm against the flimsy pajama pants she still wore. She shivered.

Eyes as silver as the reflected moonlight took her in. "I'm scaring you now."

It wasn't a question, but she answered anyway. "Yes."

"I can tell. Your scent changes." He stepped back, his nostrils flaring, hands flexing. Everything about him said he was losing the battle with his self-control. "That first night, in the alley, you truly believe you could have killed me?"

"Yes." At least she had then.

"Would you, had you felt it necessary?"

She tensed but replied, hoping the affirmation would convince her too. "Yes."

He scrubbed a hand across his face. "Good. You may have to yet."

Her jaw opened slightly. That wasn't the direction she'd thought he'd been headed in. There seemed to be no correct response, so she just watched him, waiting for whatever interesting thing he might say next. She was not disappointed.

"There are enough hours of night left to visit your aunt. You need something more appropriate to wear though. Maybe Doc has something."

This time, she had words and a little bit of fear. "Why do you want to see my aunt?"

"She was comarré, wasn't she? She may know something that might help you." He paused, and his mouth bent. "That might help *us*."

Those two small letters, that one tiny pronoun, changed everything. It redefined her relationship with the vampire. It made them a unit. A team. A couple. Sweet heaven, she did not like the sound of that, but she imagined she'd get used to it. She'd gotten used to much harder things in her life.

"And then...we...do what?" Despite her misgivings, she was thrilled to have his help. To be an us. A we. However she looked at it, it meant she was no longer alone in this fight.

"Then we go to Corvinestri."

"Corvinestri?"

"That's where you're from isn't it? The seat of the House of Tepes?"

"Yes."

The bend of his mouth increased. Obviously, that was one city he didn't relish visiting. "We go to return this ring and see about proving your innocence."

"You're anathema. You won't be able to get past the city wards."

"I can take you as far as the wards then." He pointed a finger at her. "And when this is over, blood rights or not, we go our separate ways, understood?"

"Yes," she agreed, but he was already gone.

# Chapter Eighteen

Insistent knocking woke Maris. Where was Velimai? Maris glanced at the bedside clock. Not quite 3 a.m. Not that she was really sleeping anyway. Not with Rennata's vague warning note and Dominic's disappointing report swirling around in her brain. How Chrysabelle could place her trust in that vampire was beyond her. The creature was anathema. More knocking. She chided herself as she sat up and swung her legs around. So was Dominic, and look how long she'd stayed with him.

She picked up the journal she'd been writing in before bed and tucked it into her nightstand drawer. There was much Chrysabelle needed to know about Maris's past, but now was not the time. Not yet.

Velimai floated in and solidified. She held the handles of the iBot to keep it steady, a completely unnecessary gesture for several reasons, one being the iBot was as stable as a rock.

"Who's at the door?" Maris lifted herself onto the seat.

Velimai moved back into Maris's field of vision and shimmered into a ghostly replica of Chrysabelle. It was like Chrysabelle was an old-fashioned movie and Velimai was the screen, still visible behind the image.

"Why haven't you let her in? Why hasn't she let herself in?"

Velimai tapped two V'ed fingers against her chest, the sign for vampire, then her image changed again into the visage of a male vampire.

Maris wanted to spit. "She's brought him here? No wonder she hasn't come inside. She knows better than to bring a vampire into my home." No vampire, friend or foe, had ever been given an invitation to cross her threshold. If she hadn't made an exception for the one vampire she'd been sleeping with, she wasn't about to make an exception for the one Chrysabelle had deemed her new protector.

Maris wheeled out of the room and down the hall. "If she thinks I'm letting him in, she's mistaken. I don't care if he is helping her."

Velimai, gliding ahead and back in her own skin, shook her head furiously. She opened her mouth, her lips peeling back in a wide snarl.

"No, you can't kill him. As much as I dislike the idea of Chrysabelle aligning herself with this creature, it's her decision."

Velimai crossed her arms as the iBot maneuvered down the stairs.

"Go back to bed, Velimai. I can handle this." She prayed silently that her niece had not done something so foolish as turn over her blood rights. Maris would know soon enough. If this vampire had drunk from Chrysabelle, Maris would smell it on him. A cold thought shuddered through her. What a stupid old woman she'd become.

No doubt Chrysabelle had recognized the blood scent surrounding Dominic as her aunt's. And now she was here for an explanation. Who could blame her?

Velimai bowed slightly and left with a not so subtle roll of her eyes. Stubborn wysper. Still, the girl was worth her keep for her ability to decimate vampires and keep secrets. In her own way, Velimai was the perfect companion. Quiet, deadly to vampires, and a worthy gin opponent.

The knocking sounded again as Maris reached the door. She opened it, wondering if she shouldn't have come brandishing her sacre. That would give the anathema something to think about.

"Chrysabelle, I know you must have questions after… after." Something about her niece looked off. The breeze shifted, bringing the faint bitterness of ash with it. "Are you feeling all right, my dear?"

"Yes, Aunt. I feel very well, thank you." Chrysabelle's stony face suddenly burst into a smile that didn't reach her eyes, unlike the vampire behind her who'd been grinning like a madman since Maris had opened the door. So this was the anathema her niece had aligned herself with. Maris immediately disliked him and hoped her face reflected that.

"Good. I was worried something was wrong since the hour is so late." Maris studied Chrysabelle, but she stood just out of the light. Odd. Chrysabelle had never seemed so short before. Or so thin. Something was going on. Perhaps Chrysabelle didn't want to say in front of the vampire. Perhaps she couldn't get away from the vampire. Again, Maris yearned for her sacre. "This one with you, he's the one helping you?"

Chrysabelle glanced back at the vampire and smiled. "Yes, he is the one helping me."

The vampire bowed slightly. Maris snorted air through her nostrils. As though putting on manners would impress her. "Why don't you come in, dear?"

A genuine smile blossomed on Chrysabelle's face. "I thought you'd never ask." She started forward, the vampire behind her following.

Maris raised a finger in warning. "That invitation is for Chrysabelle only. No vampire will ever cross this threshold."

Chrysabelle walked into the house and laughed. "Oh, I think that's about to change, comarré."

"What?" Maris rocked back, moving her iBot a few paces away. And then, without warning, Chrysabelle wasn't Chrysabelle anymore.

The figure of her niece morphed into an unfamiliar female vampire. Maris's breath came in hard, fast gasps. "Velimai," she screamed. "Velimai!"

The female laughed, fangs glistening. "Don't worry, comarré. I'm not going to drink you dry. Yet." She grabbed Maris by the arm.

Velimai shot into the room behind the female, took one look, and charged forward in solid form, the only form in which she could scream.

"Tatiana!" The male vampire stuck outside leaned against the invisible threshold barrier as though it was a pane of glass. "Behind you. A wysper."

Tatiana pulled Maris out of the iBot and into a rough embrace, then spun to face Velimai. Her fist caught Velimai across the jaw, sending her to the floor with a split lip. Tatiana's knuckles were scraped raw by the wysper's sandpaper skin, but the marks vanished a second later. Velimai stayed down, face contorted in pain and anger, but held her solid form and opened her mouth as she shuffled backward. Maris tensed, prepared to have her eardrums blown out.

Velimai's shattering cry ripped through the room. Maris winced. The sculpted glass coffee table shattered, spraying safety glass through the room like confetti.

Tatiana's fingers dug painfully into Maris's flesh. "Mikkel, do something," she shouted to the male.

Instantly, he lifted his arm toward Velimai and spoke a few words. The air shimmered darkly around his hand, but nothing happened. The male must be House of Bathory to wield the black arts he'd attempted, but without an invitation neither he nor his power could enter the house. Fortunately, Velimai's scream had no such boundaries. The veins in his neck and hands began to throb.

Blood oozed from Tatiana's ears. She howled in pain and dropped Maris, stumbling over the glass-covered floor to get to Velimai. Tatiana's hands went around the wysper's throat, choking off the sound, then Tatiana slammed Velimai against the wall. She dropped to the wood floor, crumpling like a rag, her throat ringed in bloody handprints.

Tatiana wiped her abraded palms on her trousers. "Disgusting creature."

Maris had little time to mourn before Tatiana leaped back to her side and grabbed her viciously by her upper arms. Maris twisted, trying to get away. Tatiana spun her around, biting back a sob of anger.

"So much for your house pet, comarré." Tatiana leaned into Maris and inhaled. "You may not last that long either."

Maris jerked away as best she could, managing to get an arm's length away from her captor. "What do you want?"

Tatiana's face went cold. "Your niece. Where is she?"

"I have no idea." Maris had heard of Tatiana but never crossed paths with her until now. Rennata's warning rang in Maris's ears. This vampiress was more than trouble. Maris would not be cowed by this bloodthirsty female, not in her own home. "And even if I did, I wouldn't tell you."

Tatiana scowled. "Do you know who I am?"

That much Maris recalled. "You're Lord Ivan's pet."

"You dare speak to me that way?" Tatiana laughed and looked at her partner outside. "How soon they forget their manners."

"You don't deserve my respect, leech."

Tatiana cracked Maris hard across the face. Blood spilled into her mouth from the inside of her cheek. She swallowed it down. These vampires didn't need the added incentive the scent would give them.

"Then neither does your niece deserve mine, comarré."

"I haven't been comarré in years."

Tatiana peered at her with ravenous eyes. "Then that makes you kine." She danced her tongue across her fangs. "And I have only one use for kine."

"Get out of my house." Maris struggled not to tremble.

"Don't worry, I'm leaving. And you're coming with me."


Mal stroked the oilcloth down the length of the blade as tenderly as he'd once stroked his daughter's cheek. He moved like a machine, no thought for the action, falling into the past and a wash of memories normally kept tightly checked. Except for rare moments like this. Cleaning this sword, so like the one he'd earned his living with when he'd still walked in the sun, always had that effect. The pain of those memories wasn't without benefit. Pain like that held the voices to a dull hum.

What more would he feel if he were able to find the same blade he'd once used to earn his keep? Not that he probably ever would. Nothing remained of his human life, and as the years ticked by, it became harder to remember what being human felt like. He'd long forgotten the sun's warmth on his skin and the scent of a spring day in his daughter's hair. At times, holding on to the image of his sweet Sofia's face was like trying to grasp fog.

The spicy scent of the Japanese Choji clove oil saturating the rag usually calmed him, but after his talk with Chrysabelle, his insides were torn by the need to be left alone and the hunger for companionship. No, he told himself, his desire to help her stemmed from his search to remove his curse, not for any other reasons. A sharp pain erupted in his fingers. He snatched them off the weapon where they'd come to rest over the blade's inscription. *Deus misereatur.* May God have mercy.

Where was his mercy? He'd never asked for this life, such as it was. He'd never asked to become a creature so vile he'd thought numerous times about ending his own existence. This life had been thrust upon him like a disease. And he'd become its carrier, spreading the infection to his beloved wife.

"Shaya," he whispered her name, something he never allowed himself, and his dead heart burned with her

memory. His beautiful Gypsy wife. What a scandalous
creature she'd been. He'd saved her from the gallows. He
shook his head. As though being a Gypsy was a crime
worthy of death. She'd been a good wife. Faithful. Given
him a child. And yet he couldn't deny he'd questioned
more than once if she'd loved him because he'd saved her
life or because she'd seen something more in him. Something worthy. He wanted to think it was the latter, but
deep down, he wasn't sure.

She'd married him when no one else would and that
was all that had mattered, but for what reward? He'd lost
her. Lost her to the same monsters who'd taken his life.
He slammed his fist on the desk, making the blade clatter
against the wood.

If only...if only...but he wouldn't let himself go
down that path. He'd been right not to turn Sofia. Eternity
was hard enough in an adult body, but for a child...he
shook his head. No. This was no life for such an
innocent.

And this was why he'd help Chrysabelle, for the
chance to find those who'd destroyed his life and make
them pay. If he lost his life again, so be it. He had lived
too long already.

He took up the oilcloth again. Someone knocked at the
office door. Chrysabelle, by her scent. Stronger than
usual. Odd. He refocused. She must have found clothes.
She'd certainly taken her time.

"Come in." *No*, the voices screeched.

The door opened, and with one hand behind her back
she slipped inside wearing her white trousers and a shirt
of Doc's, probably the only white one he owned. The perfume of her blood hit him hard. *No, no, no*...Oil oozed

between his fingers from the rag in his hand. He eased his grip.

"Here." She planted a tumbler full of crimson liquid in front of him. Her gaze hovered on the long, two-handed sword he'd been cleaning, causing her hand to pause. A small nick marred the inside of her pale wrist. She tucked it to her side and lifted her chin. "Don't argue. Just drink it."

No wonder her scent had been so strong. *Kill her.* He stared at the glass, fangs jutting into the edge of his tongue, saliva pooling. He pushed his chair away from the desk, but stayed seated. "I said—"

"It's not like drinking directly from the vein. If you don't want it, dump it down the sink. But we both know you need it." She turned on her heels and walked out, shutting the door firmly.

Memories forgotten, his mouth came open as he inhaled, dragging the honeyed fragrance over his tongue. His gums ached. The voices railed. His fingers wrapped around the tumbler before he realized what he'd done.

The heat from the glass shot into his gut like a fist. For some reason, he hadn't expected that, but of course it would be warm. It was fresh. *Spoiled.*

He pulled his hand away, dragged his fingers through his hair. He should empty the blood into the sink, turn the faucet on and wash it away. Or just throw the whole lot overboard. *Yes, yes, yes...*

The scent burrowed down his throat, filling his lungs with thick, sweet pressure.

His fingers strayed back to the warmth. The thought of pouring that blood out, of wasting it, seemed like blasphemy. That wasn't just any blood. That was comarré blood. Freely given. Chrysabelle wanted him to have it. *Wants you to die.*

He stared at the glass. Tapped his fingers against it. Inhaled the heady aroma already infusing his body with need. Hell and damnation, it smelled good.

One taste wouldn't hurt, would it? *Yes.* Like she said, it wasn't as if he was taking it from her vein. No chance he'd drain her dry.

But what if one taste was all it took? What if that one taste made him hunt her down and…the sweetness of it fogged his head with a strange euphoria, blocking out the voices? Unlike the time Preacher had been present, or she'd pricked her leg to get his attention, this blood was no longer forbidden fruit. It was his for the drinking.

So he should drink it.

He lifted the tumbler.

Put it to his mouth.

And took a sip.

He swallowed and a sound so animalistic welled out of his throat, he wasn't sure it had come from him. His body tensed like he'd been electrocuted. Heat and cold rushed through his veins. His face shifted, his muscles throbbed. He lifted the glass again and drained it in one long draught.

A thrum rose up around him, a pulsing, thumping noise that filled his ears until he heard nothing else.

His heart. He slammed the glass down onto the desk.

For the first time in more than five hundred years, it pumped with life. He didn't have time to question how that was possible when the pain kicked in. It started in the marrow of his bones, radiated through his veins and into his muscles until it burnished his skin with a searing heat.

His hands dug into the arms of his chair. Sweat dripped down the back of his neck.

And then, just as quickly as it had flashed through him, the pain left. In its place was a lingering warmth and sense of well-being unlike anything he'd felt since being turned. Strength suffused his body, and the voices, at least for the moment, remained miraculously still. Not even the low hum of their presence remained. Not that he could hear over the beating of his own heart.

Chrysabelle was at the door. He knew, not because of her unique scent or the familiar rhythm of her heart, but because he could *feel* her. Sense her in a way he'd not sensed anyone. None of the human donor blood he'd gotten through Sweets had caused this sort of reaction, but then comarré blood was as different from that substance as oil from water.

He moved to the door, shocked at his own speed, and opened it. Her hand was lifted, prepared to knock. The subtle glow that had always surrounded her now radiated with new force.

"Oh." She stared up at him like she was seeing him for the first time. Had her blood changed him that much? "You drank it."

He frowned, reluctant to admit the truth. "Yes."

She glanced down each length of the hall, then stepped inside and shut the door. She sucked in her right cheek, her hands twisting the hem of her borrowed shirt.

"What?" Obviously, she had something to say.

She smoothed the hem of the shirt, then crossed and uncrossed her arms. "You have to kiss me. Now. While your heart's still beating."

"What?" He backed up and swallowed, ingesting a

breath of Chrysabelle-flavored air. His body tightened. He cursed himself for not pouring the blood out. He should have known there would be strings attached.

"You took my blood. You can give me this."

"I didn't take it, you offered."

"Same difference. Now kiss me."

"No. Why?" Kissing her would be ... wrong.

She sighed and looked thoroughly exasperated. "It's part of the exchange."

"I didn't agree to that. I didn't agree to any of this." Irritation nibbled away at the euphoria her blood had given him.

She threw up her hands. "Fine. I'll just start to age, the quality of my blood will deteriorate, and I'll be unable to defend myself. But that's just fine."

"What are you talking about?" Beyond the ship's confines, the night called to him more strongly than it had in decades. He wanted to join it, to revel in its comforting black embrace.

Peering at him intently, she nodded. "You want to be out there, don't you? In the night. Part of it."

"What? No." He shook his head while taking one step toward the door.

She blocked his path. "Not until you kiss me." She licked her bottom lip. "You owe me."

His eyes stayed on that lip, studied the deep crimson that evidenced the richness of her blood. Would she taste the way she smelled? Would her lips be as soft as they looked? He'd not kissed a woman in many years.

She notched her head back, lightly rapping it against the door behind her and shaking him from his thoughts. Without realizing it, he'd backed her into the door, pinning her with his arms. Her pulse jumped beneath her skin. He growled softly, making her jerk.

"Just get it over with." She lifted her chin and closed her eyes.

"Not until you tell me why I owe you." He moved his hand to trace a finger across that succulent bottom lip. She shivered under his touch. He was scaring her again, and this time, he didn't give a damn. She should be afraid. She asked too much.

Opening her eyes, she bent her face away. "It's the rule of the exchange. I give you blood, you give me saliva. If you'd taken from my vein…" She paused, and he knew she wanted to say *the way you were supposed to,* but didn't. "If you had, that part would already be over."

"What does it matter?" His fingers followed the swoop and curl of her signum across her cheek and up to her temple. The beat of her pulse stroked his fingertips, beckoning in a steady, erotic thumping that meshed with the one still filling his body.

"My blood gives you life. Your bite does the same for me. Keeps me from aging. Makes me strong." She dropped her chin, forcing his fingers into the silk of her hair. "I am only human, you know."

"A kiss will replace a bite?"

"Yes." Her head stayed down. He would have thought the idea repulsed her, but her scent carried the heavy sweetness of lust and the sharp, tinny edge of shame. She desired him and hated herself for it.

The realization made him want to punish her. Prove her right.

"Fine." He grabbed her shoulders and pushed her against the door as his mouth ground down on hers.

She made a small, startled sound and tensed. It didn't slow him. He was careful for nothing, save to keep his fangs sheathed so he wouldn't nick her. He couldn't risk that.

She tasted the way she smelled, whiskey strong and honey sweet. She was soft and pliant and dangerous. The tension left her body, and she moved into him with a willingness his body instantly recognized.

He pushed away, ending the kiss as quickly as it had begun. "Get Doc and Fi. We're going to your aunt's." He raised his brows. "Unless you require more of me?" His tone was cruel even to his own ears.

"No," she whispered. "That will do." She seemed dazed. Her heart raced in his ears, faster than his own. Without question, she'd found the kiss pleasurable.

Unfortunately, so had he. Before he did something he would regret, he turned back to his desk. His insides seethed. She remained behind him. Too close. Far too close. "Go," he said, more gruffly than he meant to.

There was no movement behind him. "I want my blades back."

"My room. In your bag."

The door opened and closed, and he was alone. The way he should be. His fingers wrapped the hilt of the sword he'd been cleaning before her interruption. She was slowly destroying the small, fragile peace he'd salvaged. Tearing down the protective walls he'd constructed to keep the need for companionship at bay. He turned the blade, watching the subtle play of candlelight on its surface. He hated her for it. Hated himself for feeling anything toward her but indifference.

Pain was a great dampener of other emotion. One

could only feel so many things at a time. He slipped his palm across the blade then lifted it away. The thin line of blood left behind disappeared almost as quickly as it had been formed.

He needed to be rid of her just as fast.

# Chapter Nineteen

Doc whistled low and long from the driver's seat. "Your aunt must have some serious coin to live out here."

Fi and Mal crouched on either side of Chrysabelle on the ancient sedan's floor. She was surprised Mal owned a car, but not surprised how substandard it was. The interior smelled like mildew and gasoline. Cracks webbed the leather seats and grime filled every crevice. At least it ran, and hopefully, with the darkly tinted windows and the cover of night, her extra companions would go unnoticed.

"Doc, you're supposed to be my driver. None of this should affect you." Chrysabelle eyed the gatehouse ahead as they rounded the corner and headed over the bridge that connected Mephisto Island to the outskirts of Paradise City. The light was on inside the building, but from this angle she couldn't see the guard. "And I'm a guest, so I can't bring anyone in without my aunt putting them on the list."

"You have to be on a list? Doc's right. Serious coin," Fi said.

"Hush." Doc and Fi's comments didn't bother Chrysabelle half as much as Mal's silence. Since the kiss, he hadn't spoken more than a few words to her, as though she'd caused some great rift in his personal well-being.

As if he had any personal well-being.

That kiss was her due. Not that an anathema would understand the exchange between a comarré and her patron. Not to mention that if he'd been vampire enough to take from her vein, that awkward kiss would have never transpired.

Her blood had changed him. She could see it in the fullness of his muscles, the increase in his speed, the surety of his stride. She'd made him as close to whole as he'd been in a long time.

And his kiss had torn her to pieces.

That kiss should have been such a simple way to complete the exchange since he refused to bite her. How wrong. Kisses were not simple. Not that one. Not in any way. But then she'd never had another kiss to judge by. Comarré who valued the purity of their blood remained chaste until such time as they were selected for the honor of breeding. Patrons understood that as well. Very few wanted to depreciate their investment by bedding their comarré. Some didn't care, but those patrons, and the comarré who acquiesced, were the exceptions.

The car slowed, and Doc lowered the window. Still no sign of the guard.

Mal's head came up, his eyes glazed with silver. "I smell blood."

"You always smell blood," Chrysabelle answered, clasping her hand over the spot on her wrist where she'd drained earlier even though her wrist blades were back in place and covered the mark.

Doc nodded. "I smell it too." He groaned softly. "Varcolai blood."

Mal slid into the seat beside her, but his head swiveled toward the building. "Recently spilled, by the scent." His eyes half-closed before opening fully. "There's nothing alive in that guardhouse."

Fi unfolded from her crouch and moved to the seat, tucking herself against the door. She reached up and squeezed Doc's large shoulder.

Chrysabelle inhaled. The wild, coppery tang mixed with the perfume of the night-blooming flowers dotting the landscaping. A chill skittered down her spine. "I had no idea the guard was varcolai." She'd seen him in passing but hadn't paid close attention. "Had to be vampires, since their powers wouldn't work on him to get them entrance."

Doc met her eyes in the rearview mirror. "Not to mention, nobles will take any chance they get to cap one of us. Present company excluded."

Mal said nothing.

She reached across Fi for the door handle. Mal got to it first, twisting to face her and pressing himself into the back of the driver's seat. "What are you doing?"

She pulled her hand away. Her knees were touching his thigh, but her back was already against the seat. "One of us has to get into the guardhouse to open the gate." She had to get to her aunt's. If anything happened to Maris because of her...

"Doc will do it."

Behind him, the shifter made a low growl but threw the car into park and got out. Mal thankfully moved back to his side of the seat. Using the hem of his T-shirt as a glove, Doc opened the shack's door and went in. A moment later, the gates swung wide. He returned to the car and shoved it into drive, his face blank, but his eyes haunted.

"I'm sorry you had to see that." Couldn't be easy for one varcolai to see another dead.

"Me too."

She leaned forward and pointed down the side of the forked road that led to her aunt's estate. "That way. Hurry."

Doc punched the gas, snapping her back. Fi squealed at the sudden start. At the turn, Chrysabelle slid across the seat and into Mal. His hands closed on her upper arms as he caught her. They were warm. From her blood.

Chrysabelle flinched. "Let me go."

His hands opened, and she moved away, slightly mortified she'd had any reaction. He couldn't have meant anything. Grabbing her was just an involuntary response. She scooted forward again to give Doc directions and to try to ignore that Mal was even more in tune with her emotions now that he'd ingested her blood.

At the second gate, she motioned toward the sidewalk that ran around the island. Her skin itched with dread. "Park here. If we drive up, we'll tip our hand."

Mal raised his brows a fraction as they all piled out of the vehicle, but said nothing. Did he expect her to go in guns blazing? What if someone was in the house? Years of training, she wanted to remind him. Training she'd paid close attention to and excelled in. What else had there been to do?

A minute after they arrived, Chrysabelle was up and on top of the stucco security wall that surrounded her aunt's estate. Mal leaped up behind her. Still on the ground, Doc cleared his throat.

She looked back. "What?" she whispered. "You can clear this, no problem."

He flicked his eyes at Fi. "Some of us need a hand."

"Maybe Fi should stay with the car." It would be safer for her there if the security had been breached and someone was still in the house.

"And leave me defenseless?" Fi asked.

"Fine, but don't do anything rash." Mal reached down and gestured for her hand.

Doc lifted her up then the vampire pulled her to the top. Chrysabelle leaped to the estate grounds, leaving Mal and Doc to get Fi down. Mal and Doc landed as silently as Chrysabelle had, but Fi made a small *whoof* when she hit. Chrysabelle put her finger to her lips.

Fi rolled her eyes, but Mal nodded and spoke at almost inaudible levels. "She's right. No more noise or talking unless necessary."

Chrysabelle refrained from fainting. Maybe that kiss hadn't been the train wreck she thought it was. Heat fought with the chill of her nerves. She forced down any thoughts that weren't immediately important. Her aunt's safety was all that mattered.

Mal bent and dragged his fingers over the ground, stirring up swirls of dust. She bent beside him. Not dust, ash. It clung to the grass where it had drifted from a larger pile. He sniffed at the residue he'd picked up, then nodded. "Brimstone." He rubbed his fingers together, sending the ash into the wind.

"Nothos," she whispered with a shudder. Something bad had happened here.

Mal stood and surveyed both sides of the grass path that separated the outer wall from the interior landscaping. His gaze stayed locked on the left side as he moved forward. Again he bent and scooped ash from the ground.

She pushed to her feet. "Another Nothos?"

He shook his head. "Vampire." He inhaled again. "Fringe." He pointed farther down. "Another pile there."

"Three down," she murmured. Who'd killed them? Velimai? And where had the fringe vamp come from? Nobility used fringe as guards, but with a Nothos? Seemed like overkill.

The group followed her through the extensive landscaping, skirting the lighted areas, until she stopped them before the palms opened up to make way for the lawn. The fronds overhead shooshed against each other with a sound like gentle rain. Insects added a few clicks and buzzes, and lizards skittered through the foliage around them. The breeze was starting to pick up like a storm might be coming, but no clouds muted the stars.

She scanned the house and the surrounding grounds. The first time she'd seen the estate with its stately columns and Mediterranean styling, she'd been amazed. Now, it seemed merely an extension of the grandeur her aunt had once known. Nothing looked out of the ordinary. No cars were parked on any portion of the long circling drive that kept the house hidden from the gated street entrance.

She half-glanced at Mal, enough to get his attention without making eye contact. "How many heartbeats in the house?"

He stared intently for a moment. "Only one. Your aunt is safe."

She exhaled the breath she'd been holding. "Or dead. My aunt has a live-in assistant."

"Then perhaps the assistant is dead." He shrugged.

Why would he care? Death must seem ordinary to him. Putting that thought aside, she nodded gently, not ready to accept either possibility. She turned to include Doc and Fi in her plans. "All of you stay here until I motion for you, otherwise the security cameras will pick you up."

Mal rested a hand on her bare ankle. "You shouldn't go alone."

She dug a fingernail into her thigh to keep from reacting to his touch. "You have a better plan?"

He frowned.

"I thought so." She pushed through a stand of jewel-toned crotons and jogged to the front door. She punched in her code, then eased the front door open.

Velimai leaped out from behind one of the large Oriental floor vases flanking the entrance, Maris's sacre in hand. Chrysabelle jumped back, snapping her wrist blades into place. Only her superior eyesight saved her from being cut in two.

Behind her, she heard Mal snarl. She raised her hands, dropping the bone daggers back into their sheaths. "Velimai! It's me, Chrysabelle!"

The nearly transparent wysper stopped, chest heaving, face bruised and bloodied. She dropped the sword to her side, and her eyes filled with tears.

"What happened? Where's Maris?"

Velimai's free hand began moving in the complex rhythm of signing, when suddenly she went solid, pulled Chrysabelle into the house by her shirt, and brandished the weapon again.

Mal stood just beyond the threshold. His eyes flared slightly when he realized what Velimai was.

Weapon pointed in defense, the wysper opened her mouth. An eerie howl screeched out of her, a sound like nails on gypsum. A crack snaked through one of the massive Oriental vases. Mal staggered back, clamping his hands to his ears.

"No!" Chrysabelle spun, her heart racing. "No, Velimai."

The wysper's cry ceased, but her mouth stayed open.

"He's a..." Chrysabelle couldn't bring herself to say "friend." "He's helping me. He's not here to hurt you. Or me. I promise. He's protecting me."

Velimai snorted, but thankfully shut her mouth.

Chrysabelle glared at the wysper, who glared right back at her before returning her sooty gaze to the vampire scowling beyond the door. She didn't look one bit convinced Mal wasn't the enemy, but Chrysabelle didn't have time to smooth wysper-vampire relations.

"Mal." She tried to get Mal's attention, but he was staring at Velimai as hard as she was staring at him. "Mal." He looked at her quickly, then back at the creature who'd almost destroyed him with her voice.

"I heard you the first time."

Doc and Fi walked up behind him, trying to see into the house. She ignored them for the moment. "Try to cross the threshold."

Without taking his eyes off Velimai, he stepped forward and met a sheer wall of resistance. "Your aunt is alive."

Relief flooded Chrysabelle.

Fi's brow scrunched. "How do you know that?"

Mal stepped back. "A vampire may not enter a human's home without permission. Only if Chrysabelle's aunt were dead could I enter unhindered."

Chrysabelle nodded. "And since you can't come in, will you check the grounds?" She knew she didn't have to explain what to look for. Mal was probably as capable as she was in a situation like this. "Doc, Fi, come help me in here."

She turned back to Velimai and guided her into the living room. Doc and Fi filed in behind her.

"Man, this place is tight," Doc said. "Or was."

Judging by the pieces of the glass coffee table covering nearly every surface, Velimai had done her best to stop whatever had happened. Magazines spilled across the rug, their electronic covers flickering. A little farther back, Maris's iBot stood empty. Without Maris at the helm it seemed more like a useless sculpture. "What happened?"

Velimai pointed at Doc and Fi, lifting her bruised chin in question. Both of them looked as curious about the wysper. The chance they'd come in contact with one before was slim.

"They're friends of the vampire." She pointed at Doc. "He's varcolai." As though Velimai couldn't tell. Then she wiggled her finger at Fi. "She's . . . sort of attached to the vampire. Or was. It's a long story. Anyway, she's human."

Velimai nodded and dismissed them with a blink of her eyes. She brushed glass from the leather sofa before sinking down on it and cradling her head in her hands. Her shoulders began to rock gently, her body flickering like a candle flame. Chrysabelle half-expected her to go to mist. For all her strangeness, Velimai's obvious distress over whatever had happened to Maris touched Chrysabelle. Perhaps the wysper wasn't such a fearsome creature after all. Unless you were a vampire.

She glanced toward the still-open door. No sign of Mal. Fi lifted her hands, a silent, "What next?"

"Fi," Chrysabelle said softly, in a voice she hoped would make it clear now was not the time for snappy comebacks.

"Yeah?"

Chrysabelle notched her head to the right. "There's a bathroom down that hall, second door. Would you get a damp washcloth?"

"No problem." With a sympathetic look at Velimai, Fi exited toward the bath.

"Doc, maybe you could fix some tea?"

Doc raised one brow and made a face that clearly implied she was crazy for asking.

"If you can make spaghetti, you can make tea." Velimai wept in great shudders now, her small body more sheer than solid. Chrysabelle pursed her mouth. Tea wasn't that hard. "Kitchen's behind me. Teapot's on the stove, tea and sugar in the canisters on the counter, and cups in the cabinet left of the range."

Scowling slightly, he disappeared into the kitchen as Fi returned with the damp washcloth.

"Thank you." Chrysabelle moved to sit beside Velimai. The sound of cabinets being opened and closed and things being moved around came out of the room behind them. "Doc's in the kitchen, trying to make tea. Can you help him?"

"Sure." Fi left, seemingly happy to have a new task.

"Here." Chrysabelle nudged the washcloth toward Velimai's hands. "I'm so sorry you've been hurt, but I need to know what's happened to my aunt."

The flickering stopped as Velimai solidified and took the cloth, pressing it against her skin then wiping her eyes. She folded it neatly and laid it on her knees, then began to sign. Her hands flew.

"Wait, wait." Wysper hand signs were not one of the required comarré language lessons, but maybe they should be. "Even when you go slowly I only get every third or fourth word." Instinctively, she reached out and gently captured Velimai's shifting hands with one of hers. The wysper's skin was like frozen sandpaper. Chrysabelle's own snagged painfully against it. Immediately, she released Velimai and flipped her hand over. Tiny ruby drops glistened on her palm and fingers.

A guttural rumble brought her head up. Mal glared from the door, held back by the lack of invitation. "I smell blood. Yours."

Chrysabelle tucked her hand down at her side and offered him a weak smile. "It's just a scratch. Did you find anything yet?"

He shook his head, glowered at Velimai, then vanished into the shadows he'd come from.

Fi came in carrying a steaming cup. Doc trailed her. She set the tea on the brushed steel side table. "What happened to your hand?"

"Nothing. Watch the glas—"

"Nothing? There's blood all over it." Fi popped her hands to hips. "You okay?"

"Fine." Chrysabelle grabbed the washcloth from Velimai's knees and swabbed the blood away. "See? All gone."

Dawn was coming. Time was running out. "Velimai, can you tell me what happened to Maris without signing?"

Velimai stood and took a few steps toward the middle of the room, shards of glass crackling under her feet. She turned to face Chrysabelle, spreading her arms slightly. Her form wavered, then shifted into a very recognizable female vampire.

"Tatiana." The name soured on Chrysabelle's tongue.

Doc peered closer. "That is freaking amazing."

Fi gasped. "How's she do that?"

"It's a wysper thing."

Velimai shifted again. This time into a male.

"Huh," Fi said, tipping her head. "There's something familiar about those two."

"Yeah, they're vampires." Doc tapped Fi lightly on the arm and she smiled, turning toward him.

"I get that. But I feel like I know them. And not in a good way."

"That feeling makes perfect sense." Chrysabelle gestured toward the image flickering over Velimai's skin. "That's Mikkel." Of course. Tatiana's House of Bathory male was the perfect mate. Equally bloodthirsty and a master of the dark arts. "Is his power how they got access?" she asked Velimai.

Velimai shook her head and became Tatiana again. It was like watching an old movie, before holodiscs. Then the image of Tatiana became Chrysabelle.

"Wait. That's me. I don't understand." Chrysabelle peered closer. Doc and Fi were caught up in some other conversation.

Shifting back to herself, Velimai shook her head, then held her hand up. She lifted one finger, then turned into

Chrysabelle. She raised her hands toward her face and wiped them down her body, erasing Chrysabelle's image and replacing it with Tatiana's.

Chrysabelle gasped softly. "Do you mean Tatiana was disguised as me?"

Slowly, Velimai signed out a few simple words. *She was you.*

"No, she doesn't have that power. Unless Mikkel cast some sort of spell over her. Was he disguised too? Did Maris invite him in?'

*No.*

"Then his power wouldn't have extended into the house." Chrysabelle tapped her fingers against her leg. "That means Tatiana has a new power." The phrase she dared not utter trickled through her brain. Castus Sanguis. Only the ancient fallen ones could bestow that kind of power. If Tatiana was working with them, for them, whatever the case might be, that made things drastically more dangerous. She sighed. "At least they didn't kill Maris."

*No.* Velimai spelled out the word "kidnap."

"They hope to draw me out."

*Yes.*

"Then we have to figure out where they took her and get her back." She glanced at the housing of the crystal clock that had once sat on the coffee table. The crystal was broken away but the clock still worked. "Sun will be up soon. They'll have to find shelter somewhere."

She stood. "Doc, bring the car in. I'll open the gate. Fi, find Mal and tell him what's going on."

The pair nodded and took off.

Velimai trailed Chrysabelle to the door and waited beside her while she punched the gate code into the keypad. Picking up Maris's sacre, the wysper tipped her chin toward the door.

Chrysabelle shook her head. "Velimai, you can't go. I can't take the risk that you'll let loose again and kill Mal. I know you want to help but I don't need another vampire death on my hands."

She leaned the sword against the wall and signed furiously.

"Slow down. Please."

This time Velimai spelled things out. *Why do you care? He's anathema.*

Chrysabelle cradled her forehead in her hand for a moment. This wasn't something she wanted to share. "In a roundabout way, he's my new patron." There was no point elaborating. It wouldn't change the situation.

Velimai's mouth hung open. Her hands stopped fluttering. Her gaze snapped from Chrysabelle's face to her neck and wrists.

She wasn't going to explain that he refused to take from her vein either. Sharing information that portrayed one's patron as weak was strictly forbidden. "I didn't intend for it to happen and oddly enough, neither did he. But it did, and now I'm stuck with him. And he with me."

Velimai picked the sacre up and held it out, feathery eyebrows raised in suggestion. Chrysabelle knew exactly what that suggestion was.

She shook her head. "You know the price Maris paid for libertas."

The wysper shrugged as if to say it had been worth it.

Careful not to make contact with Velimai's skin, Chrysabelle took the gleaming sword. She hefted its familiar weight, wrapped her fingers around the hilt with ease. The grip was fitted to Maris, but it wasn't uncomfortable; the weapon's blood magic was tuned to her aunt but not unresponsive. Chrysabelle sliced it through the air, testing, remembering. This sacre was no different from her own, save the blood that filled the hilt and the gold that decorated both her aunt's body and the wafer-thin blade. The red leather–wrapped handle, the signum dancing over the metal...even the sour-sweet tang of the weapon was the same. Except that this sacre had been used to kill. *To gain freedom.* Again, she shook her head.

"Only as a last resort. Only...only if there is no other option." Somehow, she knew there wouldn't be. Whether because of Mal's lurking dementia or her own desperate need to separate herself from this mad life, she would end up raising her blade against him. The feeling sank into her bones, spreading a lingering sadness through her.

Velimai retrieved the sword's red leather sheath from behind the cracked vase and handed it to Chrysabelle, who took it without protesting further. The weapon was valuable, and Velimai certainly didn't need it.

Of all the vampires she'd ever known, Mal was the first she'd ever felt sorry for. No, not sorry for. That wasn't it. She empathized with him. His desire to be free. She understood it. Wanted it for herself.

She sheathed the sword and slung its crimson strap over her shoulder and across her chest. Her body welcomed the subtle weight like the embrace of an old friend.

Despite everything she knew about him, everything he'd been, everything he'd done, he seemed...the most in need of help. A vampire in need of help. She'd never entertained such a thought before.

Perhaps he wasn't the only one going mad.

# Chapter Twenty

Mal had found nothing useful around the grounds, except a better understanding of how wealthy a woman Chrysabelle's aunt was. The yacht parked in the deepwater slip had to cost an unbelievable sum. It made his own accommodations look reef-worthy.

He ended his search in the shadows at the front of the house and settled against a palm to watch Chrysabelle inside. She'd left the door open. Perhaps so he could see her? Interesting, but unlikely. Probably to allow for a quicker exit.

Her perfume wafted past, borne on the breeze, and he indulged his basest needs by inhaling until he was full. Now that he'd had Chrysabelle's blood, her scent didn't raise the same wildness in him. Instead, the effect was something new and not altogether welcome. The feeling of strange satisfaction, of knowing he'd tasted her, that didn't bother him. It was the possessive pang of need to have her again that set him on edge. Whether that uninvited urge came from tasting her blood or her mouth, he didn't know. What he did know was that their kiss should not have happened. His lip curled in disgust, but the sweetness of her mouth still played across his tongue.

Chrysabelle stood in the foyer, the wysper at her side. The wysper had given Chrysabelle her aunt's sword, and she now balanced the sword with a grace that testified to her years of training. Flashes of reflected silver danced over her face. The glimmer mixed with her signum and made her look like some otherworldly goddess cast in precious metals.

Only her conversation with the wysper ruined the effect. The emotion he felt from her confused him, so he ignored it. Too many female-free years had gone by for him to bother trying to understand a woman now.

He narrowed his eyes. If she thought to challenge him for her treasured freedom, she wouldn't find him a very available opponent. Not that he wouldn't fight her if need be, he just didn't expect to live through this trip to Romania. Corvinestri was the seat of the House of Tepes. The vampire who'd sired Mal was from there. The vampire he'd *killed*. There was little chance he could show up in that hidden city without a reckoning. After all, the nobility had tried to eradicate him once before and had thought they'd succeeded. Proving them wrong would be a terrible blow to someone's ego. And that someone would want to put things right. If that meant the chance to take Shaya's murderer down with him, so be it.

He was done living anyway. He'd had enough of this hell on earth. How much worse could the real one be?

Chrysabelle sheathed the sword, threw the strap across her body, and made motions to leave. He peeled off the palm and headed toward the house. Fi came around from the side yard.

"There you are," she called.

"Here I am."

Doc pulled the car alongside the house and jumped

out, leaving the door open. "We gotta roll, man. Sun's coming."

"I know. I can feel it."

"I know *you* can, but Goldilocks in there might not be aware."

Chrysabelle stepped out of the house, thankfully leaving the wysper behind, who quickly shut the door. "I know what time it is. The vampires who took my aunt certainly do too. I need to find where they could have gone to spend the day."

She glanced at Mal. Something ugly flashed through her gaze and rolled over him. Pity? Sympathy? Whatever it was, he wanted none of it. She broke eye contact to adjust the buckle on the sword's strap, now nestled between her breasts. "Who would know the locations of those kinds of safe houses?"

Mal looked at Doc. Doc shook his head. "No way. I'm not asking that man for any favors. I'm not getting in his debt again. Ever."

"Whose debt?" Chrysabelle's head came up, interest replacing all other emotion in her eyes.

"No one," Doc answered.

"Dominic's," Mal said.

"Don't." Doc's hands flexed against the car roof. Fi moved in closer, putting a hand on his side.

Mal ignored Doc. Overhearing Chrysabelle's willingness to kill him had put him in a foul mood. Fouler than usual anyway.

Chrysabelle rolled her cherry lips in, then out on an exhale. "The way I see it, Dominic owes my aunt. I'll ask him. I don't know why you think Doc should do it anyway."

"Because Doc used to work for him."

Chrysabelle's brows shot up.

Doc cursed softly and smacked the roof. "That's history. Let it be, vampire."

"Yeah." Fi nodded, coming down on Doc's side. What a shock.

Apparently, it no longer mattered that if not for being part of Mal's curse, she'd be six feet down instead of cuddling up to the shifter. Females. He shrugged. "History or not, doesn't change what happened."

"Does it matter?" Chrysabelle tapped her watchless wrist. "Time's wasting. Unless you've decided to give tanning another chance."

Mal hooked a thumb in his belt. He hadn't packed enough weaponry if they were headed to Dominic's. "We might need Doc's help to get to him."

Doc growled. "I'll take you to the club, but then you're on your own."

"Thank you. I'm sure Dominic will be willing to see me," Chrysabelle said, smiling at Doc before glaring at Mal. Like he cared what she thought.

Doc guided Fi around him and into the sedan's front seat. She slid over, then he got in and slammed the door.

Chrysabelle took a few steps, reaching for the handle to the back door.

"Not so fast." Mal lifted his chin toward her newly acquired weapon. "That goes in the trunk."

Her fingers toyed with the strap, an insolent smile curving her mouth. "Big bad vampire scared of a little old ceremonial sword?"

The next instant he was in front of her, his hand latched to the back of her neck to keep her eyes on his. Heat from the blade pricked his skin. "I am afraid of nothing. Not you. Not your hot blade. Not even leaving you with *no option*."

Her breath shuddered in her throat, and her pulse jumped a tick. "I'm not afraid of you anymore either."

"No?" Thunder rumbled in the distance, followed by a flash of heat lightning that lit her eyes like two icy-blue flames.

"No."

His thumb shifted until the tip nestled over the tender flesh below her ear. He stroked the spot, enjoying the erratic vibration beneath her skin. "Then that must be lust causing your heart to beat so fast."

Her eyes narrowed. "Yes, that's it." Sarcasm dripped off her voice. "My desire for you is so strong I can barely contain myself. Every comarré dreams of the day she'll have an anathema of her very own. One who can't stand her. One whose demons want her dead." She fluttered her lids and shook herself with a fake shiver. "I'm such a lucky, lucky girl."

He tightened his grip. "You lie."

"Not this time, vampire." She grabbed his wrist and tried to move his hand but failed. "You should be able to feel that much."

"What I feel is your temperature rising." And desire mixed with revulsion. The same mix of emotion he'd felt from her before. Did she love to hate him or hate to love him? Maybe he should push the issue and find out.

"Because you're making me mad," she spat.

"You felt nothing when we kissed?"

"Nothing. Does that disappoint you?"

He released her and forced a laugh. "On the contrary. It relieves me."

"The sword stays with me." She grabbed the car door and yanked it open. "Now if you don't mind, I'd like to go save my aunt." She slid into the dark interior, leaving him alone as the first drops of rain pummeled down.

Tatiana stood in the hangar door. Storm clouds rolled over the horizon, diluting the coming dawn. Behind her, Mikkel exited the plane.

"She's secured?" She flexed her hand against the slight remaining soreness. Interrogation was hard work. Washing the blood from her hands instead of licking them clean had been easy enough, but the blood splattered on the plane's interior had tested her control. The perfume of comarré blood would linger for days, tainting her dreams as she slept in the plane's light-secured bedroom.

"Very. I tied her up and locked her in the bathroom." He winked, a puerile gesture she could have done without. "Not even Houdini could escape those knots."

"Good. Did you get anything more from her?" she asked, already knowing the answer. If she couldn't get the old bat to spill more than the name of some remnant errand girl, what chance did he have?

He shook his head and looked acceptably displeased. "Nothing. She's going to be a hard one to crack."

"I'll make her talk eventually. I'm just too hungry to concentrate with all that blood. I'd hate to slip and drain her before she gets a chance to tell me everything she knows." She laughed and Mikkel joined in, nodding.

His smile faded. "Do you think her blood is still good after this much time?"

Tatiana's belly growled, and she narrowed her eyes at

him. Pretty did not always mean brains. "Of course it's still good. And all this talk of blood isn't helping. Especially knowing the girl is out there, somewhere, with a vampire helping her." The old comarré had given that much up when she'd thought Tatiana was her niece. "It just makes me want to hunt that much more." The vampire helping the rogue comarré would be ash as soon as she found him.

Mikkel glanced at the sky. "The Nothos should be back soon."

"Good. Then it can track down the female remnant and bring her in." She sighed. "I can't believe those two vampire guards took down my other Nothos. Whoever sent them clearly trained them, although the element of surprise was on their side."

"Training fringe." He shook his head. "What a waste."

"Except that it obviously works." All nobles, including her, kept a contingent of trained fringe guards. She eyed him, wondering if the flight had affected his brain. Since gaining her new power, she'd felt a distance between her and Mikkel. She grimaced. "The Americas' abundance of fringe is just one more reason not to live here." Fringe vampires weren't worth notice, except when they stood in the way of what she wanted. Then they made excellent practice for hand-to-hand.

The smell of brimstone wafted in with a gust of rain-tinged air. She inhaled the familiar scent. "Finally."

The Nothos stalked in, a limp kine under each corded arm. It dropped them at her feet with a slight bow. The female kine whimpered as she hit the concrete.

"Well done." The kine were deliciously young but not children. That was a line she would never, ever cross. She spoke to the Nothos while watching the pair slowly rouse. "You are to find a female remnant named Nyssa. She works as a black market errand girl. Half shadeux, half wysper, believed to be mute, but use the iron mesh ear-plugs anyway. I can't afford to lose another of you."

The Nothos stayed still.

"Do you need iron shackles?"

"No, mistress." It patted a pair of the rusty bracelets hooked to its belt.

She glared at it. "Then go."

The Nothos nodded and leaped into the now pouring rain, its strange loping gait carrying it swiftly into the last bit of remaining darkness. Tatiana envied the creature's indifference to sunlight. Hard to believe the only thing separating their kind from hers was a bit of human DNA. The walking horrors didn't deserve such a boon any more than they deserved their invisibility to human eyes. One more thing breaking the covenant would remove.

The male kine groaned. His eyes flicked open and he reached for his head. "What happened?" His hand came away red and sticky.

The sweet perfume of hot blood brought her fangs down hard. Tatiana bent toward the male kine until the sil-ver of her eyes reflected in his. Could there be a kine some-where worthy of sacrificing to the ring? One pure enough to activate the ring's power? Doubtful. Kine were weak. Far from pure. Good for one thing and one thing only. The male trembled at her closeness, and his fear sent liquid pleasure spilling down her spine like the finest silk.

"Where are we?" he asked. "Who are you?"

She smiled broadly. "You're in hell. And I'm the devil."

# Chapter Twenty-one

Twenty minutes later and a world away, Doc rolled the sedan down an alley that reminded Chrysabelle of the one where she'd stabbed Mal. Despite the rain, two large, hairy men flanked a rusted metal door long ago stenciled with Seven. At the sedan's approach, both straightened. One flicked a cigarette to the ground and exhaled a thin curl of smoke.

"What's Seven?"

Doc glanced into the rearview mirror. "Dominic's club. As in seven deadly sins."

"This is where Dominic lives?" Based on the way the vampire dressed, she'd imagined something more in keeping with her aunt's estate, not the slums.

Doc shifted the sedan into park. "Yes, this is his club and his home. There are more levels than you'd guess."

Beside her, Mal rolled his head from shoulder to shoulder like a man loosening for a fight. "Take your shirt off."

"What? Why?"

He kept his eyes on the two guarding the door. "Put the sword on beneath it. With the shirt's length and your hair over the handle, it won't be as noticeable."

She raised her brows but did as he said. That he wanted her to keep the sword he'd been adamant she leave in the trunk minutes before spoke volumes. He expected trouble. That made two of them.

Doc checked his watch. "Dawn can't be more than forty-five minutes out."

"We won't be that long." Mal looked at her, his eyes silver, his fangs kissing his bottom lip, his human face long discarded. "You ready?"

"Yes." She stared at his fangs longer than she should have. Already the blood was building in her again, weakening her flesh. Being in such close contact was ruining her cycle.

"Follow my lead."

She nodded. She'd do what seemed right, whether it was his lead or not, but she wasn't going to tell him that.

"Be careful," Fi said, scooting closer to Doc. "Both of you."

Putting his arm around her, Doc lifted his head to look at them in the rearview mirror. "Watch out for the twins."

"Will do." Mal opened the door and slid out. He waited in the rain for Chrysabelle, then shut the door and rapped lightly on the hood. Doc pulled the sedan farther down the alley into the shadows.

Immediately, the scent of the two men by the door hit her. She blinked water out of her eyes. "Varcolai," she whispered, knowing full well Mal had probably made them already.

"Wolf," he whispered back, confirming they both knew what they were dealing with. "Stay behind me."

Bristling slightly, she hung back at his right shoulder. Did he still think she couldn't take care of herself?

Granted she didn't have much human-world experience, but judging by the two varcolai guarding the club door, this wasn't exactly the human world.

The shorter guard jerked his chin at her, glinting light off the platinum hoop in his ear. "No weapons. No exceptions."

Mal put his arm out and held Chrysabelle in place, his hand coming across her body to rest on her hip. "We have no weapons." His voice had a mesmerizing quality that danced over her skin. "There is nothing unusual about us. When you let us in, you'll forget you've seen us."

The guards stared blankly, nodding as though the movement took thought.

She shivered as the rain penetrated her shirt. Holy mother. Mal had just glamoured the guards. Impossible. Vampire powers didn't work on varcolai.

One guard opened the door, then stepped aside. Mal snaked his arm behind her and pushed her forward. The moment they were through the wards and the door shut, she spun to face him.

"How did you do that?"

"Do what?"

She resisted the urge to slap him. "You know what I mean."

He shrugged. "It's just something I can do."

"How?"

"Don't worry about it."

Fine, he wanted to act like it was nothing, she'd let him. But not yet. "Doc know you can do that?"

"He knows." He pushed past her and toward a red-lit corridor.

She grabbed his arm. "You ever do that to him?"

He pulled her close, a move she recognized as an attempt to scare her into acquiescing. He could try all he wanted, but she'd begun to figure him out. "You have more questions? Because if you do, we'll leave. Dawn's coming. Your aunt can handle that, wherever she is. I can't."

Not breathing him in was impossible this close. She turned her face away. "No more questions." For now. She let go of his arm and he caught her wrist, keeping her in place.

"This is not a safe place. Stay close. Understood?"

"Yes, *patronus*."

His mouth bent slightly at her condescending tone, but then he was off through the corridor and she was hurrying to catch up. Several yards down the hall they came to a set of double doors, steel like the exterior one and in no better shape.

"This place is a dump."

He snorted and knocked three times. A peephole in the door opened. The faint rumble of music drifted out. If someone inspected them, she couldn't see. The peephole closed.

The door was unbolted and swung wide. A heavily armed fringe vamp greeted them with a curious gaze and a respectful bow. "Enjoy yourselves."

Mal's arm settled around her waist. She opened her mouth to protest, but he shook his head slightly, his eyes full of warning. With her pressed to his side, they made their way through a set of heavy velvet drapes.

Everything changed.

The room unfurled into a sultan's harem. Luscious fabrics covered the walls, tufted floor pillows surrounded low tables of burnished wood, all glistening beneath elaborate crystal chandeliers. A heavy, seductive rhythm thumped loud enough to prevent eavesdropping. Several varieties of othernaturals danced on top of platforms throughout the space and the sweet copper scent of blood drowsed the air like opium. Vampires—all fringe—mingled with various types of fae, some varcolai, and an assortment of beautiful human men and women dressed in white with blond hair and ruby lips and...

Glints of swirling gold.

"This is new," Mal muttered.

Her heart thudded with realization. Her hand shot for her sacre, but Mal caught it before she reached the weapon's handle, interlaced his fingers with hers, and drew her in as though they were embracing. "Relax," he whispered in her ear.

She struggled against his cold grip, working her fingers loose. "Those are comarré. Serving fringe. They've got to be here against their will."

"Shh..." He shook his head. "Look closer."

"I need to help—"

"Look," he whispered again, this time cupping her cheek and gently turning her head.

She stared, heart beating with the need to rescue her brothers and sisters. Being tied to nobility was bad enough, but fringe? After a long minute, her heart slowed. The signum weren't quite right. Some of the red lips were smudged. Dark roots shadowed pale locks. She relaxed her hand, splaying it against his chest to steady herself. "They're counterfeit."

She'd never seen such a thing. Never imagined it. Still pressed to him, she stared harder, picking out the subtle ways they were different. "Do they glow?"

"No. Not like you." His mouth was above her ear now, causing his voice to reverberate through her hair. His mouth moved against her scalp as though he wanted to say something else, but he kept silent.

"Fake comarré." She spat the word. Seeing the impostors doused her with a cold splash of indignation. Being comarré was not something to play at. It wasn't a game. Wasn't a costume that could be taken on and off at will. Had Mal felt this way that first night at the club, surrounded by humans pretending to be his bloodsucking brothers?

"Not fake exactly, but not real either. They're a sort of fringe, like the masters they serve." He inhaled and the movement of air lifted a shiver from her. "They don't have your perfume, your glow...your..." He swallowed, a purely reflexive action. "They're nothing like you."

She should pull out of his embrace. "I don't like it."

"I don't either, but this is not our world." He made no move to release her. "You're not going to hurt anyone, are you?"

*Our* world. How staggering three letters could be. "Not at the moment, no."

"Then I'm going to let you go, but you've got to stay close to me. I doubt they've seen a genuine comarré before." Still, he held her tight. "If they think I'm your patron, they'll leave you alone."

"You are my patron." Where they touched, his body had warmed to the same temperature as hers. She wondered if the heat was a boon or a bother.

"You know what I mean." He sighed, ruffling her hair with the exhale. "One of these vamps thinks you're available and we're all going to be breathing ashes."

"Understood."

With a reluctant slowness, his hands loosened and his arm returned to her waist. "Let's find Dominic."

The main room had seven arched doorways, each labeled with one of the seven deadly sins. Vanity had glistening gold-mirrored curtains covering the entrance, Envy had gilded chain mail, Sloth had nothing. Wrath's doors were riveted steel and guarded by an armed shadeux fae, which was kind of like igniting both ends of a stick of dynamite—completely unnecessary and bound to result in someone getting hurt.

Mal directed them toward Lust. Beyond the heavy suede curtain, a red glass bar curved against the far wall. Vampires lay on embroidered chaises while the fake comarré flitted around them. Chrysabelle's gut soured at the sight.

As she and Mal approached the bar, a woman came toward them, every inch of visible skin hennaed in delicate fae runes. Her sheer silks were trimmed in gold like a storybook genie's, but her pointed ears and overlarge eyes gave away her true lineage.

*Haerbinger fae.*

Chrysabelle's gut went from sour to ice-cold. The fae extended her hands palms up, the chains connecting the rings on her middle fingers to her wrist bracelets swaying. Why wasn't she wearing gloves?

"Surely this must be a special occasion for the noble Malkolm to grace us. Or have you decided to return to the Pits?"

"Satima." Mal gave the fae a curt nod. His hold on Chrysabelle tightened. What were the Pits? He'd flinched just the tiniest bit at that question. "Where's Dominic?"

Satima laughed, a lovely tinkling sound offset by the sharp teeth glistening behind her wine-stained lips. "Still the same charmer, I see." She turned her voluminous chocolate eyes on Chrysabelle and leaned in. "Hello there, pretty one. I don't think I've met you before."

Without thinking, Chrysabelle took a step behind Mal and grabbed hold of his leather coat. Haerbinger fae drank blood. Something he obviously knew too, as he moved to shield her further.

"Satima." Mal's warning echoed like distant thunder, rippling through Chrysabelle where she clung to him.

"Now, now," Satima said. "There's nothing wrong with a little sharing among old friends."

Mal's body completely blocked Chrysabelle's view of the haerbinger. She leaned closer, putting her head down. His hands fisted. "I don't share, and we've never been friends."

Chrysabelle twisted against him, putting them back-to-back for better defensive position. Instantly, his body tensed like he'd been shocked. One hand reached back and pushed her away enough to separate them.

"Hmph," she snorted. He hadn't had a problem with touching her earlier. Beneath her shirt, she adjusted the sacre's strap where it dug into her should—she stopped, realizing she'd rested the blade against him. Had he actually felt its heat through the leather sheath and the fabric of their clothes? Was that possible? But then she'd never known a vampire who could charm varcolai. Mal was one surprise after another.

Satima laughed again. "You're wise to hide your pet in here. Come out, pretty one. I won't bite unless asked. Or your patron gives his blessing."

Chrysabelle stayed where she was.

"Which I won't," Mal assured her. "Now get Dominic before I start looking for him myself."

"Dominic's not here," Satima said.

"He's here," Mal countered. "Get him. Now."

Chrysabelle's fists itched to teach the haerbinger a lesson about what a real comarré could do. Unfortunately, hitting the fae wouldn't dissipate the attention they were already attracting. She snuck a glance around Mal. Satima sauntered away. That didn't keep heads from turning to watch them or conversations from quieting in an attempt to hear what was going on. A few of the fringe vamps eyed her with more than curiosity.

Especially the one stalking toward her.

She tugged at Mal's coat. "We have more company." Large company, with fangs showing, flames shaved into his close-cropped hair, and tiny gold hoops glinting at each earlobe.

The fringe vamp stopped in front of her, appraising her like she imagined one might a racehorse. Or a steak dinner. He held out his hand. "Come with me."

"Like hell she will." Mal turned, his words a twisted snarl. "She's mine, Ronan."

She ignored the subtle charge of his claiming her. Little point in reveling in a pretense. "You know this fringe?"

Ronan dropped his hand and hooked a thumb in the waistband of his leather pants. An unwanted thrill rippled through her. Curse her fickle blood. No, curse Mal. Until he pierced her skin and truly became her patron, she'd waver every time a new set of fangs showed themselves.

"Yeah, he knows me." Ronan leaned in and smiled. His fangs weren't as long as Mal's. The fire inside her cooled a bit. "Which is why he's not going to fight me over you. Not to mention I'm head of security here now." He grabbed her bicep and hauled her forward.

Mal grabbed her other arm and yanked back.

"Hey!" She jerked her arm from Ronan's grasp, falling hard into Mal. The sacre made contact again and he sucked in sharply. She moved away quickly but still stayed close. Maybe she should unsheathe the weapon and dissect this fringe's C1 and C2 vertebrae. Holy mother, she wanted to hit something. The need to lash out coiled in her muscles.

Mal held her hand. Possessively. Like she was his property. Which, technically, she was. "I don't care what you're the head of. Touch her again and I'll kill you."

Ronan laughed. "You mean you'll try. Don't forget who came out of the Pits a victor, old man." He reached for Chrysabelle a second time.

"Things have changed since those days, whelp." Mal's fist slammed Ronan's head back, dropping him before the fringe made contact. Mal curved his arm around her, gently moving her behind him as Ronan shot to his feet.

Her sense of relief didn't last long.

Fingers lifted a section of her hair. "Pretty."

She spun and came face-to-face with a male version of Satima. Sweet sunlight. Another haerbinger. At least he couldn't make skin contact thanks to the flesh-colored leather covering his hands. Henna runes decorated his arms but turned into a swirling phoenix design on his bare chest.

"Don't get any ideas, haerbinger." Her fingers itched for her wrist blades.

Mal glanced over his shoulder. "Pasha only drinks from Satima."

Chrysabelle studied the new fae. A subtle glow that had nothing to do with the club's lighting system emanated from his eyes. "Are you...?"

"Gemini?" Pasha smiled, his teeth as sharp and white as a wolverine's. "Yes, I am."

Chrysabelle shuddered, ignoring the scuffling going on behind her. Paradise City just got better and better. "That makes Satima your twin." No wonder he only drank from her.

Gemini haerbinger were rare. When twin haerbinger fae were born, one twin carried the power to read futures while the other carried no power at all, but unless the gifted twin's blood remained pure, the gift would be lost. Which meant feeding from the ungifted twin. Usually, the ungifted twin killed the other.

Before Pasha could respond, Satima sidled up to him, sliding her arms around his waist and pressing the length of her body against him. She kissed his neck and winked at Chrysabelle. "Dominic will see you now."

"Very good." Freaks. She turned to get Mal. He was holding Ronan off the floor by his throat. "Satima said—"

"I heard." Jerking his arm, he threw Ronan into a flank of low couches, scattering patrons. Mal smoothed his coat. "After you."

They followed Satima and Pasha until it became clear the twins were taking them to the door to Wrath.

"There are other ways to Dominic's office." Mal's voice grated with an undercurrent of anger.

Satima shrugged. "He asked me to bring you this way."

*Liar,* Chrysabelle wanted to shout. Even without the true connection of patron and comarré, she could feel Mal's discomfort. Was there something behind that door he feared or was it the temptation of wrath itself? She reached for his forearm and gave the corded muscle a squeeze.

Satima laughed. "How touching. Look, Pasha, the pretty one seeks to reassure her master. So precious."

Chrysabelle snatched her hand back. "Take us to Dominic. Now."

Pasha's grin softened. "Or what? You'll get us drunk on your blood?"

"Enough." Mal silenced the twins. He shot a dark glance at Chrysabelle, but she refused to acknowledge his displeasure. So touching him was the wrong thing to do. It wouldn't happen again.

"Fine." Satima sniffed. They didn't stop until they stood before the scarred metal door to Wrath and its fae guard.

Mal cursed under his breath then nodded. "Mortalis."

The shadeux fae notched his head slightly to one side, his murky green eyes unblinking. His six-fingered grip tightened around one of the blades tucked into his belt. "Malkolm."

Chrysabelle had never seen a real live shadeux, only drawings. The horns that curled from his forehead down to his jaw line had been capped in filigreed silver, but their points were as sharp as daggers. He was charcoal-blue wherever leather didn't cover skin, and the high-pointed tips of his ears, also capped in filigree, peaked through his ebony shag. The hilts of a matched pair of fae thinblades jutted over his shoulders. His stormy-sea eyes shifted to her. "Comarré."

She lifted her chin slightly. This creature would not cow her, no matter that his visible blades outnumbered her hidden ones. "Shadeux."

His thin mouth angled at one side, then smoothed out. He returned his attention to Mal and gestured him closer, holding a hand up to the twins to keep them back. Chrysabelle stayed with Mal. The fae kept his voice low. "Your comarré is armed."

"So are you," Chrysabelle whispered back through gritted teeth.

Mal grabbed her arm without taking his eyes off the fae. His fingers pressed the sheath of her wrist blade into her skin. "Name your price."

Chrysabelle tugged her arm away, giving Mal her most evil glare. Unfortunately, he wasn't looking at her.

The fae stared at her then shook his head. "Your comarré is poorly behaved."

"Thanks for the bulletin. You going to let us pass or not?"

"For one of her varcolai bone blades, yes."

Now Mal's attention was on her. His eyes held a million things—surprise, distrust, anger. "Give him one."

"No." She was already woefully under-armed.

The fae crossed his arms. Barbs protruded along the lengths of his forearms. "Then no access."

Chrysabelle advanced until the barbs were a breath away, then lowered her voice and pinned his gaze with hers, hoping the thumping music would keep her words from being overheard. "Let us in to see Dominic or you'll have more access to my blades than you want, understood?"

The fae just stared. Chrysabelle's body tensed, a thousand different fight scenarios cycling through her brain. He dipped his chin. "Foolish or brave, I do not know." He reached behind him and opened the door. "Go."

She pushed through, keeping watch on the shadeux until Mal blocked her view. The twins did not follow. The downward sloping passage was narrow and hot and lit with red phosphorescent coating on the walls and ceiling, bringing to mind the entrance to hell.

Mal grabbed her shoulder, turning her. "What did you say to Mortalis?"

"I threatened him. Why, is he an old friend of yours?"

His hand left her shoulder. If her mocking tone bothered him, he didn't show it. "Do you know what a shadeux fae is capable of?"

How stupid did he think she was? Anyone remotely othernatural knew what a shadeux fae could do. "You mean the way they can latch onto your soul and suck it out of you, or the way they can slip inside a soulless creature and kill it before it even knows they're there?"

He grunted. "Are you really carrying varcolai bone blades?"

"Yes."

"Why varcolai?"

"Remember how it burned when I sank one into your shoulder?"

He frowned. "Yes."

That should be enough explanation. "Doc doesn't need to know, understand?" Her victory with the shadeux spurred new confidence. She turned to go. "We're wasting time. Which way?"

He grabbed her again, this time pulling her to him. "Don't ever do anything so foolish again."

She laughed softly, but inside her nerves tingled hot and wary. "Your concern is touching, but I don't need protecting. I don't know what your experience with women has been, but when it comes to me, don't apply it. I'm not like any woman you've ever known." She struggled to break the bonds of his hands. "Do you think we could get on with it? My aunt's life is at stake."

His grip tightened, and he brought his face within inches of hers. "So is yours." The red phosphorescence gave him a devilish glow. It suited him. Made her body ache to be bitten.

She shook her head, searching for something, anything, to diffuse the prickly heat of being so close to him. "If this is what you think passes for romance, no wonder you don't have a woman."

"Romance? Why the hell would I romance you?" He barked out a short, humorless laugh. "And getting a woman isn't the problem. It's keeping them alive."

# Chapter Twenty-two

Glad Chrysabelle didn't respond, Mal strode past her, trying to deny the odd feeling of uncertainty building in his gut. Other than himself, he had never known anyone to face down Mortalis and live. Did he really want this woman at his back? *No.* The voices whined like hungry children.

He looked over his shoulder. She chewed her bottom lip. Not exactly the picture of a fear-inducing warrior. He cocked his head. "This way."

How many times had he walked this passage, knowing what lay ahead meant pain and humiliation? *Not enough.* How many times had he done it to survive? How many times had he done it, half-hoping he wouldn't?

Taking Chrysabelle's blood meant never facing that kind of sacrifice again, but her blood came with too many strings. *Too many! Too many! Drain her now.* Of all the bloodsucking beings under the covenant, he was the last one who should be responsible for a human life. The voices roared their approval.

The passage widened. The jeers and cheers of a distant crowd threaded his memories as his steps took him closer to the Pits. He'd always dreaded this walk, but this time the dread clawed into him, shredding his resolve. He shook his head; the sounds of the crowds remained. Hell. The sounds weren't just memories. The Pits were in use, and in a few yards he'd have to decide which way to take Chrysabelle—through them or through the holding cells. The crowds would probably ignore her if he kept her close and they didn't look too hard, but she'd see into the Pits, see the match raging below, the beings within desperate to maim or kill in order to claim victory and the purse attached to it. Taking her through the holding cells would mean walking her past the combatants awaiting their turns. They would *not* ignore her. And she would know he'd once been behind those bars. *Animal.*

He preferred neither direction, but there was no other way to get to Dominic at this point. He stopped to weigh the choice. Chrysabelle's soft form collided with his.

"Hey," she muttered. "You could give a person some warning." She tucked her fingers into the strap of her sword. The red phosphorescence gave her signum the glint of live flame. "Judging by the lack of any discernable office, I'm guessing we're not there yet, so why did we stop?"

"You talk a lot." *So silence her.*

"And you don't answer questions."

He ground his back teeth together. "We have to go through the Pits to get to Dominic. Stay close, don't talk to anyone, keep your eyes on me."

Her mouth bunched to one side. "You really don't get it, do you? I'm not helpless." She rolled her eyes and shook her head. "Can we just go?"

"That's what I've been trying to do."

She snorted. "Right."

He whirled. "You think I'm trying to drag this out for some reason? That I want you around any longer than necessary?" *All that blood, yours for the drinking.* "Things have to be done a certain way here. You should understand protocol." He retook the route to the Pits, fists clenched. Bothersome woman.

"Protocol and stalling are two different things, vampire."

He said nothing, kept marching. Footsteps rushed up behind him. She snagged his arm. He yanked it away, pace unaltered. "Stay close, don't talk to anyone, keep your eyes on me."

"I heard you the first time." She marched beside him, righteous anger wafting off her in hot waves. "I don't know why you have to be so—"

"Quiet." He put his arm out to stop her before she pushed through the doors that led into the Pits. A sudden cheer rose from behind them, and her eyebrows lifted. The place sounded packed, the crowd bloodthirsty. Chrysabelle bobbed her head, trying to see through the crack between the doors. He moved in front of her, catching her eyes. "How would a patron typically indicate his possession of a comarré?"

Her eyes narrowed. "Why?"

The back of his head throbbed. The voices laughed, taking delight in his pain. "Once we get inside, it needs to be very clear that you are not available."

She crossed her arms. "There's a ceremonial collar, but that's not going to help you now."

"What else?" *Bite her. Drink her. Drain her.*

Her mouth firmed into a hard narrow line.

"What?" Ramming his fist into the concrete wall would be less painful. "Tell me or I swear—"

"Your hand on the back of my neck." She swallowed like she'd just downed a mouthful of bad eggs.

"Your sword might get in the way of that."

She perked up, shrugging with an all too obvious joy. "You asked."

"Stay close." He grabbed her forearm, feeling the business end of one hidden blade.

"I know the drill."

He just hoped she'd follow it. Leading with his shoulder, he pushed through the double doors and into one of the many places he'd never intended to return.

The din swelled up around them, a fog of noise that blended into a cacophonous gray cushion between him and the voices. At least that was a plus. He kept to the wall, but the stadium setup meant the view was good at any angle, despite the shoulder-to-shoulder audience. The twenty-foot-wide pit currently held a fringe vamp and a remnant. Judging from the creature's six-clawed hands, horns and gold eyes, he was some sort of shadeux or smokesinger fae mixed with varcolai. The remnant lunged, driving the fringe back into the chains of iron and silver that ringed the arena. His cry of pain as the silver bit into his flesh barely registered above the crowd's noise. Mal's back burned in remembrance. Silver for vampires and varcolai, iron for fae. Both for remnants if their blood was unlucky.

"Ow," Chrysabelle said softly, prying at his fingers where his hand clasped her arm.

Her whisper filled his head, blanked out the memories that had nearly caused him to forget her presence.

"You're hurting me." She stared, peering into him like he'd suddenly become transparent.

Surrounded by the dirty concrete walls and hazy air, her eyes seemed bluer than he remembered. Her face more beautiful compared to the ugliness around them. He eased his grip. "I didn't mean to." He hadn't meant to come to a stop either, but they had.

"You fought here, I take it."

"Yes." What point was there in denying it? She'd heard what had been said in the club.

A fresh cheer went up from the crowd. Mal turned in time to see the remnant lift the bloody threads that had once been the fringe's throat, then the remains went to ash, trickling from the remnant's fingers.

The spectators turned to one another, exchanging congratulations and commiserations as bets were cashed in. A few glanced in the direction of Mal and Chrysabelle. Their eyes skimmed him to stop on her. One fringe deliberately inhaled. His eyes fluttered closed, then widened with hunger. His body tensed into a slight crouch.

Mal propelled Chrysabelle toward the door at the other end. "Go."

The fringe landed in front of them. "Haven't seen you around here in a long time, Malkolm."

Mal's hand slid beneath her hair to clasp the back of her neck, barely avoiding her sword. Heat radiated off it, prickling his skin. Her pulse jacked higher.

"Move, fringe." He couldn't come up with a name, but the Pits were always crowded. He couldn't be expected to know the name of every lowlife who'd ever seen him fight.

The fringe stayed put. "Looks like you've got yourself a pet." He tipped his head, smiled, and ran his tongue over his fangs. "What have we got here? A new flavor of comarré? Dominic's been holding out on us."

Three rows deep into the crowd all eyes were on them. "I said move. I won't say it again." Beneath his fingers, Chrysabelle's pulse smoothed out. His gut told him that was a signal. Of what, he didn't know.

He figured it out when her fingers brushed his knuckles on the way to her sword. He snagged her pinkie with his and brought her face around. "I will deal with this."

For a moment, her lips ground against each other in a thin line. "As you wish." Her hand slipped back to her side, but her eyes held deadly intent.

The fringe laughed softly and dug a wad of worn plastic bills from his pocket. "How much for a taste?"

The sudden urge to reassure Chrysabelle, to tell her everything would be all right, staggered Mal. The voices, barely audible over the din, moaned. This was not the time to contemplate the meaning of such thoughts. Keeping Chrysabelle on his right, he ignored the fringe and pushed past him.

"I asked you a question, Malkolm."

Some fringe didn't know when to give up. Mal kept Chrysabelle headed for the door. The air on his left shifted, telegraphing the fringe's move. Mal feinted to avoid the fist as it shot past, then grabbed the fringe's arm and snapped it cleanly.

The fringe howled. The crowd closed in around them. Damn. Maybe the holding cells would have been a better choice. Too late now. He held up his free hand, his other still securely fastened to Chrysabelle's neck and burning like fire from being so close to her blade. "Back up and let us through and no one gets ashed."

The crowd went still. A second later, familiar laughter broke the silence. Bodies parted and Katsumi, fringe vamp and former wife of a yakuza boss, strode through shaking her head. When she stood apart from the crowd, she stopped and smoothed the high-necked, long-sleeved black gown that hid a full body suit of tattoos. "Malkolm."

*"Ane-san."* Little sister, once a yakuza term of respect, now he used it to needle her. Back in the day, Katsumi had made mountains of yen off Mal's fights. So much so that she'd shared a portion of her take with him. Enough to keep his strength up. Enough to keep him fighting.

She clicked nine long crimson nails together, the pinkie on her left hand missing from the last knuckle, a yakuza ritual done to atone. For what, Mal didn't know. "Have you come back to fight?"

"No."

Her nails stopped. "You're sure? Not even one?"

"No."

"Pity. What then?"

"Not your business." He took his hand from Chrysabelle's neck to move in front of her. Katsumi was not known for delaying her gratification.

She smiled, mouth closed. "No, I suppose it isn't." Turning back into the crowd, she waved her pinkieless hand in the air as if stirring an already boiling pot. "Kill him then."

The roar deafened, the surge of bodies like a crashing wall of fangs and fists. A high, piercing cry cut through the bedlam. Chrysabelle. She leaped into position next to him, wielding her sword one-handed. Her other hand found his, pressed a bone dagger into his palm.

"Take it."

It stung, but he didn't argue. There would be time later, when the killing was done and Chrysabelle was safe.

The fringe with the broken arm came at them first, sneering at Chrysabelle. A distant look glazed her face. Like she'd detached. That could be very bad. She tossed her sword into the air, reversed her grip on the hilt as it came down, then rammed the blade into the fringe's heart. His sneer vanished into ash. Maybe detached was good. Depending on which side you were on.

She flipped her grip on the weapon again, this time waving the blade at the suddenly hesitant crowd. "Who's next?"

Mal eyed her with new appreciation. She hadn't flinched at killing the fringe. More than that, she'd done it with a steady hand and an unnerving grace. Maybe she deserved a little more credit for her training.

"No one is next." The words echoed in the new silence, reverberating threat and menace.

All eyes shifted upward to a private balcony that overlooked the arena. Dominic's hands gripped the glass rail, knuckles white. Mal had seen the tumultuous look on his face a few times before. It didn't bode well.

"You and you." Dominic's gaze pressed heavy on Mal and Chrysabelle. "My office, now." With a forced smile, he addressed the rest of the crowd. "Please accept my apologies for this incident. Your accounts have all been credited with a thousand dollars in additional funds."

A new cheer arose, and the double doors opened, ushering in a slew of servers carrying trays laden with pints of blood, shots of alcohol, and tabs of the various alchemical drugs Dominic made his living from. Chrysabelle blew the remaining ash off her sword before returning it to its scabbard.

Mal glanced at Dominic. Dominic stared back. Hard. Chrysabelle grabbed Mal's arm, turning her face away from Dominic and keeping her voice low. Her eyes held none of the distance they had when she'd pinned the fringe. "Am I in trouble?"

The question disarmed Mal. An instant ago she'd been an avenging angel blithely decimating her attacker, now her brows bent in uncertainty, yet he sensed no duplicity in her. He shook his head. "Dominic can't hurt you."

Mal wouldn't let him. As much as Chrysabelle had disrupted Mal's life, as much as he wanted to be rid of her, he wouldn't let Dominic prostitute her like the rest of his homemade comarré. Chrysabelle was too good for that. What else might become of her, Mal couldn't say. He handed her the bone dagger. "Sheath that and follow me."

The blade vanished up her sleeve. "I told you I could protect myself."

He nodded, feeling the weight of truth upon him like a blanket of fresh snow, cold and clean. "So you did." Now was not the time to explain that stabbing a wounded fringe in no way compared to taking on a full-powered noble vampire with a few hundred years of age on him.

She'd find that out for herself when they walked into Dominic's office.

# Chapter Twenty-three

On the inside, Chrysabelle's nerves buzzed against her skin like a swarm of bees trying to escape a burning hive. She'd killed fringe before, but always in practice sessions, never in a situation where her life was clearly in danger. The feelings unsettled her—she was at once proud of her ability to protect herself so well and yet stunned by how easily she'd ended a life. She'd never felt that way in training, but maybe the steps she'd been taking away from her comarré life were changing her in more ways than she was aware.

She shook off the strangeness as best she could. Time to focus on getting Dominic's help, something that might be a little harder now that she'd offed one of his customers.

Beside her, Mal walked with purpose. He knew where he was going because he'd been here before. Been in those Pits before. She cringed inwardly. The idea of him there made an unused part of her ache. She glanced at Mal. His eyes stayed straight ahead. "I'm guessing it doesn't always end in death."

"What doesn't?" He turned, obviously caught off guard.

"What happens in the Pits."

"No. Death, a draw, or one combatant admits defeat."

Or, she was guessing, one combatant kept the other alive so he could be defeated and humiliated repeatedly. "Did you ever beat Ronan?"

A brief silence. "No."

"You could now."

He stopped, narrowing his eyes, then turned, and for a moment she thought he was going to argue. Instead, he pushed his hand against the wall behind him. A door opened under the pressure of his touch.

"After you."

She went through, bracing herself. Dominic had not reacted well to what she'd done to one of his paying customers. No telling what he would do in the privacy of his office. The door only led to another passage and, farther down, another door. Just as she was about to question Mal, the door swung open.

Dominic glared at them, moving aside enough to allow them entrance. He wore his true face like a king wore a crown. How he must despise Mal for being another displaced noble, a possible usurper to his throne. To the fringe, they were equally grand.

Another thought occurred. Had Dominic had a hand in Mal's subjugation? Certainly Dominic and his harem of fake comarré could have supplied Mal with an endless supply of human blood. Why hadn't he?

Head full of new suspicions, she stared back as she made her way forward, glad for Mal's presence at her back. Dominic said nothing as she brushed past. Leather and silk upholstery decorated the expanse beyond him, mixing with marble floors and honey wood-paneled walls. Near the right-hand wall and diagonal to a set of gilded French doors—presumably the ones that led to the balcony over the Pits—an antique Renaissance-style desk held court, its slick marble surface like vanilla ice cream swirled with caramel. Behind it, a chair of thronelike proportions. She took a seat in one of the burgundy silk armchairs opposite the desk, adjusting her sacre so its point canted to the side.

Mal was not yet seated when Dominic slammed the door and twisted to face them. The menace in his eyes lifted the small hairs on the back of her neck.

"*Porca vacca!* How *dare* you come into my home and execute—"

Mal snarled, body tensing. "We were attacked in your home—"

"None of that matters." Chrysabelle leaped to her feet. "They've taken—"

"Of course it matters," Dominic raged, approaching them. "My word is law, and you've broken that law. Brought weapons into my club—"

"They've taken Maris." Chrysabelle waited a moment for that news to sink in. "Do you still think a dead fringe matters?"

Dominic's mouth hung open midsentence, and he paled, an incredible feat for a vampire who'd not seen the sun in his many years. "When?"

"A few hours ago. Velimai showed us. It was a vampire named Tatiana and one other noble, Mikkel."

He stumbled toward the desk, groping for the tall chair behind it like he'd suddenly lost his sight. Collapsing onto the stocky gilt frame, he stared vacantly at the space behind Chrysabelle, finally blinking and returning his gaze to her. "Why didn't you come sooner?"

His accusatory tone set her nerves on edge. "We came as soon as we could."

Beside her, Mal sprawled in the seat like he hadn't a care in the world. "Your staff did their best to keep us from getting here at all."

Dominic, face now wiped of all trace of shock, lifted one brow. "As well they should, considering what I pay them."

Chrysabelle wanted to smack the pompousness out of his voice. How dare he act so cavalier when her aunt's life was at stake?

Mal tugged her hand, motioning for her to sit. "We found the remains of two fringe and a Nothos on the perimeter."

"The fringe were mine. I sent them to protect her."

"They did a wretched job of it," Chrysabelle said, settling into the chair and adjusting her sacre again.

Dominic steepled his fingers. "They took down a Nothos. Not an easy task."

She blew out through her nostrils. "My aunt is still gone."

He peered over his hands. "What else do you know that might be of use?"

"Tatiana is House of Tepes. The vampire with her was Bathory. He tried to use black magic on Velimai, but without an invitation his power couldn't penetrate the house."

"How did Tatiana get in?"

Chrysabelle shook her head. "Apparently, she can mimic appearances."

Dominic's brow wrinkled. "No vampire has that power."

"Think harder." Chrysabelle stroked the silk covering the chair's padded arm. The burgundy fabric was shot through with green and gold. "Higher up." She lifted her face then so she could watch his.

His eyes widened for the briefest of moments. "You think she's aligned herself with . . . she wouldn't."

"To get the power she wants? Of course she would. You don't know her like I do."

Dominic flexed his hands into fists, then gripped the arms of his chair. "This is your fault. If not for you and that ring—"

"This is not her fault." Suddenly, Mal's casual sprawl took on a predatory tension. He bent his head, gaze arrowed in on Dominic. "She could not have predicted what has happened. If you're not going to help, say so. The sun will be up any minute."

Dominic laughed with the prickly air of superiority. "The sun's been up for half an hour. I pump certain *things* into the air system to suppress the internal clock."

"Vampires don't breathe," Mal said.

"It gets in through the skin." Dominic looked at Chrysabelle. "Why not just give Tatiana this ring?"

"That's the plan right now. Although . . ."

Mal nodded. "Tell him."

"Tatiana wants to break the covenant. If this ring has anything to do with that . . ." Chrysabelle shook her head. "I don't want to stand idly by and let her have her way either."

If the news shocked Dominic, he didn't show it. "She won't break the covenant." He threw his hands up. "*Maronna*, the chaos it would unleash."

"She will, and you're an idiot if you think otherwise." Chrysabelle rose and paced to the French doors. Anger flooded her veins, tightened her jaw and neck and shoulders. She forced a modicum of calm into her body before speaking again. "We're wasting time. Maris is out there and needs our help."

Dominic stood, shoving the ornate throne back across the floor with a loud scrape. Mal tensed, but Dominic's attention belonged to Chrysabelle. "You will not talk to me that way."

Mal unfolded to a standing position and slowly rolled his shoulders, a move that held a remarkable amount of menace. "She'll talk to you any damn way she pleases. She knows these nobles and what they're capable of better than either one of us. Are you going to help or not?"

Dominic pressed a button on his desk and spoke into a receiver. "Send Mortalis in." Then he answered Mal. "I will help in whatever way I can. Your comarré may not know this, but I loved her aunt very much. For Marissa I willingly turned my back on the House of St. Germain and became anathema, leaving with her after she won libertas."

Chrysabelle saw Dominic with new eyes. "You're the one Maris went through libertas for?"

"Yes. I nursed her back to health, made money whatever way I could to provide for her. I did what I had to do, because I loved her. I still do."

Chrysabelle snorted. "You've got a strange way of showing it."

Dominic's gaze steeled. "*Ogni moneta ha due facce.* Every coin has two faces. Perhaps you should ask your aunt what happened between us before you judge me."

"I'll do that. If I ever see her again."

A knock sounded, but not in the direction of the door they'd come through.

"Come," Dominic called.

From the opposite side of the room, a new door opened. Mortalis strolled through and stopped beside Dominic's desk. He nodded at Mal, then gave his attention over to Dominic.

"Two noble vampires kidnapped Maris. They may have Nothos with them; we know they had at least one. We need to find them and get Maris back."

"I'll start with the known safe houses, work from there." An unsettling smile broke over Mortalis's face. He stroked one horn. "A Nothos, eh? Now that's the kind of fight I like."

What did Dominic have on the shadeux to get him to obey so readily? Chrysabelle looped her fingers through the sacre's strap. "I thought you said the sun was up?"

"It is," Dominic said.

She tipped her chin at Mortalis. "Then what good is he?"

Mortalis strummed his fingers over the hilt of a black-handled blade tucked into his belt. "The common belief that shadeux cannot abide sunlight is false. We cannot be *seen* when the sun rules the sky, but we may certainly travel beneath its rays." His six fingers stopped strumming and gripped the hilt. "You'd be wise to keep that knowledge to yourself."

She filed the nugget of info away. "You don't scare me, shadeux. You don't instill trust in me either. I'm going with you."

Mal grabbed her arm. "No, you're not. That's exactly what these vampires want is to draw you out. You'll stay here until Mortalis gets back. Based on what he finds, we'll reassess."

Dominic kept quiet, but Mortalis laughed softly. "Well done, vampire. You may learn to control her yet."

She opened her mouth, but Mal spun her around to face him before she could respond to the fae. She glared at Mal. "My aunt needs me."

"She needs you alive." Something in his eyes and the tone of his voice softened her temper. But that was foolish, wasn't it? That look in his eyes was nothing more than the need for sleep, exacerbated by the sun's rise and too little rest over the past few days. One draught of her blood did not a whole vampire make. Nor, without question, had it created any sort of empathy in him for her.

She jerked her arm away. "Fine." She looked at Dominic. "I want a report the instant he gets back."

Mortalis ignored her and spoke to Dominic. "I will return as soon as I can."

As the shadeux left, Dominic came around from behind the desk. "You might as well sleep until he returns, Malkolm. There is nothing else you can do. Come. I have a room you may use. It's safe. We're several stories underground on this level."

"Fine." Mal held out his arm, indicating Chrysabelle should go ahead of him. So lack of sleep made him more human? Or was he putting on a show for Dominic?

They followed Dominic out of the office by the door through which Mortalis had entered, then down a long hall. Finally, Dominic stopped at a door near the middle of the corridor. He twisted a brass key in the lock, then opened the door. "I'll let you know as soon as Mortalis has returned. Chrysabelle, I'll have food brought up for you shortly."

She crossed her arms. "I'm not staying in there with him."

Already inside, Mal looked around the room but not back at her. "Yes, you are. It's not safe for you in the club alone."

Dominic nodded. "He's right. It might not be safe for my guests either." He glanced at the red strap crossing her chest. "That's Marissa's sacre, is it not?"

"Yes," Chrysabelle whispered. What memories swirled in that brain of his?

If his eyes seemed oddly liquid, it was only for a moment. "I will find her and I will punish those responsible for taking her. Marissa earned her freedom once. She will not do it alone again." He tipped his head toward the door. "In. Please, *cara mia*."

"I'm not Maris. Your pretty words mean nothing to me." She curled her lip at him as she reluctantly stepped over the threshold. "If he eats me, it's on your head."

Dominic pursed his lips. "My head? His skin, you mean." Dominic winked and shut the door firmly. A second later, a small snick followed.

Chrysabelle tried the knob. "He locked us in. That pompous old—"

"What did you expect? You snuffed one of his patrons." Mal's voice held a shade of humor.

She whirled. "Are you serious? You think he locked us in because of me? You're the one they all want to fight. I was protecting you."

"Protecting me?" The humor disappeared. "Bloody hell. You're not just annoying, you're also delusional." He threw his hands up and walked away to sit on the king-size four-poster bed. He bounced a few times, testing the mattress, then pushed back, swung his legs up, and lay down. He crossed his arms behind his head and closed his eyes. "I'm not one of those vampires that sleeps like I'm dead."

"And I care how you sleep because?"

He opened one eye. "Because I tend to wake up in attack mode."

"Whatever." She shivered, clasping her wrists to feel the blades secured there. "Just so you don't wake up hungry."

Both eyes stayed shut. "I always wake up hungry."

# Chapter Twenty-four

A flicker of sensation darted through the blackness cradling Tatiana. She shifted, and it was gone.

Another flicker. Stronger. Pounding. A voice. "Mistress."

She struggled to shed the coma of daysleep, but it clamped down on her like a drug. She waded through the thick morass masquerading as her brain and found enough energy to mumble, "What?"

Then the stench of brimstone hit her.

The Nothos.

"Shall I return later?"

"No." With new determination, she fought through the fog and pulled herself upright. The wall clock showed she'd been down barely two hours. Not enough, but it would have to do. Grabbing the headboard, she lurched to her feet. Mikkel remained motionless, as deep in daysleep as a corpse in death. She stumbled toward the door until she leaned against it, fighting the urge to close her eyes.

"What is it?" Bloodlust cramped her muscles. The kine last night had done little to assuage the heightened thirst that had accompanied her new power. She should have brought her comar along, but the fewer who knew of this trip, the better.

"Mistress, I have the remnant."

"Is the plane secure?" She snatched her robe and hastily tied it on. Not the best attire for what was sure to be another bloody interrogation, but this shouldn't take long.

"Yes."

Tatiana retrieved a set of earplugs and fitted them in before easing the door open. The Nothos stood in the center of the cabin, slightly bent to keep its head from touching the ceiling. The dim lighting made a cartoon of its grotesque form. The remnant dangled from its fist, her six-fingered hands secured at the wrists with iron shackles to bind her powers. Suddenly, Tatiana felt very awake. She pulled the earplugs free.

"Drop her and strip her silver."

The Nothos released her and the girl collapsed in a heap upon the carpet. It reached down, hooked its claws beneath the glittering chains skirting her neck, and yanked the links free. Wisps of smoke trailed off its skin. It growled softly but kept on until the remnant's ears, wrists, fingers, and navel were decontaminated. Lastly, it removed the two etched bands circling the ends of her horns. After depositing the offensive metal into a bin, the Nothos bowed slightly, lacerated palms up, then walked backward until it exited the plane.

Tatiana fought the urge to smile. This would be most enjoyable. She bent over the tangle of blue-gray skin and lean muscle cowering on the floor and traced a finger down one of the girl's slim horns. Blood welled from the scratches and tears in the hybrid's skin where the silver had once been. Fresh need clawed Tatiana's throat, but she'd never stooped to feed from a remnant before, and she was not about to start.

She rapped a nail against the horn. A circle of tarnish shadowed where the silver adornment had sat. The girl's gaze was empty of emotion. Almost dead. "You do not fear me?"

The girl's eyes narrowed, but she said nothing. Her fingers moved, fluttering against each other like dying moths.

"Ah yes, that's right. You're a mute, aren't you?" Tatiana sighed. "You mongrels are such a bother. Yes or no questions it is."

She seized the girl by the horn and jerked her up until her feet came off the carpet. Tatiana's robe ruffled against her legs with the sudden movement. "Lie to me, and I'll kill you. Understood?"

The remnant stayed still. Perhaps she realized Tatiana planned to kill her anyway.

"Very well. Let's begin, shall we?" Tatiana tossed her into one of the seats bordering the cabin and brushed her hands off. "I'm looking for a rogue comarré and the vampire that's helping her. Have you seen—"

"Mistress!" The Nothos's voice screeched like a bird of prey's. It bounded back into the cabin. "We have company."

"So deal with it."

"Yes, mist—" A silver dagger lodged in its windpipe. Blood and smoke leaked from the edges of the Nothos's stretched mouth. It yanked the blade free, then gargled, "Shadeux," before leaping out of the cabin.

*Shadeux fae.* Tatiana rushed to the door. The Nothos grappled with an unseen force, its head snapping back, its punches finding only air. Bloody bollocks. She reached to shut the door, then thought again. She needed more than a

closed door to slow the intruder down. Scooping up the
discarded silver blade, she ignored its searing heat, hauled
the remnant up by her hair, and plunged the weapon into
the girl's chest. The remnant jerked, her mouth gaping in
a silent cry of pain.

"Here, shadeux!" Tatiana held the girl in front of the
open door. "Come get what you came for." She shoved the
girl down the stairs, then slammed the door and locked it.
Clenching her stinging fist, she ran back to the bedroom.

"Mikkel, get up." She tore the covers from his body
and slapped him. "Wake up."

He mumbled something unintelligible.

Sluggard. "Wake *up*. We've got to get out of here. Now."

"Um-hmm..." He rolled over.

She grabbed his ankle and whipped his nude body off
the mattress. His head smacked the floor with a hard
thunk.

He curled upright, clutching his head. "What the hell?"

"There's a shadeux fae in the hangar. The Nothos is
probably dead or about to be. Get in the cockpit now or I
will tear your arms off and beat you to a pulp with them."

Mikkel rose to his feet, grabbed his discarded leather
pants, and tugged them on. "Is the hangar door open?"

"No, you'll have to drive through it."

"I can't drive through it." His exasperated tone grated
on her already fraying nerves. "Not if you want the plane
to still be airworthy."

She planted her hands on her hips. "Then I suggest you
get out there and open it."

He smiled like he'd just won a prize. "I don't need to,
my sweet. I can do that from right here." He thrust out one
hand and a ball of black fire danced over his palm.

The tension drained out of her, and she smiled back. At last something was going her way. Mikkel really was worth his weight in blood. She leaned in and planted a quick kiss on his mouth. "Then let's get out of here, darling."

His hands cupped her backside. "What about the old bag?"

"She's coming back with us." Tatiana nipped his bottom lip, piercing the tender skin. "Once her niece returns to Corvinestri to save her aunt, I'll have the blood whore seized and put on trial." She sucked at the wound. "I will be Elder before the blood dries on the executioner's sword."

Chrysabelle stood at the bedside, staring down at Mal. After two hours of examining the suite, she'd finally given in to her curiosity. There was nothing else as interesting in the room anyway. His claims of not sleeping like he was dead seemed a bit overreaching. He looked exactly like every sleeping vampire she'd ever seen. Not that those numbers were so high. Vampires typically slept under pretty heavy security, considering the near paralysis daysleep put them in.

She pursed her mouth. He didn't truly look *exactly* like every sleeping vampire she'd ever seen. He looked nothing like Algernon, who'd been turned well into his later years and bore the according lines and touches of gray.

No, Mal had been turned at the prime of his manhood. Not a strand of silver tarnished the rich black of his hair, not a wrinkle cracked his treacherously handsome face. His sizable frame wore the thick muscle of a body used to physical labor. Certainly used to guiding a heavy sword through flesh and bone. He must have been something to behold as a human, because the beauty that suffused all vampires at their turning had outdone itself with him.

If the serpent in the garden had looked anything like Mal, Eve's sin would have been far worse than devouring a single apple.

Chrysabelle's index finger traced the line of her lower lip. She bent closer to study the mouth that had kissed her and inhaled. Her eyes closed involuntarily. His dark spice whispered promises to her blood, awakening the need she'd worked so hard to temper.

*Thump, thump, thump.* Her pulse sang in her ears, a demanding anthem all comarré knew. The desire to feed the vampire who claimed her was inborn, but the personal cost of feeding this one outweighed the intrinsic urge. He was *not* the proper, austere vampire that Algernon had been. Mal didn't care about rules and propriety. He would not—could not—simply drink from her as if she were nothing more than a vessel. She doubted he would ever be satisfied with taking from the wrist as was the custom with most patrons. No, Mal would want much more intimate access than that.

A cold realization straightened her. He would take and take until he killed her. Or worse, until he possessed her mind, body, and soul. Parts of her had already begun to weaken. Why had she never felt this way about Algernon? Shoring her defenses against Mal had become an hourly job.

And yet, she must sustain him until her life was freely hers again. How long would that take? How long could she keep herself from wanting more? How long before she fell completely into his darkness? Was this how Maris had felt for Dominic?

Already the veins in her wrists grew fat and ripe, the

blood thickening with an intoxicating yearning to be spilled. Mal was not the only one with demons.

*Oh holy mother, protect me from this creature. Bind my heart in ice. Numb my body. I cannot walk my aunt's path. Please.*

A knock came at the door and she jumped, yelping like a startled child. Mal didn't move. She flattened a hand over her heart, willing it to slow as she moved away from the bed. The door opened, and a male remnant, hybrid indiscernible, entered carrying a tray laden with covered dishes, a large bottle of water, and a goblet. Behind him, Ronan stood in the hall, arms crossed. He raised his brows over eyes hot with messages she had no desire to read.

"Shouldn't you be sleeping?" She glared back with as much frost as she could manage. How dare that fringe think himself worthy of her? How dare he think himself better than Mal? Her sacre and wrist sheaths, slung over one of the dining chairs, seemed miles away.

Ronan nodded toward the bed. "You mean like lover boy there?" He laughed. "What a knacker." His gaze slipped south of her face. "Sleeping's the last thing I'd be doing with a fancy piece like you in the room."

A wanton thrill zipped through her belly, but it was not lust for Ronan she felt. "You're right about that. You'd be too busy dying to sleep."

His gaze snapped back to her face, some of the previous fire snuffed out. "You need to learn your place."

She walked toward him a few steps, unwilling to quench the angry heat nipping at her spine. "You mean like those pretenders in the club? I am as different from them as Malkolm is from you, fringe. He and I are superior creatures, not poorly crafted copies or inferior kin."

"He is anathema." Ronan spat the word like a curse.

"And yet he is still your better." Anathema or not, Mal was still noble.

Ronan's upper lip curled, showing his fangs.

She laughed softly. "Fangs neither impress nor scare me. Noble vampires are capable of a great many things far more terrible than a simple show of teeth."

Behind her, the remnant who'd brought in the tray cleared his throat. She moved to let him pass, then with a condescending smile closed the door on Ronan. The lock clicked a second after. Her shoulders slumped, and she exhaled through her mouth as the tension in her body melted. That exchange had served no purpose but to antagonize a fringe who already hated Mal, so why had she done it? With a sickening realization, she knew the answer. Because she'd begun to consider Mal's enemies as her own. The feeling was a symptom of the protectiveness a comarré felt for her patron. Although she'd never felt it that strongly for Algernon.

Foolishness best forgotten.

She tipped her head back to stare at the coffered ceiling. Hard to believe they were underground, but she'd pulled the curtains back from the tall windows. Nothing but brick on the other side. This suite, for all its rich appointments, was nothing more than a glorified cell.

The scent of meat reached her nose, and her stomach growled. She hurried to the table and removed the silver dome from the first plate. Her mouth watered. Pale red juices pooled around a thick porterhouse. A snowy mound of truffle-flecked mashed potatoes and a lattice of slim haricots verts accompanied the steak. She flicked her napkin open, settled it onto her lap, then lifted her knife and fork to the task.

"Something smells good."

For the second time in just a few minutes, she jumped. Her knees bumped the table, clattering dishes and glassware. Composing herself, she glanced toward the bed.

Mal lay propped on his side, still wearing his true face. Eyeing her much as she imagined she'd just stared down the slab of beef on her plate.

"How long have you been awake?" Concentrating on her food, she pierced the steak with her fork then cut a piece. The meat was so tender the knife was hardly required. She bit down, juice oozing over her tongue. The muscles in her cheek tightened in savory pleasure. Was this what Mal had felt the first time he'd tasted her?

"Long enough."

She swallowed and used her fork to trench a valley in her mashed potatoes. Being watched greatly diminished her appetite. For food. "If I woke you, I apologize. I shouldn't have said anything to Ronan—"

"Don't apologize for that. Listening to Ronan get his back teeth handed to him by a woman he considers a gourmet meal made my year."

Her fork stilled. So he had heard that much. "Do you think of me that way as well?"

He didn't answer for a long moment. Finally, she looked at him. The bright light of hunger flared in his eyes like a platinum beacon. She turned back to her plate. Disappointment she had no right to feel clogged her throat. "Evidently, you do."

"Don't." Need thickened his voice.

"Don't what? Don't state the obvious?"

"Don't judge me for what I cannot control."

At the edge of her peripheral vision, she caught his

movement as he sat up. Warmth spread in her veins. She almost laughed at her traitorous body.

He bent his head into his hands. It looked like he was squeezing his temples. "I don't think of you as food, but..."

She put her fork down to watch him. "But if you lost control—"

"I'd kill you. The voices are begging me to do it now." He lifted his head, still cradled in his hands. "You're wrong, you know. I'm not superior to Ronan."

"Of course you are. You're nobility." Perhaps reminding him of that would—

"You think that means jack to me?" He scowled and slid off the bed to pace to the far side of the suite. "I'm a monster. The sooner you get that, the better."

So much for the reminder. The thrumming of her pulse once again filled her ears. "You don't have to be a monster."

He spun and stalked back toward her. "My curse says otherwise."

"You're hungry." It was like another part of her had spoken those words. Almost cooed them. And laced them with the clear intent of where his sustenance should come from. Holy mother, she was doomed.

He stopped. Took a step toward the door. "Dominic has resources."

Need pushed her to her feet. "And let it be known that we are not patron and comarré in truth? You said yourself I was safer if the others believed—"

"I know what I said." But he stayed the same distance from the door.

She rolled her sleeve up, revealing a few inches of gold vines and star-shaped flowers. "I need to drain this blood anyway. And you need the strength."

"No." He shook his head but his gaze was fixed on her wrist and the shadowy blue lines beneath the gold.

Her thumb skipped over the tiny switch on her ring with a nervous tremor. Opening a vein in front of a hungry, erratic vampire wasn't the wisest thing, no matter what her body felt like doing. "Then I'll just go into the bathroom and drain off the excess into the sink."

Her foot hadn't touched the floor after her first step when he responded. "Don't." He glanced away, swallowing hard, jaw working like he already had her between his teeth. "I'll drink it." He shot her a hard, silvered look. "From the glass."

Nodding, she reached for the goblet, wrapping her fingers around the chilled glass. She rolled it in her palms to warm it. "I'll be right back."

She strode past him and into the marble and porcelain bath, then shut the door behind her. The glossy-painted wood cooled her fevered skin as she leaned back. This was what she wanted, wasn't it? Without her blood, Mal wouldn't be strong enough to do the job she needed him for. And if things went well these next few days, she'd never have to see him again. If she could ignore the fact that she technically owned her blood rights.

Setting the goblet onto the counter, she then positioned her wrist over it. Just a few more days. She flipped open the hidden blade in her ring. Two, maybe three more drainings at best.

The blade pricked her skin like a tiny fang. Except it wasn't a fang. And no fangs meant she'd have to endure another kiss or grow weaker, something she couldn't risk until her aunt was safe and her life was her own again.

Another kiss. His mouth on hers.

The tremor returned to her hand.

# Chapter Twenty-five

*D*rainherkillherdrainherkill—

Mal grabbed the sheathed blade of Chrysabelle's sword. Searing heat snarled through the leather and bit his palm, snuffing the voices out like wet fingers on a wick. He released the blade, flexing his stinging hand. Since he'd woken, the voices had pounded his skull. The hunger whipped them into a frenzy. But so did being near Chrysabelle.

And lately, he'd been very near her. Filled with her scent, wary of every shift of her body, every flash of golden light that glinted off her skin and the glow that surrounded her like sunlight. He closed his eyes and rolled his head from side to side, trying to listen to the subtle movement of his bones instead of her heartbeat, but it was still there. Always there. Even now he could hear the ethereal softening of her pulse as she bled herself into the goblet.

Drinking her was only going to make things worse.

*Not if you drink her to death.*

His teeth ached, but not as much as other parts of him. He was a fool to pretend he didn't want her. But a bigger fool to pretend he could have her. That she would want him back. When this was over, she'd be gone. *Good.* That's what he wanted. What he'd told her he required if she wanted his help. Alone was what he was most used to anyway. *What you deserve.* It was the easiest. The safest.

The scent of blood overwhelmed his senses. The goblet must be nearly full by now. He swallowed the saliva pooling under his tongue.

No wonder she thought he viewed her as food. The beast inside him definitely did, but not the tattered remains of the man he'd once been. That infinitesimal part of him recognized her for the woman she was, and then reminded him he'd never been the kind of man any decent woman wanted. This time, the only voice in his head was his own. *Not then, not now.*

He shook his head in disgust. Thoughts like that were a disservice to his beautiful Shaya's memory, rest her soul. She had been a decent woman. *Whore. Thief. Cheat.* He squeezed his lids together, desperate to ignore the voices. No, she hadn't been a decent woman by society's standards, or they wouldn't have put her on the gallows.

Chrysabelle was a very different woman from Shaya, that much was certain. So different, that deep in that charred, grizzled place that had once held his heart, a speck of longing had taken hold. A hope so small, he refused to acknowledge it. *You don't deserve hope.* Why should he? Wasn't there enough pain in his life? *No.*

"Mal?"

He whirled, caught off guard for a rare moment. "What? I wasn't—" The blood scent hit him hard, tightening his body with white-hot need. The voices leveled to a soft whine.

Chrysabelle stood waiting, goblet in hand. Two punctures marked her wrist. She'd purposefully pierced herself to make it look like he'd done it.

"I called you twice." She met his eyes as she raised the goblet, peering at him like he'd become someone else. "It's going to get cold if you don't…" She shrugged and reached to set it down on the table.

He took it from her, brushing his cold fingertips over her warm ones. The brief contact magnified the cravings already echoing through him. He steeled himself against the need. "Thank you."

Her brows lifted, but she said nothing. Was it such a surprise that he could show gratitude? Perhaps it was. Let it be. The shock was good for her. She shouldn't grow comfortable around him. That way led to danger.

He lifted the glass to his lips, then stopped and stared back. "Do you like watching?"

"What? No." She turned away, but not before the skin on her gilded cheeks colored.

He hadn't expected her to be shy about this, of all things, and as proof of his depravity, needling her gave him pleasure. She wanted him to drink. She could bear a little suffering for it. Especially since he seemed to be the only one of them struggling with this strange partnership. "You can if you want."

"I don't." She walked to the bed. Her hands smoothed the bed linens where he'd rested.

"Why not?" Even in Doc's big shirt, the lean, feminine lines of her body were pleasing. Not that Mal cared.

"Because." She fluffed the pillow.

"That's not an answer." The warmth seeped through the glass into his hand. Her warmth. He groaned inwardly.

For a moment, he forgot which one of them he was torturing.

"I don't want to. That's all." She stood by the bed, eyes focused on anything but him.

"You should." He brought the goblet to his nose and inhaled. This time, he couldn't muzzle the groan. The rattling in his head grew louder.

"Why?" That got her to face him. Her jaw was set in a stoniness matched only by her eyes. "For what purpose?"

"You should know what you do to me." If he wasn't already on a slow train to hell, that certainly guaranteed his ticket.

"I know very well what *my blood* does to you." She rolled her eyes and had the audacity to look amused. "Now drink. The flirting isn't getting you anywhere."

"Flirting? Is that what you think I'm doing? Not bloody likely." He hadn't flirted with anyone since he'd given up the vein, and he wasn't about to start with a woman who'd stated more than once her willingness to kill him. Annoyed, he knocked the glass back, downing the contents in several rapid swallows.

The power of her blood slammed into him like a fist.

Arcing pain shot from joint to joint, flaring through his muscles. He ground his teeth to keep from vocalizing, but the sheer volume of agony doubled him. He went to his knees. The glass slipped from his grasp, spraying red droplets over the Persian carpet. By the time the goblet had stopped rolling, the pain that had come so fast had disappeared. A new clarity invaded him, filling him with invigorating strength. His head cleared of all but his own incredulous thoughts. The voices vanished, buried beneath the rarest of all sounds—the beating of his heart.

Sweat cooled the back of his neck. He lifted his head. Chrysabelle stood directly in front of him, arms crossed, and smirking.

"Feeling better?" she asked.

He pressed his hand to his chest. "It's beating. I can't get used to that."

"Here." She handed him the bottle of water off the tray.

"I don't need that." Life, real life, coursed through him.

"Yes, you do. You have to kiss me, and you just downed a glassful of blood. My blood, but still. That might work for you, but I don't particularly want to taste it." She pushed the bottle closer. "Drink."

"It didn't bother you the first time." He jumped to his feet. Maybe it was the hot rush of blood, the new burst of energy or the beautiful woman in front of him, but suddenly, kissing her didn't seem like such an awful thing to suffer through. He'd been angry the first time. Unsure of himself and the way her blood had affected him. This time, he wasn't angry. If kissing her was the price he had to pay for feeling this strong and this powerful, so be it.

"It didn't occur to me the first time."

He took the bottle, wrenched off the cap, and drank. He swallowed with gusto and held out his arms. "Happy?"

"Not particularly, no." In fact, she looked downright terrified. "Just get it over with."

"Now who's flirting?" He tossed the bottle aside and reached for her. The honeyed perfume that surrounded her enveloped him with a fresh wave of intoxication. His hands fit to her waist like they'd been there a thousand times before.

Tentatively, her hands found his arms, resting on his

biceps. Keeping him at bay. Without any real effort, he assumed his human face and retracted his fangs. "Better?"

"Just do it, please."

He bent his head and brushed his mouth across hers with a gentleness he hoped would forgive the first time he'd done this to her. Her lips parted under his press, and he tasted the same warm sweetness he'd just drunk, but purer. He lifted one hand to her neck, threading his fingers into her hair and grazing his thumb across the pulse that trembled beneath her ear. The skin there was so warm and soft he had to fight to keep his fangs retracted.

Her grip tightened on his arms. Her head tilted a little farther back.

And then a sharp realization pierced him. She wasn't food. She was *life*. Brilliant and sparkling and powerful. No one had ever made him feel—

The door swung open. At the noise, she pushed away and scrambled for her weapons. Her cheeks flushed and she bent her head, swinging her hair down to hide her face as she strapped the blades on.

Ronan stood in the open door, leering at Chrysabelle like the bloody fool he was. He laughed rudely. "Looks like you're not so superior after all, princess. At least Dominic's whores get paid."

Mal took a step toward the whelp as Chrysabelle twisted toward him in a blur of white and gold. Something shot from her hand. Ronan howled, grabbing at his suddenly bloody shoulder. A bone dagger protruded from it, sending up wisps of smoke.

Mal looked at her in amazement. "I barely saw you move."

She shrugged. "It's the kiss. I'm always fastest after a

fresh infusion of power. Not usually that fast, but you're a lot stronger than Algernon was. He never had the benefit of his drained sire's powers."

Oh good. At least he had that going for him.

She walked to Ronan, yanked the blade out of his body, and wiped it on his shirt. "Was there a reason you barged in without knocking?"

"You little whore." He reared back, fist raised.

She punched him where the dagger had been. Dropping his hand, he groaned and staggered back, smacking into the door. "Answer me, or it's Malkolm's turn to take a shot."

Now that sounded like fun.

Angry vapors wafted off Ronan, but a quick glance at Mal kept him from reacting further. His lips curled back in an evil sneer. "Mortalis is back. Your aunt's ticket's been punched."

"Where is she?" Chrysabelle shoved through Dominic's office door. He and Mortalis were bent over a small figure on the couch. The Asian woman from the Pits slouched in Dominic's desk chair. Chrysabelle's stomach roiled with panic. "What happened? Is she okay?"

The vampire and the fae moved to face her, giving her a clear look at the blood-covered figure. She stopped dead and released the breath she'd been holding. "That's not my aunt."

"That's Nyssa," Mal said behind her.

"Is she going to be okay? I know that name. Who is she?"

"She's a runner for Jonas Sweets. And she should be fine."

Jonas was the guy Maris had contacted. A numbing chill settled into her belly. Had they already broken Maris? "He's the guy who sent me to you."

"Yes," Mal answered.

Mortalis turned back to Nyssa, but Dominic approached Chrysabelle. She started in before he could speak. "Ronan said Maris's ticket had been punched. What did he mean? Where is she? What's going on?"

Dominic held his hands up. "Ronan is a heartless fool."

"There's a lot of that going around," the Asian woman said. She twirled a jeweled letter opener in her fingers.

"Katsumi." The warning in Dominic's voice matched the flicker of silver in his eyes. "Mortalis trailed a Nothos back to an abandoned hangar in one of the old private airports. There was a plane parked inside, evidence of two human kills, and the heavy scent of comarré blood. Before he killed the Nothos, he saw two noble vampires, one male, one female. The male used black magic."

Mortalis lifted his head from Nyssa's side. "The female is the one who hurt Nyssa."

"Mikkel and Tatiana." Red edged her vision. If they'd harmed her aunt in any way, she was going to kill them both. Maybe stake them to a field of sacred ground and wait for the sun to come up. "What are we waiting for? You must have a sun-proof vehicle. How long will it take to get to the hangar?"

"We're not going to the hangar."

"What? Why?"

"The plane took off. They're headed back to Corvinestri."

She stepped back, shaking her head. "They're going to kill her."

Mal's hand settled on her shoulder. "Not if we kill them first."

Dominic nodded. "We need a plan. We can't just stampede in and hope for the best."

Chrysabelle sank into the nearest chair. She leaned back and blinked hard to clear the tears threatening to spill. The sacre pressed into her spine. Maris's blade. Chrysabelle swallowed. What defense did her crippled aunt have against those two monsters? Especially back on their own soil. This was all her fault. "I should go alone. Get the ring. Tatiana will give up Maris if I offer her the ring and myself."

"You will not offer yourself. Or go alone." Mal's voice shook her with its vehemence.

"I still have to retrieve the ring from my suite at the Primoris Domus. I can't leave it where it is—look how much trouble it's already brought." Her house could not become the focus for Tatiana's anger.

Mal shoved a hand through his hair. "I'm starting to think no good can come of giving Tatiana the ring."

Chrysabelle had begun to think that too. "At the very least, I will get it and destroy it. Then Tatiana can twist in the wind over her precious ring."

"But not alone." Mal's stance broadened into something battle-ready. "I'm going with you."

"Agreed." After all, she had promised to talk to the Aurelian about his curse. He might as well be there to hear what she had to say. She rubbed her forehead. What was she thinking? The Aurelian wouldn't tolerate Mal's presence any more than Madame Rennata would allow a vampire beyond the great room of the Primoris Domus. And Chrysabelle would be lucky to get an audience with the Aurelian if Madame Rennata found out about the danger Chrysabelle had put the house in with that stupid ring.

Dominic said something. Chrysabelle glanced up. "What?"

"I said I'm going too." Dominic's gaze shifted to a mother-of-pearl-handled falchion on the wall. The sword looked like it had never been used. "I'm not without skills myself. And I will not allow them to hurt Marissa."

The letter opener fell out of Katsumi's hand and clattered to the desk. The woman leaned back in the chair, and crossed her arms, looking very much like a woman scorned.

Chrysabelle tucked her hair behind her ears. How long had Dominic and Katsumi been sleeping together? "That's all well and good, but you're both anathema. The wards will keep you out of the city. I'm basically going alone anyway."

Dominic's rich laugh brought her head up. His finger wagged at her like he was talking to a child. "But you see, I have a secret weapon." He turned and gestured into the dark recesses of his office.

A broomstick of a man emerged from the shadows, the pale skin of his face and hands marred by oddly shaped freckles. Bottle-glass green eyes took her in. For a moment, she stared. Then her brain caught up with what she was seeing.

Dominic swept one hand wide toward the room's newest occupant. "Chrysabelle, meet Solomon, one of the few pure-blooded cypher fae."

*Cypher fae.* Those weren't freckles. Those were numbers. She held out her hand to the rare creature. "Pleasure to meet you."

He splayed his six-fingered hands in front of him. "I am not gloved."

Still holding out her hand, she shrugged.

Solomon's brows rose and his eyes widened. "You would voluntarily touch me?"

"I have no codes to hide."

"Codes?" Mortalis snorted. "He'll strip out every bit of personal info in that pretty little head of yours, including passwords, relevant numbers, and the personal configurations necessary to deceive wards that recognize you. And some that don't."

Chrysabelle's hand dropped to her side.

Solomon sighed. "My unfortunate kin tells the truth. But your trust is endearing."

Mal stepped up next to Chrysabelle. "And you're going to help us why?"

She shot him a look that hopefully he understood as shut up and be nice. "He can get all of you into the city."

"I understand that," Mal said. "But why should he? What's in it for him? No one does anything for free."

"Indeed," Katsumi interjected.

The smile returned to Solomon's face. He lifted one shoulder. "There is much I can glean in Corvinestri."

"Yeah, that, and Dominic has his number." Mortalis kneeled beside Nyssa, taking her hand in his.

Impressive. Getting a cypher's number was no easy feat, but if you could find the sum of their freckles, you owned them. What alchemy had Dominic used to achieve that?

Mortalis scooped Nyssa into his arms. "I'm going to take her to the physician, then I'll be ready to leave."

"Is she going to be okay?" Chrysabelle couldn't help but hope so, even if she didn't know the girl.

Mortalis nodded. "She's half shadeux. Very resilient. If the Nothos hadn't put iron cuffs on her, she probably could have taken it out on her own."

As Mortalis left, Mal questioned Dominic. "How soon can we leave? I assume you have a plane?"

"I do," Dominic answered. "It will take half an hour to get to the airfield, but the plane and pilots won't be ready for another hour and a half. I don't know if Tatiana had time to refuel or not before they left, so that may mean another stop for them before they hit Corvinestri. Either way, we won't be far behind."

"Time to get back to the ship and get Doc," Mal said.

"I need my bag too." Not to mention the body armor in it. "And my Golgotha blade."

"I have a few alchemical weapons to prepare as well." Dominic nodded. "Then I'll call for a car. We'll head for the plane as soon as you return."

"Good." Mal grabbed Chrysabelle's arm. "Let's go."

"Us? The sun's up." Chrysabelle stared at Mal. Tried not to focus on his mouth. "How exactly are *you* going to get from the car to the ship without turning into vampire flambé?"

Mal stayed silent for a moment, then cursed and shook his head. "Doc will know what weapons I want." He cursed again. "Hurry back."

# Chapter Twenty-six

One varcolai, one comarré, one former ghost, two fae, two fringe, a second anathema, and the ever-present host of disembodied voices. All of them, save the comarré at his side, the fringe pilot and copilot, and the voices in his head, huddled around a large table in the conference area of the plane, debating the best way to extract Chrysabelle's aunt without getting any of them killed. Fortunately, Dominic had left Katsumi in charge of running Seven so Mal didn't have to deal with her too. He sank lower into his seat. How had his life gotten this freaking crowded? At least his recent feeding meant the voices weren't thrashing his brain.

Beside him, Chrysabelle sketched what she remembered of the floor plan of Tatiana's home. Her pencil lifted off the paper, and she paused. "Could I ask why you're growling?"

"I didn't growl."

She erased a line and added a window, nodding the whole time. "Yes, you did."

Maybe he had. Considering the circumstances, growling was the least he should be doing. He stared at one particular member of the group around the conference table. "You shouldn't have let her come."

Chrysabelle glanced at him, rolling her eyes, darkened by the helioglazing on the plane windows. "For the last time, I didn't *let* Fi come. She bullied her way here. You of all people should know how Fi is when she wants something. Besides, she actually went shopping for me. She was so thrilled to find out she's not attached to you anymore, I can't believe she'd choose to be near you again. I guess she couldn't bear to be away from Doc."

"Have you looked at the clothes yet?" Chrysabelle still hadn't changed out of Doc's borrowed shirt and her original trousers. Both pieces were covered in dirt and blood spatter. He wondered if the items beneath those were still as pristine white as the day she'd sauntered through the gym, taunting him to bite her. The memory caused him to shift uncomfortably.

"No, but I'll worry about that after I finish this plan for Mortalis."

"You might not be so benevolent after you see what she picked out. Fi's taste can be a little...extreme. And you still shouldn't have let her come."

Her pencil lead broke. She clicked out a new length. "You know Doc didn't do anything to stop her, I might add, but I don't see you giving him grief."

"I will."

She stabbed her pencil toward the aisle. "Want me to let you out so you can start that now?"

"No." He crossed his arms and tried again to get comfortable. Dominic's private jet was plush, but nothing about this trip made it easy to relax.

"Don't you need to sleep, what with the sun being out and all?"

"I slept earlier." *Before I kissed you*, he wanted to say, just to see if she'd blush again. Other than the coloring of her cheeks, she hadn't seemed as affected by the second kiss as she had been by the first. Or maybe he'd imagined her initial reactions. Or maybe she was too worried about her aunt to think about anything else. That was probably it. What did he know about anything anymore? The world around him now matched the chaos of his head.

"Only two hours." Her face softened and she laid her hand on his arm. "Don't be a hero, seriously. I have great faith in your ability to smite the bad guys, but you need more sleep than that."

At her touch a soft whine whispered through his cranium. "No, I don't." He'd never needed much sleep. He'd always chalked it up to the residual power he'd siphoned off his sire. Since taking her blood, the hours required had dropped even more.

Her brows cocked along with the side of her mouth in a blatantly incredulous expression. "Just because you don't want to sleep where Dominic's slept..."

He shifted in his seat to lean closer and lowered his voice. "It's one of *those* things. Like what I did at the door of Seven when we first got there."

"Oh." She nodded slowly. "An inherited trait from your sire." She grinned, nearly knocking him back with the way her eyes lit up. "Or should I say an ingested trait?"

"What?" Her smile was amazing. Or more bloody likely it was just such a rare thing to see a smile aimed in his direction. A smile wasn't anything special. Which was why he was going to stop staring at hers very soon.

"Never mind." She went back to the paper, tracing rooms and doorways. A few strands of hair escaped her braid to fall around her face, the pale silk crisscrossing the whorls of gold on her cheeks and neck. The tip of her tongue peeked out between her lips as she concentrated.

Unable to bear the ache in his soul, he looked away and stared directly into his reflection in the window. It was the first time in a long time he'd seen himself. He kept no mirrors on the ship in the compartments he frequented. Why should he? He couldn't afford gold-backed ones, and seeing his true reflection—the only reflection silver-backed mirrors showed—was unnecessary torture.

Seeing his face reminded him of everything he'd lost. His true face, the one he wore without effort, was the face of a monster, not a man. His human face was just a mask. One he'd worn countless times in hundreds of years to lure the unsuspecting to their deaths. Neither face was worth looking at.

He closed his eyes, but the image of the savage he'd seen in the window was burned in his mind. *Killer. Murderer. Beast. Butcher. Bourreau.*

His thoughts had stirred the voices and for once, he let them rail. He couldn't deny their words. Death had been his human trade. If only he could hide behind the hood now. He glanced at Chrysabelle. She had handed off the schematic to Mortalis and now covered herself with a blanket. She claimed to know his history but hadn't said much about it. Did she think he'd gotten what he deserved?

In his human years, how many murderers had he dispatched? How many thieves? Rapists? Many from his time had believed the weight of the condemned's vile deed passed over to the headsman upon death. No wonder the women of his village refused him. Despite the hood, they knew who he was. What he did. Even in the tavern, he'd sat alone, relegated to a tankard reserved solely for him so that no one else might have to drink from the same cup.

"Are you not talking to me?"

Her question brought him out of his thoughts. "What? No. I didn't hear the question."

"I asked you to tell me about the night you were turned." Her shoulders lifted slightly. "If you want to."

"That's not a story you need to hear now."

"Your persuasion doesn't work on me, remember?" She pulled the blanket up to her chin. "Besides, we might not have a later after this trip."

He focused on the weave of her blanket. If she wanted to know how he'd become a monster, so be it. "It was late, well after midnight, when I finally arrived home. I entered our cottage and went first to see..." He swallowed at the tightness in his throat. "I went first to see my daughter, Sofia. I always checked on her first."

"You had a child?"

"Yes, I had a child." An angel. That's what Sofia had been. Everything that was worthwhile in his world had narrowed to that tiny, giggling human being. The first time her soft hand had wrapped his pinkie finger, the fierceness of a thousand warriors had leaped up inside him with the need to protect her. And yet he'd watched her die.

She shook her head. "Never mind, go ahead, I won't interrupt again."

But he was too lost in the rising emotions of that night to care. The swell of fear, panic, helplessness, and grief would have suffocated him had he still been mortal. "A dark shape bent over Sofia's bed. Too large to be Shaya. I grabbed him, pulled him away. Even in the moonlight coming through her window I could tell something was wrong with Sofia." His sweet angel had been as pale as the bed linens, her perfect rosebud mouth gray, her body limp.

"The creature overpowered me. He bit me, started draining me. I cried out and the sound brought Shaya running in. The vampire left me and attacked her. I found enough strength to beat at him, but not enough to stop him. He finished with Shaya, then told me that one as strong as I would be perfect for his family. He tore at his own wrist and fed me his blood." The bitter memory ran down Mal's throat. It was the last time the taste of blood had turned his stomach.

"Power surged through me, and when I realized that he was saving me, I couldn't stop drinking. I determined I would save Sofia and Shaya as well…" He'd thought only for them. For their salvation. "Too late, I tasted death in his veins. I had taken everything.

"I mimicked what he'd done and fed Shaya from my own wrist. As soon as she revived, I scooped Sofia into my arms. There was still breath in her, still a trace of life. But then I couldn't do it." He shook his head slowly and blinked hard, trying not to remember the exact moment the spark of life had died in his precious child's eyes. Had she thought he'd let her die? Or had she understood what he'd saved her from? All the years he'd spent chained in that ruined dungeon couldn't compare with the agony of not knowing.

"I knew what I had become. I could not pass that curse to my own child. I could not damn my own flesh and blood." His innocent Sofia. Better she die and cross heaven's threshold than live a cursed existence. Better he live with the guilt than she find out the monster he'd become. Or hate him for turning her into one too. "Shaya never let me forget I could have saved Sofia. Never."

"You made the right choice in a very hard decision."

He snorted softly, hating himself for that night all over again. Aching to feel Sofia's arms around him once more. To hear her soft "Papa" whispered in his ear. To inhale the scent of grass and sun in her hair after she'd been playing outside. Pain wracked his chest. Let Chrysabelle think what she wanted, but truth was truth. "Don't romanticize it. I let Sofia die."

"At least Sofia had a chance to know you and Shaya. Comarré never know their parents. Or any of their blood family, for that matter. You gave her that much."

"What about your aunt?"

"She's not really my aunt, that's just what we call the older comarrés, but she is the comarré who was assigned to me when I was born. She's about the closest thing to a mother I've had." Chrysabelle picked at the blanket's stitching. "What happened after you realized what you'd been turned into?"

"I didn't know anything about the curse involved in drinking one's sire to death, but it didn't take me long to figure out I couldn't feed without killing." His lip curled. "I didn't care. Drinking my victims to death gave me pleasure. I reveled in it. After all, I knew exactly what humans were capable of. Punishing their sins was my livelihood. At first, Shaya begged me to stop, to spare them. Then she joined me. The bodies we left behind meant we couldn't stay in one place for long."

Chrysabelle showed no signs of disinterest, but he'd gone beyond the tale of his turning. "You want to know more?"

"Yes." She bit her bottom lip. "If you don't mind."

Did he mind? He wasn't sure. Part of him wanted to keep his history to himself, but another part wanted someone to understand what he'd been through. To know how vile the nobility could be. "Europe became our banquet hall. Out hunting one night in a small village, Shaya met a noble vampire and, after talking to him, determined that the vampire who'd turned us had been House of Tepes, one of the strongest of the noble Families. To our amazement, that meant we were noble as well.

"The life this noble showed us was beyond our comprehension. Hidden cities devoted solely to vampire society. Mansions and servants, fine clothes, art, jewels. Shaya wanted to stay, but my inability to feed without killing undid me. When the others discovered I'd drained my sire, they pronounced me anathema. Some talked of chaining me in an open field and letting the sun take care of me. I had to go. So I slipped away and left Shaya there. It was a far better life than what I could give her. Besides that, my need to feed and kill grew stronger with each passing year. I was afraid if she stayed with me..."

"That you might kill her?" Chrysabelle asked.

He nodded. The fear had almost realized itself several times before he'd left Shaya. But he hadn't harmed her, and that was all that mattered. "Then, about fifty years ago, a pair of nobles found me in northern England. Lord Ivan was one of them. They had Shaya with them. Said that my killing had gone on long enough, that I was making things difficult for all nobles. That my inability to control my bloodthirst risked rousing the kine against them all. If I didn't go with them, they would kill Shaya. So I went.

"They took me to a ruined fortress and pronounced my punishment. I would not be killed as vampire law holds that no vampire should kill another. Instead I would be chained in the dungeon and left to rot until the hunger drove me insane. They blindfolded me and shoved me to my knees. Shaya cursed and screamed, begged them to let us go. I heard them hit her, knock her down.

"I begged them to spare her. They refused. She fought them hard." The plane disappeared, replaced by the crumbling castle walls. "I recognized the sound of the sword being pulled from its sheath. Shaya cried out. Air brushed my cheek as the blade sailed past me and met its target.

"Blood spattered my face." The broken stones bit into his knees. "Shaya went quiet."

Blindfolded and shackled, he'd listened helplessly to the sound of her dropping to the ground, smelled her turn to bitter ash. Black ice sprang up through him, filling his veins and encasing his heart. She had been the last bastion against his accursed hunger. Removing her had opened a portal of surging hatred and murderous intent. In that moment, he became more of a monster than he'd ever been before.

Had he not already been in chains, he would have killed every last one of them before destroying the village surrounding the ruins. Man, woman, and child, he would have ended every life he came upon.

Chrysabelle's soft voice broke through, the slightest quaver of horror evident in the timbre. "Oh, Mal. I'm so, so sorry for what they did."

He scrubbed a hand across his face. He was not in that dark place. Had not been there for a very long time. "Then they took me to the dungeon and chained me there as promised. The one who wasn't Lord Ivan spoke an incantation over me—that was the curse that would give me these names and these voices—then they left, sealing the passage behind them."

"Holy mother," she whispered. A tear streaked down one cheek. "That's where Fiona found you?"

"Yes. And killing her triggered the second curse. It woke the voices and etched the names into my skin."

Dominic and Mortalis walked toward them. Company was the last thing he wanted. He nodded and shifted his body away. "Go to sleep."

A few moments later, a soft weight pressed his side. He scowled as he turned. Why couldn't they just leave him alone? The sight of Chrysabelle's blonde head using his shoulder as a pillow drained the temper out of him in a cold rush.

He listened over the hum of the engines and the chatter in the cabin and focused on her breathing. Soft and steady. She slept. She'd probably have nightmares after what he'd told her.

Hating his own weakness, he leaned in carefully so as not to disturb her and inhaled. Her perfume held more than just the allure of blood now, but he didn't think on it for long. Thoughts about her, about the possibility of what could be between them, about what the future might hold, were pointless. His past proved that. His curse hung over him like a bird of prey waiting to snatch anything good from his life and devour it.

He turned again to the window and closed his eyes.

Even without the curse, there was no reason to think of her as anything more than a temporary blip on his radar, because if this trip went as he assumed it would, his future would end within Corvinestri's walls.


A hand jiggled Chrysabelle's shoulder. Then a voice spoke from somewhere very close to her. "Time to wake up. We're almost there."

Mal's voice. The sudden rush of everything he'd told her swept over her. She wanted to comfort him, tell him everything would be okay, but none of that would help. She didn't know everything would be okay. Doubted it, actually.

She rubbed her eyes as she sat up, only to realize she'd been leaning against him. Sleeping on him. No wonder she'd dreamed of him. Of what he'd been like before he'd been turned. Of what it would have been like to…Her face began to heat. She'd not had those kinds of dreams about Algernon, that much was for sure.

"I'm up." She stood under the pretense of stretching. Desperately, her mind searched for something else to think about other than the horrors Mal had endured. "How much longer before we get there?"

Dominic sat across from them. If he had an opinion about her snuggling up with Mal, his face didn't show it. "Forty, forty-five minutes. You need to strap in."

She shook her head and reached into the overhead for her bag and the two shopping bags of stuff Fi had purchased. "I've got to change first." She trekked to the bathroom, thankful for the excuse to put some space between her and Mal. After the tenderness of his last kiss, she'd been shocked. Now he'd confessed his past to her, then let her sleep on his shoulder. She was downright worried.

Locking the door turned the bathroom light on automatically. Quite a bit different from the commercial jet she'd flown to get to the Americas in the first place, the bathroom on Dominic's plane bordered on luxurious. The shower alone could have held three or four people. She set her bags on the polished glass countertop. The gold-backed mirror ran the length of the wall, reflecting her bedraggled image.

She frowned. Her clothes were beyond ruined. Dirty, stained, speckled with blood. Even a few small tears. Completely unbecoming for a comarré. Madame Rennata might not even see her if she showed up looking like this. Chrysabelle stripped down to her underwear and used a damp washcloth to clean up as best she could. What a relief to have fresh clothes waiting for her.

Time to see what Fi had gotten her, then she'd peel on her body armor and get dressed. She plunged her hands into the first shopping bag, reached beneath the tissue paper, and pulled out—

Sweet heaven. She closed her eyes and sent up a silent prayer. *Forgive me, holy mother, but I think I'm going to kill a mortal.*

Black leather pants with some kind of corset-style lacing on the back. Or the front, she couldn't tell which. A matching leather vest and a long black leather duster lined with burgundy fabric. A tank top with a deeply scooped neckline. At least that was white, except for the flowered skull embroidered on the front. Three more tanks just like it in red, gray, and black—each with its own hideous embellishments. The urge to weep welled up like a hot bubble in Chrysabelle's chest. The tanks would barely cover her cami bra.

The second bag held a large shoe box. She pulled it out and tossed the lid away. Short, lug-soled black leather boots that zipped up the side. What were they called? Combat boots? Shaking slightly, she set the box on the counter next to the other unacceptable items.

Disappointment weighed her down. The purchases were obviously Fi's idea of cool, and for that, Chrysabelle did her best not to be angry. But these wouldn't do. She just…couldn't wear these things. The clothes reminded her of those worn by the pretenders at Puncture.

She took a few calming breaths. In through the nose, out through the mouth. Then she called through the cracked door, "Fi! Could you come here, please?"

Half a knock and Chrysabelle opened the door and pulled Fi into the bathroom.

"Hey, what's up?" Fi smiled at the clothes laid out on the counter. "Hot threads, huh?"

"About those." How to put this. "I'm not comfortable wearing such *hot threads*."

"Why not? You'll look great in them. It's what all the sexy vampire slayers are wearing." Fi scratched her arm, then her eyes went wide as if she suddenly realized Chrysabelle had on nothing but underwear. "Wow, you really are covered with those gold tattoos, aren't you?" She reached out toward the butterfly hovering near Chrysabelle's navel.

Chrysabelle backed up. "Too sexy is part of it. It's also that comarré are only supposed to wear white. Just like I put on the list with my sizes, remember?"

With a little grin, Fi shook her head. "I hate to tell you

this, but all that long-sleeved, loose, and flowy white stuff makes you look like a Palm Beach grandma on her way to yoga."

Chrysabelle clutched the back of her neck and massaged the knotting muscles. "Fi, it's what I'm used to. What I feel comfortable in. I know it must be hard to understand, but—"

"Plus those clothes you wear are no good for fighting. A blade could slice right through that thin fabric."

"I've never trained in anything else. And I need those clothes to cover the body armor I'll be wearing." By not covering it, she'd be breaking yet another rule.

"Leather makes great body armor. Plus white gets dirty fast. Shows the blood." Fi frowned, her mouth bunched to one side. "I'm sorry you don't like them, but trust me, you're going to look great. Very intimidating."

"I believe you. But I have to have something else." She calmed herself, still the edge didn't entirely leave her voice. "It's very possible that my house, the Primoris Domus, could disavow me for breaking a law I have sworn to uphold."

"How are they going to know what you're wearing?"

"Because the Primoris Domus is the first stop I must make." Chrysabelle leaned against this wall. This was not going well.

Fi grimaced. "I had no idea. I don't want you to get into trouble. Especially after everything your blood has done for me. Let me go see if there's anything on the plane. Maybe Dominic has something."

"Thank you, that would be wonderful." Chrysabelle smiled as a small weight lifted off her.

"Right back." Fi headed out, shutting the door behind

her. She returned a few minutes later, her expression dour. "I'm sorry. All Dominic has is a dark gray suit."

Chrysabelle nodded. "Thanks for checking. I guess these will have to do."

Fi left and Chrysabelle surveyed the pile of unacceptable clothes, hands on her hips. She had no choice but to wear them. There was no time or place to get anything else. Apprehension worried her shore of confidence.

Resigned, she shoved the clothes to one side, then opened her personal bag and extracted the white zippered pouch that held her body armor. The pouch was slightly larger than the palm of her hand, but twice as thick. She unzipped it and shook the precious contents onto the counter. The whisper-thin silver mesh body suit slipped out, light as a promise and far stronger.

A few minutes and some carefully practiced moves later, the suit covered her from just beneath her jaw to her ankles and wrists. It fit as closely as a layer of paint, except that it breathed and moved like a second skin and had the durability of steel and holy magic. She'd worn it before, to practice putting it on and taking it off and to accustom herself to fighting in it, but this time its ability to save her life might be tested.

If Madame Rennata didn't rip it off her for letting it show beneath her clothes. The comarré body armor was a closely guarded secret. Or had been, until now. Chrysabelle sighed. She would do her best to explain, but what did it matter? She'd already revealed secrets to Mal she shouldn't have. Told him about the training. Maybe Madame Rennata wouldn't care. Maybe Chrysabelle shouldn't care. She had to break from those rules sometime, didn't she? She sighed. To just stop being a comarré was nigh impossible when it was the only life she'd known for a hundred and fifteen years.

Of course, if Tatiana succeeded in breaking the covenant, the time might come for the true purpose of the comarré to be revealed to all. The world would need someone to stand up against the vampire nation, to protect human life. Who better than those warriors already embedded behind enemy walls?

Just because she'd chosen to leave that life behind didn't mean she couldn't be counted on when the call came.

Even if she had let him kiss her. Twice.

That second kiss…no, none of that mattered. Not her past, not her future, just her present. Maris needed her to be brave and strong and ignore all else. If Mal could endure losing his child, surely Chrysabelle could suffer the smaller slings and arrows. With that thought on repeat, she reluctantly began to dress.

# Chapter Twenty-seven

For the first few moments, none of them said a word. Mal, like the rest of them, just stared at her. At what she was wearing.

Chrysabelle had emerged from the bathroom and now stood in front of them, looking slightly disconcerted and very...un-Chrysabelle.

He finally found his voice. "I...That's...Huh." No, he had nothing. Just the usual noise in his head. Her new look defied immediate description.

Her jaw tightened. "No comments, please. It is what it is."

The rest of them nodded. Doc held his hands up in some kind of surrender. Only Fi spoke, her tone overly bright. "I think you look awesome."

"Thank you." And with that, Chrysabelle pushed through the group and went back to where she and Mal had been sitting, tossing the coat over her arm onto the seats. Mal followed, but hung back a little. She popped the overhead bin and threw the shopping bags inside, then set her personal bag on the seat, opened it, and started extracting weapons and slipping them into her outfit.

And what an outfit it was.

A fine silver mesh, almost like body glitter, encased all visible skin except her hands and head. What the mesh was exactly, he couldn't tell, but then fashion was Fi's thing, not his. Black leather enveloped the rest of Chrysabelle.

Black. Leather. The contrast between that and her signum was startling. She was sun and shadow, day and night. Good. And evil. The voices howled in agreement.

Over a white tank top, a snug vest cinched her trim waist. The pants that hugged her legs laced up the back like an old-fashioned corset. The image was not an unpleasant one. Looking at her like this, covered and yet somehow totally revealed, he'd never realized how much lean muscle she carried. The time she'd walked into the gym nearly naked, he'd been a little too overwhelmed by the startling amount of signum and bare skin on display to take in that detail.

Perhaps that was why she favored the loose tunic and wide pants, to hide her athletic build. He started to wonder if the generally accepted idea of the comarré as some kind of vampire geisha wasn't actually a misconception the comarré themselves perpetuated. As a cover story went, it was a good one, except geisha weren't trained to kill the men they entertained.

He walked up beside her as she tucked the Golgotha blade beneath the lacing on the back of her pants. "It's not as bad as you think."

"You have no idea." She strapped on the sword across her body, adjusting the strap to fall between her breasts, now clearly delineated by the vest's uplifting abilities.

"I promise you, no one's going to care if—"

She spun, her eyes holding more angst than he'd expected. "You promise me? You do *not* understand." She glanced back at the rest of the group and the steam seemed to leave her a bit. "I didn't mean to snap, but this is more than just an outfit. It's a blatant disregard for everything I've been raised to hold sacred."

She was right about him not understanding. How anyone could be so upset about clothes was beyond him. "Maybe we can—"

"No. Forget it." She shook her head. "I will deal with whatever ramifications come. All that matters is freeing my aunt."

He wanted to say something to make it better, but his vocabulary hadn't included those kinds of words since his human life had ended. She reached for the coat lying across the seats, and he went to get it for her at the same time, his hand almost brushing her arm. His fingers prickled with heat.

She jerked her arm out of the way. "Don't touch me."

He scowled. Didn't she understand he'd been trying to help? "Fine."

"That's not what I meant." Her voice lowered. "This… body armor is spun from fine silver and imbued with holy magic. It will burn you." She picked up the coat, carefully keeping her distance. "I just thought you should know."

That explained the sensation in his hand. "Silver body armor." Perfect protection against vampires. No wonder it covered her throat. How many more toys did she have? "Another comarré weapon?"

"Yes. Another guarded secret, actually. When worn, it's to be kept hidden. One more rule I'm breaking." She pulled the coat on and adjusted it over her sword. The red-leather-wrapped handle stuck out next to the base of her braid.

The combination of black leather and visible weaponry did more than change her look. It erased the veil of innocence that had clouded his judgment concerning her. He'd somehow been unwilling to accept that this pale, gilded creature could be anything more than a source of life and power, thinking that she would certainly perish without his help. Now he saw her more clearly than he ever had. She was a killer, not to the extent or purpose that he was, but she and her kind were certainly just as lethal. Or could be, when the need arose.

The thought should have unsettled him. It didn't. Neither did the lack of understanding as to why such a side of her would even be necessary.

Instead, he felt a kinship with her that he'd never expected. In that moment, he saw her as an equal. A woman who could face the tribulations of the life he lived. Son of a priest. The last woman he'd thought that about, he'd married. If he didn't watch himself, Chrysabelle was going to be a hell of a lot harder to get rid of when this was over. Assuming she wanted to stay in the first place. Which she wouldn't.

He almost laughed. The noble vampire Families really had no idea what kind of creatures they paid to nourish them. Wouldn't they be surprised to learn their docile comarré were such well-trained, well-equipped warriors, ready to slit the throats they fed at a moment's notice?

She popped her collar, hiding the sword handle a little more. "I guess I'm as ready as I'm going to be."

He rested his forearm on the overhead bins and leaned in, a thousand words dancing on his tongue, but none of them seeming right. "We'll get her out. Even if we have to kill every one of those undead bastards to do it."

That brought a smile to her face. "You know you're still one of those, right?"

He could look at that smile a lot and not get tired of it, even if it was brought on by the idea of killing vampires. *Maybe she'll kill you.* "I'm undead bastard anathema. Big difference."

She laughed softly. "Point taken."

Dominic called to them from his seat. "*Per favore,* you must sit down and buckle up, we're about to land."

Mal nodded at him, then sat and buckled his lap belt. Not that a crash would kill him anyway. *Too bad.*

Chrysabelle took the seat beside him, moving the point of her sword out of his way. She clicked her belt, then glanced at him. "Just so I can be prepared, are you going to"—she waved her hand at him—"do that thing where the voices take over?"

*Yessss.* "No. Not ever again." Not if he could help it. *Give her to us.* Not around her. *All over her.* Invisible teeth gnawed on the interior of his skull. Whines of hunger drilled into his ears from the inside out. He closed his eyes and leaned back, trying to quench the cravings the voices stirred up. Deep within him, the beast shook off the chains Chrysabelle's blood had bound it with and reared its head.

Unfortunately, she was the one thing the beast most craved.


Tatiana stroked Nehebkau as she strolled circles around the old comarré. The albino cobra lay draped around Tatiana's shoulders, his head on her chest and his tail wound down around her arm in a serpentine embrace. It was good to be home. She'd missed her precious boy. "Your niece should be here soon, and when she arrives, I'm going to kill her. And you're going to watch. I want you to think about that."

"Get staked, bloodsucker." The blood whore lifted her head defiantly. Against the dusky backdrop of bruises covering her face, her signum sparkled in the sanctuary's artificial light. The makeup she'd used to cover them had worn off long ago.

"I'm going to kill the vampire that's helping her too." Tatiana continued to walk, her high-heeled boots soundless on the leaves and moss of the simulated jungle floor. "And then I'm going to kill you." She stopped in front of the chair the comarré was tied to. "Unless you want to tell me where the ring is."

"I told you, I don't know anything about a ring."

"Liar." Tatiana backhanded her. Nehebkau hissed and flared his hood at the sudden movement. She smoothed her fingers down his creamy throat. "It's all right, my darling. Hush now."

The old comarré spit out a mouthful of blood and tipped her head back to stare at the sanctuary's fiber optic night sky. "The stars are beautiful but they can't compete with the sun. Don't you miss the sun shining down on you? The bright light of day? That warmth?" Her voice was irritatingly pleasant. Fool.

Tatiana leaned close and grabbed the kine's chin, tipping her face until they were only inches away from each other. Nehebkau's tongue flicked in and out, tasting the air. Could he sense the blood feast hidden beneath the old woman's skin? Tatiana dropped her hand from the comarré's chin and bared her fangs in a hiss of her own. The comarré merely squinted and turned her head. Killing this one could not come soon enough.

Anger at the kine's cavalier attitude ate into Tatiana's good mood. "I am going to drink you slowly, old woman. So slowly you can feel the life seeping out of you, slipping away down my throat."

Her finger traced a gold vine from the woman's temple to her cheek, stopping beneath her eye. "The way each swallow stabs at your heart, dragging your pulse down, weakening you until . . . nothing."

She pressed her fingernail into the woman's skin until red spilled forth. Flicking the bead up with her nail, she brought her finger to her mouth and licked it clean. "Already you taste like death to me."

The kind of death that would infuse her with more power. The comarré might be old, but her blood hadn't suffered from time spent without a patron. The potent heat of life still throbbed within her. Oh yes, power dwelt in this woman's veins. Power that would soon be Tatiana's. A giddy shiver tickled her skin. Power was everything. Power was *life*.

The sanctuary door opened and Mikkel stepped halfway into the room. He tipped his head to one side, requesting her presence outside. She nodded, then turned back to the old woman. "I won't be gone long." She smiled and unhooked Nehebkau from around her neck, easing her darling to the floor. "But I'll leave you a little company. I wouldn't make any sudden movements if I were you."

A shadow of fear flickered in the comarré's eyes as the serpent reared back and stared her down with its bright red gaze. How dare that old whore fear Nehebkau but not his master?

Tatiana suppressed her growing rage as she walked away to join Mikkel in the hall. Securing the door behind her, she raised her brows. "What is it?"

"I have good news, my sweet." He smiled, hands going to her hips and pulling her close. "Mmm...you smell like fresh blood. You know what that does to me."

She almost dug her nails into his arms to push him away, then stopped. Mikkel often saw pain as an aphrodisiac. Instead, she gathered every last remaining ounce of patience. "Later, my love. What's the good news?"

He nuzzled her neck, undeterred. "I've got a new team of Nothos scouring the city." His fangs scraped her skin. "If the girl is here, we will have her very soon." He bounced a finger off the tip of Tatiana's nose. He was lucky to keep it. "And then I will present her to you to do with what you will."

At last, Tatiana's smile came willingly to her lips. "You do know how to please me." Maybe she would take him to bed after all. "But I hope it doesn't take long. Waiting to kill this one grows harder and harder. Especially when the threat of death doesn't seem to faze her. It's like she wants to die."

"Then why wait? If the old comarré wants to sacrifice herself for her niece, I say let her." His hands crawled up beneath her shirt.

Tatiana froze. That was it. And this whelp had inadvertently figured it out. The sacrifice had to be a comarré. Pure untainted blood. And why use the comar she'd paid good money for when she had another one? One that no one would miss.

She threw her head back and laughed, dislodging Mikkel's palpating hand. "Of course!"

"What?"

"Nothing." She kissed him hard, then grabbed his hand and led him toward her chambers. He deserved a reward for his efforts, and what was better than being allowed to pleasure her?

Maris stilled her hands as Tatiana's laugh echoed through the door. A minute passed, then another, but the vampiress didn't return. Maris resumed struggling with her bound wrists. She no longer cared if she spilled her own blood in the effort or not. Nothing mattered now, except warning Chrysabelle.

Whatever this ring was that Tatiana so desperately sought, it couldn't be used for anything good. Maris had no idea if Chrysabelle had it or not, but she'd searched Chrysabelle's things after the girl had arrived to be sure there was no kind of tracking device planted among them. There'd been no ring. Chrysabelle could have had it on her person, but Maris had seen no evidence of it.

Did the vampire helping Chrysabelle know about it? Chances were good that if he did, his "help" would be more for himself than for her niece.

Her heart ached at what had transpired since Algernon's death. *Chrysabelle, forgive me.* This was not how things were supposed to have gone, but Maris would atone. If it took her dying breath, she would make things right at last.

The rope scoured her wrists, but she dismissed the pain. It was no worse than her swollen eye or what she feared was a cracked cheekbone. Her libertas battle had almost killed her, but she'd survived it. Now she would fight for Chrysabelle's libertas.

Tatiana's pet watched, its beady red eyes ever vigilant. That dangerous creature would be the first thing Maris dispatched when she got free. And she *would* get free. If she had to tear flesh and break bone to do it, she would free herself and do as much damage as she physically could to Tatiana and her house.

If only Maris had her sacre. But she'd seen swords decorating the walls of this house. One of them would have to do. The time for pretending was over. The time for protecting had come. *Holy mother, please allow me this one last effort.* She dug a fingernail into the weave of the rope, fraying it piece by piece.

The snake slithered closer, flicking its tongue out.

One of the benefits of being a cripple was being under-estimated. Tatiana had not secured Maris's feet. She snapped her good foot out, catching the cobra and sending it flying into a teak chaise with a satisfying thump.

Of course, there were greater benefits in only pretend-ing to be crippled. After her libertas, she'd been confined to a wheelchair while her body healed. Staying in the chair after she'd learned on her own to walk again had been a difficult decision and an even harder secret to keep, something she'd only ever entrusted to one other—her sweet, volatile Velimai. Bitter tears burned Maris's eyes, but her anger forced them away. Tatiana and her paramour would pay for what they'd done to Velimai.

With a final burst of effort, she snapped the rope and loosed her hands. Red marks circled her wrists. She flexed them, marveling at how the signum still sparkled after all these years. How she'd despised those marks, worked to hide them so she could move in the mortal world undetected and live a normal human life. The life she'd wanted for Chrysabelle. Poor Dominic. He'd never understood her need for that mundane normalcy, but she'd never expected him to. He reveled in being the creature he was, and a normal human life had stopped being an option for him the day he was turned. He'd gone from prince to king. Comarré were born serfs. How could he understand?

She stood slowly, giving her bad leg a chance to catch up. It took longer for the circulation to return to her old muscles these days. Paying Dominic in blood had given her a welcome boost of virility. Keeping her strength up while living her life as a cripple had been a test of will made bearable by Dominic's occasional visits, but today would make all those years worthwhile.

The cobra shifted, coming back to life. Foul creature. Maris limped over and snatched it behind the head and by the tail. "You and your mistress are quite a pair, aren't you? Cold-blooded killers."

The cobra spit, and the sharp tang of venom tainted the air.

"Just like your keeper. Reeking of poison and death." In one quick motion, she released the snake's head and spun the creature around by the tail, bringing its skull down against the bench with a hard, final snap.

She dropped the limp body. The serpent writhed at her feet as the nerves twitched reflexively in the final throes of death. If only Eve could have done as much. Maris wiped her hands on her dirty, bloodied clothes.

"Now for your mistress."

# Chapter Twenty-eight

The apprehension building in Mal's gut had grown the
farther into the city they'd driven. The cypher fae,
Solomon, had gotten them through Corvinestri's wards
without incident, but that didn't mean they weren't being
watched. Even the voices' ever-present droning had taken
on a nervous hum. Something wasn't right. Besides the
fact that two anathema were now within the walls of one
of the power centers of vampire nobility.

The grounds around the Primoris Domus house, if you
could call such a structure a house, were so well lit that
the night didn't leave a single shadow. He almost expected
to see armed guards, but what good would they do against
vampires?

He'd never been to a comarré residence before, let
alone imagined one could be as impressive as the houses
nobles lived in. Maybe more so. How many acres did the
property entail? At least three other buildings dotted the
landscape. Training facilities maybe? Dorms? Armies
could have been barracked inside buildings that large. He
glanced at Chrysabelle. Maybe that's exactly what the
buildings held.

"Nice joint," Doc said. "Your kind don't like small spaces, I dig."

Chrysabelle's eyes stayed on the building, focused yet distant. She raised her hand to the window and rested her fingertips on the glass. "Within that house, hundreds of comarré live their lives. They're born here, raised here, trained here. This is our world. Our home."

Doc shot a look at Mal as if to say it seemed like a sheltered life. He couldn't disagree, but Chrysabelle had handled herself well in the human world. Perhaps she'd been trained for that too.

Their driver, the plane's pilot, pulled the limo to a stop just beyond the large circular drive in front of the main house, staying in the shadows of the tree-lined entrance. The second vehicle, driven by the copilot and holding Dominic, Mortalis, and Solomon, parked behind them. Fi might as well have been in that car too, for all she'd said. Since the incident with the clothes, she'd been quiet and mopey.

"I'm going in alone," Chrysabelle announced, reaching for the door handle.

Mal grabbed it first. "Like hell you are."

Finally, she looked at him. "Do you honestly think you're going to be granted an invitation to come any farther than the threshold? At best I can get you into the foyer and the great room, but nothing beyond that. This place is a sanctuary against vampires." She shook her head. "I go alone."

"Tatiana has a comar from this house, yes?"

Her brow furrowed. "Yes, but what does that—"

"Would she have been given an invitation to enter at some point or not? How does the process of obtaining a comarré work?"

An inkling of his direction shimmered in her eyes.

"She would have come to the house at some point to meet the available comars, negotiate the blood rights price, then again to pay." She tapped her finger on her thigh. "It's not unheard of for someone else to act as a go-between, but knowing Tatiana, she probably did it herself."

"Are the invitations rescinded once the blood rights are purchased?"

Defeat clouded Chrysabelle's gaze. "No." She looked at the house again. "Tatiana could have already come here with her Nothos. We have no way of knowing whether the house has been breached."

He hit the button to lower the window and forced himself to inhale. "I don't smell brimstone." Yet. His gut told him the night air wouldn't stay untainted for much longer.

"Me either," Doc added.

Chrysabelle nodded and slid toward the door. "Very well then. Mal, you can come. But don't be..." Her mouth pursed in frustration.

"Don't be too me?" He understood. And he didn't blame her for it. "I'll be on my best behavior."

"Whatever that is," Doc said. He sprawled out, propping his feet on the edge of the seat Chrysabelle was about to vacate and slipping his arm around Fi. "We'll hold down the fort here."

Mal opened the car door for Chrysabelle, letting her exit ahead of him. When she was out, he turned to Doc. "Don't get comfortable. If we're too late—"

Doc raised his fingers to his forehead in a casual salute. "I got this, bro."

"Good enough." Mal slipped out of the vehicle and shut the door. He let Chrysabelle go in front with enough paces between them so anyone watching could see she wasn't being coerced. At the door, he stayed a few steps back and waited while she knocked.

She shifted uneasily, clenching and unclenching her hands. Was she that worried about what he might do? What scene was going through her mind? Him attacking the whole house?

"I'm not going to do anything to embarrass you," he said, shifting into his human face. How easy that was to maintain with her blood in his system.

"Don't worry, I've taken care of that myself." She plucked at her long leather coat. "These clothes…" She shook her head.

What an idiot he was. Of course she wasn't just worried about what he might do. There was no way the comarré house was going to let slide the fact that Chrysabelle was wanted for murdering her patron. The muscle in his jaw twitched. If anyone in there tried to hurt her—

The door opened. A female about Chrysabelle's age peered out. A tiny gold sparrow flew over one eyebrow. Still, she had less than half the signum Chrysabelle did for as much of her as Mal could see. Her brows lifted, lofting the sparrow higher. "Chrysabelle? What are you doing here? Why are you dressed like that?"

"Hello to you too, Saraphina. I need to come in."

Saraphina's gaze strayed to Mal. Her eyes widened. "Madame Rennata doesn't allow visitors after dusk, you know that."

Chrysabelle exhaled and visibly straightened. "He's my visitor and last time I checked, this was still my home, so move out of the way." She shoved the door open, pushing the other comarré farther into the house. The girl sputtered in protest, muttering in what sounded like Latin.

A few steps in and Chrysabelle turned back to him. "Are you coming?"

"Am I invited?"

"No," Saraphina spat.

"Yes," Chrysabelle said. "What she says doesn't override what I say, so get a move on."

Saraphina gasped. "I'm going to get Madame Rennata."

"Yes, you do that." Chrysabelle rolled her eyes as Saraphina stalked off. "This new generation. I've forgotten more than that girl knows. Come on."

Mal entered.

And cringed.

The sweet, honeyed fragrance of comarré blood flooded every pore with hunger. His muscles ached with it. He swayed, drunk on the deluge. The voices screeched and clawed, rabid with need. *Kill, drink, drain, devour, blood, blood, blood.* Deep inside, where the darkness flourished, the beast lifted its head and inhaled. Mal squeezed his eyes shut, jaw tightening. Not here. Not now.

Light pressure on his sleeve. He opened his eyes to slits. Chrysabelle.

Her voice washed over him, a soothing balm. "I know this must be hard for you, but try to relax. You are my patron now. That means you're not an outsider in my world anymore."

Her words calmed him, but they were pretty lies and he knew it. An anathema would never be allowed a comarré. He was her patron by accident, not by purpose. He responded through gritted teeth. She must not know how he struggled, how little control he held on to. "I will do my best. I told you that."

She smiled and patted his arm. *Maybe later she'll give*

*you a cookie*. He shut out the voices with new will. After all, he could have her blood whenever he wanted it. All he had to do was ask. And be willing to kiss her.

"Chrysabelle, what is the meaning of this?" An older woman approached, bearing heavily on a cane. Her visible skin was more decorated than Saraphina's, but still not as much as Chrysabelle's. Her long white robes swayed as she stopped. She glared at Mal while addressing Chrysabelle. "Why have you invited this creature into our house?"

Then her gaze shifted back to Chrysabelle. "Holy mother. Why in heaven's name are you dressed like some cheap kine whore? Your appearance is appalling. I should have you removed for that alone, but I imagine you've got a reasonable explanation given your recent circumstances."

Mal bristled at the woman's comments. Chrysabelle looked nothing like a whore, but for her sake, he kept silent.

Chrysabelle bent slightly from the waist. "My apologies, Madame Rennata. No explanation except that I had little choice in my clothes, I'm afraid. Considering the money my blood rights brought to the Primoris Domus, I'm sure you can overlook this indiscretion for the moment. I've only come to access my suite, where I assure you I will change, and then I will be gone. Tatiana has kidnapped Maris. I intend to rescue her."

"Tatia—rescue her? No. I forbid it."

Chrysabelle stiffened. "What do you mean, you forbid it? My aunt's life is in danger. You know what Tatiana is like."

"Exactly why I forbid you to attempt such a thing." Rennata glanced at Mal quickly. "Everyone knows comarré are not equipped for such…endeavors."

Mal stifled a retort. Not equipped. Like hell. Chrysabelle

walked around with a freaking arsenal strapped to her. Obviously, Rennata didn't think he knew that, and she didn't want to risk exposing comarré secrets by letting Chrysabelle talk about it either. He wondered... did Rennata know about the ring? Was she stalling to keep Chrysabelle from discovering it had already been removed? Would the woman have given it to Tatiana? No, that wasn't likely. Tatiana wouldn't still be pursuing them if that were the case.

"You cannot forbid me from this." Chrysabelle planted her hands on her hips.

Rennata lifted her chin. "There are risks one accepts when one lives the life of a comarré. Your aunt accepted them and so have you. Now is not the time—"

"Hmph." Mal lowered his head to hide his anger until he could better control it. "Did either of them have a choice to live any other way?"

Rennata's mouth opened slightly. "I beg your pardon, vampire. This is comarré business." She spoke to Chrysabelle. "And I am still unclear what he's doing here."

"We didn't know if Tatiana had come here yet or not. He's with me in case I need help." Chrysabelle slid closer to Mal.

"Tatiana's already visited. I fail to see how a strange vampire could help you with that."

Chrysabelle tilted her head. "She's been here? When? What did she want?"

"Right after Algernon's body was discovered. She came to see if you were still alive."

"But how..." The fingers on Chrysabelle's right hand curled into a fist. "She wanted to enter my rooms, didn't she?"

Rennata laughed. "Don't worry, child. We took care of things."

What did that mean? There was a tone in the woman's voice that clearly indicated she meant something only Chrysabelle would understand.

"You didn't take care of things that well apparently. She found Maris and would have kidnapped me too, if I hadn't been with…"

Rennata's brows rose. "With whom, dear?"

"With me." Mal sensed Chrysabelle didn't want to use his name. He didn't particularly want his cover blown yet either. The longer he had before the nobles who had cursed him knew he was in Corvinestri, the better.

Rennata focused her piercing blue gaze on him. "And who are you again?"

He turned to Chrysabelle. This was getting old fast. "Get what you came for and let's be on our way."

Chrysabelle raised her palm, as if she needed more time. "Did you take Tatiana to my suites or did you mock up one of the cells?"

Rennata's face blanched. "I will not discuss such things in front of this unknown. You have changed since Algernon's death, Chrysabelle. I do not care for it."

Mal laughed bitterly. "Changed? You're bloody right she's changed. Being accused of murder, hunted by Nothos, and having a family member kidnapped will do that to a person."

"Chrysabelle has not been accused of murder. Not officially." Rennata's nostrils flared. "You carry the scent of a noble, but I don't recognize you."

"Do you know every vampire in this city?"

"Every one that lives here, yes," Rennata replied with

a haughtiness better suited to his fanged brethren. "Except you."

He took a few steps closer, impressed that the older comarré didn't step back or flinch. "I am Chrysabelle's protector." He refrained from using the word "patron." That was more information Chrysabelle would probably rather he not share. He couldn't blame her. "And if she hasn't been officially accused of murder, why does the House of Tepes seek her? Or does Tatiana work alone?"

"Tatiana never works alone." Rennata sniffed and placed both hands on the head of her cane. "You don't know anything about Tatiana, do you?" She peered at him. "Who are you, vampire?"

"He is my patron. That is all you need to know."

Mal turned before his face could register his surprise. Chrysabelle's mouth bent down for a brief moment, then she swallowed and stared defiantly at Rennata.

"That cannot be." Rennata rapped her cane on the floor, narrowly missing Mal's foot. "This…this…unknown is your patron?" She glanced at him and revelation flared in her eyes. "Holy mother, preserve us. You're anathema, aren't you? That's why I don't know you."

Mal gave up the pretense of his human face and growled, showing his fangs. The elder comarré retreated a few steps to one side, but the look of judgment on her face remained.

Chrysabelle came up behind him, touching him lightly on the elbow as she moved to stand beside him. "Madame Rennata, I'm going to my suite. If you'd like to accompany me, we can talk on the way. Otherwise, this conversation is over for the time being. My aunt needs me and my time is running out."

"And leave this creature here? I think not—"

"Stop calling him a creature. He's a bloody vampire," Chrysabelle snapped.

Rennata gasped. "You will not take that tone with me, nor use such language. Not in this house or anywhere else. And leaving him here is unacceptable."

"My apologies." Chrysabelle sighed. "He cannot go beyond the common areas. The wards prevent that."

Interesting. Mal gave Rennata the once-over for good measure before speaking to Chrysabelle. "How long will it take you to do what you need to?"

"No more than ten minutes."

"Fine." He glanced at the mantel clock. "I'll wait outside for that long. You don't show by minute eleven and hell breaks loose." He shot Rennata the toothy grin he'd once used on victims right before going in for the kill. "And you're not going to want that."

This time she had the good sense to flinch.

He swiveled for the door as the two women headed farther into the house. At least this would give him a chance to get away from the torturous perfume rattling his control. He paused in the foyer for a moment to study a portrait of one of the earliest comarrés. Their history paralleled the noble vampire Families, as though some higher power had created them to keep the vampire hungers in check. For the most part, it had worked. Until someone like him had come along.

He stood thinking as the minutes ticked by. He shook his head. He really had no right to be in this place. Chrysabelle hadn't wanted him to come in, but he'd insisted on it. And hadn't kept his mouth shut. Better get to the car before Rennata had him thrown out.

Mal had the door open two inches when the stench hit him.

Brimstone.

He wheeled around and chased after Chrysabelle but came to an abrupt halt in the great room. Several doors fed off the room and he had no idea which way led to the suites. He listened for her, hoping to home in on which direction she'd gone.

Eerie silence greeted him.

Not her heartbeat, not Rennata's, not the girl who'd opened the door, no one's. How could that be? Certainly there were plenty of comarré here. Chrysabelle had said as many as several hundred.

Frustration bore down on him. This was not the time for guessing games and comarré secrets.

He leaned back, opened his mouth, and yelled Chrysabelle's name.

# Chapter Twenty-nine

Chrysabelle lengthened her stride as she and Rennata left the great room and Mal behind. Making him wait wasn't a very good idea, but what else could she do? She needed this time with Rennata, if for no other reason than to smooth things so that upon her return, she would be able to access the Aurelian on Mal's behalf. He deserved that for what he'd been through.

Suddenly, she realized Rennata had said something. "I'm sorry, what was that? I've got so much going on in my head, I can barely concentrate on putting one foot in front of the other."

"Understandable, given the circumstances." Rennata, cane long ago discarded, kept pace beside Chrysabelle. "I was saying that if you attempt to rescue your aunt, you will expose us. Do you expect the Families to believe you're an aberration? That you trained yourself to fight and kill in your spare time?" She sighed with great effort. "I cannot allow you to jeopardize all for the sake of one. I am sorry."

Chrysabelle shook her head. "I'm sorry too, but I will not allow my aunt to die because of something I've done."

Rennata stopped and grabbed her arm. "You mean you killed Algernon?"

"No. I just meant because of my running after I discovered his body. This mess wasn't made any better by my actions." She eased her arm out of Rennata's grasp. How far had she fallen in this woman's eyes? "Do you think I'm capable of murdering my patron?"

The older woman's brows lifted slightly. "We are all capable of that." She started walking again, and Chrysabelle joined her. "And you did bring that unwelcome creature, er, vampire into our house."

"He is not unwelcome. He's my patron."

"He's anathema. How under this heaven does a comarré of your value end up with a vampire like him? Of all the comarré in this house . . . You were raised better than that. You were our best." She shook her head. "You have much to explain, including how he came to hold your blood rights. I'm sure it's a very interesting story."

Rennata had been like a parent to Chrysabelle, a very strict one, but a parent nonetheless. Still, there was a time for being scolded like a child and a time to understand that lives were at stake and things needed to be dealt with. Now was strictly the latter. "You're right, it's very interesting. Perhaps we can sit down over tea when this is all over."

"At the very least, I'd think."

Saved by the proximity of her suite, Chrysabelle reached for the handle of the door to her rooms and turned. "If you'll just excuse me, I won't be a moment."

"We've brought your sacre back."

"Thank you, I appreciate that." Chrysabelle shut the door, glad to get away from Rennata's line of questions.

She had no intention of explaining what had happened unless left with no other choice.

The suite was almost the way she'd left it. A few insignificant things were missing, no doubt taken to furnish the cell Rennata had used to throw Tatiana off. Her sacre rested across the foot of the bed. Chrysabelle laid Maris's sacre on the bed beside it, then stripped off her clothes and boots and changed into a high-necked white suede tunic and trousers and new slippers. She grabbed her sacre and slung it across her body. As good as it felt to be in her own clothes again, the weight of her personal sword felt doubly good.

She added Maris's sacre over her own, then slid out the drawer in her bedside table and tapped open the hidden panel in the bottom, releasing the ring into her palm. She turned it in her fingers, wondering what power the band held for Tatiana to want it so desperately. It must be great. No matter. If handing the ring over to Tatiana was what it took to get Aunt Maris home safely, so be it. The ring could be dealt with later. Certainly the heads of the Families would be interested in knowing what one of their children was up to, no?

The sound of her name being yelled at ear-piercing decibels rattled the door. She dropped the drawer, shoved the ring in her trouser pocket, and yanked open the door. Rennata stood facing the way they'd come, her face a horrified mask, a gold pocket watch in her hand. "It's not been eight minutes yet," she muttered.

Chrysabelle flew past. Something was wrong. Mal would have given her the time allotted otherwise. She burst into the great room, her heart pounding, and skidded to a stop beside him. "What happened?"

"Nothos. I smelled brimstone as soon as I opened the door. We need to go now. Did you get—"

Rennata rounded the corner. "What's going on?"

"Nothos." While Rennata crossed herself, Chrysabelle nodded to Mal. "Let's go."

"Wait," Rennata called.

"What?" Mal hesitated.

Rennata gripped the door frame as though she might tear it from the building. "If you go against Tatiana, you must kill her." She pointed a look at Chrysabelle. "That is the only acceptable outcome."

Chrysabelle and Mal both nodded, and with the speed only a vampire his age could manage, Mal disappeared from the room. Chrysabelle chased after him, following through the open door and out into the night. She caught up to him behind one of the massive oaks lining the drive.

Neither of them said a word.

Two Nothos, one on each car roof, trails of vapor leaking from their nostrils. They were hideous. Wrongly jointed and excessively muscled. And not one iota human. Brimstone fouled Chrysabelle's throat. She envied Mal's ability to forgo breathing.

The closest Nothos reared back, its massive hand aimed claws down. Mal pointed at Chrysabelle, then to the Nothos about to jam its talons into the car roof, indicating he would take the one farther back. She nodded and reached for her sacre. Her hand trembled slightly as her fingers closed around the hilt. This was no weak fringe she was about to take on. *Holy mother, help me.*

The handle warmed in her grasp, reassuring her. This weapon was tuned to her, its hollow hilt filled with her own life's blood to marry the blade to her as though it were an extension of her arm. It quivered in her hand, ready to taste her opponent's flesh.

She started forward, but Mal held his palm up for her to wait.

The Nothos plunged its fist into the car roof. Metal screeched. From inside the car, Fi screamed. Mal slashed his hand down.

They both leaped out from behind the trees. In one silent jump, Mal landed on the roof behind his Nothos. Chrysabelle ran toward her target, a calm settling into her veins. She was meant for this. With a steely sense of purpose, she vaulted onto the car with a thud and raised her weapon.

Her Nothos yanked its hand, trying to free it, but failed on the first try. That bought her enough time to bring her sacre down on his shoulder. The hot blade bit into the beast's stinking flesh but sizzled to a stop against bone. The open wound smoked, releasing a brand-new stench into the air.

The creature howled. Car doors opened. She unstuck her blade as the Nothos's free hand slammed into her side and swiped her to the ground. The pain and impact sucked the air from her lungs. She lay there gasping, watching the beast's shoulder knit back together in an oozing line of flesh and hair. That shouldn't be possible. A hot blade left a lasting mark. Slowly, the creature turned, its yellow eyes scanning the night, looking for her.

Doc stepped in front of her, roaring like a jungle cat. His body had partially shifted into a half-leopard, half-man state and his fingers now sported lethal claws. The Nothos roared back, reaching for Doc. She pushed to her feet and whipped a bone dagger into the beast's eye.

Fluid exploded, coating the side of the creature's face and Doc's right arm. With a yowl of pain, the Nothos fell to its knees, denting the hood. It grabbed the dagger and pulled. The punctured eyeball came out with the blade, leaving a gaping, wet hole.

The Nothos flung the dagger at Doc, eyeball and all, but missed.

Doc hissed and was about to pounce when Chrysabelle grabbed him and pointed to Fi, the last person besides the drivers still in the vehicles. Chrysabelle yelled to her, "Get out of the car."

Fi shook her head, shivering against the leather seat. The Nothos pounded a fist into the roof and she jumped.

Chrysabelle turned to Doc. "Get her out of there and into the house."

"Will do." Doc reached in, grabbed Fi, and, tossing her over his shoulder, took off in a run for the main house. Rennata had better let them in.

Mortalis sprang onto the roof next to where Mal exchanged staggering blows with his Nothos. "Get back."

Surprisingly, Mal did, jumping across to the other car and knocking the one-eyed Nothos off the roof and onto the hood. Sword in hand, Chrysabelle launched herself onto the snarling creature. Her knees met bone and sinew slippery with retinal fluid. Fighting for balance, she hefted her sacre two-handed and plunged it into the creature's heart.

It curled upward like a spider, its great mouth gaping into an abyss of teeth. Shrieks tore at her eardrums. Claws raked down her arms, shredding the sleeves of her suede tunic but glancing off the body armor underneath. Vile yellow sludge seeped up around the blade. She wrenched the blade in deeper, gouging the hood beneath its body. Metal whined against metal. The screeching intensified. The sludge blackened, bubbled, and turned to smoke. The Nothos went rigid, its remaining eye fixed on her.

A second later, her knees smashed into the hood and a cloud of ash rose up around her. She sneezed, spit out a mouthful of bitter dust, then stood, blade aimed to take on the last Nothos.

It lurched atop the other car, wavering like a drunken sailor, eyes alternately rolling up into its head and locking onto her. Dominic stood off to one side, his short blade brandished, Solomon behind him. Since cyphers were basically defenseless, Dominic was Solomon's only chance. Mortalis was nowhere to be seen. Had the Nothos killed him? Time to end this thing. She flicked out her remaining dagger and was about to let it fly when Mal stopped her.

"Don't. Mortalis is in there controlling it."

Her hand dropped to her side. "He can occupy a Nothos?"

"Not as thoroughly as a fringe or with the same consistency as a noble," Mal said. "But yes."

She'd never seen a shadeux possess anyone. Heard about it. Read about it. Understood what they were capable of, but this . . . this was amazing.

The Nothos let out a gut-deep growl, its protruding lower jaw dripping strands of saliva. Had Mortalis ever tried to slip inside Mal and take control of him? What would happen if a shadeux tried to take over someone who had a soul?

With jerky movements, the Nothos jumped off the car and landed in a crouch. It straightened as though puppet strings pulled it upright. A voice spilled out of it, half

Mortalis, half raging Nothos. "Do you want me to kill it, or should we use it as a Trojan horse?"

Dominic and Solomon had come around to stand closer to Chrysabelle. Only the drivers remained in the cars. Dominic sheathed his falchion. "I like the Trojan horse idea, but can you keep control of that thing long enough?"

The Nothos nodded jerkily and spewed out a yes.

Chrysabelle failed to see how the Nothos could work as a Trojan horse. No one but Mortalis could possess it that way. How were the rest of them supposed to get into Tatiana's estate? Maybe it was time to tell them about the underground access. Rennata would have Chrysabelle banned if she revealed the tunnels. Maybe the Nothos idea was worth some discussion. "Explain it to me."

Mal notched his head toward the foul creature as he closed the distance between them. "Mortalis steers the thing through the front doors with you as his prisoner. If it goes well, they throw you in with your aunt. We charge in after and I follow your heartbeat to wherever they're holding you both and we clean house. Solomon can get us in wherever we need to go once we know where we're headed."

She rested the point of her sacre on the dented hood. "And if things don't go well?"

"That's why it's up to you." He brushed a few flecks of stray ash off her sleeve. The gesture startled her almost as much as seeing the two Nothos had. "You decide."

"Please, *bella*," Dominic said. "It might be our best chance to find Marissa."

Mal scowled. "And what if it gets Chrysabelle killed?"

What if? What if she didn't do it and Maris ended up

dead because they didn't get to her in time? "I can take that risk." She moved closer to Mal. "There's just one thing."

"What?"

She reached into her pocket and wrapped her fingers around the ring, then extended her balled fist in the small space left between them. She opened it. "This. Tatiana will expect me to have it. If you hold on to it that might buy me some time to negotiate." As though that was even possible with Tatiana.

"You sure letting her have it is the best solution?"

"I'm not sure of anything right now, but it's a plan."

"What makes you think I can keep it safer than you?"

"Because if it comes down to it, you can let the demons inside you loose." Even if it meant the death of the rest of them. Her spine iced at the thought of Tatiana getting that ring, but if it meant freeing Maris...

"You know what that might mean."

"I do."

He held out his palm. She tipped hers, letting the circle of gold slide into his hand. He winced slightly when the metal came into contact with his skin.

"You okay?" she asked. "I know it's sacred, but Algernon had no problems touching it. That I know of."

"Algernon didn't have a chorus of banshees in his head." He closed his fingers over the ring and tucked it into his jacket. "Let's just say they're not crazy about this particular piece of jewelry."

"Don't worry, I'm going to want it back."

Black rimmed the silver in his eyes. "You'll get it without a fight."

She turned to face the Nothos. One corded arm hung

slack at its side, the other scratched a hole in its horse-shaped head trying to get at the fae inside it. This was going to be interesting to say the least.

"Hang on to that thing, Mortalis. We're going in."

The fair-haired male struggled under Tatiana's mouth, his heartbeat weakening to a thready rhythm that sang in her ears like a choir of castrati. The blood was sweeter when the victim teetered on that narrow edge between life and death.

"Enough, mistress, please," he whispered.

This was not a victim, however. This was her comar, and it had taken her years to repay Ivan for the cost of his blood rights. Well worth it, though, for his blood was exquisite. Reluctantly, she drew one last mouthful from his wrist, then pushed him away and collapsed back onto the chaise.

Clutching his wrist, he lurched to his feet, bowing slightly as he backed away. "Thank you, mistress."

She was only vaguely aware of the pale blond kine stumbling out of the room. His heartbeat receded as he shut the door and left her to absorb the strength of his blood.

The rush of power hit her with its familiar numbing warmth, needling through her veins with the stinging prick of morphine. If vampires had a drug, it was comarré blood. She closed her eyes and gave herself over to the heady swirl of life. Her heart began to beat. She listened to the bleak cadence and was reminded of how weak she'd been as a human. Of everything she'd had to endure. That life was thankfully behind her. She had been twice reborn as a creature of unparalleled power.

Power that would see her through the coming battle.

One of the Nothos scouts had reported two others lost in a fight at the Primoris Domus. Losing the two Nothos was unfortunate, but all that mattered was that the girl was *here*. And coming to her. Even now, Mikkel watched the perimeter for her approach. Once the girl was secured, he would be free to decimate the rest of her party. It seemed the least reward Tatiana could offer him for his help.

The perfection of it all thrilled her. Her greatness was immeasurable. How long would it take before there was no vampire more powerful than she? None would be better suited to rule. The House of Tepes would rise to terrifying heights under her guidance. Another swell of power rippled through her. She would rule all the Families.

The girl would bring her the ring and take her aunt's place as the sacrifice. Why use the old comarré's blood when Tatiana could have the younger one? Was the old woman even still alive? Tatiana hadn't checked on her since bedding Mikkel. Why bother? With the niece on her way, the old woman no longer mattered.

Sweet, dumb Mikkel. How wonderful that he'd been the inadvertent key to her figuring out the sacrifice.

How clever that comarré blood would unlock the ring. How had she not seen it before? Pure blood. Pure power. *The covenant shall be broken.* Then all manner of hell would be unleashed. Tatiana laughed, unable to contain the wicked, heady joy filling her soulless body. What would it feel like when she slipped that ring onto her finger? She craved it with an almost greater hunger than she desired blood.

A powerful presence filled the room, followed by an

unmistakable scent. She forced herself not to shudder. The time was at hand. All fear had to be pushed aside. The fearful did not rule, only the strong.

"Master," she whispered, opening her eyes and slipping off the chaise to bow.

He held out his hand for her to kiss his ring, and after she had, bid her, "Rise, my child."

She did as asked, keeping her head down. Tremors of excitement skittered over her skin. She was so close to getting everything she desired. For once, she did not dread the presence of the Castus. She would do their bidding and gather her reward.

The room darkened around him as though his being overpowered the light. "You have just fed?"

"Yes, master. I am prepared. The ring and the sacrifice approach."

"You are sure?"

"Yes." She raised her head. Nothing could stop her. Everything was in place. Everything was perfectly aligned.

The Castus smiled. Tatiana forced herself not to look away. "How soon?"

"Within the hour." She assumed. She hoped a more accurate answer wasn't required.

"Very good. The prophecy will be fulfilled at last." He laughed, shattering the mirror over the mantel. Glass rained down, slicing a thousand tiny cuts into her. They healed quickly, leaving traces of blood behind.

He lifted her hand and dragged his forked tongue over the beads of blood on her hand and arm. "Now then, when you have the ring and the sacrifice in hand, this is what you must do..."

# Chapter Thirty

Maris inched down the hall, careful not to scrape the heel of her bad leg on the floor. She'd found enough weapons along the way to arm herself with a short dagger and a cutlass. Not her first choices, but those had been the easiest and quietest to remove from their mounts.

The house reeked of vampire. Not the subtle spice she'd once found so alluring on Dominic, but the pervasive mustiness of death and decay. Like old paper money left too long in a damp place.

Tatiana had killed in this house. There was no other explanation. Maris's lip curled in disgust. This Tatiana lived like the world owed her something and she was determined to claim it.

A noise up ahead sent Maris into a side room. A small guest room, nothing more. No closet either, just an armoire that would cause considerable pain to her hip should she have to climb into it. She pressed her ear to the door and listened as footsteps went by.

She opened the door a slit and peeked into the hall, gripping the dagger close to her side. A servant disappeared down the corridor. She ducked out. Time to move.

She couldn't expect to remain undetected forever. At some point, someone would realize she was no longer tied to that chair and an alarm would be raised.

The hall split north and south. The stench grew stronger to the north so she went that way. Assuming Tatiana killed in her quarters was taking a leap of faith, but Maris had nothing else to go on. Step by arduous step, she closed on Tatiana, praying it wasn't much farther. The beatings had left her bruised and weary, her hip a knot of pain.

An interior door opened and closed. Frantic to find a hiding place, Maris tried the closest room, but it was locked. Snapping herself against the wall at the side of a large display cabinet, she readied herself to attack. The cutlass blade rested against her cheek, the hilt held snugly by her breast. From here, she could strike out and slice the throat of whoever came by. Maybe even decapitate them.

Footsteps approached. Soft. Sluggish. Weak. Not the stride of a vampire. At least, not Tatiana. Her steps were much more determined, full of arrogance and carelessness.

Maris held her weapons, waiting to see…the air changed, the mustiness tempered with a sweeter scent. More like home.

A comar stumbled past. She couldn't see his face, but one hand clenched his opposite wrist. Blood stained his gilded fingers. The wound would heal, but his wobbly gait indicated the blood loss had been great. Her heart went out to him for a thousand different reasons, but she had work to do and little time to accomplish it.

Bittersweet emotion filled her. She now knew where Tatiana was, and that Tatiana had just fed. She would be strong. Hard to defeat. But Tatiana's careless use of her comar stirred Maris. The vampire needed to die. She was a blight on her own kind.

Maris swallowed down her fear. She'd lived long enough anyway. When the comar was safely past, she stepped out into the hall and walked as boldly toward the way he'd come as her bad leg would let her. That boldness didn't mean she'd willfully throw away the element of surprise however.

She pressed her ear to a flat spot on one of the carved double doors he'd likely exited from. A distant conversation reached her ears, too muted to understand. Sounded like it came from far inside the room. Beyond the room, maybe. She eased the door open and listened again. Definitely another room. Satisfied the first room was empty, she slipped in and closed the door quietly.

A small salon, well furnished but ill smelling. Another set of double doors. She listened at those and heard more clearly the conversation that had eluded her.

"...after the ring is on your finger"—a deeply scarred male voice rasped. Maris winced. The voice grated like teeth scraping bone—"you will drain your sacrifice to death."

"Yes, master," a female voice replied. Tatiana. "I only hope the elder comarré lives long enough to watch me do it."

The horrid smell increased and the crack of a slap reverberated in reply. Then the harsh male voice spoke again. "Your only hope need be that what I ask of you is done."

*Holy mother.* Her hand went to her mouth. The sudden recognition of whom that odor and voice belonged to sucked the strength out of Maris. Cold fear burrowed into her joints. The weapons in her hands became thousand-pound weights, her own body difficult to support. Her bad leg trembled like a sapling in a stiff breeze.

If Tatiana was willing to subjugate herself to those ancient evils, there was no limit to what she could do. And whatever this ring was, it was going to bring about something awful. The ring Tatiana believed Chrysabelle had.

Maris eased her way out of the room, desperate to put distance between herself and the monumental evil in the next room.

She scanned in both directions. All clear. But which way to go? She scoured her mind for the lessons drilled into her so many years ago. The fog of time lifted and the logical answer showed itself. Now to find a way into the bowels of the estate. She moved in the direction the comar had gone. Something made her think Tatiana had not reserved the best rooms for him.

Was he the comar Tatiana planned on using for a sacrifice? Herself? Chrysabelle? Holy mother, not Chrysabelle.

Maris shivered as she hurried down the empty corridor. This revelation changed everything. She had to stay alive long enough to warn Chrysabelle of Tatiana's dangerous alliance. Maris had done too much and gone too far to allow that wicked bloodsucking autocrat to harm her niece. Tatiana had to be stopped. Permanently.

After that, Maris would find a way to die usefully. Like covered in the ashes of as many vampires as she could take with her.


"So much for the Trojan horse idea." Mal shook his head as he stared into the car. A more loathsome display of innards he could not recall. Even the voices recoiled. It was as though the Nothos had somehow exploded. Fortunately, they were parked on the public road that ran through Corvinestri's human cemetery. Not much chance of disturbing anyone here.

Dominic peered in beside him. *"Mamma mia."*

"I didn't have a choice," Mortalis grumbled. "I've never tried to possess one for that long. Hell, until yesterday, I'd never possessed one at all." He scraped his hands along his arms, depositing big sticky clumps of Nothos remains onto the limo floor.

Doc stuck his head over the car door and wrinkled his nose. "That's just nasty." He smirked at Dominic. "Glad I'm not paying that cleaning bill."

Dominic smirked back. "As if you could."

"Enough," Mal said. Chrysabelle approached, but he held up his hands. "Stay over there with Fi and Solomon. You don't want to see this. Or get any closer to the smell."

Shreds of Nothos plastered the car's interior. Pools of yellow blood soaked the carpet. Strings of sinew and tendons hung from the bar. Rusty black bones lay strewn about. Lots and lots of bones. Mal's eyes watered from the stench. *Too bad it's not you.*

"I'm sure I've seen worse. And I can already smell it." She stopped next to Mal, blinking hard. "Wow, that is nasty."

"Yes, thanks for pointing that out again." Mortalis wiped more entrails off his face.

Chrysabelle poked at a lump of flesh on the interior door handle. "Wonder why it didn't turn to ash?"

Mortalis tapped the tip of one filigreed horn. "Too much silver contact, maybe."

The driver pushed his door open and rushed behind a

marble monument. The sounds of vomiting followed. Mal lifted a brow. Stepping off the public road and onto the hallowed cemetery ground would be like walking on razor blades. Maybe fringe didn't feel it as strongly as the noble-blooded. Or maybe the driver thought getting sick in front of everyone else was worse. Mal had never seen a vampire—even a fringe—lose his accounts over a little gore. He looked back at the car's interior. Okay, more than a little gore.

The driver hurried back to the road. Wisps of smoke curled off his skin. No way was stepping foot on that soil better than puking in front of people.

Mal grimaced, then turned back to Mortalis. "What did you do to it exactly?"

"I turned it inside out." Mortalis climbed out. Everyone backed up. "Trust me, it was halfway there on its own trying to get at me."

Dominic cursed in Italian. "Now what? That Nothos was our way in."

Mal shut the car door. "We'll figure out a different plan." Maybe they could force their way in?

"We're wasting time," Dominic said. "Marissa could be dying. There's no telling what Tatiana will do to her." He patted his chest and glass clanked from his breast pocket. "I came prepared to blast us in if need be."

Mal snorted. "So much for subtlety."

Dominic scowled. "You have a better idea?"

"I know another way in." Chrysabelle squinted and rubbed her forehead as though a headache pounded the back of her eyes. "There are underground tunnels that connect the major estates. I can get us in, so Solomon can stay behind."

"You've known this all along?" Anger flickered in Dominic's eyes. "Why didn't you say something sooner?"

Chrysabelle's hands went to her hips and the pulse in her neck jumped. "You of all people should understand about comarré keeping secrets."

*"Stupido."* Dominic threw his hands in the air.

"Apologize, Dominic." Mal's temper flared hot beneath his skin. The beast lifted its head. He understood Dominic had a personal stake in this, but Mal would not abide Chrysabelle being disrespected. "Talk to her like that again and I'll break your neck. Or she can do it herself."

Looking less than penitent, Dominic sketched a shallow bow. *"Scusi."* Blowhard. The vampire must have been a real joy before he turned anathema. What had Chrysabelle's aunt ever seen in him? *More than Chrysabelle will ever see in you.*

Mortalis flicked a piece of skin off one of his horns. "Well, I'm out. There's no way I can go in there smelling like this. They'll scent me immediately."

Mal pointed at him. "You stay here and protect Fi and Solomon. Solomon, cyphers can set wards as well as break them, correct?"

Solomon bowed his head. "Yes, of course."

"Then set one around this perimeter. Chrysabelle, I assume you know how to get to these tunnels from here?"

Her eyes stayed on the ground. Clearly, she was not happy to have revealed this secret to so many. "I can guide us in from the village sewers."

"Good." Mal glanced at Doc. "You and Dominic need to put the past behind you for tonight."

Dominic stood at the edge of the road, staring into the

headstones and monuments. He looked back and shrugged one shoulder. "For Marissa, of course."

Doc nodded. "So long as I get to kill something."

"All right then, Mortalis, you're in charge here. You've got the map Chrysabelle drew. Get the car in the proximity of the estate in an hour." Mal glanced at the others as they gathered around him. "Let's go."

A half hour later and the four of them slogged through ankle-high brown water and debris that Mal didn't want to look too closely at. Weak solars spaced every few yards offered little light and dripping water echoed through the dim tunnels.

He was surprised Chrysabelle could see to lead them as well as she was. She hadn't faltered once, only slowed. A rat scurried past along the pipes bolted to the wall, squeaking its displeasure at the strange intruders.

Doc's stomach rumbled. Mal shot him a look.

Doc shook his head. "Don't go there with me, vampire. You drink blood."

"Quiet." Chrysabelle held her hand up and stopped before a fork in the tunnel. Both sides of the divergence were gated. "I need better ears. Do you hear voices coming from either of these tunnels?"

Mal heard a lot of things—the buzz in his head, the pleasurable hum of her pulse, the drip and splash of the water, the patter of vermin feet—but he listened past all that and focused on what the paths held. Faintly, like rain falling on a distant window, the drone of conversation reached him. He nodded. "I hear voices coming from both."

She frowned. "That means they've kept the staff on at Algernon's. I thought they'd have shut the house up."

"Do you know which direction or not?" Dominic asked.

"Chill, man. Let the girl do her thing." Doc flicked open his switchblade and began cleaning under his nails, carefully avoiding Mal's direction since he'd obviously violated the temporary peace treaty.

Dominic muttered in Italian.

She ignored both of them and asked Mal, "Can you smell death from either direction? Algernon's house should carry that odor. Tatiana's... hopefully not."

Mal inhaled. The sewer stank, but nothing like the exploded Nothos. Again he nodded. "I smell death." *You should know.*

"In which direction?"

He hated his answer. "Both."

Her face crumpled for a brief moment, then steeled. "Very well. I will have to guess—no, wait. Is the scent of comarré mixed with either one? Maybe more strongly than another?"

He pulled the air in, unraveling the layers of scent as if they were intertwined strands of thread. The honeyed perfume of comarré was strong in both, but only one tunnel carried the particularly sweet fragrance he'd come to know as Chrysabelle. The other carried an oddly familiar scent. Not completely unpleasant. It reminded him of something or someone from his past. The noise in his head ticked up. He sniffed again. The scent was familiar, but also different. Off. He ignored it for the moment. Chrysabelle needed him to get this right.

"There." He pointed to the left. "That way carries your scent."

She offered him a sliver of a smile before shifting her gaze to the other tunnel. "Then we go right."

Mal stepped in behind her but grabbed Doc's arm. "Keep it civil with Dominic. I mean it."

Doc flipped the switchblade closed and tucked it away. "Noted."

She turned to face them all. "From here on in, no talking. If you can hear them, they can hear you. Understood?"

Apparently satisfied with their nods, Chrysabelle walked up to the locked gate and stood very still in front of it. A moment later, a small snick signaled the gate had unlocked. She pushed it open, stepped over the raised threshold and headed into the tunnel. Mal stayed close to her, with Dominic and Doc keeping some distance from each other.

"How did you unlock that?" he whispered.

She just shook her head and kept her silence. Another comarré secret?

As the minutes ticked by, the path descended lower and lower and the tunnel narrowed. Water rushed by. The solars disappeared, replaced by gently pulsing phosphorescence that reminded Mal of the hallways that led to the Pits at Seven. The subtle sounds of occupation strengthened deeper in, and the soft voices of servants penetrated the thick barrier of stone between them and the residence. A few times, Chrysabelle's eyes shifted upward. Could she hear them? Or was she thinking of her aunt and what the next few hours might bring?

At last, when they were somewhere in the dark underbelly of Corvinestri, they came to a four-way split. The path directly across from them led into a small, dark room. Chrysabelle motioned them in.

The empty space was carved from the surrounding rock and still bore the marks of whatever tools had hewn it. Moisture seeped from the walls. Nothing denoted the room as anything special and, more interesting, there was no way out except the way they'd come in. He glanced up. Nothing on the ceiling either. Judging by the look of frustration on Dominic's face, he'd figured that out too. If this was the way into Tatiana's estate, they were going to need dynamite, shovels, or magic. He held his hands out to Chrysabelle in question.

Exasperation thinned Chrysabelle's mouth. She splayed her fingers, pushing her palm toward the floor. Mal nodded. She wanted them to wait, be patient. He could do that. He'd waited this long to extract his revenge on the nobles who'd cursed him, he could wait a little longer.

She positioned herself in front of the back wall and off to one side.

He tried not to stare, but even in the gloom, she shimmered with the soft glow only a comarré could produce. Her braid bared the sides of her face, revealing the delicate gold lacework tattooed there, and despite the twinkling silver body armor covering her neck, the ache in his gums made him bite down until his fangs jutted into his lower lip. Not the time. *Always the time*.

She pushed up her tunic sleeves to roll the silver mesh back past her elbows, exposing her signum, then bending her arms, she locked them together vertically in front of her face like a shield, fists facing inward, the flats of her forearms facing the wall. She closed her eyes and mouthed words. He couldn't see her lips, but it seemed like she was praying.

Dominic sighed. Mal glared at him. If he didn't shut up, Mal would give him a bloody reason to. He turned back in time to see the wall shimmer in front of Chrysabelle.

She opened her eyes as it wavered for another second then melted away to reveal a doorway into an extensive wine cellar. Weak light spilled into the space.

The cellar held more than wine bottles.

Near the back of the room, amid the racks and oak casks, another older comarré limped toward them. Her clothes were dirty and torn, her face bruised and bloodied, her weapons raised in a fighting stance. Her eyes widened and her mouth fell open as she took in the group of them.

Dominic rushed forward. "Marissa!"

"Holy mother," Chrysabelle whispered, reaching for the wall. "You can walk?"

# Chapter Thirty-one

Fi wandered the cemetery, reading names and dates as best she could by the light of the moon. How many of these people owed their death to a vampire like she did? She traced the carving on one headstone, her fingers catching on the weathered stone as she glanced back toward the cars. She would have felt better if Doc had stayed. Hanging out with the fae was fine, but the drivers were still vamps. Vamps she didn't know. Friendly or not, she wanted some distance. Especially since one of the drivers, Leo, had managed a few minutes on hallowed ground to toss his cookies, even if he had come out smoking like a burned pot roast.

She shivered and pulled her coat tighter. If Doc were here, he'd have his arm around her, keeping her warm. Hopefully he was okay, wherever he was. Mal would protect him, wouldn't he?

Sighing, she strolled past the rows of tombstones. The relative safety of the holy ground didn't stop the old cemetery from being a smidge creepy, especially at night, but it wasn't enough to suppress her interest. This was exactly the type of place that would have piqued her curiosity when she'd been studying to be an anthropologist.

She frowned. That stupid drive to unearth some exciting, previously undiscovered thing had gotten her killed. Why couldn't she have been a computer engineer? Or an accountant?

Her mind wandered to the day she'd discovered those ruins in northern England. The terror that followed. She shook her head to make the memories go away. This was not the place for those kinds of thoughts. Her feet carried her farther away from the car and the four othernatural males who were currently playing some kind of dice game. There was a huge crypt in the corner of the cemetery she was dying to see.

She smiled. *Dying to see.* Now that was funny. Doc would have thought so.

The crypt was illustrated on all sides with flowers and people and depictions of life, all brightly painted like the headstones in the famous Merry Cemetery in Sâpânṭa. Had this family moved to Corvinestri from that part of Romania? What would make them do that? It must pay very well to work for the nobility. It would have to. She walked around the crypt slowly, studying the pictures and wishing for a headlamp and a sketchbook. How many of the family were still alive? Still working for the vampires who controlled this hidden city?

A soft mewling caught her attention. She looked in the direction of the sounds. Beyond the wrought iron gates of the cemetery sat a tiny striped kitten. He cried again and Fi missed Doc more than ever, remembering the day Mal had brought a torn-up Doc in cat form back to the freighter. Mal had thought the cat would give her something else to focus on besides tormenting him. He'd been right, but neither of them had known Doc's true nature.

He'd been too wounded to shift into human form. Once he had...well, not exactly the pet Mal had been counting on.

She grinned and hurried to the gate. "You poor thing. Where's your mama?"

The kitten sneezed and blinked at Fi, meowing for attention. She stuck her hand through the gate but couldn't quite reach him. "Aw, c'mere, baby. Do you have a wittle cold?"

But the kitten stayed put and answered her with more pitiful meowing.

"Hang on, I'm coming." She glanced back at the men. Still busy with their game. The tall fae had warded the whole area. There had to be some overflow that covered the area beyond the gates too.

She opened the gate and stuck her head out to scan the area. No one lying in wait, nothing unusual in either direction. The kitten flopped onto its side and began to purr.

She slipped out but stayed close to the gate. "Here, kitty, kitty. Come on, come to Fi. I'm good with cats, you'll see." She took a step toward the little ball of fluff, prepared to scoop it up and dash back through the gate, but no one jumped out of the bushes. Nerves were making her silly. She laughed softly and bent to pick up the kitten. "There you are—"

A hand closed over her nose and mouth. The kitten vanished into curls of black smoke.

Her fingers flew up to pry the hand away but found nothing, no physical being. She whirled, still scrabbling at her mouth, trying to wedge it open to no avail. The air prickled with dark magic, but she was alone. The unseen force pressed down harder. Her lungs burned with the need for air. The need to scream.

She concentrated on going spectral and, for a moment, the force seemed to weaken. Then it lifted her free of the ground and the invisible hand clamped down harder. She screamed but the sound came out weak and muffled. A dark shape appeared out of the shadows, the creature's hands outstretched toward her. Her head spun with sparks of light and the clawing ache to breathe.

She tried to scream again as her body floated through the air in the creature's direction. Numbness spread through her like a fog, closing down her vision until the last pinpoint of light winked out.


A thousand questions tumbled through Chrysabelle's mind. Had her aunt always been able to walk? Why would she hide such a thing? Had Dominic known?

"She's down here," a voice called out behind Maris.

Maris limped forward, almost stumbling. She turned her head in the voice's direction, then back again. Panic filled her eyes.

"We've got her," the voice called out again, this time followed by the sound of multiple sets of footsteps running down stairs.

Maris held Chrysabelle's gaze and touched her fist to her heart, then shook her head sadly. In a smooth motion, she dropped her weapons and brought her arms up in front of her face with her fists and elbows together. Her sleeves slid back to reveal her signum. The opening between them vanished.

Maris had closed the portal.

Chrysabelle slammed her fist into the rock wall, barely containing the scream chafing her throat. They'd been so close. She punched the wall again, but her fist hit flesh.

Mal's palm cushioned the space between her hand and the rock wall. She tore her hand away, anger pulsating in her veins. She'd been within yards of her aunt. A net of helplessness closed around her heart.

Mal motioned to the wall as if to say, "Just open it again."

But she couldn't. The wards had a built-in safety measure. Once a door had been opened and closed, it couldn't be reopened for fifteen minutes. She shook her head at him. They'd have to go through a different one, one that wasn't as conveniently located in the house.

She charged out, waving her hand for the others to follow. She didn't care at this point if Doc and Dominic came along or not. Maris's near escape would certainly cost her. Tatiana would have her punished. Maybe killed outright.

Those thoughts moved her quickly another thirty feet down the tunnel and into the next room. Mal, Doc, and Dominic were right behind her. This was not going to be pleasant. Especially if the room beyond had been used recently. She positioned herself in front of the correct wall according to the map in her head and put her arms together before her so the signum inscribed on her forearms lined up. *Please, holy mother,* she mouthed.

The portal opened.

The weak luminescence from the room they were in refused to penetrate the total darkness in the space beyond. She tipped her head, motioning the others through. Their vision would have to guide her because she would be blind in there. She entered behind Dominic, turned, and reactivated the ward, closing the portal.

"We can talk now," she said, trying to breathe through her mouth. The musty reek of carrion and ash crawled down her throat anyway. Things had died here. Not all of them human. "This area is completely silver-lined."

"Yes," Dominic answered from in front of her. "That's the protocol for any dungeon built in a vampire estate." He laughed softly. "No one wants to hear the screaming."

"Or smell the stench," Doc choked out. The squeak of vermin echoed from the corners of the space.

"Why did you shut the door?" Mal was a few feet to her left.

She reached for him, hoping for his sleeve, but grazed his hard stomach instead. She curled her fingers away, ignoring the burst of sensation touching him aroused in her. "So we could talk. If we manage to make it out of this house alive, I'm thinking we'll be able to get out the front door. If not, I can try to reopen this door or the one in the wine cellar, but there's no guarantee. The wards get sticky with too much use. They're mostly meant for one-way trips."

Carefully avoiding her body armor, he guided her hand to his arm. "Is that why you didn't reopen the one your aunt closed? I assume that was your aunt."

"Basically, and yes." She looked in what she thought was the direction of Dominic. "Did you know she could walk?"

"No," he answered. The word was too bitter to be a lie, and the simplicity of the response confirmed his shock at seeing Maris ambulatory. How was he feeling about the woman he claimed to love? Betrayed? Deceived?

Chrysabelle felt a bit of that herself, but she had to focus on why they'd come. Maris might be willing to sac-

rifice herself for Chrysabelle, but Chrysabelle wasn't
okay with that. Maris was family. As real a family as a
comarré could get. Chrysabelle needed that. Plus, Maris
being able to walk made getting her out easier. Dominic
could wallow on his own time. They had to move. "I can't
see a thing, so one of you is going to have to find a way out
of here."

"Be glad you can't see," Doc said. "This joint ain't
pretty. Doesn't look like it's been used for a while though."

"I'm sure the dungeon is too lax a punishment for Tatiana's enemies. She's known to be a bit prickly about getting dirty." Chrysabelle glanced upward into the darkness,
wondering where in the estate her aunt might be. "She's
probably got a nice clean holding cell up there somewhere."

"Then let's find it." Mal moved forward. The muscle
beneath her hand tightened. "Watch your step."

Her foot sent something clattering across the floor.
"What was that?"

"A femur," Mal answered.

"Great," she said. She squeezed Mal's arm lightly.
"This can't be fun for you," she said softly.

He grunted.

She wasn't sure how to take that. Did this dungeon
remind him of the ruins where he'd been imprisoned? She
hoped not. "How far are we from the door?"

"We're there. It's locked. Is it guarded from the
outside?"

"If the dungeon is empty, probably not. Do you sense
any life in here?"

"Nothing more than a few rats," Dominic answered.

"One of you is going to have to break the lock. As quietly as you can."

"What's our plan when we get out of here?" Doc asked.

Chrysabelle took her hand from Mal's arm and rubbed her chin. "We're two levels down. The living areas in this estate are on the north side, so we'll head that way once we hit the main floor. Tatiana's had the estate modified somewhat since she took it over, so we'll start checking rooms once we get up there."

"Maris could be anywhere," Dominic said.

"Yes," Chrysabelle answered, "but you can home in on her heartbeat, can't you?"

Silence for a brief span. "I can still do that."

"Then that's the plan. All right, break this door down and let's go."

"Stand back," Mal said, taking her fingers in his hand and pulling her to the side.

She moved a few steps away and Mal dropped her hand. Something scurried over her foot. The suffocating blackness closed in. She refused to acknowledge the childish fear knotting her belly. Instead she stroked her fingers over the daggers at her wrists and concentrated on what lay ahead. The pressing dark receded enough for her to breathe.

"Doc, take the top hinge, I'll take the bottom," Mal said. "Dominic, grab the door as soon as you can slip your hands through the opening to keep it from falling. Ready?" A brief pause. She assumed the other men nodded. "Now."

The sharp hiss and acrid smell of silver-burned flesh filled the air. Dominic cursed in Italian, and Doc let out a feline spit.

"Solid silver," Mal growled. "Bloody hell."

"Watch out." She pulled her sacre free. The weapon

hummed in her grasp, grateful to be free, eager to taste flesh. She pointed it at what she thought was the door.

Doc snorted. "What are you going to do with—"

"Aim me toward the hinges and get out of the way."

"A little more left," Mal said. "Now forward. A little more."

The tip of the blade scratched the door, catching the seam between door and frame.

"Right there."

"Stand free," she cautioned them. When the sounds of their movement stopped, she rammed the blade halfway into the seam and jerked upward. The structure screeched in protest. A spray of sparks illuminated the line of warped silver left behind as she drove the blade higher, severing the hinges. Her shoulders ached with the effort. Sacres were designed to cut through any material, but flesh and bone were far easier than metal.

Finally, she tugged the weapon free. Fuchsia spots danced before her eyes as the sparks died and the darkness returned. She blinked to clear them.

"So much for the element of surprise," Doc said.

"Let's hope Tatiana thinks it's her staff." Chrysabelle sheathed her sacre, then kicked the door down. It crashed forward, sending curls of dust into the dimly lit stairwell beyond. Faint phosphorescence outlined a decrepit railing, warped stairs, and the trio surrounding her.

Doc wore his in-between face, his eyes green-gold with full-blown pupils to combat the sheer darkness, his nose and cheekbones more pronounced. But it was the almost saber-tooth overhang of fangs that sent a shiver down her spine. Teeth that big would leave dime-size holes. Good to know the varcolai was on her side.

She went first, carefully picking her way up the steps. The second from the top gave beneath her foot. She grabbed the railing. Flakes of rust coated her hand. It grated loudly as the bolts stressed and the entire length bowed out into the air. Unbalanced and about to fall, she released it and struggled to right herself. Mal caught her wrist. His palm sizzled against the silver mesh, but he held on until she stood firm.

"Thank you." She pulled her tunic back over the armor.

He flexed his twice-burned hand and shrugged. "Pain brings clarity."

She nodded. "Then I think we're all about to get really clear."

# Chapter Thirty-two

Fi struggled against the vampire she recognized from Velimai's replay as Mikkel, but her efforts were useless. He held her at arm's length and the black magic hand that had clamped onto her at the cemetery still squeezed her into a state of numbness. No matter how many times she told herself to fight him, willed her legs to kick or her arms to strike out, her body stayed limp. Even trying to go ghostly had lost what little effect it had had.

She had only just become real again, and now she was going to die for the second time. At the hands of a freaking vampire. If she came back as a ghost again, she was going to make this one's life truly miserable.

She just hoped dying wasn't going to hurt as much as it had the first time. She shivered inside and wished for Doc.

Mikkel carried her through a set of double doors and dumped her on some fancy Oriental rug. She winced as she hit the floor. Momentum rolled her faceup, enabling her to see the back of another vampire, this one female. *Please don't let it be—*

The female turned. *It was.* Fi's numbness turned to a bitter chill, and the niggling feeling that she knew these two beyond what Velimai had showed them at Maris's house filled her again as it had that night. Where had she seen them? Even her mind felt numb.

"Look what I brought you, my sweet," Mikkel said.

Tatiana wiped the blood off her knuckles with a towel. "I'm too busy to eat."

That good news was tempered by what sat behind Tatiana. There, tied to a chair and looking like a bloody rag, was another comarré, her gilded face swollen and bruised, her clothing torn and dirty. Chrysabelle's aunt? Fi almost hoped not. The woman looked half dead, but maybe she was just sedated.

Mikkel frowned. "I found her in the kine cemetery." His lids lowered and the corner of his mouth perked up as though he was about to reveal some great tidbit of info. "In the company of some fringe and a pair of fae, one I didn't recognize. But one I think was the shadeux fae who took down the Nothos in the hangar."

Tatiana's face blanked. "You're sure?"

"Absolutely." Mikkel seemed pleased with himself.

"Did you kill them?"

"No. They had the area warded, and she fought my magic hard. I almost didn't get her out. Plus I thought I should bring her to you immediately."

"Hmph." Tatiana bent down and stared into Fi's eyes. She couldn't help but stare back. It was like looking into an abyss. A vile, familiar abyss. "Is the other comarré with you? The girl? What about the vampire helping her?"

Fi lay there, helpless to answer. Not that she would have anyway. If she was going to die in the jaws of a vampire for a second time, she certainly wasn't going to give either of them any help hurting her friends.

"Ignorant chit. You think you can best me?" Tatiana slapped Fi across the face. Pain radiated through her cheek, causing a shocked tear to spill over the stinging skin. Anger blossomed in Fi's belly. Warm, comforting anger. And the renewed urge to fight. She definitely wasn't giving this bloodsucker any help.

"Answer me," Tatiana screamed, spittle flying into Fi's face. Disgusting. If she'd been able to move, she would have spit back.

Mikkel shook his head. "She can't. I've got her bound with one of my spells at the moment."

Tatiana rolled her eyes as she stood. A muscle ticked in her jaw. "Then unbind her before I slit both your throats."

That got him moving. Good to know who wore the pants in that relationship. He whispered something, and the numbness seeped out of Fi like ice melting. Before she could wiggle her fingers, Tatiana scooped her up by the front of her hoodie and held her so close Fi could count the eyelashes fringing her possessed silver eyes. Those eyes...

"Where. Is. The. Girl."

It wasn't a question, it was a demand for an answer. So Fi gave her the same answer that used to make her parents crazy. Nothing. She added a yawn for good measure.

Tatiana shook her. "Answer me."

"Don't...tell her anything..." The words drifted from behind Tatiana, slow and labored. The woman had to be Maris.

Tatiana whirled, clutching Fi one-handed like a rag doll. She backhanded Maris, snapping her head to the side. "Shut up, old woman." Tatiana inhaled what sounded like a sob. "You're lucky you're still alive after what you did to my precious Nehebkau."

Wincing at Maris's pain, Fi wished she had one of those Golgotha blades like Chrysabelle carried. Or Doc's switchblade. This close, Fi could have easily buried it in Tatiana's heart. Her hands twitched with the thought.

Maris's eyes fluttered closed as her chin sagged to her chest.

Tatiana returned her tarnished gaze to Fi. Her nostrils flared and her lips curled, showing off her fangs. "Tell me what I want to know and I'll spare your life."

Fi flared her nostrils. "You should brush more."

Tatiana shifted hands to take Fi by the throat. Her icy fingers closed over Fi's neck like a vise grip. She smiled, and Fi's bravado took a small step back at the expanse of teeth. "I like to play games too. Maybe we should play one together." She pulled Fi closer and dragged a nail down her cheek. The burning left behind meant Tatiana must have cut her. A second later, Tatiana licked a drop of red off her finger. "You should know I always win."

"Then let's have a tanning competition. You go first." Where was Doc? Even if he couldn't shift into anything more than a house cat, his half-and-half stage was pretty damn scary. And she could use some pretty damn scary on her side right now.

Tatiana opened her mouth and pressed her tongue into the sharp tip of one fang. Blood welled up instantly. "Do you have any idea how much a vampire bite hurts? How razor-fine fangs are?"

"Actually, you dumb cow, I do. Do you know how much a varcolai bite hurts? You're going to, because my boyfriend's teeth are way bigger than yours."

With a shriek, Tatiana flung Fi across the room. She fell into a low table, her arm snapping beneath her as she landed. The pain sucked the breath from her lungs but only for an instant. Giddy with the irony that she was about to die a second time at the hand of the undead, Fi opened her mouth and laughed. Living in Mal's head had exposed her to horrors no creature should have to see. If Tatiana thought a few broken bones were going to—

Fi stopped laughing. It was entirely possible that Mal and the rest of them had made it into the estate. They could be in the building. If she yelled loud enough, maybe he or Doc would hear her. Both of them had pretty amazing hearing. She smiled at Tatiana. "You are so dead."

Tatiana smiled back. "It's amusing when my food talks back."

Lifting her good arm, Fi flipped Tatiana the bird before screaming as loud and as long as she could. A snap of Mikkel's hand cut off her air. Bits and pieces of her life flickered in her vision, a mash-up of her memories and a few that had to belong to Mal. Her mother's face morphed into one of Mal's victims. Her college boyfriend changed into a vampire holding a blindfold. As her world went dark again, she suddenly realized why Mikkel and Tatiana seemed so familiar.

Mal bent his head sharply to the left and right, cracking the bones in his neck. It didn't help. The voices scraped against Mal's skull like teeth on steel. Some of them howled. Some of them cursed. Some of them wept. And each step deeper into the house made them louder. Concentrating had become a chore. He glanced at Chrysabelle.

Maybe he should grab her body armor again. The sting of silver cut through the chaos, if only until the wound healed.

Pain to fight pain. If he'd still been human, he would have gone insane long ago.

Maybe he already had.

He closed his eyes for a moment against the gnawing inside his head. The beast was awake. Hungry. It bore up through his gums, made his teeth ache to bite, made his throat tighten at the remembrance of blood. This whole house stank of it. And death. He opened his eyes, newly bitter. For a house this large to carry such a smell meant its mistress was careless with her kills, greedy with her feeding. And yet he was the one considered anathema.

Invisible jaws chewed at his joints. *Feed, kill, drink, blood, blood, blood.* What he wouldn't give to be free of th—a scream rang out through the estate. Human. Familiar.

Doc's hand closed over the blade sheathed at his belt. "That was Fi," he ground out. "They hurt her, I'm gonna rip them apart." He stretched his jaw, showing off teeth that made Mal's fangs seem like a starter set. "And I'm going to enjoy it." His pupils were razor-thin slits, his body spring-loaded. Whatever got in Doc's way was going to end up dead.

And Mal would be happy to help. He gripped the handle of his long sword. He'd not hefted the blade in anything but practice for too long.

Chrysabelle motioned them forward as she broke into a jog toward the direction of the scream. Mal and Doc went after her, with Dominic bringing up the rear. Silently, they covered two halls and a set of stairs, stopping before a pair of double doors.

Nodding at Mal, Chrysabelle tapped the side of her nose, then pointed toward the doors.

Mal inhaled. *No, no, no, no*... The scents of vampires, comarré blood, and Fi mingled in his nostrils. A piercing whine filled his head, lighting his nerve endings with fresh fire. He nodded and reached for his long sword, holding up his other hand and counting down with his fingers.

On one, they burst through the doors, then through a second set and into the room beyond. The last pair of doors slammed shut behind them. Chaos erupted. Chrysabelle whipped out her sacre but stayed at his side. Doc charged the male vampire standing over Fi, who sprawled unconscious on the carpet, a bruise purpling her cheek, her arm jutting out at an unnatural angle.

"Maris." Dominic rushed to the center of the room where Chrysabelle's aunt was bound to a chair, also unconscious and badly beaten.

Behind Maris, a female vampire had her back to them. She was spreading things out over a table, but at the noise, she spun and flipped a slim dagger into Dominic's belly. With a groan, he crumpled at Maris's feet, muttering, "Laudanum." No other nonmagical drug slowed a vampire so much as the ancient tincture of opium. Mal had found that out the hard way more than once during his life.

The female's eyes locked onto Mal's a second later.

Her jaw dropped.

As did his. "Son of a priest."

The wailing in his head blocked out all other sounds. The beast within flexed its muscles. His vision darkened around the edges, narrowing to focus on her and her alone.

Disbelief closed his throat. All this time, he'd mourned her. Endured the guilt of her death like the weight of a thousand worlds. The beast roared to be let out. Not yet. But soon. The beast's anger spilled over, giving Mal a voice again.

"How in hell's name are you still alive?"

Tatiana stared back, eyes reflecting the anger he was feeling. "I could ask you the same thing, *husband*."

# Chapter Thirty-three

Chrysabelle almost dropped her sacre. With some effort, she formed her confusion into words. "What did she just call you?"

"Husband," Mal whispered, his gaze pinned to the vampiress now brandishing a sword in their direction. To one side, Doc snarled, claws deep into Mikkel's chest, a healthy gash opened across one cheek.

Chrysabelle stared at the woman Mal had once called wife and saw her with new perspective. This dark, exotic beauty had once been Malkolm's wife. Chrysabelle hated everything that meant. "You said your wife was dead." Severing a vampire's neck was about as final as you could get.

"She is. Was. Is." He shook his head, never taking his eyes off Tatiana. "They beheaded you. I heard the sword. I smelled the blood, felt the heat of it—"

"Guards!" Tatiana yelled as she stepped over Dominic's drugged body and, sword firmly aimed at Mal's chest, walked toward them. "Mikkel cast a mimicry spell on a fringe to look like me, then he beheaded her. I'd already fed her enough of my blood to mingle our scents. Genius, really."

"Mikkel?" Mal glanced at the vampire struggling against Doc, then back at Tatiana. "He was the one with you that night. He and Lord Ivan."

She scoffed, shaking her head. "You were easy to fool. So lost in your madness, you didn't know the difference."

The sword point pricked his jacket. "But then you never were one to see things clearly, were you? You probably thought I loved you too."

"Shaya—"

"Don't call me that." She jabbed the sword through the leather. "My name is Tatiana."

"I made you what you are."

Bitterness sparked in her eyes, her mouth twisting. "You brought me into this life, but that past has been erased. The taint of your blood has been wiped away. I have been given navitas. I've been re-sired by another." She leaned in. "I have been reborn."

So it was true. Tatiana had actually survived navitas. Chrysabelle had never known a vampire who'd undergone the ritual. Nobles who wanted to change houses could theoretically do so if they found an older vampire from that house willing to sire them. It was supposedly a very painful process, and considered an affront to the original sire. It was also rarely done because it often left the resired vampire insane. As evidenced in Tatiana.

"I saved your life. They would have hung you." Mal's voice went dead of emotion. Something in him had switched off. Or was about to switch on. "Yet this is how you repay me."

"I spared you, didn't I?" She bore down on the sword. It slashed deeper through the leather and had to have pierced Mal's skin. He didn't flinch. "I could have had you killed, but I left you in that dungeon instead. Along with another of Mikkel's special spells." She grinned widely. "He supplied the magic, but the blood that made it work was mine. The voices were my idea too. How long did it take you to figure out your new victims turned into spirits?" She looked past him as though she expected to see a crowd of ghosts hovering around him.

Chrysabelle wanted to cut her. How dare Tatiana pretend that leaving Mal in those ruins to rot was somehow kinder than slitting his throat! And to be proud of that curse. Chrysabelle's sacre hummed in her hand, the vibration of her anger sung back to her by the sword's blood magic. How could Mal have ever loved this woman?

"You didn't kill me because killing me would have made you anathema too." Still he didn't move. Didn't raise his voice.

"I should have killed you. I'm sure the council would have forgiven me. But leaving you alive kept my hands clean. Besides, letting you live with your demons seemed a great punishment for what you did to Sofia."

"I saved her from this nightmare."

Madness invaded Tatiana's eyes and she jerked. "You killed my child."

A strong, spicy metallic scent drifted past Chrysabelle. Blood. Tatiana's sword had bitten through to Mal's flesh. He'd not reacted one bit. She studied the skin visible above his jacket collar. The first tendrils of black script unfurled like deadly ribbons. She almost shuddered, remembering the last time the names had possessed him. Did Tatiana have any idea what she'd done to Mal when she and Mikkel had cursed him? Any idea of the beast she'd created? Chrysabelle guessed not.

Wouldn't Tatiana be surprised? Chrysabelle snorted a soft puff of air through her nostrils, unwittingly attracting Tatiana's attention.

The vampire studied Chrysabelle, disdain clear in her eyes. She turned back to Mal. "I might spare your life again for bringing the blood whore to me. You could be useful for my future plans, but her I'm just going to kill. I already have the sacrifice I need, and justice must be met for her patron's death."

"Death," Mal muttered, but the word sounded like it had been spoken by a ravening crowd. The beast was coming awake.

The doors burst open behind them and a cadre of fringe guards spilled into the room.

Tatiana's smug face spoke volumes. She backed away, tearing the sword free and slicing through Mal's jacket. "Seize these—"

With a clang, the ring hit the wood floor and bounced once, spinning to a stop with a soft whirr.

"Aha!" Tatiana snatched the ring up triumphantly, lifting it above her head with an unsettling smile.

"No," Chrysabelle whispered. The sword must have cut his pocket open.

"Yes," Tatiana crowed. "Hold them," she directed the guards as she retreated toward Maris. "I want them to watch while I usher in the new age of vampires."

Hands grabbed at Chrysabelle, only to be yanked away at the sting of her body armor. One foolish guard tried to take her sacre. His hand burst into flames. They resorted to simply surrounding her and Mal with a ring of swords and crossbows. Doc was hauled off Mikkel and put into shackles.

Chrysabelle trembled with rage. "I know what you mean to do, Tatiana. You won't succeed."

"Won't I?" She shook salt out from a clay pot on the table and into a circle around herself and Maris.

"Nothing you do matters," Mal growled with the cadence of a thousand voices speaking together. The seams of his jacket split as the beast took over his body, his face contorting into something out of a nightmare.

Tatiana faltered, dropping the soil she was adding to the salt circle. "What the—"

The inky names spread like a stain until blackness covered him entirely. The beast laughed with its chorus of voices. "This is what you made me."

"Stay back." She shook her head, looking unsure for the first time. "I have work to do, and I will not be stopped."

"Please, Mal, do something," Chrysabelle begged.

The beast looked at her, his eyes two deep pits of unrelenting black. "We will not kill her. She brought about our curse, she may be the key to its undoing."

"*I* am the key to its undoing." Maybe Chrysabelle was, maybe she wasn't. But she needed him—them—to be on her side, not Tatiana's.

The beast scowled, baring wicked fangs. "You are the key to our demise."

So much for that. She had no idea why his voices thought she was such a threat, but she was about to press her sacre's silver blade against Mal's skin to see if she could shock him back into control. A hissing sound stopped her.

A shadow spun up behind Tatiana. Smoky wisps of darkness spiraled out of the ground and converged into a weak shape.

True terror suffused Chrysabelle for the first time since they'd entered the estate. The mass crystallized, revealing an unholy evil she'd never dreamed she'd come face-to-face with. One of the ancients. A Castus. The drawings didn't come close to the horror of the creature in person. Nothing in her years of training had prepared her for this. Mal—or rather, the beast he'd become—seemed unfazed.

The Castus laughed as it became solid, a horrid, grating sound that scratched at Chrysabelle's ears. Fortunately, its attention was devoted solely to Tatiana. "Proceed, my child."

"The light and the dark shall collide." Tatiana grabbed a handful of Maris's hair and notched her head to one side.

The words sounded familiar. Like one of the old comarré prophets or—

"Sorrow shall bind the darkness." Tatiana slipped the ring onto her finger. She gasped as blood welled up over the gold band. The scale–like prongs inside must have dug into her skin.

"Continue, child," the Castus demanded.

"It shall devour the light." With a guttural cry, Tatiana fell upon the unconscious woman before her, stabbing her fangs into Maris's gilded neck.

Chrysabelle cried out as Maris's eyes shot open. She jerked against the ropes binding her until she saw Chrysabelle. Sadness and regret welled in her gaze. She mouthed the words, "I'm sorry" as her eyes started to roll back in her head.

"No," Chrysabelle screamed. She surged forward, using her armored forearms to deflect the guards' swords and shove them away. Her hands slammed into an invisible wall. She pounded, meeting nothing but air.

Mikkel snickered, his hands outstretched toward her.

Helpless to do anything but watch, Chrysabelle's heart broke at the sight of her dear aunt and Tatiana's cruel use of her. Tatiana drank until Maris was pale and still. At last, Tatiana raised her head, not bothering to wipe away the blood drenching her mouth and chin. "And the covenant shall be broken."

She rubbed her fingers across her face, letting the blood drip down her fingers to mingle with the blood spilled by the ring. "Now shall the darkness arise reborn. So be it written, so be it done."

The Castus howled with pleasure.

Trumpets blared and a brilliant light flooded the room. Every vampire cowered, clapping hands over their ears, save Mal's beast who just seemed stunned. Fi bolted upright. Inside the light, another shape began to develop. Wings of pulsing white fire spread out behind the being.

"Michael," the Castus spat. "So good of you to come, *brother*."

"We have not been brothers since you were cast out, Samael." The creature leaned on an enormous glowing sword and shook his head. "How far you are fallen from heaven. How dim the Morning Star has become."

*Holy mother.* She bowed her head. Only one kind of being was powerful enough to call the Castus by his names without retribution. Her hands trembled at the presence of the archangel, glad his blazing radiance prevented her from seeing his face. There was little doubt in her mind such a sight would overwhelm her. Or blind her. Still, his presence brought comfort. As though he were there to protect her.

"Who breaks this covenant created between the Sons of God and the Daughters of Man?" Michael asked in a tone ripe with power and peace.

Chrysabelle shivered. The covenant had been put in place after the Great Flood, to protect the dwindling numbers of Castus against the rising swell of human population in exchange for the othernaturals leaving humans in peace.

"I do," Tatiana spoke through bloodstained lips. She raised her hand to show the ring she wore. "I am bound by sorrow. I have devoured the light. Now I break this covenant and will arise reborn with the power inherent in the ring of sorrows."

"You must abide by the rules of the covenant, brother," the Castus taunted.

"And so I shall."

The shadows shrank back and his radiant countenance shifted toward Tatiana. "The covenant protects mortals as well as your kind. Do you understand this?"

She lifted her chin. "The noble houses don't need protection."

He tipped his head at Maris. "Mortal, you consent to this, fully understanding what the breaking of the covenant means?"

Tatiana shook Maris, rousing her. Maris nodded weakly, her eyes shifting toward Chrysabelle. *Forgive me*, she mouthed before her eyes fluttered shut again.

"So be it. You must live with the consequences." Michael spoke to Samael. "The blood ritual for breaking the covenant is accomplished, but not the ritual for the power of the ring of sorrows to be granted. That cannot yet be fulfilled. Not in the one you have chosen." He pointed the holy blade at Tatiana. "This one is not the darkest of her kind." His aim shifted to Maris. "And this one is no longer the light."

"What?" Tatiana's face dissolved into disbelief. She pounded a fist against her chest. "I defy you to find another darker than—"

Michael laughed. "You are as blind as your master."

A squalling sound erupted from the Castus. Shadows leaped from the corners of the room toward the archangel. "How dare you deny—"

"I deny nothing. The covenant is broken." And with a second great flash of light and a peal of thunder, the archangel was gone.

An immense ripple of power burst through the room like a shock wave. The Castus disappeared, the guards fell, and Tatiana slammed into the table behind her. Mikkel's invisible wall vanished, rocking Chrysabelle forward. She caught herself, then hurdled Dominic, and rushed to Maris's side. Chrysabelle slit the ropes binding Maris and pulled her limp body into her arms, scattering the circle of salt and earth.

"Come on, Maris, hold on." Chrysabelle pressed her palm against Maris's neck to staunch the trickle of blood. A weak pulse still beat in her veins. "Stay with me, Maris, please."

Mal, free of the beast, flew past them toward Tatiana.

Maris's eyes fluttered open and she smiled weakly. "Too late, my darling child. I'm sorry it's come to this. I made Tatiana promise to leave you alone if I helped her break the covenant."

"Shh. We'll have time to talk when we're on Dominic's

plane back to Paradise City." Tears burned Chrysabelle's eyes. Maris could not die. She could not.

"No, let me. I have much to say and no time to say it." Her cold hand rested on Chrysabelle's wrist. "You are not my niece—"

"That's never stopped me from loving—"

"You are my daughter."

Shock stilled Chrysabelle. "What? How can you know that?" Comarré births were shrouded in secret. Mothers didn't even know the sex of the children they birthed. A hundred questions bounced through Chrysabelle's head, blocking out the clash of weapons and words erupting around them.

"Ask Velimai for my journals."

"If you knew, why did you leave?" Chrysabelle held Maris tighter, willing life into her, praying some miracle would keep her alive. *Holy mother, let her live. Please. I need her. She's my mother. My mother.*

Tears spilled from Maris's lids. "I wanted a better life for you. A life outside this world, but . . ." Her voice faded, her breath coming in shallow gasps. "I made a mistake. I didn't know it would turn out the way it did."

"What would turn out the way it did?" Silent tears trailed down Chrysabelle's cheeks. Her heart ached. Her mother. All these years of not knowing—

"Algernon." Her hand slipped from Chrysabelle's wrist. "Forgive me."

"There's nothing to forgive." Maris had nothing to do with Algernon becoming Chrysabelle's patron, but if talking kept her from dying, Chrysabelle would talk for as long as it took to get help. "Algernon was a good patron. Kind, considerate—"

"The Century Ball. I was there...to bring you home."
Maris's eyes slipped shut. "He refused your freedom."

"Don't," Chrysabelle pleaded. The word snagged in her throat.

"So I killed him," she breathed. Her head lolled back, her voice a dying whisper. "To free you when he wouldn't."

The pulse beneath Chrysabelle's fingers disappeared.

# Chapter Thirty-four

The burst of power locked Mal's voices down hard and fast, shoving their ever-present hum into the recesses of his mind and locking the beast back in its dark cage. He shook his head, blinking to clear the black haze clouding his vision.

The sight before him wasn't any better. Pandemonium ruled the room. Two fringe guards leaped to their feet and leveled their swords at him. "Move and you die," one snarled.

He almost laughed until he saw Chrysabelle crumpled on the floor a short distance away. She held her aunt in her arms while trying to staunch the flow of blood from a gash in Maris's neck. It was a losing cause. The woman's heartbeat slowed with each passing second as her life ebbed. Behind them, Sha—Tatiana, blood smeared across her mouth, unsheathed a stiletto and took aim.

Anger fueled his speed. He cracked the guards' heads together and dropped their bodies to the floor. A second later, he pinned Tatiana to the table behind her by her lying throat. "Not so fast." Her pulse hammered his palm, her smooth skin as warm as the last time he'd bedded her.

Life thrummed within her. Life she'd gained from Maris's blood.

"You're not mad about that little dungeon incident, are you, lover?" She laughed, sweet and coy, tipping her head back. A gold locket slipped into the hollow of her throat. The locket he'd given her with the portrait of Sofia inside.

Could it be the same one? He'd spent a fortune on that trinket, but he'd loved her then. That time was gone. "Undo the curse and we'll talk about that."

"I have nothing to say to you. Except that you should have withered up and died down there." She swiped at him, slicing the stiletto toward his face and catching his forehead.

Blood trickled into his eye, but already he felt the wound knitting closed, the sting fading. He grabbed both her wrists, immobilizing them against the table. "Then I'll have to kill you and see if that removes the curse."

"It won't," Mikkel answered. Across the room, he pushed a blade up under Fi's chin. A thin line of red oozed down her pale skin. "But if you kill her, the kine dies too."

One of Fi's eyes was swollen shut, the bruise surrounding it melding into another on her cheek. She smiled bravely. "Stake her, Mal. For me."

"No," Doc yelled. He strained against the shackles and the guards holding him on either side. The muscles in his neck corded with the effort. He hadn't shifted even slightly. Those restraints must be silver-lined.

Maris's heartbeat went silent. Chrysabelle shuddered, exhaling a soft sob as she clutched her aunt to her. The guilt and sorrow flooding the comarré's soul was a palpable thing.

New rage burned in Mal's gut. He summoned a little

of the beast's darkness into his eyes and stared Mikkel down. "Kill her and you both die."

"Go ahead and try it." Tatiana laughed. "But if you fail, I'm going to drain your little blood whore dry." She shimmered and suddenly he was holding Chrysabelle prisoner. Somehow Tatiana had become Chrysabelle. She winked at him. "I see how you look at her. How you crave her."

He jerked back out of shock. Tatiana shed Chrysabelle's image and scissored her legs up, trying to catch him around the head.

Mal ducked but kept her hands pinned to the table as she flipped over it. Her wrists snapped with a resounding crunch as she twisted to get her feet under her. The stiletto fell from her useless fingers. Mal released her. He had to save Fi.

"Bloody hell," Tatiana yowled in pain. "Kill her, Mikkel. Now."

Doc roared, hissing and spitting and slamming himself into the guards holding him as Mikkel ran his blade across Fi's fragile mortal skin.

Mal arrived in time to catch her body. Mikkel dropped the bloody dagger and ran for Tatiana, but Mal caught his leg and jerked him back, slamming him into the far wall.

Fi collapsed over Mal's shoulder. Blood bubbled from the gash in her throat, soaking through the ruined seams of his jacket and warming his skin. Holding her with one arm, he reached for the dagger in his boot, but a bone dagger whipped past him and into the guard on Doc's left. The fringe burst into ash. A set of keys dropped to the floor next to the blade.

Mikkel staggered to his feet, one arm dangling from a shoulder knocked out of joint.

Mal staked the second guard to ash, then scooped up the keys and unlocked Doc's restraints. The minute he was free, he pulled Fi into his arms. The grief on his face almost undid Mal. "Get her out of here. I'll take care of Mikkel."

"Stay with me, baby," Doc whispered. Eyes like glowing embers, he cradled Fi against him and closed his hand over the wound. She was dying and they both knew it. He caught Mal's gaze for a second. "Make it hurt."

Mal nodded and Doc took off with Fi. On the other side of the room, Chrysabelle held Tatiana at the end of her sacre, but she wasn't much of a challenge at the moment. Broken bones took time to mend even for a vampire like Tatiana. Mal unsheathed his long sword as he turned and beckoned to Mikkel. "Time to die, vampire."


Chrysabelle moved on instinct built up from years of repetitive training. She clung to it, because she had nothing else left besides the pain that tightened her skin across her muscles and made her ache to inflict that same pain on the one responsible for her mother's death. Her sacre buzzed with the need to taste cold flesh. It struck out like a deadly extension of Chrysabelle's rage, biting at Tatiana, leaving bloody cuts that sizzled into scars.

Tatiana clutched her arms to her chest, her hands hanging limp like rags, the bitter flash of the gold ring taunting Chrysabelle every time Tatiana avoided the blade. "Whore," she spat. "You'll never get out of here alive."

"That's not one of my concerns."

Tatiana tried to retrieve a dagger off the table, her face

gnarling in pain as she failed, but already one wrist had begun to straighten as the bones mended.

Chrysabelle took advantage of the opening, thrusting fast and notching the sacre's point against Tatiana's chest. "Tell Mikkel to reverse Mal's curse. It's his magic. Make him remove it and I'll let you live," she lied.

"Never." A wisp of smoke coiled off Tatiana's skin. A few more rose up behind her, coalescing into a larger shape. The stench of brimstone and decaying flesh filled the room.

The Castus was returning.

Tatiana's nostrils flared and an insidious smile curved her mouth. She laughed like a child. "When the master is through with you, I'm going to present your body to the council as proof of your guilt."

Dominic stirred with a soft moan. He eased the dagger from his belly, rolled to his side, and vomited. The smell of bile and heady, sweet laudanum drifted through the room.

The Castus solidified behind Tatiana. Chrysabelle backed up. Tatiana moved to the side and the fiery-eyed Castus stepped forward, its cloven hooves cutting through the rug and digging into the wood floor. The room darkened as his shadowy presence filled it.

The blood in the handle of her sacre boiled. A switch inside her clicked and a new boldness overtook the numbing fear coursing through her. She raised her sword, fully aware it was likely for the last time. "Stay where you are, hell spawn."

The Castus stilled. Then threw its horned head back and howled with laughter. Tatiana joined in until tears rolled down her face.

The sound of metal singing through the air shut her up. Chrysabelle followed Tatiana's horrified gaze.

Mikkel fell to his knees, eyes wide, mouth open, his body riddled with cuts that seemed in no hurry to heal. Then his head slid off his shoulders and rolled toward Dominic. A second later, all of him went to ash. Blood dripped from Mal's sword.

*"Molto bene,"* Dominic murmured. "You still have the touch."

Tatiana shoved one useless hand toward Chrysabelle. "Kill her," she commanded the Castus.

The Castus turned. "How dare you order me—"

"No," Tatiana backpedaled, "I didn't mean—"

Chrysabelle whipped her Golgotha dagger into the demon's temple. The blade sank deep, bursting into flames.

Screeching, the Castus stumbled backward. It latched on to Tatiana's outstretched arm, yanking her forward, its body wavering like it might vanish again. "The ring is mine. I will find another to wear it."

"Chrysabelle," Mal yelled.

Double-handing her sacre, she swept the blade in a wide downward arc, severing Tatiana's broken wrist. The hot blade passed through the shadowy Castus but seared Tatiana's flesh. The hand—and the ring—dropped to the floor intact.

The Castus vanished.

With a head-splitting wail, Tatiana scattered into a swarm of black wasps, obviously attempting one last attack before escaping. Mal, blood covering the side of his face and neck, stabbed the hand with his sword, plucking it up like a piece of refuse. The wasps dove after him, stinging relentlessly.

Dominic reached into his suit jacket and retrieved a vial. He threw it into the empty fireplace, smashing it. Smoke billowed up toward the ceiling, sending the wasps flying from the room.

Mal held the sword out toward Chrysabelle. She freed the ring from Tatiana's dead finger, then stuffed it into her vest pocket. Mal flicked the hand off his blade.

Suddenly, he jerked, his gaze going to his arm. He pushed his jacket sleeve back and exposed a strange bare spot among the names. "She's gone."

"Who's gone?" Chrysabelle asked.

"Fi," he answered. "Her name isn't on me anymore." He let the sleeve slide back into place. "I can't sense her."

Shouts rang from down the hall. Dominic got to his feet, his face twisting at the sight of Maris. He tugged her lifeless body into his arms, cradling her and whispering low in Italian.

Mal pointed his sword toward the doors. "You know the way to the front door?"

"Mostly."

He turned to Dominic. "You with us?"

"*Si*," Dominic answered softly. "I will carry her home."

"Then let's get the hell out of Dodge."

# Chapter Thirty-five

Paradise City had a few evenings every autumn when the cooler temperatures brought a chill to the skin, the winds cleared the lingering smog, and the stars twinkled more brightly. In the first of her journals, Maris had written about those nights and called them "a gift of nature."

Nothing about this night felt like a gift.

Chrysabelle stared at the lies carved into her mother's granite headstone. The real dates of her birth and death would remain the private knowledge of those who'd known her and loved her. The human world would not understand a life lived over such a span of time, not yet anyway. Maybe they would once the snarling, creeping darkness of the covenant's dissolution saturated their lives and their nightmares walked among them. Maybe then the human world could grasp something more.

*The human world.* She shook her head. The world belonged to the othernaturals now. It might be slow at first, but wars would erupt. Vendettas would be played out. Power seized. Unless humans rose to the challenge, they would become collateral damage. Pawns. Prey.

Already the news broadcast stories of strange sightings. How much longer before mortal kind fully understood their new reality? Another week? A month?

A blanket of white roses covered the grave. Dominic's doing. Any doubts she'd had about the vampire's feelings for Maris had vanished watching him grieve. He seemed lost. Like part of him had died along with her.

In her own way, Chrysabelle knew how that felt. Maris had been her beacon of hope for a normal life in a normal world. Now all of that had been ripped away by Tatiana's greed.

A jacket settled over her shoulders. "You looked cold," Doc said.

"Thank you," she said, nodding at the still-grieving varcolai. Fiona had died in his arms, sighing out her last breath, then vanishing into nothing. Doc held out hope she would return in her ghostly form and Chrysabelle prayed he was right. Not just to ease his pain, but because Chrysabelle felt responsible for what had happened. Fi didn't deserve the lot she'd been handed, and Doc didn't deserve the sorrow etched into his body like a million tiny scars.

The sun had set hours ago, but Doc kept his black wraparound sunglasses on. "I can pick you up later, if you want more time."

As far as she knew, this was only the second occasion he'd left the ship in the week since they'd returned. Maybe he thought Fi might show up here. The other time he'd left the freighter, he'd come by the house to see how Chrysabelle was doing. And to tell her Mal had yet to drink the blood she'd sent.

She understood Mal's anger, but she hadn't forgotten

her responsibility or her promise to help him. Although
with Fiona gone, Chrysabelle didn't know what that
meant for her blood rights. Did Mal still own them? And
what if Fi *did* come back? What then? The comarré rule
book didn't really cover these kinds of circumstances.
Most likely, he was still her patron. Which meant they
were still connected, whether either of them liked it
or not.

"No, I'm ready." She placed the single rose she'd been
rolling in her fingers onto the grave and turned to walk to
the car, the hilts of the double sacres on her back clinking
softly together. "Any sign of her?"

"Not yet." Doc shook his head, kept his eyes straight
ahead.

Chrysabelle gave his arm a squeeze. "I'm so sorry."

Up ahead, the devil himself leaned against the passen-
ger door, keeping well off the cemetery's hallowed ground.
Mal's arms were crossed, face a blank mask. The moonlight cut across the hollow of his cheek and sank his eyes
in shadow, but still she could tell he looked past her, not at
her. What she couldn't tell for sure was if the darkness
flickering over his skin was more shadow or the beast trying to rear its head.

An uncomfortable mix of guilt and longing washed
through her. She wanted to ask him for time, for patience.
To understand her side of things. Words hadn't come easily between them since Corvinestri, but there was plenty
that needed to be said. Mostly from her.

Mal wanted more than blood from her. She knew that.
Understood it more than he probably realized. He wanted
his freedom.

Freedom she'd hinted she could provide by way of the

Aurelian, but she'd yet to contact the ancient historian. She would. Just not yet. She couldn't return to Corvinestri while Tatiana still lived. Chrysabelle wasn't even sure if the Primoris Domus would open its doors to her again after the rules she'd broken and secrets she'd revealed. Did they even still consider her comarré?

With Mikkel dead, a visit to the Aurelian might be the only way to find out how to remove Mal's curse. He'd upheld his end of their bargain, now she owed him to uphold hers.

Her fingers strayed to the ring hanging on the chain around her neck. If Tatiana didn't find a way to kill her first, Chrysabelle *would* pay that debt.

Someday.

Soon.

# Glossary

**Anathema:** a noble vampire who has been cast out of noble society for some reason.

**Aurelian:** the comarré historian.

**Castus Sanguis:** the fallen angels, from which the othernatural races descend.

**Comarré/comar:** a human hybrid species especially bred to serve the blood needs of the noble vampire race.

**Dominus:** the ruling head of a noble vampire family.

**Elder:** the second in command to a Dominus.

**Fae:** a race of othernatural beings descended from fallen angels and nature.

**Fringe vampires:** a race of lesser vampires descended from the cursed Judas Iscariot.

**Kine:** an archaic vampire term for humans.

**Libertas:** the ritual in which a comarré can fight for their independence. Ends in death of comarré or patron.

**Navitas:** the ritual in which a vampire can be re-sired by another, to change family lines or turn a fringe noble.

**Noble vampires:** a powerful race of vampires descended from fallen angels.

**Nothos:** hellhounds.

**Patronus/patron:** a noble vampire who purchases a comarré's blood rights.

**Remnant:** a hybrid of different species of fae and/or varcolai.

**Sacre:** the ceremonial sword of the comarré.

**Signum:** the inlaid gold tattoos or marks put into comarré skin to purify their blood.

**Vampling:** a newly turned or young vampire.

**Varcolai:** a race of shifters descended from fallen angels and animals.

# Acknowledgments

I must thank my brother, Matt, for letting me pick his brain about ships; my mom and dad for their unwavering support and constant checking of my writing progress; my agent, Elaine, for her tremendous belief in me and general awesomeness; my friend Laura, whose encouragement and insistence that my agent actually see this book even though I told her I was only writing it to amuse myself were instrumental in its publication; Carrie, Carolyn, Leigh, Briana, and Dayna for reading some of the early versions and pronouncing it worthy; Alessandro and Kimberly Menozzi for their Italian translations; Bob Rivera for his Latin translations; Maria for her medical help; the staff at Romance Divas for keeping things going when I was in my writing cave; and the fabulous duo of Rocki and Louisa, who keep me going, and keep me sane. All writers should be blessed with such friends and family as I have.

Also, great thanks to my editor, Devi, her assistant, Jennifer, and the entire publishing team at Orbit, without whom this book would not have seen the light of day, nor would it have been graced with such an amazing cover. You are a pretty awesome group.

Lastly, the biggest thanks of all goes to my husband, Rick, for understanding that deadlines sometimes mean dinner comes from the drive-thru and the cleaning must be done by an outside source. You're my hero in so many ways. I love you.

# extras

orbit

# meet the author

**Kristen Painter's** writing résumé boasts multiple Golden Heart nominations and advance praise from a handful of bestselling authors, including Gena Showalter and Roxanne St. Claire. Having lived in New York and now in Florida, Kristen has a wealth of fascinating experiences from which to flavor her stories, including time spent working in fashion for Christian Dior and as a maître d' for Wolfgang Puck. Her website is at kristenpainter.com and on twitter @Kristen_Painter. The series website is at www.houseofcomarre.com.

# interview

*Have you always been a writer?*

I've dabbled in art, advertising, the food industry, modeling, teaching, you name it, I probably did it as a summer job. Despite those other jobs, I have always been a writer. Maybe not with the same proliferation that I have now, but I've never been far from pen and paper, keyboard and monitor. It's just part of who I am, a storyteller. Of course, I've gone from telling stories about my cats and pinecones that come to life and moved on to characters I hope people find a little more interesting.

*How did you come up for the idea of the comarré?*

Years ago—like college years ago—I had this idea about a mysterious girl with a gold butterfly tattoo that marked her as an assassin. But it was just an idea, strong enough to stick with me but not enough to turn into a book. It wasn't until the rest of the story hit me many years later that I could truly see who she was and what her world was like. Chrysabelle and Mal grew out of those first tendrils of thought, eventually taking over in a way that surprised even me. And now, to see Chrysabelle realized on the cover in such a stunning way...I have to say that's the realization of a dream.

*Why Paradise City?*

I knew I wanted to set the book in Florida since I live here and I love the area, but I didn't want to set it in an existing city. I decided to reimagine Miami, a Miami of the future where things weren't as bright as they were once upon a time. Paradise City seems like a place that is trying very hard to be something more than it is, trying to live up to its name and struggling with that just a little. The perfect place to loose the kind of chaos that makes urban fantasy such a fun read.

*What do you do when you're not writing?*

This is that "free time" thing people are always talking about, isn't it? Besides struggling to get some kind of regular exercise, I do a few other things that aren't writing. It probably goes without saying that I love to read, but I also love to cook. I make jewelry too—I find it's really nice to do something different with my hands than rap on a keyboard all day. I've been known to spend entire days watching movies too. As a writer, I think it's really important to refill the creative well through a variety of sources, whether that be walking on the beach, playing with my cats, or challenging my husband to some Wii. Or shopping. Retail therapy can be very good for the writer's soul.

### *How much of you is in your characters?*

That's an interesting question. Is there anyone who doesn't know the pain of loss? The shiver of fear? The joy of victory? I like to think my characters draw on all human experiences, not just my own, but of course, my experiences are going to shape them to some extent. Not entirely though. I mean, I've never killed someone, but that hasn't stopped me from offing people in my books. Is it wrong to say I find that rather enjoyable?

### *Have you ever wanted to be a vampire?*

On the one hand, it would be ridiculously cool to be able to scatter, to have some kind of inherent power and be basically invincible. On the other, in real life the sight of blood makes my eyes roll back into my head, so no. (My husband has several stories about how ineffectual a paramedic I am in the face of gushing wounds, something he seems capable of producing on a regular basis.) I do think it would awesome to have an actual gold tattoo though. So long as getting it was fairly painless.

### *Which of your characters would you most like to hang out with?*

Doc. In leopard form. I've always wanted to be on a first-name basis with a big cat. At least until he got hungry, then maybe I'd go over to Chrysabelle's. Mal scares me a little. Mostly because, like Doc, there's a good chance he'd bite me.

*What's next for Mal and Chrysabelle?*

I don't want to give anything away, but their lives won't be getting any easier for some time . . .

# introducing

If you enjoyed BLOOD RIGHTS,

look out for

## FLESH AND BLOOD

*House of Comarré: Book 2*

## by KRISTEN PAINTER

---

*Paradise City, New Florida 2067*

Tatiana needed to die. The thought pushed Chrysabelle on until her shoulders burned and her arms shook. Sweat drenched her thin white T-shirt and dampened her hair, but no matter how many times she pounded her fists into the heavy bag, no matter how hard she punished her body, nothing changed. Her mother was still dead. Tatiana was still alive. And Chrysabelle still owed Mal for the promise she'd made to him.

Over and over, she struck the bag. The sight of her mother dying in her arms still haunted her. She hit harder, but her conscience punched back, heavy with the guilt of her unpaid debt.

Mal had helped her when she needed him. And she'd done nothing to uphold her end of the deal. Hadn't even spoken to him in the two weeks since they'd returned from Corvinestri. Wasn't his fault Maris was dead. It was Tatiana's. The comarré life taught that revenge served no purpose.

Chrysabelle was starting to think otherwise.

She punched the bag again, then spun and landed a kick with a loud grunt of anger. She dropped her hands and stared at the bag, not seeing it. Just the mess she still needed to deal with.

She walked away from the bag, pushing hair off her face with her taped hands. She should be downstairs, reading through the journals Maris had left behind, trying to find some vampire weakness she could exploit to Tatiana's detriment. Instead, she was hiding out in the gym. Not hiding out. Training. For when she next met the vampiress who'd killed her mother. And with the covenant between humans and othernaturals gone, being fight ready was going to matter.

Just like Mal thought finding a way to remove his curse mattered. Which it did. She turned back to the bag and slammed her fist into it again. Most comarré wouldn't dream of creating such tension between them and their patron. Not that most comarré had an anathema vampire for a patron. If Mal even was her patron anymore. She sighed. Her life was an *unqualified* mess.

"Argh!" She whirled and kicked the bag, flinging sweat. Velimai, her mother's former assistant and now hers, stood in the doorway, watching.

*Your mother loved beating up that bag,* Velimai signed, her face wistful.

"It helps." Chrysabelle smiled at the wysper fae. They both missed Maris. Her presence filled the house.

Velimai nodded back, fingers moving. *Ready for dinner?* Wyspers were mute, except for an ear-piercing scream capable of killing vampires.

"Steak?" Chrysabelle asked hopefully. With no patron and no bite, steak seemed to keep her strength up and maintain her better-than-human senses the best of all the foods she'd tried. No wonder it was served so often at most comarré houses.

*What else?* Velimai signed, smiling. So long as she didn't sign too fast, Chrysabelle could understand most of what she said.

"I'll grab a shower and be down in five." She started ripping the tape off her hands with her teeth.

*Take ten,* Velimai signed as she left.

The hot shower felt good, but alone in the steam, Chrysabelle had too much time to think.

She'd sent Mal blood, not just because it was the proper thing to do for one's patron—however suspect his hold on her blood rights might be—but because she had to drain it from her system anyway. According to Doc, Mal's sidekick of sorts, her efforts were futile. Mal had left the blood untouched in the galley refrigerator of the abandoned freighter he called home. Maybe he thought he'd have to kiss her again if he consumed it. She grimaced at that memory and added more cold water to the mix. No, neither of them wanted to go there again. What he was doing for blood, she had no idea. She wanted to pretend she didn't care, but that was a lie. Caring about her patron was ingrained in her makeup. One hundred fifteen years of comarré indoctrination was a tough thing to ignore. The struggle between who she wanted to be and who she had been played out even in daily decisions. How many years would it be before she thought of herself not as a comarré but simply as a woman?

She rinsed the soap from her body, letting the water beat against her skin. Her thoughts returned to Mal. Did he feel that she'd betrayed him? She hoped not, hoped he realized she was just waiting for the time to be right. Going back to Corvinestri could be very dangerous for both of them. Surely he understood that.

She couldn't imagine he was in any rush to face Tatiana again. Not after finding out she was the one responsible for his curse. He probably wanted to kill her as badly as Chrysabelle did.

What must it feel like to have the person you'd married turn on you that way? It was bad enough the vampiress had killed Maris and destroyed the covenant, but for Mal to come face-to-face with the woman who had been his mortal wife, only to find out she was the one responsible for his years of imprisonment and his curse...

Maybe Chrysabelle wasn't the only one whose life was a mess.

She cranked the water off, grabbed a towel, and dried off before wrapping her hair up. She threw on a robe and opened the door. The delicious smell of steak made her stomach growl. She headed downstairs, ready to dig in.

After dinner, she settled on the couch with one of Maris's journals, but her mind kept returning to Mal. She needed a distraction.

"Screen on." The wall across from her flickered to life and the late evening news projected into the room with holographic precision.

"...*an ex-soldier in Little Havana who preaches nightly outside the abandoned Catholic church. His message? Vampires need to be cleansed.*" The anchorman smiled as though he didn't expect his viewers to believe in vampires either. Idiot. Chrysabelle peered at the footage that illustrated the story. There was something familiar about the shaved head and the glint of those dog tags, but she couldn't place them. What she did know was that ex-soldier wasn't human. He was fringe, a less powerful class of vampire compared to the nobles, but vampire nonetheless. Couldn't the anchorman tell? Or was he, like a good portion of his audience, choosing not to believe?

"*A woman at a Coral Gables Publix reported the man behind her in the checkout line had horns.*" The woman's face filled the inset screen hovering beside the anchorman's head. "*He had gray skin and a lot of silver earrings and horns. Horns!*" She made looping motions at the sides of her head. "*And it's not even Halloween yet!*"

A shadeux fae picking up eggs and milk was the least of that woman's worries. What would the public do when Halloween had come and gone but the monsters still remained? The holiday was less than two weeks away.

The camera switched its focus back to the anchorman.

*"More and more reports have been coming in from all over New Florida about strange sightings just like this one. If you've seen something unusual in your area, give our tip hotline a call at—"*

She changed the channel to another local news station. *"In a press release today, Mayor Diaz-White announced she will be forming a task force to investigate what can only be described as the paranormal happenings taking place in the city, although the mayor claims every incident can be explained."*

"Screen off." The holographic image vanished. Chrysabelle had seen enough. Paradise City was only beginning to wake up to the new reality the whole world now faced with the covenant gone. As the days ticked away, the inevitable clash between light and dark forces would come, escalating until there was no denying what was happening. No matter what the mayor told the people.

Which brought her thoughts back to Tatiana. Did a more evil, conniving, ambitious vampire exist? Chrysabelle doubted it. Tatiana had killed Maris as part of the ritual that tore the covenant away, but Chrysabelle had kept Tatiana from keeping the ring of sorrows. How long before Tatiana made another attempt to claim the ring? At least it was safely tucked away, but Chrysabelle had considered destroying it several times in the past weeks. If only she could be sure enough of its power to determine that destroying it wouldn't cause further damage to the world around them.

The swirls of gold tattooed on her skin glittered softly as her thumb rubbed the band on her ring finger. One click released a tiny blade, sharp enough to pierce a vein and drain away the excess blood in her system. Those born into the comarré life, raised to fulfill the needs of the vampires who purchased their blood rights and heavily tattooed with the special gold signum that purified their blood, produced the substance in rich, pure, powerful abundance. Without a patron, the excess blood would sicken her, poisoning her system until she went mad. She'd been on the verge once and that was enough.

She held her wrist up to the light. The veins pulsed thick and blue. She needed to drain the excess. Maybe that was why Mal had been on her mind so much these past few days.

Maris had told her that eventually her system would adjust, but Chrysabelle had twice drained her blood to feed Mal and twice he'd kissed her in return, giving her the infusion of vampire power that was her due. Those kisses had kept her body producing. Kept her thinking of him.

She should drain the blood into the sink, wash it away. And thoughts of Mal with it. She sighed softly and wished he were that easy to forget. He wasn't. Not even close. She stood and headed for the kitchen. What was one more container in the refrigerator among the others? Her blood was valuable. Whether Mal wanted it or not.

*Corvinestri, Romania, 2067*

"This is going to hurt, my sweet. Are you sure you can withstand the pain?"

"You've already told me it will hurt. And I've already told you I can withstand more pain than you can dream of." Tatiana glared at Zafir. "Do you think it was pleasant when that comarré whore sliced my hand off in the first place?" Or what she'd endured in the clutches of the Castus Sanguis? He had no idea.

"*Laa,* my darling, of course not." His lush black lashes fluttered over his olive cheeks. "I only wished to prepare you."

"Just do it. I will be fine." She lay back on Zafir's lab table, her head propped on his folded coat, her remaining hand flat on her chest where her locket lay beneath her blouse. He and his brother, Nasir, were both exceptionally beautiful in a dark, Arabian kind of way, but according to Lord Ivan who'd sent her here, Zafir was the most circumspect of the talented pair. And in this matter, discretion was of the utmost importance. Few knew her hand had been severed and she intended to keep it that way. The servants who found out had been dispatched, save Octavian, the head of her household staff. She would not, under any circumstance, be made to appear incapable or disadvantaged. She intended to have Lord Ivan's position of Dominus one day and nothing, *nothing* would prevent that. Soon she would renew her standing in the eyes of the Castus. Show them she was worthy once again. Reclaim the ring of sorrows—and the power it held—that was rightfully hers.

This new hand was the first step toward that goal.

"*Na'am,* you will do very well, won't you?" Zafir laughed softly.

She wanted to slap his face until that patronizing tone became a cry for mercy. He was no Mikkel, that much was certain. Mikkel's talents in the black arts had been exceptional. Of course, those talents hadn't kept her late paramour alive either. And if Zafir's talents in alchemy were as powerful as he claimed, he might be better than

Mikkel. If he failed to do as he'd promised, then perhaps she'd give the brother a chance. At the very least, Zafir was Mikkel's equal in bed.

Life had very quickly taught her that pleasure and power were the only real rewards for pain. Her sweet Sofia's face flashed before her eyes, something that had been happening more and more since her confrontation with Malkolm. Seeing him had stirred up the past. She reached for the locket around her neck. "Get on with it."

"As you wish." Zafir moved the meticulously crafted platinum prosthetic into place at the end of her right wrist. The gleaming hand lay open, the lines and creases on the palm mirroring images of those on her left because it had been cast from her remaining hand. The hot metal had been quenched in her blood to further seal the magic.

He painted the stump of her wrist with a foul-smelling paste that burned slightly, then he adjusted the prosthetic so that her flesh touched metal. The metal was cool, but her body was warm only because she'd fed from her comar ahead of time to give herself strength.

Using a glass spoon, Zafir scooped pale silver-white dust from a squat glass jar and sprinkled the joined area with the powder.

The pain struck in a searing wave.

A cry ripped from Tatiana's throat and she jerked away from the agony, but Zafir grabbed her forearm and kept it pressed against the metal.

"You mustn't move, my love."

Fire traveled the length of her arm and bit into her shoulder. Lava flowed through her joints, melting her bones with blinding pain. She clenched her jaw to keep from vomiting.

She could endure this. She'd endured the Castus Sanguis's punishing use of her mind and body, and would again if that's what it took to regain their favor. All that mattered was the unholy power they wielded and that a portion of it become hers. *Pain brings clarity.*

Flames licked her skin. Wisps of smoke wafted from the joint of flesh and metal. Blisters rose, filling with fluid. Her fangs pierced her lower lip and copper washed her mouth.

"Almost there," Zafir encouraged. "That's my girl."

Killing him might ease the pain. She was no one's gir—

Daggers dug into the stump of her wrist, grinding through the muscle and burrowing into her bone. She cursed loudly. Then cursed again. And just as she was about to shove her fingers into his chest and rip out his heart, the pain subsided to a dull throbbing.

She yanked her arm away from him. "Do you have any idea how badly that—"

He laughed triumphantly and pointed. "How do you like it?"

She followed the line of his gaze to the platinum fist at the end of her arm. She willed the hand to open. It did. She wiggled the fingers—her fingers—and the bright platinum digits waved back. She leaped off the table, pain forgotten.

"Oh, Zafir, this is brilliant." She stared at her reflection in the palm of her hand. Pain always seemed to make her more beautiful.

He grinned at her words, showing off his fangs. Something about the contrast of those long white teeth against his dark skin gave her a perverse thrill. He was a handsome devil. Devil being the operative word. "There's more."

"Such as?"

He threaded his arms around her waist, turning her back against his chest. He nuzzled his mouth, cool from not feeding, into the curve of her neck. "Think sword, my lush wonder."

"Sword?"

"Yes. A wicked scimitar or a deadly katana. Whatever you like." His fangs scraped her skin, and she shivered with pleasure.

"Very well." She thought of the hefty two-handed blade her husband, Malkolm, had once wielded in his mortal occupation as a headsman. She'd always admired that weapon. She should have used it on him. She sniffed. Now was not the time to burden herself further with the past. She focused on the image in her head.

Tingles of sensation shot up her arm from her new hand. She held it up toward the light. What was happening? The tingles became pressure and her fingers fused together.

She inhaled, clogging her throat with the bitter air of Zafir's laboratory. "What the—"

"Just wait," he urged. His grip increased, as if he thought she might bolt. Or turn on him. Wise boy.

Her fingers melted into a solid shaft as they elongated into a polished knife, then longer still until the blade replicated the image in her head.

"Unholy hell." She went utterly still, very aware that her mouth hung open.

He laughed softly, sending vibrations through her skin. "You should not doubt me in the future, my sweet." His hands slipped lower, only to climb again once he'd breached the hem of her silk blouse.

She pushed him away with her elbows and broke out of the embrace, all without taking her gaze off the sword growing from her wrist. She slashed it through the air. Perfectly weighted. "Bloody amazing. How is this even possible?"

He shrugged. "Does a magician tell his secrets? Of course, such magic comes with a price."

The blade glinted like sunlit water, but she managed to pull her gaze away to stare him down. "We discussed no price."

He whispered something in Arabic as he pulled her into his arms again. The sword shrank back to a hand.

She arched a brow, warm tendrils of suspicion growing along her spine. "How did you do that?"

"I am not a fool." He kissed her cheekbone.

Neither was she. The fact that he'd built in his own controls angered her beyond the point of reason. Red tinged her vision. Had Lord Ivan put him up to this? If so, they both deserved to die. No one dictated what she did. No one. "What is this price you speak of?"

"The only payment I require is more of what you've already been paying me." He cupped her body against the hard lines of his own. "If Nasir could see me now, he would be very jealous indeed."

Barely restraining the urge to tear his throat out, she tipped her head back to let him kiss her neck. How dare he think to control her? "Does Nasir know what you've done for me?" She'd insisted their relationship remain a secret, telling him she wasn't ready to be scrutinized by the rest of society until her hand was restored.

"Mmm," he hummed against her skin. "And give him a chance to tell me how I should be doing things? *Laa*, my darling, I've kept you for myself."

"Good." In that much, Lord Ivan's assessment had been correct. Her metal fingers stroked Zafir's chest, drawing circles over his unbeating heart. "There's something you should know about me."

"What's that?" His hands strayed to her rib cage.

She straightened. "No one controls me." She'd had no control of her life as a mortal and had fought too hard to wrest control of her vampire life to have it taken from her now, no matter how small a thing it might be.

His face stayed buried against her neck, his mouth hungry on her skin. "Of course not, my precious."

"Remove the controls you built in."

He laughed. "You think I'm a fool? To give you such power freely? No."

She threaded her fingers into his hair and jerked his head back to look at her. "Bad decision." Her metal fingers stilled, pressing against his chest. She whispered, "Sword."

Zafir's eyes shot wide as the blade pierced him. He jerked once, then disintegrated into a small pile of ash.

Tatiana turned the sword back into a hand and shook her head at the sooty pile on the laboratory floor. "Let's hope your brother's not as stupid." She liked intelligence in her male companions, but not so much that their ambitions ran roughshod over hers. She needed devotion, not competition.

She tipped over a few Bunsen burners, staying long enough to be certain the blaze would devour all traces of her actions. Vampire law stated that killing another noble was an unforgivable crime. She'd come to believe the only real crime was getting caught.

She slipped out the door and pulled up the hood of her

cloak, staying in the shadows of the small overhang. This part of Corvinestri was deserted as far as she could see down the cobblestone streets. Zafir was not a wealthy, high-ranking member of the St. Germain family and his neighborhood reflected that, something that suited her purposes rather well.

Out into the night and down a dark alley to wait a little while longer until tongues of flames licked the windows. Lights came on in the house next door. Perhaps the stone wall adjoining the two buildings had already grown hot. From her hiding place, she scattered into a cloud of black wasps and resettled herself with great dramatic flair on Zafir's doorstep.

She made a show of knocking. "Zafir, Zafir, are you home?"

After a moment of restless waiting, she banged on the door. "Zafir, you must get out!"

Neighbors began to trickle out of the homes.

Satisfied with the amount of witnesses, Tatiana tipped her head back and yelled, "Fire!"